To Mom and Dad,
who always remind me not to overthink it.

Float

kate marchant

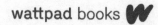

wattpad books **w**

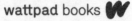 **wattpad** books

An imprint of Wattpad WEBTOON Book Group.

Content Warning: language, death,
discussion of drowning, teenage drinking

Published in Canada by Wattpad Books, a division of Wattpad Corp.
36 Wellington Street E., Toronto, ON M5E 1C7

www.wattpad.com

First Wattpad Books edition: February 2022

ISBN 978-1-98936-597-7 (Trade Paper original)
ISBN 978-1-98936-598-4 (eBook edition)

Library and Archives Canada Cataloguing in Publication information is
available upon request.

Printed and bound in Canada
1 3 5 7 9 10 8 6 4 2

Cover design by Sarah Salomon
Typesetting by Sarah Salomon

Chapter 1

The scorching midafternoon Florida sunshine battered my bare shoulders.

If I didn't find some air conditioning soon I was going to pass out and end up sprawled across the concrete pickup platform outside Jacksonville International Airport, where eventually some poor security officer might stumble upon my unconscious body and have the unfortunate duty of reviving me.

I knew I was overthinking it—my mom always said my best talent was working myself up over nothing—but I was the only person who'd been stupid enough to step out of the cool airport terminal and head to the parking lot, where temperatures had to be in the hundreds. And I was way too stubborn to turn around and admit my mistake, so instead I stood in the narrow shadow of a lamppost and squinted along the heat-baked road for any sign of my aunt, Rachel, feeling like an idiot. A damp, sticky idiot.

Would I *ever* stop sweating?

Jeans really hadn't been the right move. When I'd boarded my flight back in Alaska, I'd tried to wear clothes that were understated and aggressively normal—which was probably my first mistake. My family was hardly normal. Jeffery Lyons and Lauren Fitzgerald, both professors of environmental science at the University of Alaska, were well known in Fairbanks for their opposing stances on climate change, their torrid affair (the products of which were numerous inconclusive research papers and, tragically, me) and their cataclysmic divorce. Every summer since I'd turned eight they'd taken turns dragging me along on expeditions up to the Arctic. If my time zone math was right, both of my parents should've been arriving at the research station right about now, unpacking their equipment and counting out rations for the long month ahead.

Normal wasn't exactly in my repertoire.

But I had dressed like *someone* from Fairbanks, land of the aurora borealis and the midnight sun, would. This meant at least three layers and, for good measure, a lightweight raincoat.

I hadn't realized anything was wrong with my choice of outfit until noticing I was the only one on the flight who wasn't dressed like they belonged on a promotional pamphlet for a tropical resort. While I'd managed to strip off most of my upper layers in the cramped airplane bathroom, leaving just a spaghetti-strap tank top, I didn't exactly feel like peeling off my jeans and parading around in my underpants. Airport security wouldn't have appreciated that. Three separate guards had already given me the stink eye when they'd heard the stuttering wheels of my suitcase screech against the terminal's linoleum floor.

Turns out, lugging one tiny roller bag back and forth between my mom's place and my dad's place for nine years really wears down the wheels. Go figure.

I'd started to really hate that abomination of a suitcase. It was small, black, and had given me absolute hell to find at the baggage claim. Maybe I could paint it. Something neon, or striped, or animal print. Anything to help me find it when I returned to Alaska at the end of the summer.

Aunt Rachel probably had some art supplies to spare. She was a freelance painter and graphic designer. My dad, who cared too much about equations and predictability to be anything other than a researcher, had never wanted to accept the fact that his younger sister was a creative spirit. She moved from state to state whenever she felt like a change of scenery. She'd ended up in Florida when she'd dated an amusement park engineer. He'd dumped her while at Disney World, of all places, and she'd settled down in Holden to collect herself.

After staring down at my crummy little suitcase for a minute or two, trying to decide whether to go for stripes or polka dots, I looked up and was practically blinded by the sight of the neon-green Volkswagen Beetle barreling toward me.

My hand flew up to shield my eyes from the reflection of the sunlight off the car's exterior. The Beetle, once I thought about it, would make a pretty good model for my suitcase renovations. How could you possibly miss something that color?

The car drew closer and slowed to a slightly more legal speed. The front tire rolled up onto the curb at my feet, and the car finally came to a stop.

A woman smiled sheepishly at me through the open passenger's side window. I only had to take one look at her to know who it was—the tangled brown hair and scattered freckles were familiar from all the family pictures dad had strung up on the walls of his apartment.

"I hit the curb, didn't I?" Rachel asked.

"You might've tapped it."

"Oh shit," she hissed, then hurried to say, "I mean *shoot*."

"Aunt Rachel. I'm seventeen. I've heard it all."

Rachel looked up from the evidence of her horrible parking job and gave me a once-over. I figured I'd probably changed a lot since she'd last seen me. I was taller now, obviously, and I'd like to think I'd started to look less like a splotchy-faced, braces-clad adolescent and more like a worldly young woman with an expansive knowledge of curse words.

Rachel seemed to agree, because she nodded and said, "Well, then, shit."

By the time I managed to pop out the retractable handle on my rickety little suitcase, my aunt had jumped out of the driver's seat of the car and wrapped her freckled arms around me in a quick hug so tight it made me wheeze.

"Oh, Waverly, you're so tall!" she cried, holding me at arm's length to look me up and down. "The last time I saw you, I don't think you were over four feet. Look at you! You're like—like a *real person*. Practically an adult."

Practically felt like the key word. Rachel and I were both on the taller end of the female spectrum, but she was in her thirties and had learned how to carry herself. I was still recovering from my freshman growth spurt. You'd think by the summer after my junior year I'd have gotten used to being nearly six feet, but the bruises that dotted my shins could attest to the fact that I hadn't quite figured out what to do with so much body.

But I'd take her assessment as a compliment.

"Well, my darling little polar bear, let's get you in some air conditioning," Rachel said, grabbing the handle of my suitcase before I could tell her that my arms were working just fine. "I want to get you settled in before dinner. I'd like to take you out to my favorite place, if you're up for some seafood."

The thought of going out to a restaurant in this heat, after being wedged in a tiny airplane seat for the last twelve hours surrounded by people, sounded like inhumane torture. But this was no time for cowardice. Back in Alaska, I was Waverly Lyons, the aggressively untalented and anxious offspring of two brilliant, bickering minds. The quiet kid with no best friend, only a small collection of people she traded notes with. The dead weight. The kid whose parents had finally cracked and called up a distant relative to play babysitter.

But for the next twenty-eight days, I was four thousand miles from that girl.

I could be *anybody*.

So as Rachel and I rolled back over the curb and pulled away from the platform to begin the hour-long drive south to my home for the month, I tried to do what I'd never managed to do before: not overthink it.

O

Holden was right at the edge of the Atlantic Ocean. And I'd never seen it before, so I couldn't help but roll down my window, lean out, and crane my neck in hopes of spotting the water as we drove past strip malls and suburbs. Eventually, the streets became narrower and greener and palm-tree lined, and then, all at once, we turned a corner and there it was: a gently sloped beach and a perfect expanse of blue-green straight out of a travel commercial. I took a deep breath and tasted salt at the back of my mouth.

"Not bad, huh?" Rachel asked from the driver's seat.

"It looks like a postcard," I said.

"You might want to get your head back in here, though. We're about to hit downtown traffic, and I'd hate to have to explain to your father how exactly you got decapitated within an hour of being in my care."

I almost laughed, but considering Rachel's earlier display of general lack of regard for curbs, maybe her remark was a little bit less of a joke and more of a serious warning.

The downtown area of Holden was small and sand dusted, but brimming with color. The shops were all painted in bold primary colors and pretty pastels, the windows and doors trimmed in brilliant white. I spotted an ice cream parlor, a bookstore, and a long boardwalk perched over white sand where sunbathers lounged on beach towels and a small crowd of teenagers made use of a volleyball net. Out in the water, surfers waited patiently for the next big wave.

"You won't stay inside and read the whole time, will you?" Rachel teased. "That's what your dad always did when we came out here on vacation. The rest of us would be at the beach for hours, but he'd coop himself up in the motel with his little science books."

"I don't know. Sounds like a nice vacation to me."

Rachel laughed, thinking it was a joke. But what else was I going to do to pass the time? I had no friends here, I wasn't artistic enough to shadow Rachel, and the only thing I could do at the beach was burn.

I couldn't swim. I'd never even set foot in a body of water that wasn't a bathtub. While the ocean might've been at my fingertips, it was still decidedly off limits.

"Have you texted your mom and dad to let them know you landed okay?" Rachel asked.

I went rigid in my seat. I'd been hoping to avoid the topic for as long as possible—maybe even the whole trip—but that'd been naively optimistic of me.

"I actually left my phone in Fairbanks," I said in a very small voice.

"You're kidding. You forgot your phone?" I expected Rachel to simmer for a while in anger and disappointment before she snapped and told me, in a misleadingly calm voice, that my disorganization was unacceptable. That was what my dad would've done. But instead, she laughed. "Oh, honey, I'm so sorry. You got the short end of the gene stick. Your grandmother? Wonderful woman. *Horrible* memory. She left me and your dad at a Kroger once. We were there for four hours before she noticed she hadn't gotten us home with all the groceries. Here. My phone should be at the bottom of my purse. Go ahead and text your dad so he doesn't panic."

I scrambled in her bag. No need to tell her that I hadn't left my phone behind by accident—or that I doubted my parents would care if I'd landed safely or had died in a fiery wreck somewhere over the middle of the country.

The text I sent was short and utilitarian: *This is Waverly. Landed and with Aunt Rachel.*

Rachel's phone vibrated with a response a minute later.

At base camp, Dad wrote back. *Just sent you an email about a marine biology internship for high schoolers. Something to do while you're in Holden? Would look great on your college applications. Let me know if you want me to email the director of the program.*

The last thing I wanted to do was spend my summer vacation voluntarily subjecting myself to more academia. I shoved Rachel's phone back in her purse. I'd figure out an excuse later. Or maybe I'd just get bold and wait until Dad came to Holden to pick me up so I could tell him, to his face, that I hated science and math in all their forms. But that idea was more anxiety inducing than empowering.

"Here we are!" Rachel announced, giving me a split second to brace my hand against the car door before she pulled up to the curb and hit the brakes. "Casa de Lyons."

Her house was bigger than I'd expected for a single woman surviving on an artist's salary—two floors, wrap-around porch, modest front yard with a pair of plastic flamingos hidden in the front flower beds. And here I'd been thinking I'd spend the summer in a beach shack with buckets of paint stacked into makeshift furniture. The houses on either side of it were nearly identical, aside from being gentle pastel shades of blue and green. Rachel clearly wasn't one for muted color palettes. Hers was a brilliant sunset orange.

"We'll drop your stuff off and I'll show you your room," she said as we climbed out of her car. "Then you can change and I'll take you out to dinner."

"I'm good to go now."

Rachel's gaze dropped to my legs. Her nose scrunched.

"What?" I asked, worried that one of those giant Florida mosquitoes I'd heard legends about had attached itself to my leg.

"Are you sure you're okay in jeans?"

"I don't have any shorts."

"You didn't pack any shorts?"

"No, I don't *own* shorts."

"Right. You usually go up north with your parents on their trips," Rachel said. "I guess you guys must be in snowsuits all summer. You know what, I'm sure I have some old shorts you could try on."

The inside of Rachel's house was just as colorful as the outside. Nothing in the living room matched—not the blue and white gingham couch or the green velvet armchair or the paisley wallpaper. The shelves on the far wall were cluttered with books stacked sideways between pieces of pottery and clay figurines. It was chaotic, bright, and unabashedly cheerful.

"Kitchen's through there," Rachel said, pointing at the narrow archway leading into the next room. I caught a glimpse of nonstick pans and irregularly shaped mugs on an island counter before she started up the staircase in the front hall.

"This'll be your room," Rachel said as she dragged my suitcase to the room at the end of the second-floor hall. It was, thankfully, more muted than the living room, and held only a single bed, a small desk, a chest of drawers, and one very kitschy seashell alarm clock.

"Is this all mine?" I asked.

"Yeah. Sorry it's so small—"

"It's *perfect*."

"Here. I've got a few boxes of my old clothes in the closet."

Rachel rummaged until she found a pair of denim shorts with a rhinestone-speckled butterfly embroidered on one of the back pockets. She held them up for my approval. I'd never been on the cutting edge of fashion, but I knew it'd been a solid two decades since bedazzled back pockets had been a thing. Still, I didn't want to be a burden.

"I had some good times in these," Rachel said.

I took the shorts without asking for the backstory. She left me to change, closing the bedroom door—*my* bedroom door—as she went. The space felt too big, somehow. Cavernous. I'd never really had a room that was totally and completely my own. Dad used the second bedroom at his place as an office when I wasn't around, and Mom just had a studio apartment, so I slept on a pull-out couch in the dining nook. And the majority of my summers were spent in communal bunks, so this was sheer luxury in comparison.

The bedroom might've been too big, but Rachel's shorts proved to be a near-perfect fit—which was good, because accidentally flashing my underwear wouldn't exactly be the best first impression to make on the good people of Holden. Especially while they were eating dinner. I walked into the bathroom—*my* bathroom—and stared at myself in the mirror for several seconds before groaning. Everything was wrong. I did not look like the mysterious, cool, jet-setting newcomer I wanted to be. I had bags under my eyes from the long flight, a butterfly on my butt, and not a tan line to be seen.

I was the same loser I'd always been, just in a different climate.

"You ready?" Rachel called from somewhere out in the hall.

No, I was *not* ready. But I went downstairs anyway.

Rachel and I were halfway out her front door when I noticed a white couple standing on the porch next door: a man who looked to be in his early fifties, and who was sweating through his golf shirt, and a platinum-blond woman wearing five-inch heels. She looked young—Rachel's age, maybe. I frowned, trying to figure out how they might be related, when the guy in the golf shirt leaned over and kissed her on the mouth. Okay, so *not* his daughter.

"Howdy, neighbors!" Rachel called. "You two look all dressed up. What's the occasion?"

"Date night!" the blond woman called back. "His treat."

A voice in my head whispered, *Sugar daddy.* That's what my mom would say. But it seemed unfair to make any judgment calls on someone else's life choices when I was the one in bedazzled loaner shorts.

"Chloe's joking, of course," the man told Rachel. "She got another promotion, so dinner's on her. I think she said she's treating me to lobster tails and a margarita?"

"Like hell," Chloe said, swatting at his arm. "George is the designated driver tonight. If anyone needs a margarita, it's *me*. What are you up to, Rach? Don't tell me you're headed out to Marlin Bay this late. You're going to ruin your eyes if you keep painting in the dark."

"Don't worry, I'm taking the weekend off. My niece—oh gosh! How rude of me. This is my niece, Waverly." To me, she said, "These are my neighbors, George and Chloe Hamilton." She turned back to the Hamiltons. "I picked Waverly up at the airport about an hour ago, so I'm taking the kid to dinner out at Holden Point before she starves."

"That's where we were headed," Chloe said. "Why don't we eat together?"

"We wouldn't want to barge in on your date—"

"You're not barging," George said.

"I could *really* use some social interaction," Chloe seconded. "Between this new client who can't make up his damn mind about the way he wants his living room to look and Isabel's obsession with *Dora the Explorer* reruns, I don't think I've had a real conversation in weeks. I don't even care what we talk about, as long as it's not carpet samples or Swiper the Fox."

"You could tell us about Waverly's trip," George suggested. "Where'd you get in from?"

"Alaska."

George let out a low whistle. "How are you taking the change in temperature?"

"I'm managing." A complete lie. I felt like I was about to pass out.

"What grade are you going into next year, Waverly?" Chloe asked.

"I'll be a senior."

"Oh, you're Blake's age! George's son."

"Where is he tonight?" Rachel asked. "The kids having another beach bash?"

"I'm sure they are," George said, "but Blake is babysitting."

Chloe opened her mouth to add something but was interrupted by a high-pitched screech of mischievous delight. A toddler dressed in tiny pink overalls waddled onto the porch and made a break for it. Chloe lunged and caught the kid before she could launch herself off the steps.

"Blake," George hollered. "I think you're missing something!"

I glanced at my aunt to see if she was concerned about the fact that this Blake guy was obviously a mediocre babysitter, but Rachel was just chuckling to herself as she rummaged through her purse in search of her car keys.

And then a boy appeared in the Hamiltons' front doorway, his arms folded over his chest and his expression a mask of brooding teenage apathy. He was tall, broad shouldered, and dark haired—a true triple threat—and he was easily the most beautiful boy I'd ever seen in person, which I knew wasn't a very impressive statement given that there was a grand total of 228 kids enrolled in my private high school back in Fairbanks. But I hardly knew how else to quantify just how much the sight of him struck me. The air left my lungs, the world stopped turning, the stars fell. Every awful metaphor I'd ever heard seemed applicable.

"Could you at least *try* to keep an eye on Isabel?" George asked in the trademark disappointed dad voice I recognized from sitcoms.

"I told you, I don't want to watch her," Blake said. "I have to go to the beach."

"No, you don't," Chloe snapped. "Hand over your phone."

She transferred the toddler, Isabel, into one arm and, with her free hand, reached for the phone in question. Chloe sounded shockingly authoritative, given that she was about six inches shorter than Blake, even in her five-inch heels. Rachel, who was studiously giving the Hamiltons some privacy by riffling through her purse, didn't seem surprised.

"No way."

"Blake. Phone." He didn't hand it over. "Now," Chloe snapped.

Blake shoved his hand into the pocket of his shorts and pulled out his cell phone. He slapped it into Chloe's waiting palm. Triumphant, she passed the phone to George, then held out Isabel until Blake reluctantly accepted the toddler into his arms.

"Bubby!" Isabel cried in a happy baby gurgle.

"You've got to be kidding me," he muttered, jerking his head back so she couldn't grab his hair. Isabel, unperturbed, batted at his nose instead.

Rachel laughed and called out, "You're making me miss my big brother."

Blake, who apparently hadn't spotted Rachel and me yet, startled and looked our way. He grimaced. I'm fairly certain I grimaced back. This was *not* how I wanted to make my social debut in Holden.

"Blake," Rachel said, "this is my niece, Waverly. She's visiting through August. I think the two of you are the same age! You'll have lots to talk about, with your college apps and your—I don't know. What do kids your age do now? Are you still on Facebook? I can't keep up."

Blake smiled tightly—almost mockingly. Chloe thumped him across the shoulder.

"Nice to meet you," he ground out.

Too afraid to say anything, I bobbed my head in response. I'd never been good at making conversation with anyone, let alone boys with perfectly symmetrical faces whose tone of voice could best be described as *hostile*.

"All right, Blake. We're heading out to dinner with Rachel and Waverly," George said, turning to his son, "so keep an eye on Isabel. We'll be back in an hour or two, and if you want me to even consider letting you go to the party tonight, you'd better behave."

"Fine."

"We'll meet you at the grill?" Rachel asked, at last extracting her car keys from the depths of her paint-stained purse.

"You lead the way!" George said, taking Chloe's hand in his.

As Rachel and I pulled out of the driveway, the couple next door hopped into the front of a cute little silver sedan parked in front of their house. I watched in the rearview mirror as their son stood on the front porch, sighing in annoyance as Isabel tried to climb on top of his shoulders and grab a fistful of his dark hair.

I might've gotten off on the wrong foot, but at least I was going to have more fun tonight than Blake Hamilton was.

Chapter 2

There was one last drop of chocolate milkshake in my cup, but no matter how I moved my straw, I just couldn't reach it. I was pretty certain that all my slurping had caused the people sitting in the booth next to us to watch with raised eyebrows, but that didn't matter to me. What mattered was that I had just chugged down the best milkshake of my entire life.

"Should we order you another one?" George asked.

I tossed my straw onto the table in defeat. "No, thanks. I'm good."

"I told you the food here was delicious," Rachel said.

The restaurant out on Holden Point was perched on stilts that elevated it over the beach, high enough above the sand that people could walk underneath it. It was very bougie, by my standards. But considering that I spent most summers eating prerationed provisions out of foil packets, I wasn't a very reliable food critic.

"How long will you be in Holden, Waverly?" Chloe asked.

"My dad's coming to pick me up the second week of August."

"A whole month with your aunt," George said. "That's something special. It's nice to have that family time. Will you be around to see Rachel's mural down in Marlin Bay?"

Rachel nodded. "Should be ready by then. Even if we get some summer storms, I'm determined to have it done and unveiled before she goes!"

"What's Waverly going to do while you're painting?"

Great question.

"She might try to find a summer job," Rachel offered helpfully.

"Oh! Blake has one of those," Chloe said. "He's a lifeguard."

Not an option for me.

"Maybe she could shadow him for a while," Rachel said. "Get the hang of the town."

Yeah, no thanks.

"Oh, don't be silly," Chloe said, my guardian angel to the rescue. "I'm sure Waverly will make her own friends soon enough. And Blake's barely around these days. I swear, he spends more time with his girlfriend and their little group than he does at home."

My hand twitched in my lap. Holden was a small town, which meant the kids who live here had probably known each other for years and had inside jokes and interwoven family histories I could never hope to understand. I was an outsider. And between my lack of a Holden-appropriate wardrobe and my painful introduction to Blake Hamilton, my admittedly grand plans of self-reinvention were already crashing and burning.

I'd need to dig deeper to architect a new persona for myself.

"Is Blake still with Alissa?" George asked, still on the subject of his son's girlfriend. "I thought he said they'd broken up."

"That was last week, babe. They're back together now."

"I give up trying to keep track of it," George declared, placing his napkin on the table and leaning back in the booth. "I think it's about time to head home."

"Agreed," Rachel said.

"I'm picking up the check," Chloe insisted. "George wasn't kidding. This is on me."

After she'd paid, the four of us gathered ourselves and slid out of the booth, groaning as we stood up, realizing we had all eaten way too much. At this rate, I was going to have to buy a bigger parka when I returned to Alaska.

Outside, it was sunset. The sky was purple, the ocean below it painted orange in the glow. There were a few surfers out in the waves who looked like they weren't going to leave the beach until it was too dark for them to see their own feet.

"Isn't it gorgeous?" Rachel asked, nudging me with her elbow.

"Yeah," I replied, unable to tear my eyes off the water. It looked like something out of a listicle entitled "Top 10 Places I'd Like My Ashes Spread." Beautiful, yes, but also massive and unforgiving and very good at reminding me of my own mortality. Even if I *could* swim, I didn't think I'd have the guts to stick more than a toe into that wall of sea foam.

Off in the distance, farther down the coastline, there were lights out on the sand. A growing crowd, tiny and dark like ants from this distance, marched across the beach.

"Is it that late already?" Chloe frowned. "I thought those kids wouldn't start the beach bash until after dark."

"Beach bash?" I repeated.

"The kids in town like to have them during the summer," Chloe explained. "Oh, Waverly, you should go!"

"Oh, no—"

"You absolutely should, Waverly!" Rachel agreed. "It's a Holden rite of passage."

Panic choked my throat. I wasn't ready to meet people. Not yet. I needed to run a brush through my hair, get my hands on some different shorts, and practice being anyone other than myself.

"Maybe Blake could take you," Chloe offered, completely misreading my hesitance.

If I thought he looked miserable before, how was he going to feel when his parents made him drag me, the weird new girl, along with him to a party? Before I could compose myself enough to put up an argument, Rachel looped her arm over my shoulder and gave me an encouraging squeeze.

"She'd love to."

"Great," Chloe said. "I'll send Blake over to pick you up once we're home."

With that, the Hamiltons slipped into their sedan and pulled out of the parking lot, speeding off before I could truly process what I'd just been talked into.

"Come on, Waverly!"

Rachel turned on music for the ride home—an unspoken signal that there was no pressure to fill the silence with chatter. I kept imagining a million different scenarios, all in which I ended up embarrassing myself in front of every kid in Holden. By the time we pulled back into the driveway in front of Rachel's house, my stomach was in knots. How was I supposed to do this? How was I supposed to walk into a party with my head held high when the only person there whose name I actually knew clearly wasn't a fan of me?

"What do I wear?" I blurted. "I mean, I feel like I should change—"

"You look fine. It's just a casual thing."

I wanted to ask if I should bring anything with me to the party but was interrupted as the Hamiltons' front door swung open and Blake stepped out. He wore a white T-shirt, a pair of dark shorts, and a scowl. I shrank down in the passenger's seat, hoping he wouldn't notice me. But I'd forgotten that the vehicle I was sitting in was neon green, which meant that the first thing Blake noticed was, in fact, me, squashed down in my seat, a pained expression on my face.

"Look, there's Blake!" Rachel said. "Why don't you go out and say hello?" She reached across me and pushed open my car door. I remained frozen in my seat. "You kids should head down to the beach soon. The parties usually start as soon as the sun sets."

My feet acted against my will. Before I knew it, I was standing upright on the sidewalk. Blake hadn't moved even an inch from his spot on the porch and looked about as happy to see me as I was to see him, which I took to mean Chloe had called him and told him he was going to let me tag along to this party.

"Hi, Blake!" Rachel called.

"Hey, Ms. Lyons." Then, to me, he said, "You ready?"

"Yes?"

Blake came down the front steps of the porch and marched across the lawn. On even ground, it was clear that he was taller than I'd realized. It was rare that I had to tip my head back to look at someone, but Blake Hamilton dwarfed me. It was intimidating. And as if the sheer size of the boy wasn't scary enough, he was still looking at me like I was something he'd scraped off the bottom of his shoe.

From her porch, Rachel said, "Have fun, kids!"

I felt like calling after her, begging her not to make me go to this bonfire party, but I couldn't force any sound to come out of my mouth. So instead I watched, silent and helpless, as my aunt disappeared into her house. Without a word, Blake turned on his heels and marched to his family's sedan. I hurried after him, struggling to keep up with his long strides. *Who is this kid? A professional speed walker?*

"Are we driving?" I asked.

Blake didn't respond but pulled a ring of keys from his pocket and clicked a button to unlock the car. The taillights flashed as he threw open the driver's side door and hopped inside. He slammed it closed behind him, making it clear that he had no intention of politely opening the passenger's side door for me.

Hurrying to the other side of the car, I opened my own door. Before I'd even buckled myself in, Blake hit the gas and sent the car flying backward so fast I nearly smacked my forehead against the dashboard.

Douche.

As we barreled down the street, the lights on the beach grew closer. The silence in the car felt like a physical weight, crushing me.

"So, how was babysitting?" I blurted.

I'm not sure why I felt the need to speak at all. But the question tumbled out of my mouth before I could stop it. Blake didn't say anything in response, but his fingers clenched the steering wheel a little bit tighter.

"Yeah, I don't like babysitting either," I powered on. "I always end up covered in washable marker and oatmeal residue."

This was bad. This was very bad. I couldn't stop talking.

Blake kept his eyes locked on the road, completely ignoring me. Usually, I would have been scared into silence by his cold attitude, but for some reason, the silence only made me talk *more*.

"Your little sister seems sweet, though. She can't be too much trouble."

Blake scoffed and muttered something under his breath that I didn't catch.

We pulled into a small but bustling parking lot by the side of the beach. In the distance, the orange glow of a roaring bonfire out on the sand illuminated a crowd of teenagers. Blake cut the motor of the car and stepped out, slamming the door behind him and leaving me sitting alone in silence. For a moment I thought he was going to let me stay there, safe and out of the way of any social interaction.

But then Blake turned back to the car, his arms folded over his chest impatiently. I fumbled to open my door. As I emerged into the warm air, I was hit by a wall of sound. Voices, laughing and gossiping, mixed with the rumble of the waves from the beach and some very loud pop music blasting out of someone's speakers. My stomach flipped as I realized that this party, just a little farther down the beach, was *very* crowded.

And I didn't know anyone.

"I'm serious about your sister," I said, hurrying after Blake. Somehow, jabbering to him made the knots in my stomach loosen. "She seems well behaved. A few years ago, I babysat these twins while our parents were at some conference for the Alaska Wildlife Alliance. Anyway, they set my hair on fire. The twins, I mean, not the committee. But it's all grown back now. See?" I lifted up a clump of my tangled brown hair.

"Do you always talk this much?"

I was so surprised by Blake's sharp voice that I missed a step at the edge of the parking lot where the concrete met the soft sand and tripped forward. I managed to keep my balance by flailing my arms wildly and avoided face-planting.

Blake sighed.

In the distance, farther down the beach, a bonfire was glowing orange. I fell into step alongside my aunt's grumpy neighbor. Out of the corner of my eye, I saw him glance down at me, assessing. *Here's the part where he realizes how much of a loser he'll seem like if he walks into this party with me at his side.*

"Blake!"

Never before had I heard a human voice reach such a high octave. A tiny girl with long, shimmering black hair broke away from the crowd and bounded across the beach, kicking up sand behind her. In the faint glow of the bonfire, I could see she was olive skinned and dressed in a black bikini top and a pair of adorable white cut-off shorts.

I glanced up at Blake, expecting to see that pinched expression of annoyance I was growing so accustomed to. But he didn't look annoyed. In fact, he was *beaming*.

"Alissa!" he shouted back, stepping forward to throw his arms around the girl's tiny waist and lift her feet off the sand, inciting a round of high-pitched giggles.

I stood beside them, my hands balled into fists, smiling awkwardly. Did I introduce myself? Did I wait for them to finish up? *Oh God. Please don't let them start making out.* When Alissa met my eyes over Blake's shoulder, I froze.

"Oh hey," she said. "Who's your friend, babe?"

"This is my neighbor's niece, Waverly." Blake lowered Alissa to the ground. "I just gave her a ride."

I hoped the look on my face came off as warm and confident and *not* like someone on the verge of a panic attack. Alissa looked me up and down, assessing.

"I'm gonna do a lap," Blake announced. "You coming?"

He kept his eyes locked on his girlfriend, making it clear that it was an exclusive invitation. The idea of being left alone at a party full of strangers was even more terrifying than third wheeling Blake and his girlfriend. But thankfully, Alissa didn't ditch me.

"Go ahead, babe," she said. "I'll find you later, yeah?"

Blake reluctantly left us to venture into the crowd, where he was greeted by people calling his name and hugging him. Shit. He was popular. That meant that his opinion of me—which clearly wasn't glowing—could be disseminated among his peers, and my plans for my summer rebranding would be over before they'd truly begun.

"Where are you from, Waverly?" Alissa asked.

It occurred to me, briefly, that I could lie. The quintessential mysterious new girl wouldn't come from Fairbanks—she'd come from Paris or Tokyo or Rio de Janeiro. But as soon as the thought flickered through my head, I had to admit that faking an accent was not a bright idea.

"Alaska," I answered. "I just landed today. Twelve-hour flight."

"Wow. Is it, like, really cold up there this time of year?"

Say something clever, I thought. What came out was: "I don't know."

Alissa's eyebrows pinched.

I scrambled. "I mean, I don't really spend summers there. My parents and I always travel."

"I'm usually not around for summers either," Alissa said, flicking her hair over her shoulder. I got the sense she thought of this as a competition. "My mom and I were planning to go to Greece next month, but I think she's going to break up with the guy whose yacht we were going to stay on. Have you ever been on a yacht?"

"No, I sort of avoid the—"

"Do you want to come get a drink?" Alissa interrupted, jabbing her thumb over her shoulder toward the bonfire. I'd never had a sip of alcohol before, but she didn't need to know that.

"Of course," I said.

Alissa led the way to the bonfire and into the crowd, where I was witness to all the horrific details of the party. There was pop music blasting out of a few large speakers that were attached to orange extension cords that ran up to a shack at the edge of the sand. A group of boys hanging around one of the speakers stacked red plastic cups into a pyramid, then poured beer over the structure, letting it waterfall. Everyone looked like they'd come straight from a two-for-one sale on self-tanner and teeth-whitening strips. It was like I'd wandered onto the set of a terribly clichéd teen movie with actors in their late twenties pretending to be my age.

Alissa tossed out greetings left and right to people we passed as she led me to one of the many silver barrels scattered around in the sand. Kegs. I recognized those from the movies too.

"What are you doing in Holden?" she asked me as she grabbed two red cups.

No one had asked me that yet. Why I was in Holden, I mean. I had been hoping nobody would, because I didn't want to have to explain to anyone that my environmental science superstar parents were divorced, and that I, their disappointingly ungifted daughter, had been so much of a burden on their research that they'd sent me to the opposite corner of the country.

"Just visiting my aunt."

"Yeah, yeah. Blake's neighbor. He said."

Alissa fumbled with the tube attached to the keg. I wondered, for the first time, if she'd had a few drinks herself. When she gave up and turned to pass me a half-full cup of beer, she spotted someone over my shoulder and waved her arm high in the air.

"Lena! Over here!"

An intimidatingly pretty girl with corkscrew curls, dark skin, and lean limbs pushed through the crowd, eyes flashing with annoyance when a drunk boy stumbled across her path and she was forced to lift her red cup high over her head so it wouldn't spill.

"Girl, I need you to stop running off on me," she told Alissa when she reached us.

"I know, I know. I'm sorry. Have you seen Ethan?"

I had no clue who Ethan was.

"He was with Jesse by the speakers."

I had no clue who Jesse was.

"Please tell me that he isn't here with that *bitch*."

And I had no clue who this bitch was, but I probably needed to figure it out fast if I wanted to avoid any social faux pas.

"Oh shit! So rude. Waverly, this is Lena. Lena, this is Waverly." I hadn't expected Alissa to introduce me to anyone, so I was a little surprised when I heard my name.

"Hey," Lena said, holding out a hand for me to shake. "You look new."

"Just got in today."

"From where?"

Here we go. "Alaska."

"Oh damn. How long is that flight?"

"It's about twelve—"

"Are you gonna drink that?" Alissa interrupted, eyes locked on the red cup in my hand.

"I don't think so. Do you want—"

Before I'd even finished the question, Alissa snatched the drink, threw back her head, and downed it in a few long gulps. She then slammed the empty cup down into the sand—an assault that made the environmentalists' daughter in me flinch—and marched away, her eyes locked on a group of boys standing beside the speakers.

Lena sighed. "You'll have to excuse her."

"What's she doing?" I asked, watching Alissa stomp up to a short, muscular boy in a tank top and board shorts. The two of them snapped at each other for a moment before the boy grabbed Alissa's hand and tugged her toward the parking lot.

"Probably hooking up with Ethan."

I did a double take. "I thought she was with Blake."

"She is. For now."

"*Oh.*"

I'd been at a party for all of ten minutes and already it felt like an episode of some reality television show in its eighth season—far too late in the game for me to catch up with all that'd happened.

"It's not always this crazy," Lena assured me, noticing my horrified expression. "It's just that Alissa's been having this identity crisis recently, and she feels like she's torn between two guys or whatever. I don't know. It's so obnoxious. I didn't even want to come to this thing tonight."

"I didn't want to come to this thing either," I admitted, the honesty tumbling out before I could check if it was the cool thing to say. "I don't know anyone. My aunt said it's a Holden rite of passage, or something, but honestly? I'm from a tiny high school. I mean, *tiny*. And everyone's too obsessed with AP exams and getting into Ivy Leagues to party. This"—I gestured vaguely—"might as well be the moon."

"I feel you. I just came along to be designated driver," Lena said, leaning back against the table beside the keg, where packages of red plastic cups sat waiting to be opened. "Alissa's a little self-destructive sometimes, but she's my best friend. I can deal with the boy drama, but the last thing I need is her getting herself in *serious* trouble, you know?"

I nodded, even though I didn't know. I'd never had a best friend, really. I didn't know what the responsibilities and requirements were. The Huntington Preparatory Academy—my school back in Fairbanks—was packed with the children of professors, scientists, doctors, and other miscellaneous holders of graduate degrees. We didn't have *friendships*. We had alliances. We were a complex network of competing study groups, and, with my mediocre grades and lack of meaningful extracurriculars, I'd never been in high demand.

So, yeah. The concept of watching over someone at a party was new to me.

"You wanna do a lap?" Lena asked me. "I can introduce you to people."

"That's okay," I said, my voice high pitched and airy.

"Or I can just point people out and tell you their drama," she offered.

I knew, then, that I was going to get along with Lena.

She led me past the drinks table and around the keg stands, pointing out different clusters of partygoers (like the boys' JV lacrosse team and the two feuding halves of the school's dance club) and a few key individuals (like the bespectacled student body president who Lena admitted, with a grimace, had been her first middle school crush). I wondered how someone might introduce *me* during a breakdown of Huntington Prep's student body.

I wasn't an active member of any clubs or teams, and I didn't have any noteworthy talents or achievements.

"Those are the surfers," Lena said, pointing out a group of particularly beachy-looking kids. "My brother usually hangs out with that crowd. I'll introduce you to him when we see him, but you have to promise not to judge me for having a really lame twin. It's not his fault I absorbed all the brains, beauty, and brawn in the womb."

I laughed. Then, before I could stop myself: "And where does Blake Hamilton fall?"

"He and my brother have been best friends since kindergarten," Lena said, tossing me a quick look I couldn't decipher. She was too perceptive. And I was too obvious.

"What about those guys?" I asked, pointing to the nearest cluster of red-cup-toting friends.

"I don't recognize them, but they probably go to our school too. I mean, I think."

"You *think*?" I repeated. "How big is your high school?"

"I think there are two thousand and something kids. I forget the number. Someone told me there are supposed to be six hundred and fifty-three seniors this year and that we're the biggest class in the school's history. Graduation's going to take *hours*." Lena tilted her head at me. "What's your school like?"

Competitive. Claustrophobic. "There are about fifty kids in each grade."

"Oh shit," Lena said suddenly, and for a moment I thought she was just stunned by our below-average class sizes, but then I noticed that her eyes were locked on something over my shoulder.

It wasn't difficult to tell what she was staring at. *Everyone* was staring, from the boys crowded around the speakers to the girls gathered around the keg. Even the sloppy make out sessions in the darker corners of the party had ended, because across the beach, Alissa stood between Blake and the guy in board shorts she'd run off with, one hand on either boy's chest.

I'd never been to a party before but I knew—instinctively—that this one was over.

Somewhere in the crowd, a chant started.

Fight! Fight! Fight!

"Oh, this'll be good," I heard.

Someone else said, "I hope Hamilton gets his ass kicked."

Oh, *absolutely* not. Blake Hamilton was my ride home. He knew how to get back to our houses. I didn't. So as hostile as he'd been toward me, I needed him to, you know, *not* get his ass kicked.

"Lena, we have to stop them," I said. "He's my ride."

Lena, who had obviously run on a beach before and knew just how to maneuver through the sand, took off toward her best friend. I followed, sinking with every step and trying desperately not to roll an ankle. By the time I got closer to the fight, Lena had pulled Alissa out of harm's way and was standing between the boys.

"Cut it out! The both of you!" Lena hissed, pushing Blake's chest. He stumbled backward. Lena turned to the boy in the board shorts. "Ethan, stop. You'll get arrested again."

Ethan, who seemed unbothered by the prospect, spat into the sand. "He attacked me."

"You've been fucking with my girlfriend," Blake shot back

The scowl he gave Ethan was ten times worse than any s.. he'd given me. It was petty, but I took some comfort in kno.. wasn't at the very top of Blake's shit list.

"Ethan, go home," Lena said.

Board shorts boy, Ethan, flipped Blake the finger before stalking off to the parking lot. We all stood around, listening to the sound of crashing waves and pop music until we heard a car rev its engine and tear off down the street, signaling Ethan's departure.

"All right, babe, let's get you home," Lena said softly, shepherding Alissa toward the parking lot. Over her shoulder, she called: "I'll see you around, Waverly?"

"Yeah. See you."

Blake was holding his forehead in the palm of his hand. His hair, dark and disheveled, fell over his eyes. I stood beside him while the crowd around us dispersed, murmuring in disappointment at the lack of bloodshed.

"Let's go," Blake grumbled.

He started toward the parking lot, not bothering to make sure I followed him. Blake stumbled twice, barely catching himself before he fell to the sand. I remembered every antidrunk driving commercial I'd ever seen and straightened my spine.

"You're not getting behind the wheel," I told him, surprised by the authority in my voice. "In the state of Florida, it's illegal to—"

"I know," Blake snapped. "You're driving."

I stopped in my tracks. "I can't—"

"You have a license, right?"

"I mean, I have my learner's permit, but I've really only ever driven snowmobiles—"

Blake reached for his shorts pocket. It took him a few tries, but he finally managed to get his hand in and pull out his car keys. He tossed them to me. Of course, I missed them, and they landed in the sand at my feet.

"Let's go, Lyons," Blake called over his shoulder as he marched to his car, teetering a little to the left.

I scooped up his keys and hurried after him.

Neither Blake nor I spoke as we climbed into his parents' car, although there was some muttering and cursing as Blake wrestled with the handle and his seat belt. I waited until he was still to drive. The sun had disappeared behind the horizon, leaving Holden dark and quiet. I liked the serenity and all, but could barely find my way around Holden when it was light outside—it was ten times harder to recognize where I was when it was dark. I had no clue if I was even going in the right direction. And Blake was no help, either, since all he did was groan every time I braked too hard at a stop sign.

"Hey, Blake?"

He grunted in response.

"What street do we live on?"

I glanced at him out of the corner of my eye to see that he had unbuckled himself and was slumped in his seat, holding his face in his hands. For a moment, I thought he was crying. I thought Blake Hamilton was *crying* in the front seat of his parents' car. And I felt terrible for him, because even though I personally had never been cheated on before, I knew that he had to be hurting inside.

My sympathy died when he looked up at me through his fingers and said, "Your mom."

"Seriously?" *Should've made him walk.*

"Seriously what?"

He was taunting me. But when I looked down at him, a snide remark about him on the tip of my tongue, I saw that he was smiling. And that completely drained my mind of every good comeback I had thought of, leaving me to sit there with my mouth open.

It was the first time he had smiled at me.

Then I remembered that Blake was hammered, and that he hated me.

"What is the name of your street?" I asked, teeth clenched.

"Am I annoying you?"

"Not at all," I lied, gripping the steering wheel a little tighter. I thought I might snap it in half.

"You deserve it."

I barked out an incredulous laugh. "Deserve what?"

"Me, annoying the shit out of you."

"What have I ever done to you?" I demanded, then bit my tongue. *It doesn't matter,* I told myself firmly. *He's grumpy and drunk and you don't need his validation.*

"You ruined my night," Blake slurred, kicking his feet up onto the dashboard.

"But I didn't do anything."

"Exactly."

It stung more than it should've. All I'd done tonight was try to step out of my comfort zone without stomping on any toes—and for a moment there, I'd felt like I was doing a decent job of walking the line between inoffensively normal and mysteriously cool. Lena and Alissa had welcomed me. They'd told me about their drama, taken me under their wings, and hadn't once commented on my bedazzled shorts.

But obviously I still had a skeptic in Blake. He saw through me. He saw the awkward, unremarkable girl who couldn't do anything right.

I felt like vomiting, and I hadn't even had any beer.

"Next street, on your right," Blake muttered.

"Huh?"

"Our houses."

His voice was so hard, so cold. I kept my eyes locked on the road, refusing to glance at Blake because I knew that if I saw him glaring at me again, I would break.

I *was* stupid. Stupid to have thought I could fit in with these kids from Holden. These kids who drank beer and dated each other and swam in the ocean like it was no big deal, like they'd all done the homework when I hadn't even known we had any.

When I finally spotted Rachel's neon-green Volkswagen down the street, it felt like a beacon of light at the end of a dark tunnel. I sped toward it, eager to get away from Blake before I could do something really stupid, like start crying. The moment we came to a stop in the Hamiltons' driveway, I tugged the keys out of the ignition and slammed them on top of the dashboard. Then, without looking back at Blake, I jumped out and into the warm, humid night air.

"See you later," I called.

But I hoped I wouldn't. *He* obviously didn't want to see *me* ever again.

I took off toward Rachel's front porch. Behind me, the gravel crunched under Blake's feet as he headed to his door. The sound spurred me on to walk a little faster, climbing the front steps of the porch two at a time. When I reached the front door, I slammed my fist against the doorbell. Rachel's soft footsteps echoed through the house from the other side of the door, growing closer until finally the front door clicked open.

"Thanks for driving," Blake called, almost regretful.

I really didn't want to give him another second of my time, but the unspoken apology in his voice made me turn over my shoulder. He stood in the driveway, staring after me and looking half forlorn and half frustrated.

"Waverly!" Rachel stood in her doorway, a glass of red wine in one hand and a paintbrush in the other. "You're home. Good. I could use a second opinion on this landscape."

My face warmed. *Fantastic. Another one of my shortcomings.*

"Oh, I'm not very good at art stuff—"

"You have eyes, don't you? You'll do. C'mon. Come tell me about the beach bash. Did you and Blake have fun?"

Rachel ushered me inside the house. I risked one glance back at the Hamiltons' driveway. Blake was still standing there, leaning back against the silver sedan with his head hung. He looked lost in his own thoughts. Either that, or he was starting to feel sick from all the alcohol.

"To catch you up . . ." Rachel said when the front door shut behind us, "I've been working on this little expressionist piece that's supposed to look like a coral reef when you look at it from across the room, and then when you get right up to it, all the coral is actually plastic waste! It's a bit cliché, I know. But enough about me, then—how was your night? Did you make any friends?"

I opened my mouth to tell her about Lena and Alissa, then hesitated. Had I made friends? Because even though I'd largely managed not to stick my foot in my mouth, I'd still been on the sidelines—a viewer rather than a cast member. And Blake Hamilton had seen me for what I was. A fraud. A loner. A girl who had no idea what she was doing.

"Could I tell you tomorrow?" I said. "I'm actually really tired."

"Gosh, of course you are. The time difference and everything." Alaska was actually *behind* Florida, but that seemed irrelevant right now. I was truly and utterly exhausted. "Can I get you anything, honey? Some water? Some aspirin?"

"No, thanks. Just need to put my head down."

Before I could start toward the stairs, Rachel threw her arms around me and squeezed. I was motionless for a moment, realizing that this was the first bear hug I'd received in a long time. Neither of my parents were very good at showing physical affection—we just didn't communicate that way. It felt weird to be hugged so fervently. It was almost too much. My eyes stung.

"Thanks for having me, Aunt Rachel," I whispered.

"Anytime, honey. Now go get some good shut-eye. We can see about getting you a summer job in the morning, if you want. Or we can sleep in! Perks of being my own boss."

I shuffled upstairs and into the guest room—*my* room—and wondered if I'd ever feel like anything but an outsider in this strange, ungodly humid town. I'd started off the day with high hopes of becoming a new and improved person. Instead, I was still the same Waverly Lyons from Fairbanks: a complete and utter failure.

Chapter 3

When I padded down to the kitchen in my pajamas the next morning, I found Rachel standing at the stove with a spatula in her hand and her eyes narrowed at the easel set up by the back doors. The painting she'd told me about last night was propped on the stand: an artfully composed collage of blues, pinks, and greens that, from where I stood, looked like a pleasant scene of a coral reef.

"Good morning, Waverly! I'm making eggs, but there's cereal in the cupboard, too, and tons of coffee in the pot."

I went for the coffee. "Is everyone in this family a morning person except for me?"

"You're just jet-lagged," Rachel said. "Be kind to yourself, grab some nutrition, and then we'll start our day. I was thinking I could drive you into town and see if Margie needs another set of hands at the bookstore. I'll be in Marlin Bay most days, so it might be nice for you to have something to do and some spending money."

We sat down together at her kitchen table and feasted on egg whites, sautéed vegetables, and coffee. When we were stuffed, Rachel gave me a pair of large khaki shorts and a short-sleeved shirt. Since the sun had only been up for two or three hours, it wasn't too hot outside yet, but it was still warm enough that I started sweating the second I stepped onto the front porch.

"Come on, Waverly! Lots to see, lots to do!"

As we pulled out of the driveway, I glanced back at the pale-green house next to Rachel's. For a second, I wished that the front door would swing open and a certain blue-eyed Hamilton boy would be standing there.

I closed my eyes and turned forward in my seat, sinking into the soft leather. Blake Hamilton did *not* want to see me again. He'd made that pretty clear. So why did I want to see him? Why did I feel like, if he just talked to me for more than thirty seconds, maybe I could prove that whatever first impression I'd made was wrong? But before I had too much time to start overanalyzing every word Blake had said to me the day before, Rachel made a sharp turn and I slid into the passenger's side door.

I'd almost forgotten how bad of a driver she was. *Almost.*

"Shit, kid. I'm sorry. Are you okay?"

"I'm good," I said with a laugh. "I'll walk it off."

"Yes! Walking's good. Lots of walking to do in town. Maybe you can do some shopping today, get some ice cream, sit on the beach. I want you to have fun here in Holden. Maybe you can go buy yourself a bathing suit?"

I opened my mouth to remind Rachel that I didn't need a bathing suit because I couldn't swim to save my life, but suddenly the car lurched to a stop. I flew forward and my seat belt knocked the air out of me, leaving me gasping.

"We're here," Rachel announced.

"Great," I croaked.

We'd stopped along the curb in the middle of the Holden town center, the ocean to our left and a line of shops to our right. I watched the locals strolling up and down the sidewalks and wondered if every teenager in Holden was shuttered up in their homes with a hangover—everyone in sight looked like they were on an outing from a retirement home.

"The ice cream parlor down there is really good," Rachel said longingly.

"We *just* had breakfast."

"You're absolutely no fun. The bookstore's over there, next to the corner store."

Rachel and I climbed out of the car. A little flare of panic twisted my stomach as we crossed the street. Was I qualified to work in a bookstore? I thought you needed some kind of advanced degree for that. Or was I thinking of librarians? It didn't really matter; as Rachel stepped up to pull open the glass door of the bookstore, all I could think about was messing this up.

The bell tied to the door jingled as we slipped inside. The tiny shop was everything I'd expected—rows of dark wood shelves, books stacked near to the ceiling, and the trademark peace and quiet.

Peace and quiet that my aunt shattered with a shouted: "Margie!"

"Hi, can I help you find—" Lena, the girl who'd taken me under her wing at last night's beach bash, appeared from the maze of shelves, a name tag pinned to the front of her shirt and a stack of Stephen King novels in her hands. Her eyes lit up. "Oh hey, Waverly!"

Rachel looked between us. "Did you two already meet?"

"Last night," I confirmed.

Lena nodded. "Do y'all need help finding anything?"

"Actually, we're here to see Margie," Rachel explained. "I called her the other day and she said she might have a part-time job for Waverly."

Lena's face lit up. "Are you the new sales associate? Oh, thank God—Margie mentioned she wanted to hire another girl, and I thought I was gonna have to make small talk with a freshman all morning. You'll be way easier to train."

It all happened very quickly after that. Margie Kim, the owner of the bookstore, emerged from the back room to greet us. She was a small, spindly woman with pin-straight black hair that was going grey at the roots, and she greeted Rachel with a tight hug and a quip about her *most loyal customer* being an insatiable reader. Then she turned her attention to me. I stood tall, the voices of all my teachers at Huntington Prep ringing in my head. But Margie didn't grill me.

She told me I had a part-time job, if I wanted it, and that Lena would show me the ropes.

Before I knew it, Rachel was halfway out the door with a book under her arm. "I'll be home, but if I don't answer the front door, come around the back. I'll probably be painting."

And then I was on my own.

O

Margie gave me some options for a schedule, and Lena showed me how the register worked. I didn't have a phone, since I'd left it across the country, but a grandfather clock in the back of the store told me that we were steadily approaching noon.

It was all going smoothly—until the bell on the door jingled.

And just like that, any excitement I felt was extinguished. Alissa, Blake Hamilton's now ex-girlfriend, walked into the bookstore with a half-empty bottle of Gatorade in her hand. She pushed her sunglasses up on top of her head and frowned at me. Between the dark purple rings under her eyes and the drink in her hand, I deduced that she was fighting a nasty hangover (which I'd never experienced but knew enough about from the movies).

"Someone's *right* on time for our lunch break," Lena called.

I hadn't pegged Alissa as the type to work at a bookstore.

"Don't even," she groaned. "I never use my sick days. Let me have this." Then, to me: "Wemberly?"

Close enough.

"It's *Waverly*," Lena corrected. "We met her last night. She's visiting from Alaska? Her aunt lives next door to Blake—" Lena stopped speaking abruptly and flinched. A half-second later, Alissa crumpled in on herself.

"Can we not?" she moaned. "Honestly, I don't want to hear about him or Ethan. Either of them. No more fucking boy talk for the rest of the year, okay? They're *garbage*."

I suppressed the urge to ask why, then, she'd been cheating on both Blake and this Ethan guy simultaneously.

"You know what you need?" Lena asked.

Alissa snorted out a laugh. "A nap."

"Later, sure. But how about some ice cream?"

Alissa snorted. "Ice cream is just empty calories."

"But you deserve them. And I'm sure Jesse would love some company."

I tried to remember if anyone had mentioned a Jesse at the bonfire party.

"C'mon, Waverly," Lena said. "You can come too." Lena grabbed Alissa's tanned wrist and the sleeve of my shirt to drag us along with her. Alissa and I tried not to fall on our faces as Lena marched us out of the bookstore, Margie calling out a good-bye behind us.

The ice cream parlor was a block down from the bookstore. A woman with exhaustion painted on her face shepherded four small children out the door, each of them bearing a cone the size of their arms, as the three of us slipped inside. The air conditioning was blasting. I sighed in contentment. Alissa folded her arms over her chest and stomped her flip-flopped feet against the black-and-white tiled floor.

"It's fucking freezing in here," she muttered.

"Quit being a baby," Lena said cheerily.

"Lena?"

Standing behind the buckets of various flavors of ice cream was a tall, lanky boy with a mop of dark corkscrew curls on his head and an ice cream scooper in his left hand. I knew at once that he was Lena's brother—the two of them were nearly identical.

"Hey, moron." Lena greeted him, confirming my suspicion.

"What are you doing here?"

Lena, as inconspicuously as possible, motioned to Alissa with one thumb. Jesse spotted the mascara-stained tear tracks on her face and pursed his lips.

"Double chocolate fudge?" he asked.

"With sprinkles," Alissa squeaked, collapsing onto the

red-cushioned bench that ran along the wall of the parlor. She propped her elbows on the black table in front of her and buried her face in her hands, sighing wearily.

"I'm on it!" Jesse said, saluting us with the scooper before grabbing a stack of little plastic cups from underneath the counter. He spotted me and did a double take.

"This is Waverly," Lena told him. "She's Rachel Lyons's niece. She's from Alaska. We're gonna have her helping out at the bookstore this summer. Waverly, this is Jesse Fletcher, my twin. He's a raging idiot."

"I'm also the hot one, so write that down."

"Sorry, forgot to mention—he's delusional."

I didn't have siblings, so I felt a bit like one of my researcher parents in the wild as I took a seat at the same table as Alissa. Lena plopped down next me and reached over to scratch her fingernails across Alissa's back in slow, soothing circles.

"Cheer up, girl," she encouraged. "You said what you said. They're garbage."

"Who's garbage?" Jesse asked from behind the counter.

"None of your business," Lena snapped.

Jesse frowned as he arranged a scoop of ice cream into a cup. "Did I miss something last night?"

I wondered why I hadn't seen Jesse at the bonfire last night. You'd think I would have noticed the six-foot-five kid who looked like a clone of Lena.

"Nothing," Alissa snarled. "Just that Blake is a raging douche and we're done."

Jesse's eyebrows shot up. I couldn't quite read his face—maybe frustration? Maybe a little satisfaction, like he'd known this was bound to happen?

"No snarky comments," Lena warned him.

"Not even that we all saw that one coming?"

With that, Alissa let out a little yelp. Her head fell from her hands, landing with a rather loud *smack* against the table underneath her.

For a moment, I thought the twins were about to lunge at each other and start throwing punches. It was a relief when Jesse grabbed the three plastic cups of double chocolate fudge ice cream and four small spoons and came around the counter to our table. He placed the cups in front of the three of us, then hesitated before sitting down next to Alissa.

"Sorry," he murmured.

Alissa didn't respond.

Jesse cleared his throat and turned to me. "So, you're from Alabama?"

"*Alaska*," Lena snapped. "Pull it together, Jesse."

"It's okay," I offered. "They're easy to mix up."

Jesse gazed at me like he wasn't very used to people defending him.

Lena snatched a plastic spoon from the table and shoveled up a large chunk of ice cream from her cup. "Waverly's our new co-worker, so she's gonna roll with us today."

"Oh cool," Jesse said. "Are you going to join us for beach breaks?"

"Beach breaks?" I asked.

Lena opened her mouth to respond but paused to glare at Jesse as he dug his spoon into the side of her cup. She slapped his hand away. "Aren't you in the middle of a shift?"

"It's almost my lunch break. Soon as Steven gets back from his, I'm a free man."

Jesse shoved a lump of ice cream into his mouth before Lena could stop him. She scowled and turned back to me, grabbing her cup and sliding it across the table so it was out of Jesse's reach. He rolled his eyes and headed back to the counter.

"We all go down to the beach at lunch," Lena explained.

"Sounds . . . fun. And by *we*, you mean you, your brother, Alissa, and . . ." I trailed off.

"And Blake," Jesse called from behind the counter.

Alissa, who still had her forehead pressed to the table, groaned.

"Can't you go be a loser somewhere else?" Lena asked her brother with a viciousness that made me sink lower in the booth. This was my fault. I'd set Jesse up. If anyone was the loser, it was definitely me.

"You guys are the ones who came in here," Jesse said. "Why don't *you* leave?"

"Yeah? We should."

"Be my guest."

"I don't think I can see him," Alissa said, popping up from the table. There was a pink oval on her forehead and tears shining in her eyes. "I'm not ready yet."

Jesse groaned. "You know what? You guys were toxic as hell. You're hurting and I know you're not ready to hear that, but honestly, you're both better off—"

Staring down at the plastic cup of double chocolate fudge ice cream in front of me, I started counting the number of visible chocolate chips. I'd always thought that I wanted a sibling—a co-conspirator, a friend, a person to side with me when my parents were being petty or awful or both. But right now? Never in my life had I been so glad that I was an only child.

Float

I was the only one who heard the door swing open, so I was
the first to look up and see who'd come into the ice cream parlor.
Blake Hamilton had the *worst* timing.

Chapter 4

Blake cleared his throat. The twins stopped shouting abruptly and went comically wide-eyed—Jesse with mortification, Lena with outrage. Alissa, who was already close to tears, took to examining nonexistent loose threads on the hem of her lacy shirt. When Blake's eyes landed on me, he winced before he could plaster on a smile.

"You ready, Jesse?" he asked, trying to sound casual and failing spectacularly.

"For what?"

"Beach break, of course."

Blake's eyes flickered over to Alissa for a split second. I was the only one who caught his moment of weakness, and the expression on his face told me everything. He was furious. I would be, too, if I caught my girlfriend making out with a fraternity boy in training.

"Oh!" Jesse said, faking a laugh. "Yeah, I'm ready for a beach break. Lena? You guys wanna come?"

He was only trying to be nice, but the kid was an idiot if he thought Alissa wanted to be around Blake or vice versa. They were both obviously uncomfortable. Not to mention, it seemed like drama, fistfights, and tears seemed to follow Blake wherever he went. It was probably best for us—*all* of us—to avoid him.

"No thanks, Jesse," I said before Lena could reply. "The three of us actually need to grab some lunch."

The weight of Blake's eyes on me made my face go up in flames.

"Waverly, you should go," Lena urged me.

I gave her an are you out of your fucking mind look, but she didn't pick up on it.

"Alissa and I can run to the corner store. We'll get you a sandwich or something and bring it down to the beach. But you should go! I mean, seriously. This is, like, your second day in town. You should spend it with your toes in the water, not waiting in line for a chicken club."

"Oh," I said, out of arguments. "Sure, thanks. You can just get me whatever you usually get."

"Can we hurry this up a little?" Blake asked. "I only have a half hour."

"Sure thing, your highness," Jesse mumbled as he pushed his chair back, the legs screeching against the tile floor. I jumped up from my seat and trailed behind him like a lost puppy and caught Blake rolling his eyes before he stormed out of the ice cream parlor.

"What's up his ass?" I asked before I could stop myself.

Lena sighed. "We've been trying to figure that out for years."

"He's been bitter ever since his dad married Chloe," Alissa

said. "Miserable asshole. You guys are right. This is for the best. We'll see you guys in a few."

Outside the ice cream parlor, Lena and Alissa turned right, and the boys and I crossed the street and headed for the narrow boardwalk that bridged the asphalt with the sand on the other side of some tall grass. Jesse fell in step with Blake, but I stayed a few feet behind the two of them, glaring up at the cloudless sky. Why couldn't it just rain? Then it wouldn't be so hot anymore, and I would have a good excuse not to get anywhere near the ocean.

Out on the dunes, Jesse and Blake headed for a volleyball net that had been erected on the beach just a little ways up from the edge of the water. As I trudged through the sand, my stomach twisted in a sailor's knot. What if Jesse and Blake knocked a ball into the water and told me to jump in and get it before the current carried it out into the ocean? I'd sink like a rock. And Blake Hamilton would probably laugh at me as I went.

"Do you know how to play?" Jesse asked when I reached the net.

"I played volleyball in sixth grade. It's been a minute"—and I hadn't been very good to begin with—"but I'm sure I'll get the hang of it again."

"She doesn't have to play," Blake said. "Just let her sit it out, Jess."

"We need four to play! Ethan said he'd—"

"Ethan?" Blake scoffed. "You invited *Ethan*?"

"Look, I think you guys just need to talk everything out."

"I don't want to talk it out with that—"

Blake was cut off by a loud, whooping cheer. A muscular boy with a volleyball tucked under his arm barreled over the dunes, kicking up sand behind him. Ethan. I recognized his buzzed hair, pointy nose, and affinity for board shorts in atrocious colors. Today, they were turquoise and covered in tiny cartoon pin-up models in string bikinis.

"Ethan."

Blake sounded less than thrilled at the new arrival. I took a surreptitious step back, just in case either of them lunged again. *Barbarians.*

"What's up, Blake?" Ethan called over Jesse's shoulder, his voice a little bitter. He wasn't over the fight, and by the looks of it, neither was Blake.

He tipped his chin up at Ethan, and that was the end of the conversation.

"Ready to play, gentlemen?" Jesse asked.

Ethan nodded down at the volleyball tucked under his arm. "I was born ready."

It sounded like he was challenging Blake, but I didn't speak testosterone, so I might've been misreading things. The two boys glared at each other for another drawn-out moment before I cleared my throat. Ethan's dark, beady eyes landed on me. He looked me up and down, but obviously didn't find me worth hitting on, so he turned back to Jesse.

"Who's she?" he asked, pointing at me.

I'm standing right here. Literally, right here.

"Waverly," I said, before Jesse could introduce me. "I'm here for the summer. My aunt lives next door to the Hamiltons."

Ethan hummed, uninterested. "Can we get this game started?"

All right. Maybe Blake wasn't the worst judge of character, after all.

"I call Waverly on my team!" Jesse exclaimed, lifting the net for me to duck under.

"Absolutely not," Blake said.

"Fine," Jesse said on a sigh. "I'll take Ethan. You've got Waverly."

"That's not what I—"

It was too late. Ethan met Jesse on the other side of the net, the two of them looping their arms over each other's shoulders to make a tiny team huddle. Blake turned to me with an expression of utter defeat.

"Should we talk strategy too?" I asked.

"Stand in the corner, there, and try not to get hit."

My cheeks flushed white-hot with anger. I knew I didn't exactly give off varsity athlete vibes, and it was hardly the first time I'd been singled out as the last choice in a schoolyard pick, but it still stung to have Blake and Ethan treat me like the toy no one wanted to play with.

"Do you know how to set?" he called out after me.

"Yes," I snapped. Then, more honestly: "I mean, it's been a while—"

Blake held his hands up, palms to the sky, in demonstration. I mirrored him. He seemed to think this was passable, because he nodded at the net.

"You can be setter."

The brief burst of triumph I felt was quickly followed by panic. Because now I actually had to participate in this sport without making a complete fool of myself.

Jesse and Ethan took another minute to talk strategy, then exchanged a stupid secret handshake before Ethan lined up to serve. I sucked in a breath as he pulled back his arm and tossed the ball up.

Wham!

It soared over the net. Blake took one step forward and held out both of his arms. I watched in awe as the ball bounced off the flat of his forearms and made a high, gentle arc toward me. With my heart somewhere in my throat, I bent my knees, held my hands up—palms to the sky—and tried to channel my sixth-grade coach (a former international volleyball player with a daughter on the Junior Olympic team and exceedingly high expectations for her middle school team). It wasn't a great set. It probably wasn't even a *good* set. But it got the ball back into the air, and then Blake was there—three swift strides across the sand followed by a leaping jump just in time to smack the ball over the net.

On the other side, Ethan dove.

But Blake's spike was too good. Ethan face-planted in the sand. The volleyball bounced off his outstretched fists and shot straight toward me under the net.

In a feat of human reflexes, I let out an undignified yelp and jerked my knee up just in time to send the volleyball soaring off my shin and toward the ocean. It landed fifteen feet out in the water with a small splash. I stared, open mouthed, as the volleyball surfaced and bobbed in the waves, drifting slowly out to sea.

"Aw, c'mon, Waverly!" Jesse called out, laughing.

"Sorry, I didn't—I mean—shit."

Ethan pulled a face that made me want to march over and kick a bit more sand in his face. Beside me, Blake just sighed.

"I didn't mean to!" I protested a bit harder.

"It's okay," Jesse insisted. I was eternally grateful that at least *someone* on this beach didn't hate me. "Just go get it for us. Whoever tips it in has to swim for it."

Never mind. Jesse hated me too.

"What?"

"*Go. Get. It.*" Blake said, enunciating every word in a holier-than-thou tone that seemed to be a favorite of teachers at the Huntington Preparatory Academy back in Alaska.

"Fine," I snapped.

It was just the ocean. It was just an oversized puddle, really. The volleyball was still relatively close to the shore. How bad could this be? I marched to the water's edge, kicking off my sneakers as I went.

The second I felt the cool foamy water against my toes, I balked.

"Just watch your step!" Jesse called. "The water gets deep pretty fast."

You have to be kidding me.

"Wait," I said. "I don't want to get wet."

Blake and Ethan, the newly appointed members of my fan club, both sighed audibly.

"It'd be easier if I just bought a new ball," Ethan muttered.

His tone was so dismissive, so condescending, so *familiar*. I really didn't want to care if I impressed a guy wearing cartoon pin-up model swim trunks, but the sting of failure—of being a disappointment—was too much to bear. I'd promised myself this summer would be different. I swore I wouldn't allow myself to be the same Waverly Lyons I'd been in Fairbanks.

So I turned and walked into the ocean.

The first steps were easy. Slimy and cool, but easy. I held my breath and stopped when the water was up to my hips. The volleyball was still out of arm's reach but close enough that I figured my growth spurt may finally have some use. In what had to look like a poor imitation of an Olympic swimmer pushing off the starting block, I straightened my arms and dove for the ball.

But I hadn't taken into account that volleyballs, when wet, becoming slippery little bastards.

The ball popped right out of my hands. It went up, and I went down.

My feet didn't hit sand. There was nothing but open water under me.

The woman my school had hired to talk to us about drugs and alcohol had been right: peer pressure was going to be the death of me.

O

I'm sure there are a lot of things people think about when they know that they're only seconds from death. Some people might contemplate the afterlife or wonder if they're headed to heaven or hell or pray to a deity.

I was thinking about chicken club sandwiches.

If I'd just gone to the corner store with Lena and Alissa maybe none of this would have happened. Maybe I wouldn't be caught in a whirlwind of water, kicking my feet like crazy as I tried to find the bottom of the ocean. But, just as Jesse had said, there was an apparent drop-off a few feet out into the water—and I wasn't sure how far down the bottom was, but I was sure someone would find out when they went to retrieve my corpse from its watery grave.

I was sinking like a rock.

A big, big rock.

Tied to an anvil.

Above me, distorted sunlight danced on the tops of the waves. It would've been peaceful if I hadn't been on the brink of death.

But just as my lungs felt like they might burst, something

disrupted the peace. A dark figure crashed through the waves, blocking out the sunlight and heading straight for me. I would have screamed if I'd been above sea level.

Hands reached out to tug me by my shirt. I collided with a warm, hard chest.

As soon as we broke the surface, there was shouting.

"Jesse! What did you do?"

"Why do you always assume everything's my fault?"

"I call *not* giving her mouth to mouth."

"Nobody's asking you to do that, Ethan."

"Back up, guys, give them some space."

I felt myself being lowered to the ground and tried to remember when I had been picked up in the first place. The sand was warm underneath my arms and legs. *Ground.* I liked the ground. I would've sighed in relief, but there was no air in my lungs.

"Oh God, she can't breathe!"

The heel of a palm pressed down into the space just beneath my rib cage. I coughed up water like a fountain, then gasped in a greedy lungful of air as my eyes popped open.

Blake hovered over me, on his knees, dripping wet.

"Waverly, I'm so sorry."

The voice wasn't coming from Blake. I turned my head and met the frantic eyes of Jesse, who was wringing his hands, bracketed by Lena, Alissa, and Ethan. All four of them were watching. All four of them had seen *everything*.

I couldn't tell what burned worse—the salt water in my throat or the humiliation.

"It's okay, Jesse," I croaked.

He looked more traumatized than I was. I tried to sit up, to prove I was all right, but Blake pushed me back down into the sand with a gentle but firm hand to my stomach.

"Give yourself a minute," he said. "You need more oxygen."

"What happened out there, Waverly?" Alissa might've been talking to me, but her eyes were locked on Blake's hand, which was still resting on my torso.

"Nothing. I don't know. It's fine."

"Can you swim?" Blake's deep voice seemed to vibrate down his arm, through his hand, and right into my body.

I spoke without thinking. "Of course I can swim."

My heart pounded against my rib cage. Could he feel that? Could he tell that it was a lie?

"Was there a riptide?" Jesse asked.

"Dude," Ethan interjected, "the riptides on this beach are *killer*. I once got caught in one while I was trying to chase this sea turtle. I swear, I almost drowned."

Alissa let out a sigh of admiration at Ethan's heroic tale.

I saw my chance and took it.

"There was a riptide," I confirmed solemnly. "I got caught in it."

I didn't even know what a riptide was, but if Ethan could almost drown in one, so could I. And blaming my near death on some imaginary force of nature felt like a permissible lie in the moment, because the alternative—admitting that I walked into the ocean knowing full well that I couldn't swim because I wanted a bunch of boys to think I was cool—was even more humiliating.

Jesse whistled low. "You're pretty tough, Waverly."

"Could I get a towel or something?" I asked, eager to change the subject before anyone asked for details.

"I've got one in my tote back at the bookstore," Lena said. "I'll be back."

She turned on her heels and took off across the beach, followed by a sprinting Jesse and Ethan at a leisurely stroll. That left me lying in the sand with Blake kneeling beside me and Alissa standing over us.

"Was it scary?" she asked me quietly.

My life flashed before my eyes. I didn't know that was a real thing.

I shrugged. "Not too scary."

Blake made a sound suspiciously like a scoff.

"Lissa, you can go with them," he said. "I'll walk Waverly back to the bookstore. I just have to make sure she's reoriented."

Alissa looked back and forth between us, visibly torn, but relented.

I watched her until she disappeared over the dunes. My stomach started doing backflips, but I wasn't sure whether it was because I was alone with Blake or because I'd just swallowed too much salt water.

"You know," he said, "I've been in a riptide before."

I made the mistake of meeting his eyes, which seemed to be burning holes in my skin, and quickly averted my gaze to the small scar above his left eyebrow. Had that always been there or had I just not been close enough to notice it?

"They're rough, huh?" I tried to sound casual and failed.

He knew. He knew I couldn't swim. Blake Hamilton had been out in the ocean with me, and he'd felt the same peaceful water that I'd felt.

"You can't swim," he said. Not a question. A statement.

"I can swim. I can *definitely*—"

Blake raised an eyebrow, and all the fight drained out of me.

"Please don't tell them," I whispered.

I think I surprised him. And maybe it was because he pitied me—half drowned and pale, hoarse from the salt water, no one to blame but myself—or maybe it was because he'd sworn some kind of oath as a lifeguard, but Blake let out a withering sigh and nodded.

"Fine. Your secret's safe with me."

He sounded earnest, but I was still on edge. For a second there, I'd really thought he might single-handedly drive the final nail in my summer coffin.

"Right, then." I pushed myself to my feet, wobbling a little but waving off Blake's attempt to offer me a hand. "If you'll excuse me, I have a shift to finish."

The only thing I wanted to do now was shove a chicken club sandwich in my mouth so no more lies could come out.

O

Rachel was in the kitchen when I got home that evening, a pot of spaghetti on the stove and a blank canvas on the easel.

"What happened to the coral reef?" I asked.

"I'm putting it on the side for a while. I had a new idea."

I sat at the kitchen island with a bowl of spaghetti and watched her work.

The doorbell rang—an eclectic little six-note jingle.

"I'll get it," I volunteered.

I hopped off my stool and headed into the living room. Without checking through the window to see who it was, I yanked open the front door, sending a wave of warm air crashing over me. I froze when I saw the boy standing on Rachel's front porch.

Blake.

He was dressed in the same shorts and T-shirt he'd been wearing earlier, but they were dry now. I wouldn't have believed he'd jumped in the ocean to rescue me if it wasn't for the strong smell of seaweed that still clung to him. He had some sort of flat, red foam board tucked under his arm, and frowned. His eyes scanned me up and down, like he was assessing me for visible injuries, before he met my eyes.

"How's your breathing?" he asked.

"A little salty, but fine, all things considered. Can I help you?"

I hadn't meant it as a joke, but Blake let out a strained laugh before scrubbing his fingers through his dark, wildly disheveled hair. Either he didn't like what he had to say next, or he was hoping I wouldn't slam the door in his face.

"Waverly Lyons." He sighed. "I'm going to teach you how to swim."

"You're going to *what*?"

"Please don't make me say it twice. I'm a lifeguard. It's my job to make sure people don't drown. And *you*"—he pointed a finger at my forehead—"are dangerous."

"How am I *dangerous*?"

"You could drown during my shift."

"Well, we wouldn't want you to lose your job, would we?"

Rachel came into the living room, whistling and balancing my bowl of spaghetti in the palm of her hand. She set the bowl down on the coffee table and continued whistling until she spotted me holding the front door open. Then she saw Blake on the front porch, foam board tucked under his arm and hands shoved into the pockets of his board shorts.

"Blake!" Rachel said. "What brings you here?"

"He wants to teach me how to swim," I told her in the same tone one might say, *Can you believe this guy?*

But instead of backing me up, she said: "Really? Oh, Blake, that's so kind of you."

It wasn't kind. It was suspicious. And unnerving, because I could see right through his whole you're a public safety hazard routine, but I couldn't figure out what he wanted from me. He was holding out a metaphorical hand to pull me out of the hole I'd dug for myself, and nobody went out of their way like that unless there was something in it for them.

"I don't even have a bathing suit," I protested halfheartedly.

"I have a few old suits that are probably your size," Rachel offered.

"Yeah, but you'd have to dig them out of the closet, and then I'd have to try them on—"

"Tomorrow, then," Blake said.

"I have work—"

"We can meet after dinner."

"But I—"

"She'll be ready at seven," Rachel told him.

With a nod in place of a good night, Blake turned and marched down the porch steps, slipping into the dark and humid twilight. Rachel drifted back to the kitchen, whistling a tune I didn't recognize, but I stood in the doorway and watched Blake become a shadowy silhouette on the neighboring lawn.

I'd gone seventeen years avoiding water. It'd taken less than forty-eight hours in Holden to change that.

Chapter 5

I spent the entirety of my third day in Holden distracted by the phantom sting of salt water in my lungs. Margie Kim was generously patient in showing me how to work the cash register, despite the fact that it was Saturday and the bookstore was packed, and at lunch time, Lena and Alissa invited me to come to the corner store with them to pick up something to eat.

"We should go see a movie tonight," Lena proposed through a mouthful of her chicken club.

Alissa hummed. "I've been weirdly craving popcorn, so, yes. I'm totally down."

Lena turned to me. "Waverly?"

My heart sank. I couldn't remember the last time I'd been to a theater, and the thought of missing out made my heart lurch. I hated that I'd already made plans with Blake. I hated that I had to keep them a secret. And I hated that the whole situation was a result of my own impulsiveness and shortcomings.

"Oh, I'm sorry. I can't. I—I have to help my aunt with some painting stuff."

Lena pouted and went back to her sandwich.

Great, I thought as I tore off a bite of my own. *Another lie. Add it to the pile.*

O

That night, after a hearty dinner of leftover spaghetti, Rachel gifted me with another relic from the past: a neon-pink polyester bikini. I had cool undertones, no melanin to speak of. Neon pink was not a color I could pull off. But Rachel urged me to try it on, and it fit, and that was the end of that conversation.

Blake arrived promptly at seven o'clock. I answered the front door with a grimace.

"Have her back by nine," Rachel told him.

"That's so *late—*"

"Will do, Ms. Lyons."

Blake didn't lead me to the beach, like I'd been expecting. Instead, we walked several blocks inland, to a white stucco building that sat on a giant property encircled by a tall fence. Written on the façade of the building in turquoise cursive were the words HOLDEN PUBLIC POOL. There were plenty of parking spots around the building, but not a single one of them was occupied.

"Why the pool?" I asked.

"Because it's shallow, there aren't any riptides, and no one else will show up."

I pressed my lips tight. That made sense—and now I felt dumb for asking.

But I couldn't help adding another question: "Is it always this empty?"

"It closed an hour ago."

Blake jogged ahead of me and pulled a ring of keys out of the pocket of his shorts to unlock the front door. I half expected him to hold it open for me and say something gentlemanly, like *after you* or *ladies first*, but he just walked into the building. I had to hurry to catch the door before it swung shut in my face.

The pool house was cool and dark and eerily quiet.

"Are you sure we're allowed to be here?" I whispered, watching Blake as he strode through the main lobby, which was bright turquoise from ceiling to floor, like he owned the place.

"I'm allowed to be here whenever I have lessons to teach."

"Is that what that thing is for?" I asked, pointing at the red foam board under his arm.

"It's a kickboard. I use it to teach little kids how to swim. It's probably too small for you, but I didn't have any bigger ones since I don't normally teach anyone over the age of seven."

I couldn't think of a comeback.

Out through the other end of the building, there was a massive patio sectioned off into four areas. The first, which was closest to the pool house, was set up with chairs and tables, like a casual restaurant. Off to the left, there was a hot tub. To the right, there was a small, shallow pool I assumed was the kiddie pool. And in the center of the patio was a large, rather intimidating Olympic-sized pool. The kind of pool with rows of lights on the inside so the whole thing glows ominously. The kind of pool that got nine feet deep at one end.

The kind I could drown in.

I took a shaky step toward the big pool.

"Whoa, there, big guy," Blake said, grabbing me by the back of my shirt and steering me toward the kiddie pool. "Let's start with something more your speed."

"Are you kidding me?" I protested. "It's only, like, three feet deep."

"Think you can handle it?"

I blew a raspberry at him over my shoulder. Blake lobbed the foam board into the center of the kiddie pool and gestured for me to go after it. That meant I would have to take off my shorts and T-shirt. Which meant Blake would see me in nothing but a neon-pink bikini—a fact I hadn't fully considered when I put it on.

"Um," I said, trying to stall.

I couldn't help but watch as Blake Hamilton reached for the hem of his shirt and lifted it over his head, messing up his already disheveled brown hair. His shoulders were broad and so sun kissed that they were covered in freckles. Up until that point, I'd scoffed at the phrase "the body of a Greek god." Nobody in high school was built like that. But now the phrase was all I could think of to describe the boy in front of me, lit from below in the strange blue glow from the pool. My eyes trailed down his flat stomach. I groaned internally. My stomach was probably bloated form the bowl of spaghetti I'd wolfed down.

Wait.

"I just ate," I cried as if I had just uncovered the historical find of the century.

Blake tossed his shirt onto a lounge chair. "And?"

"I can't get in the water. You aren't supposed to go in the water until a half an hour after—"

"That rule only applies when you're getting in water you can actually drown in."

I scrunched my nose. "I don't think we should take any chances."

Blake caught my arm before I could turn and run. My eyes landed on his hand, then trailed a line up his forearm, around his elbow, and over his bicep to his slightly sunburned shoulder. Either we'd never been so close before or I'd just never noticed the light dusting of freckles across his cheeks and the bridge of his nose. They were, unfortunately, very cute.

"Waverly," he said. "You'll be fine. I'm right here."

Yes, that's the problem. I groaned and reached for the hem of my shirt.

Luckily, Blake was merciful enough to turn away as I peeled it off. I tossed my clothes onto the nearest longue chair, kicked off my flip-flops, and jumped in. By the time my self-appointed swimming teacher turned back around, I was crouching in the middle of the kiddie pool with the water up to my chin. Blake jumped into the water beside me, sending a wave of chlorinated pool water splashing over my face.

"Excuse you," I spluttered.

"Sorry." He didn't sound sorry at all.

"Let's get this over with," I grumbled, rubbing water from my eyes. "How do I swim?"

Blake looked like he might laugh.

"What?" I demanded.

Blake shook his head. "Lean back."

"Pardon?"

"If you want to learn how to swim, you need to first know how *not* to drown," he said, crouching in the water beside me so our eyes were almost level.

I took a deep breath.

Then, as slowly as I could, I leaned back in the water and prayed that Rachel's bikini wouldn't betray me. I closed my eyes as the water rushed over my ears and waited for it to rush over my face. But it didn't come—Blake's hand appeared beneath my back, pushing me upward enough so that my head wouldn't sink under the water. His fingers were barely touching me, but it was enough to make my heart flutter. Blake's knee nudged the back of my legs, and I knew what had to happen next.

I lifted up my feet.

"I'm letting go now." Blake's voice was muffled by the water, but I nodded to let him know that I'd heard him.

The second his hand was gone, I sank.

I brought my feet down again and stood back up, coughing up water.

"You have to try to stay up," Blake told me.

"How?" I cried in frustration.

"Take a big breath," he said, still crouching in the water, "and hold your hands out to steady yourself. Think about distributing your weight evenly."

I groaned and leaned back in the water again, somehow comforted by the return of Blake's hand against my back. I closed my eyes and kicked up my feet again, enjoying the way the cold pool water and warm night air felt against my body. Now I could see why people actually liked swimming. I didn't even care if the glare off my pale stomach was blinding Blake; the water felt like heaven.

"You're doing it," Blake said from above me. He sounded proud, but it was probably just some weird distortion of his voice through the water.

"Doing what?"

"Floating."

O

"You know, the goal is to keep your head *above* the water."

I glared up at Blake from the shallow end of the big pool. Since I'd done so well with the whole float-on-your-back thing—a feat that he'd informed me was "impressive, if you were six"—Blake had decided I could graduate to the shallow end of the bigger pool to practice treading water. Despite the demonstration of how I was supposed to kick my legs like an eggbeater, I was getting tired of lifting my feet up, flailing my limbs, sinking under the water, and standing upright again.

Blake, however, didn't seem to be getting tired of watching me.

"I think my leg is cramping," I said upon resurfacing.

"It's been five minutes," Blake scoffed, plopping down on the end of one of the recliners by the side of the pool. "Where's your stamina?"

I took a deep breath and submerged myself up to my neck in the water. Then I lifted up my feet and began kicking furiously. I barely heard the beginning of Blake's chuckle before my head sank under the water. I put my feet back down on the bottom of the pool and stood up, chlorine burning my eyes and Blake's full-on laughter bombarding my ears.

"You know what?" I snapped. "Just because you already know how to do this doesn't mean it's *easy*. How long did it take you to learn at first? Huh?"

Blake bit back another laugh, lips quivering with the effort.

"I don't remember. You'll have to ask my preschool teachers."

He leaned back in the recliner, kicking his feet up and putting his hands behind his head. "I really don't get how someone can get to the age of seventeen without learning how to swim."

"It's never come up," I admitted, watching my legs—distorted and eerily white beneath the water—as I tried once more to tread water. "My parents are climatologists. They both teach at the University of Alaska, so we always go north on research trips over the summer. We're talking Greenland and Iceland and the Canadian Arctic Archipelago. I've never really done the whole Fourth of July barbecue and pool party thing or gone canoeing and skinny-dipping at some camp with a big lake."

I'd always wanted to, though. I'd wanted to be like kids in movies—the ones with extensive groups of friends and a golden retriever for a sidekick.

"What about gym class?" Blake asked. "You never have swim days?"

Of course, someone who had lived by the ocean for his or her entire life probably couldn't fathom the idea of not gallivanting in the water recreationally. It was a part of him. It was a part of Holden's culture.

I shrugged. "Swimming during the school year just isn't something people I know do unless they're, like, Junior Olympics level."

"That's . . ." Blake searched for the right word. "Sad."

For a moment, I let the word settle in the warm night air between us. They stung like an insult, but there was a sweet aftertaste: *validation*. I wasn't being overdramatic. I wasn't being a whiner. It really was sad that I'd gone seventeen years without living even one day the way Holden kids lived their whole summers. Blake, Jesse, Lena, and Alissa had what I'd always wanted—minus the golden retriever. Sun-soaked days and warm nights. Summer jobs that didn't involve being monitored by an adult every hour of the day (or shivering in Arctic winds). Beach volleyball, surfing, lounging by the local pool. Romance. Friendship.

I was jealous. And I was achingly, devastatingly sad when I thought about all the summers I'd never get back.

But my pity party didn't last long, because one moment Blake was in the lounge chair up on the patio, and the next, he was cannonballing into the pool beside me. I only had a split second to brace myself before I was hit with a wall of chlorinated water.

"What was that for?" I spluttered when Blake surfaced beside me.

"It's called a water fight. Thought you might want to have one."

With all the strength I could muster, I swung my arm across the surface of the pool. In my head, this was going to create a massive wave capable of knocking him clear off his feet. In practice, all I managed to do was splatter his chest.

"Truly menacing," Blake said. "Am I going to have to teach you how to splash too?"

I cupped my hands together and splashed him the way women in face-wash commercials demonstrate the products. It was surprisingly effective. And Blake, who hadn't seen it coming, ended up with a mouthful of pool water and bruised pride.

"How was that?" I asked.

Blake charged me. I let out a noise that sounded somewhere between a gasp and a horse choking on an apple as he wrapped an arm around my waist and lifted me off my feet and over his shoulder. My heart stuttered as I felt a million things at once: the heat of his body against mine, the way his damp hair tickled the inside of my elbow, the firm curve of the shoulder digging into my stomach in the soft hollow beneath my rib cage.

Oh God, I thought, *please don't let my bathing suit fall off.*

And then I was under the water, tossed like the kickboard into the middle of the pool. Maybe it should've been scary. But there was a laugh lodged in my throat, and I knew I could stand in this part of the pool, and I had a lifeguard in arm's reach. I wasn't scared. I was giddy. Bubbles tickled my skin as I somersaulted in the water, free floating.

But then a hand encircled my upper arm in a tight grip and yanked me upward.

I surfaced with a grunt and frantically scrubbed chlorine out of my eyes. When I could open them, Blake was watching me with an expression that was half horrified.

"Are you okay?" I asked. It felt a little silly that I was asking him the question, as if *he* was the one who had just been dunked in the water. But he looked odd. Regretful, maybe.

"I'm fine," he croaked.

He didn't sound fine.

"I'm sorry if I splashed you too hard."

"I said I'm fine," Blake snapped, his eyes turning dark as he took a step back from me. I flinched and took a step backward too. "You didn't do anything. I just shouldn't have done that. You can't swim. It probably wasn't the smartest idea to toss you into the water."

"It's not that deep. I'm literally standing."

Blake frowned as he noticed that I was, indeed, able to stand.

"Sorry." He shook his head again. "I just thought . . ."

"I'm fine. You've got good lifeguard instincts."

I meant it as an honest compliment, but Blake didn't take it that way. His head reared back like I'd smacked him across the face. He looked genuinely hurt. I tried to replay the last few things I'd said, picking them apart for where I'd gone wrong.

"Who told you?" he demanded.

"Told me what?"

"About my mom."

"What about your mom?"

"So you *don't* know?"

I blinked. "Wait, what happened with your—"

"Never mind," Blake said, turning his back to me and placing his hands on the ledge of the pool. He lifted himself up out of the water, his wet skin glistening in the dim pool lights.

"Wait!" I protested.

By the time I managed to pull myself out of the pool (with less grace and less upper body strength), Blake already had his shoes and shirt on. His phone vibrated on the lounge chair. I caught a glimpse of the screen—an endless column of notifications, all under the same name.

Alissa Hastings.

I watched Blake's face as he picked up his phone and read whatever she'd sent him. He grimaced, then sighed like the weight of the world had settled on his shoulders.

"Let's call it a day," he suggested with a forced smile.

I couldn't do anything but nod. Was he really ditching me to hang out with Alissa? I thought we'd been having fun. More fun than he'd have with his cheating ex-girlfriend, at least. But I guess Blake still saw me as his neighbor's socially disastrous, untalented, hopeless niece—a dead weight to be lugged around and tolerated in small doses, when she kept quiet and didn't make too big of a mess of things.

I pulled my clothes on over my wet bathing suit and followed Blake through the pool house. Neither of us spoke. The only sounds we made were the wet squeaks of his feet in his sneakers and the clacking of my flip-flops against the tile floor.

"Do you know the way home?" Blake asked as he locked up behind us.

"I'm sure I can figure it out. Small town and all."

I hoped I didn't sound as hurt as I felt.

Blake, who didn't seem sold on my navigation skills, gave me directions and repeated them twice. He probably figured the chances of me getting lost on the walk back were really high and didn't want to get in trouble with my aunt for letting me loose in an unfamiliar town.

"I'll see you tomorrow?" he asked, still looking unsettled.

"Sure," I said, eager to get away.

"Waverly."

Blake was still standing in front of the pool house, his hands thrust into the pockets of his swim trunks. It was immediate déjà vu. Last night, when I'd given him a ride home, he'd looked at me the same way. And I still couldn't understand what it meant.

"Don't get lost," he said.

I snorted. "No promises."

We turned and went our separate ways. With every step I took, my heart sank.

It wasn't like I had a crush on Blake. That was ridiculous. I'd known the guy for two days, and he'd hated my guts for half of our brief acquaintance. I wasn't *jealous*. I was just struggling to understand what made me different from Alissa. How did she have boys getting into fistfights over her one day and accepting invitations to her house the next? How did she have someone like Blake Hamilton wrapped around her finger? It just didn't add up. Not that I had an advanced degree in relationships—I'd never in my life seen an example of two people working out.

But for one brief and wonderful moment in that pool, with the burn of chlorine in my eyes and laughter in my throat, I'd felt like Blake and I might be on the brink of something.

So, fine. Maybe I had a crush.

I'd done stupider things.

Chapter 6

The bookstore was closed on Sunday so Margie could attend a family wedding, which was good, because I woke up the morning after my first swimming lesson with Blake feeling like I'd climbed a mountain. My legs wobbled. My shoulders ached. It was a little pathetic, really, that treading water had taken so much out of me.

When I finally managed to drag myself out of bed and down the stairs, I found Rachel set up in the kitchen, a tarp spread out on the floor and an easel angled so it was bathed in the reflection of the morning sunlight off the white walls.

"Coffee's in the pot," she called over her shoulder, not taking her eyes off her brush.

I poured myself a mug and took a seat at the kitchen island, wincing as my muscles and bones settled on the stool.

"Are you painting for fun, or is this work?" I asked.

"Work," Rachel said with a huff, taking a step back to examine the clown fish she'd just put the finishing touches on. "This is a commissioned piece for a new restaurant over in Marlin Bay. I tried to tell them nobody wants to have these little guys watching over them while they eat seafood, but, alas. *The client is always right*. I could use a second eye, here, kiddo. What do you think? Pink or yellow for this piece of coral in the foreground?"

"Oh," I said, blushing. "I don't know. I suck at art."

"Nobody sucks at art," Rachel said passionately. "They're only unpracticed. Or they haven't had a good meal and a full night's sleep. You don't have to be classically trained at art to pick a color for me. Just go with your gut."

I thought of her awful neon-pink bikini and blurted, "Yellow."

Rachel smiled and reached for a tube of paint. While she mixed a brilliant shade the color of butter and sunshine, I turned her words over in my head.

It was comforting to think that all the things I was awful at could be boiled down to my being hungry, tired, or inexperienced. But I didn't know if that held up. Because I'd certainly practiced things—like volleyball, that one season, or Latin, all three years of middle school (my parents thought it might help me better understand the binomial names of plants and animals)—and still managed to suck at them. There was definitely something else there. Talent. Intelligence. A natural inclination to not be mediocre at everything.

"Hey, how'd the swimming lesson go last night?" Rachel asked, tugging me out of my spiral just to remind me of another thing I was lousy at.

"It was fun," I blurted. "I learned how to float on my back. And I'm okay at treading water."

Rachel tucked her painter's palette against her hip and beamed at me like I'd told her I'd won an Olympic gold medal. "Look at you go! I knew you'd like the water once you gave it a chance. Remind me to thank Blake Hamilton's parents when I see them. That was really nice of him, offering to teach you."

"Hey," I said, already regretting my nosiness, "do you know anything about George Hamilton's first wife? Blake's mom?"

Rachel pursed her lips. "I know she was a swimmer. Think she went to the Olympics, but I *might* be making that up. God, such a tragedy." Rachel leaned toward me to say, more quietly, "She drowned. Long time ago, now. Before I even moved here."

"Oh," I murmured. "That's really sad."

I considered pressing Rachel for details, but it felt too intimate. Too intrusive. Besides, with my track record around the boy next door, I'd probably say too much and drive him away before I could figure out how to tread water. So I sat back, watched my aunt leave yellow brushstrokes across her canvas, and thought about how sad it was that a boy whose mother had drowned had gone on to become a lifeguard.

O

The next morning, Rachel dropped me off outside the bookstore for my shift. Margie was at the register helping a girl no older than ten squeeze a set of five fat hardback books into one plastic bag, which she assured Margie she could carry all by herself.

"Waverly, could you shelve these?" Margie asked me, gesturing to a stack of books at the end of the counter. "I've talked this young lady into tackling one series at a time."

I loaded the books into my arms, glad for a straightforward

task to make me feel useful. But I barely made it two steps into the stacks before I spotted two long-limbed twins. Lena and Jesse, both dressed in the same shade of canary yellow, had their heads bowed and were conversing in low, bookstore-appropriate tones.

"Did you guys coordinate outfits or something?" I asked.

Both their heads snapped toward me at the same time.

"She might know," Lena told her brother.

"Know what?" My palms went immediately clammy against the slick paperback cover at the bottom of the stack in my arms. Was this about my near drowning and resulting swim lessons with Blake? Had I already been found out?

"Do you know what happened between Blake and Alissa this weekend?"

I made a vague noise that wasn't quite a denial.

"You live next door to the Hamiltons. You didn't hear or see anything?"

"No. I was definitely home all night, though."

Lena sighed. "I'm just trying to figure out why Alissa sent me a text saying she was skipping her shift to take a mental health day."

"Do you think it has something to do with Blake?" I asked, trying to shift the weight of the books in my now-trembling arms.

"The only other option is Ethan," Jesse said, plucking a few books off my stack before my elbows gave out. "I texted him, and he said he didn't know what was going on. And Blake never texted me back yesterday. He was supposed to be on duty at the beach this morning, but I didn't see him and he's still not answering his phone, so . . ."

I hadn't heard whether or not Blake had returned home the night he'd left me standing outside the public pool. He probably hadn't. But before my traitorous brain could bombard me with mental images of what could've kept Blake over at Alissa's house all Saturday night, the bell tied to the front door chimed softly behind me.

Lena immediately slapped on her best customer service smile.

A beat later, it twisted into a snarl. "*You.*"

My heart stuttered for a beat before coming back to normal—if you consider a heart beating like a bongo drum under the hands of a very enthusiastic drummer to be normal. Blake stood in the doorway. His shirt was wrinkled like he'd slept in it and there were faint shadows in the hollows under his eyes. Maybe he just wasn't a morning person, but it seemed more likely that he'd endured an exhausting night with Alissa.

The sight of him all disheveled made me suddenly and uncontrollably pissed off.

"Where were you on Saturday night?" Lena demanded.

Blake's eyes flickered over her shoulder and met mine.

If he tells them about the lessons, I'll kill him.

"Why do you need to know?" he asked.

"None of your business. Now, where were you?"

Blake cracked a smug smile. "None of your business."

Jesse sighed and cradled some of my books to his chest as he slumped against one of the tall shelves. "Do you have any clue what's going on with Alissa? She told Lena she wanted to take a mental health day."

I caught a flicker of guilt in Blake's eyes before he disguised it. "I haven't talked to Alissa since the bonfire, so unless seeing me at the beach yesterday gave her a mental breakdown, I have nothing to do with this."

I totally would've believed Blake if I hadn't known for a fact that he was lying through his teeth. He was a good actor. Blake shot me a brief but cutting look—a silent warning not to call him out on his bluff *or else*.

Whatever friendship might've blossomed at the pool was dead.

"Didn't you hang out with her on Saturday?" I asked with mock innocence.

It was a reckless thing to do, but I wanted him to squirm. I wanted to hear how he might try to justify spending a passionate night with Alissa so soon after she'd cheated—and so soon after he'd extended me one small dose of kindness, which he surely must've known would leave me hopelessly and irrevocably infatuated.

Lena and Jesse looked between us.

"Nope," Blake said, his jaw a little stiff.

"Really? I thought I heard you leave your house."

He tilted his head. "Did I see you over by the public pool?"

My heart dropped. He wouldn't dare. If Blake told Lena and Jesse I couldn't swim, and that not only had I walked into the ocean knowing this but that I'd blatantly lied about it to their faces, we'd never recover from it. They'd forever see me as an impulsive, stupid liar. And I didn't want that to happen, because I liked Jesse and Lena. I really, *really* liked them. I couldn't let Blake jeopardize my blossoming friendships with them. I let out a frustrated groan under my breath as I realized that both Blake and I had secrets to hide, which meant that I needed to back down before Blake could let my miserable secret slip first.

"Nope," I said tightly. "Wasn't me."

"Hm. I guess we were both mistaken."

Lena and Jesse both looked thoroughly confused.

"Hey, Jesse, why don't you walk me to work?" Blake grabbed Jesse's bony arm.

Jesse let out a whine and reluctantly handed me back the rest of my books to shelve.

"Say good-bye," Blake told him.

"Good-bye," Jesse grumbled.

I took my stack of books and hurried to the children's section. Lena followed, watching me with narrowed eyes.

"What?" I asked with mock innocence as I stuffed a few Percy Jacksons into place.

"What's going on?" Lena demanded.

"Margie asked me to put these back where they—"

"No, no. Don't be cute. What was that about, between you and Blake?"

"I have never had anything between me and anyone else ever—"

I was saved by the sound of a solitary, miserable sniffle.

Lena and I turned in unison to find Alissa standing under the sign for the mystery section (fittingly enough) with puffy eyes and long hair thrown up into a halfhearted bun that'd fallen into the hood of her oversized sweatshirt. She looked like she'd spent the last two days sobbing.

"Oh my God," Lena said. "Are you okay?"

Alissa sniffled again. "Blake and I talked."

"I knew it."

"I asked him to come over so I could apologize and let him know how bad I feel about the thing with Ethan—because, I mean, *obviously* Ethan is the worst. And it was really, really awful of me to hook up with him, and I don't know why I did it—"

"What'd he say?" I asked, despite myself.

Alissa looked up and blinked at me as if she had only just noticed my presence. She wiped her nose with the sleeve of her sweatshirt and shrugged.

"He said he didn't want to get back together."

"Oh babe," Lena said.

"That's not even the worst part." Alissa shook her head, then added in a voice so watery it was difficult to understand her. "I think he has another girl. Less than three days and five fucking hours after we break up, he finds *another girl*?"

Did she know he'd been with me? Had Blake let slip that we were at the pool together? No—she'd have said something if she knew it was me. Right? Oh no. I was going to have to choose a battle: admit that I'd lied about knowing how to swim or let Alissa think Blake was running around town with some new girl.

"Maybe you should just try being single for a bit?" Lena suggested.

Alissa scoffed and shouldered past us, marching straight to the back office.

"Fuck that," she called over her shoulder. "Ethan's still answering my texts. If Hamilton wants to play that game, fine. We'll play."

Sweet Jesus. It wasn't even nine o'clock in the morning.

How did anyone in Holden survive this many social calamities before lunch?

O

Lena and Alissa spent the whole next day whispering in corners of the bookstore. I was used to feeling out of the loop, and I could respect that Alissa might want to keep things private from a girl she'd only met last week, but it still stung when I approached them and they immediately stopped talking or loudly changed the subject.

It stung even worse when they both left work early.

I waited until five o'clock—when Rachel had told me she'd head home from Marlin Bay—before I stepped out of the bookstore, calling good-bye to Margie over my shoulder, and emerged into the fresh air. It was still hot and humid enough to make me feel disgustingly sticky, but at least the ocean breeze was cool. I shoved my hands in the pockets of my loose jean shorts and started down the street in the general direction of Rachel's house.

If Alissa thought it could take Blake all of a couple days to find someone new after ditching her, how strong had their relationship really been? Although, to be fair, it made sense that he'd rebound fast. He had that brooding, attractive thing going on, and I'm sure a lot of girls were into the whole lifeguard aesthetic. On paper, I got it. But it was a bit hard to wrap my head around the idea that I'd never even kissed a boy while someone as moody and prickly as Blake Hamilton could easily turn around and find someone new within a day of a breakup.

A car horn honked behind me.

I jumped about a foot in the air, my heart lodged somewhere in my throat, and spun around to see a familiar silver sedan.

"*Hamilton,*" I hissed.

"Hey, Alaska." Blake's chipper voice replied through the open passenger's side window.

"It's incredibly creepy to follow people in your car."

"What else was I supposed to do? Drive past at twenty miles an hour and shout?"

His face was smug, his hair was disheveled, and he was wearing a sweatshirt. In this heat. Absurd. With as much dignity as I could manage, I held my chin high and continued down the sidewalk. Unfortunately, Blake decided he wasn't done just yet. His car rolled alongside me.

"This is me offering you a ride," he said. "Just so we're clear."

Suddenly, I was mad at him. And not just because he had sneaked up on me and made me feel like an idiot, but also because whatever was going on with him and Alissa, paired with the speed of his departure after my swim lessons, had left me feeling like I was ten steps behind everyone in Holden. I was so tired of feeling dumb and unprepared.

"You're a dick," I snapped, fully embracing the irrational anger.

"For offering you a ride?"

I folded my arms tight over my chest. "Just because I can't swim doesn't mean I don't know how to walk, thank you very much."

"I'm only making sure you get home safe."

I narrowed my eyes at him, trying to detect any sign that he was teasing me. But he looked like he was being serious. For a moment, my heart fluttered. It was infuriating. The smallest gesture of kindness—common courtesy, really—from a hot boy was enough to soften me, and I hated myself for it.

"Idiot," I murmured.

"That's a little harsh," Blake called to me as I started to turn the corner of a street. I didn't turn back to look at him, but I heard his car pull to a stop. "Hey, Alaska?"

"What?" I called over my shoulder.

"Where are you going?"

I knew immediately that I'd taken the wrong turn. My feet stopped, but my ego was far too large for me to turn around and admit my mistake. I waited for him to call out again. To rub it all in my face.

"If you get in the car now," he called, "I won't say anything the whole way home."

No jokes? No rude remarks? I didn't waste time questioning it. I turned on my heel, marched to the car, and slipped into the passenger's seat before Blake could rescind the offer. I didn't look at him as I pulled on my seat belt. He wordlessly clicked the air conditioning on.

"Are you cold?" I asked before I could stop myself.

He was in a sweatshirt, after all.

"I'm fine." He shrugged, keeping his blue eyes locked on the road ahead as he made the correct turn to our houses. "I just thought you might be warm. You practically live in the snow, right?"

"Alaska isn't all ice and polar bears, you know."

He shrugged. "Never been."

"Never taken geography, either, I'd assume."

It came out harsher than I wanted it to. Meaner. It was the kind of thing one Huntington Prep kid would say to another—a not-so-gentle barb about academic failure. But Blake didn't laugh it off or toss back an equally sharp comment about one of my many shortcomings. He said nothing. His cheeks seemed horribly pink. For a long moment, the only sound in the car was the soft tick of his turn signal. I dropped my gaze down to my hands, fiddling with my thumbs and wishing I knew how to stop doing everything wrong.

"This is going *really* well," I blurted.

Blake barked out a startled laugh. It was a nice sound, and it made me slump in my seat with relief. I hadn't noticed how tense both of us were until I was able to unclench my fists and tip my head back against the cool leather headrest.

"Thanks, by the way," he said.

I frowned, trying to remember if I had done him any favors recently. "For what?"

"For not telling Lena and Jesse about me going over to Alissa's house the other night."

I was about to mention that I had only kept my mouth shut because he was holding the fact that I couldn't swim against me but decided I'd let him feel indebted to me.

"Alissa told Lena everything anyway," I said with a shrug.

Blake's hands twitched on the wheel. "She *what*?"

"Well," me and my big mouth barreled on, "maybe not everything. I don't know. They were whispering most of the day. But Alissa came by after you and Jesse left, and she told Lena that you guys met up, and she said you wouldn't take her back, and then she said you rebounded already, or something. And then I think she tried to call Ethan."

This impulsive oversharing thing had never happened to me before. Only around Blake did I find myself talking so much, even when my foot felt firmly wedged in my mouth.

"She told you I *rebounded*?"

"I figure she's either superparanoid or she knows you were at the pool with someone."

"Does she know I was with *you*?" he asked, knuckles practically white on the steering wheel.

"Well, I'm alive, so no."

Blake seemed to relax a little, but his dark eyebrows were still knit together so there was a little crease between them. "This makes no sense. I didn't tell her where I was coming from on Saturday. Unless someone saw us at the pool and told her—but then she would've known it was you, and she would've said something. Right? And why does she think I've *rebounded*?"

He kept saying it that way—like the concept was absurd to him.

"She's probably just paranoid," I murmured, sinking into my seat miserably.

Neither of us spoke another word. When we finally pulled up in front of our houses, I wasn't sure whether I should thank Blake for the ride or reprimand him again for the honking.

"We're here," Blake announced.

"I know," I snapped, then winced apologetically. "Thank you."

"No problem."

I climbed out of the car and jogged across the lawn, eager to get inside before the mosquitos that sheltered in the grass could eat me alive, but somehow Blake and his long strides got to his porch steps at the exact same time I reached Rachel's. We climbed in perfect unison.

"Hey, Waverly?" he called.

I briefly considered pretending I hadn't heard him. "Yeah?"

"Be at the public pool Thursday night. Eight o'clock. You're going to learn how to tread water if it kills me."

Before I could argue, Blake slipped inside his house, leaving me to stare after him with my mouth agape and a mosquito perched on my wrist.

Shit. I was in trouble.

Chapter 7

The next morning, Lena arrived at the bookstore a full six minutes into our shift.

I'd meant to get a start on shelving the new inventory while I waited for her, but instead I'd found Alissa's stash of celebrity gossip magazines behind the register. Alissa hadn't indicated that she was going to show up to work that day, seeing as she was still on an emotional hiatus, so I took it upon myself to rummage through some of the junk she had stashed in a monogrammed bag she kept in our shared work space. She had four packs of gum and about a hundred different issues of a magazine entitled *The Daily Gossip*, which had a disclaimer printed on the back of each cover to warn the reader that their stories were satirical and for entertainment purposes only and that libel lawsuits would not be appreciated.

Upon hearing Lena stomp in, I tried to hide the magazine in my hands.

"Those things will rot your brain, you know," Lena said, not missing a thing. "But the secret celebrity siblings edition is pretty good. Although almost everything they say about twins is totally made up. I'm telling you now—we're very overrated."

I exhaled in a *whoosh*, relieved to see that she was still talking to me after her day of whispering with Alissa—and that she didn't seem put off by my snooping.

"I'd love a sibling," I said. "But I'm just reading these for the horoscopes."

Flicking to the next page, I found a collection of unflattering paparazzi shots of celebrities on vacation. The collage of bikini bottoms and sunburn lines was like a slap to the face—a sudden and unwanted reminder that I had another swim lesson with Blake tomorrow night.

"What's wrong?" Lena demanded. "Is Mercury in retrograde?"

"I don't know. I just remembered that I need to . . . buy a bikini." The way I said it made it sound a little more like a question than a statement. But it was true—I wasn't about to wear Rachel's neon-pink bikini again. And I wasn't exactly excited about swimsuit shopping.

"Alissa has some here. They all still have the tags on, if you want to take one."

"*Here?* In the bookstore?"

Lena ducked behind the cashier's desk. "She practically lives here. I see you've found the magazine stash already. I think she puts the clothes in this cabinet—"

"I can't just steal one of her bathing suits, Lena." There was no way it'd fit.

"She buys new ones all the time. Seriously, she doesn't even wear them—I think she just likes the rush of spending her dad's money. What color do you want? How do you feel about animal prints?"

I gave Lena a pointed look. "Does she have anything, you know, neutral?"

"Depends. Do you consider leopard a neutral?"

"Lena, I don't think this is going to—"

"Here we go," she cried, interrupting me midsentence to shove a navy-blue and white striped bikini at me. I caught a glimpse of a brand name I didn't recognize on the tag, followed by a price with one more digit than I was used to. Lena ushered me into the bookstore bathroom, where I stood perfectly still for a moment, staring at myself in the little mirror over the tiny sink. Tangled mess of hair, oversized Disney World T-shirt, shorts several sizes too big (Rachel had dug this particular pair up from a cardboard box somewhere at the bottom of her closet). I looked like a mess.

And once I had the overpriced bikini on, I still looked like a mess. Just a nautical one.

"Open the door and let me see!" Lena demanded from outside.

Is this what it's like to have an older sister?

"Waverly, I'm not above breaking the door down."

I'd only known Lena for a few days, but I already knew her well enough to know that she wasn't joking. She would totally break down the door. So, taking a deep breath and sucking in my stomach, I grabbed the door handle and cracked it open.

Lena looked me up and down. "You know, considering you're a solid eight inches taller than Alissa, it fits remarkably well."

"Are your sure she won't mind?"

"I'm sure. Honestly, she keeps so much stuff here, she won't notice anything's gone. And like I said—she shops. All. The. Time."

"Must be nice to have that kind of spending money," I muttered. "Why does she even work here, anyway? Is this a college apps thing?"

"She needs this job."

"She *needs* it?" I repeated dubiously.

"I mean, no. But she really, really likes being able to say that she's not just mooching off her dad all the time."

"What does he do?"

"He owns Hastings Yachts. It's a boat rental service," Lena said.

I'm pretty sure if I were an heiress, I'd spend all my time lounging around and spend all of my dad's money on books. At least Alissa had a job.

"I didn't know that," I replied truthfully.

"You learn something new every day." Lena shrugged. "Alissa seems like this big, dramatic, raging dumpster of emotions, but she can't help it. If you met her mom, you'd understand. She's been remarried seven times. So, Alissa doesn't really know what a real, working relationship is . . ."

"Which is why she can't choose between Ethan and Blake?"

"Precisely."

I wasn't sure what to think. On the one hand, I respected that she wanted to be financially independent, if only to buy herself a warehouse of swimsuits. On the other hand, Alissa had cheated on someone, and although she and Blake weren't married and there was no teenage daughter to get caught in the landslide of their failed relationship, something about her flippant disregard for the boys she played with rubbed me the wrong way. But maybe that was because I didn't like the idea that having miserable parents was supposed to result in kids who hurt other people. I couldn't bear the idea that I might somehow be more inclined than other people to be cruel. To be selfish. I didn't want to be like my parents.

Lena and I spent the rest of the morning stocking the shelves and, when that was done, taking turns reading absurd celebrity rumors to each other. For our lunch break, we grabbed chicken club sandwiches from the shop down the street and sat on a bench with our feet in the sand. Lena basked in the sun. I watched warily as a seagull circled overhead. We feasted until we were full, then trudged back to the bookstore.

"I'm never eating again," I moaned, clutching my stomach.

"Liar," Lena said, then let out a loud belch.

We were both laughing so hard that it took us a few tries to tug the door open. When we did, we found Blake standing at the front display, hands shoved into the pockets of his dark jeans as he gazed down at the arrangement of books.

"Look who decided to pick up a book," Lena singsonged.

Blake turned to face us. "I read, you know."

"I'm just teasing you. What brings you in?"

Blake kept his eyes on me for a moment longer before tilting his head up, a single lock of his dark hair falling across his forehead in an absurdly romantic way.

"I'm Chloe's errand boy for the day," he said, producing a double-sided list scribbled on a torn piece of ruled paper. "She's got me picking up all her *essentials*."

Lena grimaced sympathetically. "Bummer."

"Yeah. You wouldn't happen to have a book called *The Billionaire's Promise*, would you?" Blake asked, face bright red.

Ah yes. The essentials.

"Let me check the back," Lena said, holding up a finger before darting into the stacks.

For the first time since I'd arrived in Holden, time seemed to slow. Blake shifted his weight awkwardly. I mirrored him.

"We're still on for tomorrow night, right?" he asked.

My eyebrows shot up. He'd really meant it. He was really going to keep up with these swim lessons.

"Listen, Blake . . ." I began.

How was I supposed to put this into words? I couldn't exactly say, *I don't want to go swimming with you right now because I think I have a monumentally embarrassing crush on you and I ate a chicken club the size of my head for lunch and I'm really not in the mood to put on a stupid bikini that makes me look like a novelty sailor because your rebound girl is probably ten times hotter than I could ever hope to be.*

"Are you going to finish that sentence?" Blake asked.

"No," I grumbled.

"Good. Then I'll see you at eight."

Were all lifeguards this snarky, or was it just Blake Hamilton?

It was probably just him. I'm sure there were some perfectly well-mannered, pleasant lifeguards out there. I just had really bad luck and got stuck with a crappy one. An attractive one, I hated to admit, but a crappy one nonetheless.

"Found it!" A shrill cry interrupted us.

Lena appeared at my side, a book in her hand, and shoved it at Blake's chest. She then circled to the other side of the cashier's desk and took a deep breath, preparing herself for an epic battle against the register.

It was silent for a moment as Lena's fingers danced across the buttons.

She handed him his receipt.

"Thanks," he told her, slipping his wallet back into the pocket of his jeans. Then he turned to me. "I'll see you tomorrow night, Waverly."

"Tomorrow night?" Lena repeated. "What are you guys up to?"

Blake froze and went slightly pale.

I scrambled. "I, um, have to—"

"Rachel wants Waverly to come down and meet her in Marlin Bay for dinner," Blake supplied, quickly picking up that I was no good at coming up with bogus excuses. He, however, was a brilliant liar: "Think she wants to show her the mural. I offered to drive."

"Right." I nodded. "The mural. I mean, dinner."

"I'll pick you up at eight," Blake said, seeming to decide that if he stuck around any longer I'd end up blurting out where we were actually headed and ruin everything.

Chapter 8

This wasn't normal. Then again, I wasn't a very normal person, so what did I expect?

I glared at my reflection in the mirror in the women's locker room at the public pool. If I was a *normal* girl, I would've had the guts to trot outside, place my hands on my hips, and send Blake Hamilton the flirtiest smile he'd ever seen in his life. But I wasn't that brazen, and I'm pretty sure if I tried to smile, I'd only end up baring my teeth at him like a wild animal. So, like the coward I was, I'd been hovering in the locker room for fifteen minutes, even though I had already peed twice, washed my hands three times, and changed into my swimsuit.

I was running out of ways to delay the inevitable.

Sooner or later, I was going to have to face Blake. And I was going to have to do it dressed in nothing but a teeny, tiny, navy-blue and white striped bikini. I glanced back at my reflection in the mirror, my eyes dropping to my chest. Okay, so my boobs weren't unnoticeably small or inconveniently large. But, I swear to God, the left one was bigger than the right one. I groaned and hung my head, staring down at the pile of my clothes beside my feet. I had already thought over the possibility of fleeing, but the girls' bathroom didn't have a window for me to jump out of or a reasonably sized air vent for me to climb into, so it looked like I was stuck.

"Waverly," Blake called from somewhere outside. "Let's go."

"I'll be out in a minute!"

It was time for me to woman up. I puffed out my lopsided chest, pushed open the bathroom door, and marched to the two sets of glass doors at the back of the pool house. I managed to keep my head held high as I stepped onto the patio and into the golden light of the setting sun.

Blake was standing beside the Olympic-sized pool, his broad, bare back turned to me as he placed his belongings on one of the poolside recliners. He was wearing a pair of navy-blue swim trunks with a white waistband. My heart did a little stutter-step as I realized that we were matching. Had he planned that or something? No, of course not.

A red foam board sat at his feet. I tried to remember what he had told me it was. A kickboard, I think. To be honest, all I could remember was that he had mocked me for being the oldest kid he'd ever given lessons to.

Maybe, if I kept very quiet, Blake wouldn't even notice that I'd come out of the locker room. I could drop my things by a lounge chair and hop into the pool before he caught sight of me in the bikini I was quickly beginning to regret wearing.

But, as they almost always do, my plan failed.

I hadn't even taken three steps across the patio when Blake whipped around.

"Ready," I choked out, tentatively placing one hand on my hip and trying to look casual. My other hand tightened in a death grip around my baggy T-shirt and shorts, which I now desperately wished were on my body rather than at my side. Was it just me or had I started sweating like crazy?

"About time," Blake muttered. He bent to snatch the red board from beside his feet, muscles in his arms flexing. I realized immediately that I was staring and averted my eyes from Blake's admittedly beautiful arm muscles to his face. Our gazes locked, and I felt like my entire face had just been engulfed in flames. So quickly I almost missed it, Blake's eyes dropped to observe my bikini. And now my entire body felt like it was on fire. *Thanks, Hamilton.*

"You got a new swimsuit," Blake said. It sounded more like a statement than a question, but I couldn't be sure.

"I did, yeah. How'd you know?"

The corner of Blake's mouth jerked upward in a smirk.

"Because," he said, taking several steps toward me. He was so close that I could see the little scar above his left eyebrow again. I hadn't been close enough to see it since he first rescued me from an imaginary riptide at the beach. What was he doing? Why was he so close?

Before I could comprehend what was happening, Blake's hand reached for my waist.

My breath caught in my throat.

"You forgot to take the tag off."

With one swift movement of his arm, Blake snagged the small plastic tag that was still hanging from the string of my bikini top. It came off in his hand with a little *pop*.

"Oh," I said, my eyes dropping to the tag that Blake held in his outstretched hand. "Thanks. It's Alissa's, actually. She keeps a ton of stuff at the bookstore—I mean, seriously, you could probably survive off her candy stash for a week. I didn't steal it, though. The bathing suit. I mean, I didn't actually ask her, either, but Lena said it was fine."

Why did I always do this around Blake? This oversharing thing?

I closed my eyes, suddenly wishing I could be somewhere else. *Anywhere* else. I waited for Blake to make some snide comment about my inability to shut up, but he remained silent.

The second I opened my eyes and saw the giant, amused smile on Blake's face, my insides melted, and I was left feeling like a bowl of hot nacho-cheese dip. I opened my other eye immediately, wanting to take in the sight before me in its entirety. I wanted to remember this forever. I wanted to memorize the amused gleam in his eyes, the freckles sprinkled across his nose, the slight dimples that had suddenly appeared as if out of nowhere.

It was beautiful. *He* was beautiful.

"Do you always talk this much?" he asked.

It was the exact same question he had asked when he was driving me to the bonfire. In fact, it was the first thing he had ever said to me. But now, instead of scowling down his nose, he was beaming at me. Like we were in on a joke. Like we were friends. Like, maybe he didn't find me a complete and utter waste of space.

And I didn't know what to do with that, so I did the first thing that came to mind.

"Last one in is a rotten egg!"

I cannonballed into the shallow end of the pool.

I stayed underwater as long as my lungs would allow, which

wasn't long considering that I had never in my life had the need to hold my breath for more than a few seconds, like when my mom attempted a new recipe in the kitchen or our expedition crossed paths with an animal carcass.

When I resurfaced, I refused to look up at Blake. Instead, I leaned back and concentrated on floating. I was better than last time, but my legs still twitched violently whenever I thought I was about to sink. It didn't help my focus that I suddenly remembered I was wearing a very small navy-blue and white striped bikini, and Blake Hamilton was still standing at the edge of the pool. He had the complete freedom to check out every visible inch of my body.

Then again, maybe he wasn't looking.

I bet Alissa has symmetrical boobs.

The thought was enough to break my concentration long enough for me to forget what I was doing. I sank like a rock. I was so surprised by the sudden appearance of water over my face that I opened my mouth and gulped in a mouthful of chlorinated pool water. The stinging in my lungs nearly immobilized me.

Then something clamped down around my wrist, and I was yanked up to the surface.

"My bad—"

I would have said more, but the water lodged in my throat prevented me from further expressing just how surprised I was.

"Breathe," a deep voice grumbled from beside me.

My eyes snapped open.

Blake was now standing in the pool, the kickboard floating in the water behind him, his chest shimmering wet and his large hand clenched around my wrist. I couldn't tell whether he was concerned for my well being or annoyed that I almost drowned in three and a half feet of water.

"Clearly, we need to review our last lesson."

All right. He was definitely annoyed.

"I'm fi—"

Blake watched me as I doubled over, coughing ferociously. When I finally managed to dislodge the water from my lungs, my entire body was shaking a little.

"You good?" There wasn't a hint of mocking in his voice.

I shot him a weak thumbs-up. He turned to chase after the kickboard, which had drifted to the other end of the pool sometime during my retching.

Blake was eerily concerned with my ability to float. I mean, I knew he was a lifeguard—it was his *job*. But it seemed like an instinctual reaction sort of thing for him. And I had a bad feeling that it had something to do with his mom. Blake hadn't said it outright, but I was smart enough to connect two and two: his mother had drowned. Now, more than ever before, I wanted to ask questions. But talk about tactless. You can't just ask people about their dead parents.

Blake swam back to me, kickboard in hand.

"Here. Do some laps."

I frowned. "Laps?"

"Yeah. Put your hands on the front of this."

I grabbed one end of the board.

"The *other* front."

I spun the board around with a huff. "How was I supposed to know?"

"Now bend your knees, push off, and start kicking."

The board was made for someone half my size. That was the excuse I told myself for why, as soon as I pushed off the bottom of the pool, the nose of the board hooked under the surface and sent a jet of chlorinated water straight into my nose.

I was so bad at this. It shouldn't have come as a surprise—I was always somewhere between *bad* and *passably mediocre* at things—but I'd been hoping that something about traveling to the opposite corner of the country would fix things. Would fix *me*.

I kicked to the far wall of the shallow end, then turned and kicked back. It took a small eternity, and it was humiliating. The flailing. The thumping sound of my legs whacking the water. The juxtaposition of the enormous splashes behind me and the snail's pace of my actual progress across the pool. When I finally reached my starting point again, Blake was out of the water and seated on the end of one of the lounge chairs, face lit by the glow of his phone.

He glanced up when he realized I'd stopped.

"It's been one minute. You can't possibly be tired."

The urge to splash him was overpowering.

"Obviously, I'm not tired. I just don't see how this is going to teach me how to swim. Can we move on to whatever's next?"

"You have to learn the motions first. You're all over the place. Keep your body straight and don't lean your shoulders side to side like that."

I heaved the kickboard out of the water and slapped it onto the patio. "I don't like this."

I'm not good at it.

"Are you throwing a tantrum right now?"

"You know, you're not nearly as cool as you think you are," I snapped.

"What's that supposed to mean?" he asked, his tone far too casual and detached. I'd hit a nerve. He was trying to act like I hadn't.

"You treat me like a child because I can't swim, and the whole time you're getting into shouting matches with your stepmother and chasing around your ex-girlfriend, who *cheated* on you with a dude who acts like he's training to be in a fraternity. I mean, if one of us is childish, it's definitely not me."

Blake's face was pink in the rapidly fading light.

"Are you done?" he asked, still monotone.

No. I wasn't. "You act like it's such a *chore* for you to be here, but you know what? I didn't ask for this. I didn't ask to be your charity case."

Blake stood abruptly from his recliner and said, "Fine. Then I quit."

With that, he grabbed his shirt and started toward the pool house.

"You can't quit," I spluttered.

He didn't stop. I grabbed the ledge of the pool and went after him. I had practically no upper body strength, but the sudden jolt of adrenaline that coursed through me was enough to pull me up out of the water. I tumbled onto the tiles surrounding the ledge and then shot up and sprinted after my rampaging swim teacher.

The consequences of my anger and frustration became apparent. I thought of Jesse and Lena and how mortifying it would be to have to tell them—maybe in a few days, maybe in a few weeks—that I'd lied about knowing how to swim.

My desperation drove me to shout, "Please."

There went my pride.

Blake stopped walking and turned, arms folded across his chest. I think he wanted to look stern. But I knew I'd hurt him. I knew I'd prodded some bruises.

"Please," I said again, softer. "I'm sorry. I didn't mean—it just *comes out* sometimes. I don't know why. I'm so tired of being bad at things. I'm bad at *everything*. It's like a constant parade of disappointment with me, okay?"

Blake said nothing but sniffed once.

"I need swimming lessons," I admitted. "I *want* swimming lessons."

Blake was quiet for a long moment before he said, "All right."

I was so relieved I could have cried. And then I realized I was standing in the light of the pool house in nothing but a wet bikini, in full view of Blake Hamilton. My cheeks flushed.

"Maybe we should get back to it?"

Our eyes met, and I felt the sudden urge to look away. But his intense gaze made my entire body go rigid. I couldn't look away, and I didn't. And neither did Blake.

Then something chimed, and the tension between us was severed.

Both of us looked down as Blake reached into the pocket of his swim trunks and withdrew his cell phone. He glanced at the screen before answering and bringing the phone up to the side of his face.

"Chloe?" Blake asked, his voice hoarse. He cleared his throat and added, "What's up?"

I looked down at my feet and listened to the muffled sound of Chloe Hamilton's voice on the other end of the phone. I couldn't make out what she was saying, but whatever she said, it sounded like a question.

"I'm with a friend," Blake said into the phone.

Friend. Such a wonderful word, and yet so deeply inaccurate for our situation.

"That's so not fair," he argued. "What if I have plans tomorrow night? No, but maybe something will come up. Why do I have to watch her? I watched her the other night. Yes, I did. When you got dinner with Dad. Why does it matter if that was a week ago?"

Chloe's voice sounded shrill on the other end.

"Let me talk to my dad," Blake demanded.

I couldn't make out what Chloe said, but whatever it was, it shut Blake up. He brought his hand up and rubbed it over his eyes, looking suddenly tired. He dropped his arm back to his side and his blue eyes glanced around for a moment before they landed on me, still standing beside him. My cheeks grew hot under his gaze, and I tried to inconspicuously reach up and adjust my bikini top. A small, almost undetectable smile pulled up the corner of Blake's mouth.

"Okay," Blake mumbled into the phone. "Fine. Fine. I know."

I watched him warily.

"Bye," Blake said, smiling as he hung up and shoved his phone back into the pocket of his swim trunks. I narrowed my eyes at him suspiciously. What was with the sudden mood swing? And why was he looking at me with that creepy smile on his face?

"What did she want?" I asked carefully.

"She wants me to watch Isabel tomorrow night."

Friday with a toddler? "Bummer."

"Not really." Blake's smile was something wicked.

"Why?" I asked, eyes narrowed.

"I just figured out how you're going to repay me for these lessons." Before I could argue, he added, "You want me to teach you how to swim, right?"

I nodded weakly.

"So, I think it's only fair that you pay me back. And I know just how you're going to do it. You said you've babysat before, right? Those Alaskan twins who set your hair on fire?"

He'd remembered the story. "I mean, yeah—"

"Great. You're going to babysit Isabel for me tomorrow night."

I opened my mouth to argue.

"Say no, and I quit."

I huffed. Blake looked utterly triumphant. He had me backed into a corner.

"Fine," I grumbled. "Deal."

Blake grinned, looking pleased with himself. He was close again. So close that I could count the freckles on his nose and see the faint scar above his left eyebrow. I wondered how he had gotten that scar. Involuntarily, my arm lifted. My fingers twitched, aching to trace the tiny scar on his forehead. I probably would have done it, too, if Blake hadn't interrupted me.

"Are you okay?" he asked.

"Huh?"

"You just—" He squinted and shook his head. "Never mind. Let me put the cover on the pool and then we can walk back to my house."

I felt like I'd been scammed into this whole babysitting deal. I didn't like it. My grand plans for Friday night (watching Rachel paint while I raided her snack cupboard) had been dashed.

This thought was interrupted by Blake. More specifically, Blake's hand, which suddenly appeared at the side of my face. I froze as his fingers grabbed a clump of wet, tangled hair that had fallen over my face. His eyes remained focused on the piece of dripping hair as he twirled it in his fingers for a moment before flicking it back. When he opened his mouth, some part of me hoped for something tender and sentimental to come out.

Instead, he said, "You're getting water all over the floor in here."

Chapter 9

I'd been hoping that Rachel would help me get out of the whole *babysitting* deal, but when I pitched the idea to her over breakfast, she took it annoyingly well.

"My little freelancing entrepreneur, picking up summer jobs left and right!" she exclaimed, cradling her mug of coffee. "Oh, this is great timing, actually. I've been meaning to tackle this one part of the mural, and I *know* it's going to be a whole event—I've got to do a run to the store to get more paint, which means I'm going to have to borrow Margie's brother's truck again so I don't ruin my car. Is it all right if I work late tonight, Waverly? You won't need me?"

You won't need me? Such a foreign question—and one I was determined not to answer the wrong way. I didn't want to be a bother or a burden.

"Do what you need to do," I told her, grabbing my mostly empty bowl of cereal and completely empty mug. "I'm going to go get ready for work."

"And I'll call Margie's brother. Oh hey—do you want a ride to the bookstore?"

"That's okay," I said too quickly. "I can walk."

O

I stayed late on Friday to help Margie close. Blake picked me up again on my walk home from the bookstore. It wasn't out of the goodness of his heart—he was just trying to make sure I didn't try to back out on our deal. Still, I was thankful he hadn't actually come into the bookstore again, since Lena still seemed a little suspicious about the fictitious ride to Marlin Bay. She asked me how dinner with my aunt was, and for a solid six seconds, I'd forgotten our little lie.

If Rachel's theory about practice was true, I was going to be a phenomenal liar by the end of the summer.

By the time Blake pulled his father's silver sedan up to the curb directly behind Rachel's Volkswagen, Holden was bathed in moonlight. I locked my fingers around the edge of my leather car seat and held on for dear life, knowing that as soon as I let go, I'd have to face the fact that I was stuck babysitting two-year-old Isabel. All because stupid Blake Hamilton was blackmailing me.

He pushed open the driver's side door, letting a gust of humid air pour into the car. I sank down farther into my seat, savoring the feeling of cool leather against my bare legs. If I could just sit in this air-conditioned car forever, I would die happy.

Blake interrupted my moment of peace by poking his head back into the car.

"Come on," he urged.

I didn't move.

Behind Blake, the Hamiltons' front door swung open. Chloe stepped onto the front porch, dressed in all white and cradling Isabel in her arms. She spotted Blake first. Then she noticed me sitting in the passenger's seat like a hostage.

"Hey . . . you two," she began, obviously trying to sound cheerful rather than confused as she looked between us, her frown deepening. "Blake, honey, it's nine o'clock. I thought your dad talked to you about your new curfew—"

"I had to give Waverly a ride home. Actually, it was kind of lucky that I caught her on my way back from my shift." Once more, the nonchalant way he lied to his stepmother stunned me. "She volunteered to watch Isabel tonight. She loves kids. Can't get enough of them."

Volunteered, my ass.

"Really?" Chloe asked, her smile tight.

"It's no problem, Mrs. Hamilton," I said.

I wasn't sure, but I thought I saw Blake flinch. Whether it was because of my falsely chipper attitude or the use of his stepmother's married name, I wasn't sure. Either way, I kind of liked seeing him squirm. So I kept up with the sickeningly sweet attitude and hopped out of the car. I practically skipped up to the porch and climbed the steps two at a time.

When I reached the front door, Chloe was grinning.

"Look, Issie," she cooed at the toddler in her arms. "This is Waverly. She's a friend."

Isabel tilted her chin, her wispy white-blond curls bouncing around her head.

"Wave-ree," she repeated, testing the word.

Close enough.

"She's a little shy," Chloe said, and for a moment I couldn't tell if she was speaking to me or to Isabel. Her eyes darted over my shoulder and her smiled dropped. "Could you hold her for a moment, Waverly? I need to speak with Blake."

I let out a vague yelp of protest, but Chloe didn't notice, and instead wiped her palms against the front of her white jeans and started down the porch steps. Isabel squealed in delight and quickly grabbed a tiny fistful of my tangled hair.

Across the front lawn, Chloe and Blake were squaring off.

"Wave-ree," Isabel repeated.

"What's up, kiddo?"

She tugged at the strands of hair she had grasped in her little hand. I winced and bit my tongue before I could say a word unsuitable for my tiny audience.

"Blake, I mean it. Now." Chloe's frustrated voice carried over the lawn.

I turned to look at the driveway and saw Blake and Chloe locked in the middle of what appeared to be a heated argument. Well, that escalated quickly. Just moments ago, they'd been so calm. Now Blake was standing rigid and red faced over Chloe, who was also pink in the cheeks and was holding her hand in front of Blake's face. I watched as Blake angrily smacked his car keys into Chloe's waiting palm.

Isabel giggled.

"Your brother," I said with a sigh, "is incorrigible."

"Bad boy," Isabel supplied.

I clamped my lips together to stop my laugh. It came out through my nose as a snort. Luckily, neither Blake nor Chloe heard. They exchanged one last word—too quiet for me to make out—before Chloe turned and marched back to the porch. She smiled brightly at me, but it was a pageant smile. All for show.

"I'm going to go get George and we'll be off," she told me. "If it's not too much trouble to ask, Waverly, could you keep an eye on Blake tonight? I'd prefer it if he doesn't leave the house. Call me if he does, all right?"

Great. Now I was babysitting *two* kids.

"Sure thing, Mrs. Hamilton," I said with a pageant smile.

She disappeared into the house. With the coast clear, Blake returned to the porch.

"Mommy mad," Isabel mumbled in my arms.

Blake stormed past us through the front door.

"Blake mad too," she observed.

"Nothing new there. C'mon, kiddo," I said.

Just as I stepped into the house, two pairs of footsteps thundered down the wide staircase on the other side of the living room. I froze in the small entry hall and watched as Chloe and George arrived at the bottom of the steps, both wearing all white and sporting matching frowns. They stomped across the living room, muttering angrily to each other, and stopped suddenly when they spotted me standing in the little entry hall.

"Waverly?" George asked, his surprise evident on his face.

"Hi, Mr. Hamilton!" I chirped, trying my best to pretend I hadn't seen a glimpse of the family drama taking place in his house. I even offered him an awkward, one-handed wave.

"What are you doing here?" George asked, still sounding surprised to see me.

"Babysitting," I replied, casually nodding at Isabel as if she was my proof.

"I thought—" he began.

"Your son is cunning, I'll give him that," Chloe grumbled, "but somehow, he's gotten this poor girl to agree to babysit Isabel."

"Chloe," George let out a heavy sigh, closed his eyes, and brought up his hand to pinch the bridge of his nose. In that moment, I couldn't help but realize how much he looked like Blake; sure, he was way older and his stomach was a little bit bigger, but he had the same dark eyebrows that furrowed together so often.

"I took his car keys, George, but you know he'll find a way to sneak out tonight," Chloe said. "And last time it was a fistfight on the beach with that Ethan kid, but who knows what's next. I'm sure we'll hear about it from the other parents again. And you just know everyone in Holden is going to think I must be doing such a *shit* job—" Chloe cut herself off and took a deep, centering breath. When she spoke again, her voice was softer. "He already hates me, George. This time it's *your* turn to whip out the discipline. I'm done playing evil stepmom."

With that, Chloe turned and stalked past me.

I listened to her wedge-heeled footsteps as she flew down the porch steps. George smiled weakly at me.

"You can go on home if you want, Waverly," he said, fidgeting with the silver watch around his left wrist. "I don't know what Blake said to you, but I'll make some calls and see if anyone else can come in tonight—"

"No, Mr. Hamilton. It's fine. I've got you covered."

"Thank you," George said on a heavy exhale. "I really appreciate this. Chloe does too. I'm sorry about her, she's just—you know, she's having a rough time with Blake, and—"

"I understand."

George hopped down the porch steps, crossed the yard, and

slipped into the driver's seat of his silver sedan. Chloe was in the passenger's seat, methodically wiping her eyes and inspecting her fingertips for smudged makeup. I awkwardly shifted Isabel into one arm and used my free hand to wave at them as they pulled out of the driveway.

When their car was out of sight, I let out a deep breath of air.

"All right, kiddo," I told Isabel, shutting the front door with my foot, "time for the tour."

The Hamiltons' house was built exactly like Rachel's house: the living rooms were the same size, the staircase was placed in the same corner, and by the looks of it, the kitchen was in the same place. But where Rachel's house was clearly the house of an eclectic artist, the Hamiltons' house was something out of a home decor magazine.

It looked like at least one of them was a serious chef, because the white marble countertops were cluttered with stand mixers and wine bottles and neatly organized spice racks.

The double doors of the refrigerator were covered in a layer of schedules, school papers, crayon drawings, and grocery lists so thick that I could barely see the stainless-steel surface underneath. There were a few things on the door that surprised me. For one, Isabel's crayon depictions of Blake, George, and Chloe were spot-on. Not to mention someone had taped up what appeared to be a history test Blake took in May. I wasn't sure whether I was more surprised by Blake's immaculate handwriting, or the big, bold letter *A* written at the top of the page by his history teacher.

Satisfied with my snooping, I circled back into the living room, where Isabel requested that I set her down on the couch and turn on the television. My parents had raised me on the National Geographic channel and nature documentaries, but since I knew how I'd turned out, I indulged Isabel in some *Dora the Explorer*.

She requested juice (a word I had to ask her to repeat twice before I understood it). I shuffled into the kitchen, became immediately overwhelmed by the number of juice options in the double-wide fridge, and settled on apple.

I only made it halfway back into the living room before I froze.

Blake was sitting on the couch, as far away from Isabel as he could manage to get without actually sitting on top of the armrest. His back was rigid and he looked stiff, as if sitting so close to his half sister made him uncomfortable.

Isabel, however, seemed to be enjoying Blake's company.

"Look!" She pointed at the television screen, distressed. "Swiper!"

"I know, kid. I see him. They'll be fine."

Isabel scooted a few inches closer to her big brother, grinning up at him and sitting on her hands. Her legs were so short that only her feet and ankles hung over the edge of the cushions.

"I've got juice," I announced.

"She's not supposed to have sugar this late," Blake said, but it was too late. Isabel's chubby fist had a firm grip on the sippy cup.

"Oops," I said.

"Oops," Isabel echoed.

"You are a terrible influence on her," Blake told me.

"Wave-ree pretty," Isabel argued, as if this somehow made me a better role model.

I started to laugh, but then I met Blake's eyes, and it felt like all the air had been sucked out of my lungs. He was looking at me oddly. Observing. Scanning my face, almost as if he was seriously considering Isabel's assessment.

My heart started pounding painfully hard against my rib cage.

Did Blake Hamilton think I was pretty?

After a moment of silence, the corners of Blake's lips curled down and he returned his gaze to the television screen. I quickly shuffled back into the kitchen.

Okay, Blake Hamilton did *not* think I was pretty.

But didn't I know that already?

I leaned my back against the refrigerator and let out a long, heavy sigh. I'm not sure how long I stood there, clutching a nearly empty glass of water in one hand and bracing myself against the fridge with the other. But next thing I knew, I heard heavy footsteps coming toward me.

I straightened up immediately and stepped away from the fridge.

Blake walked in, his arms folded tightly over his chest, wrinkling his perfect white T-shirt. He surveyed the room quickly, probably assessing the kitchen for any damage I might have caused, before allowing his gaze to land on me.

"You're still here," I blurted.

He frowned. "What's that supposed to mean? I *live* here."

"Chloe said you were going to sneak out." I tried to inconspicuously edge onto my tiptoes and decrease the gap between our heights. It didn't work.

"Well, I didn't," Blake said, holding up his arms and motioning down at his body, which was very obviously still in the house and *not* at some wild teenage party. I frowned, trying to figure out why he hadn't even attempted to leave the house.

"Why?" I asked.

Blake opened his mouth then snapped it shut. He let out a grunt and ran his fingers through his dark hair, sending the already disheveled locks into complete disarray.

"I mean . . ." Blake began, then trailed off.

"Why didn't you sneak out?" I repeated. "That was the big plan, right? Why else would you need me here?"

"Because this way, I don't actually have to interact with her."

Was that really the reason? Or was I here because he'd wanted me to be? It felt like such a self-centered, indulgent idea. I couldn't shake it.

Our staring contest was interrupted when Blake's cell phone vibrated. He waved me away with one hand and dug into the pocket of his shorts with his other. As he answered his phone, making sure to turn away from me so I couldn't eavesdrop or anything, I stuck my tongue out at his back before heading back into the living room to do my supervision duties.

A moment later, Blake popped into the doorway between the kitchen and the living room.

"—try calling Lena?" he said into his phone, his tone agitated.

"What about Lena?" I asked.

"Hold on." Blake pressed the phone to his chest. "Waverly, don't let her get any juice on the—" Isabel's apple juice was dribbling. I dove for the sippy cup. Blake huffed and put his phone to his ear again. "Jesse? Yeah, I'm here . . . no, it's no one . . . just Isabel's babysitter."

Naturally, Blake wouldn't want Jesse to know that I was at his house. I tried not to take offense. It wasn't like I wanted Jesse to know I was here either.

Blake hurried out of the room.

I got up to follow him, fully embracing my desire to eavesdrop. But I was almost to the doorway when Blake reappeared in it, his scowl something awful and a sweatshirt in his hand.

"—see you soon," he said, hanging up.

It hit me. He was sneaking out.

"Oh come on," I cried, jabbing a finger at him. "Do *not* make me call your stepmother."

"You're serious?" Blake asked. He glanced down at my finger where it was planted against his chest and huffed. "I don't have time for this."

"I'm serious. I'll call Chloe."

"No, you won't—"

I opened my mouth to argue.

"—because you're coming with me."

"Coming *where*?" I spluttered.

"Ethan's party. Jesse just invited us."

That had to be a lie. For one thing, Jesse didn't know I was over at Blake's house. He couldn't possibly have invited the both of us. Not to mention, Blake didn't look like he was ready to *go have some fun.* He looked too tense, like he was ready for a fight or something. Which wouldn't be a surprise, considering he was going to Ethan's party. He hated Ethan.

"Bullshit," I accused.

"Fine." Blake huffed. "Ethan's throwing a party at his house. Jesse called and said Alissa's so drunk she can't walk. He needs help getting her home. And Lena thinks she can handle it, of course, but—look, I don't have time for this. We can talk later."

I hadn't actually been expecting him to keep me in the loop. I was never in the loop.

"Alissa's in trouble?" I asked.

"Yes," Blake said through gritted teeth. "Now can we *please* go?"

I would have thought the whole knight in shining armor act was cute, but something about the fact that Blake still cared for Alissa, his cheating ex-girlfriend, made me feel sick. And I refused to admit that it was because I wished Blake showed *me* this kind of care.

"Shouldn't I stay here?" I asked, desperately trying my best to weasel out of the inevitable trouble. "You know, and watch Isabel. Make sure she doesn't die or anything."

Blake gave me a pointed glare.

"I need you to come along," he stated, pulling his sweat-shirt over his shoulders. When his head popped through the top, I nearly laughed. His dark hair was all mussed, sticking up at strange angles. I had to shove my hands into the pockets of Rachel's shorts to keep myself from reaching up and running my fingers through it.

"Why?" I croaked miserably.

"In case you hadn't noticed, I don't have a car for the night," Blake pointed out, shoving his cell phone into his shorts and adjusting the hem of his sweatshirt.

"So?" I quirked an eyebrow at him. "Neither do I."

Blake looked up at me, a smirk pulling up the corners of his mouth.

"I know you don't have a car," he said, "but your aunt does."

Chapter 10

Florida had turned me into a delinquent. There was no other way to explain how I'd landed myself in the backseat of my aunt's *borrowed* (stolen) car, Isabel Hamilton in a car seat next to me, something called a baby go-bag at my feet, and Blake Hamilton in the driver's seat, muttering to himself as he tried to find parking on Ethan's McMansion-lined street.

"Would you stop doing that?"

Blake's voice made me jump nearly a foot into the air. I clutched my seat belt in one hand and Isabel's tiny, pajama-clad foot in the other.

"Doing what?"

"Bouncing your leg. You're shaking the whole car. Relax. Nobody's getting in trouble."

I could already picture our mug shots.

"I promise," Blake pressed on, "this will take ten minutes, tops. All we need to do is find Alissa, get her in the car, and drive her home. Then we'll go back, put Rachel's car keys on the kitchen counter right where we found them, and you can go back to babysitting in peace."

"But what if—"

"Chloe and my dad aren't coming home for at least another two hours. And you just called your aunt. She's staying late to work on the mural down in Marlin Bay. It'll take her, what? Half an hour to clean her brushes? Twenty minutes to get a lift home from one of her assistants? She'll never even know we borrowed her car."

My leg started shaking again.

"But—" I started.

"If something happens, I'll tell Rachel the truth."

"The truth?" I repeated. The hard angle of Blake's jaw was intensified by the faint bluish glow of the light from the dashboard. He'd take the blame for me? Really?

I decided to drop the subject and focus on keeping my left leg still as Blake wove through the streets of Holden. We pulled up to a stop sign, and suddenly I could feel the road shaking. For a second, I thought that there was an earthquake. Then I realized that the rhythmic thump of the ground was perfectly in time to the bass of a Katy Perry song.

Figures. Ethan *would* play Katy Perry at his parties.

It was another minute or so before Blake pulled the car onto a very crowded street. I was surprised at the abnormal number of cars parked along the curb. Then, after a moment, I spotted what I could only guess was Ethan's house—a monstrous combination of vaguely Mediterranean architecture and the American proclivity to go big or go home.

"Is that it?" I asked, praying that by some miracle we had arrived at the wrong destination, and there was someone *else* in Holden throwing a giant party at a house that looked like it belonged to a professional basketball player.

Blake parked and quickly got out. I rolled down my window to shout at him.

"Isabel and I can just wait here!" I reached out the window to pat the outside of Rachel's car, which I could now see was illegally parked against a red curb. Fantastic. Add that to the list of rules I was breaking tonight.

"Fine," Blake said. "Do you have your phone with you?"

Oh dear God.

"Waverly?"

"I . . . don't have a phone."

Blake blinked. "You're fucking kidding me."

"I'm not. I left it in Alaska."

On purpose, of course, but we didn't have time to unpack all that.

"Then you have to come inside with me. I can't leave you with my baby sister without a phone."

"But I can't bring a baby into a party."

Blake held out a hand impatiently. "Pass me the go bag."

He retrieved a pair of earmuffs—the kind people wear when they're using chainsaws or other heavy machinery—and informed me that Chloe had been taking Isabel to baseball games for a while. How different could it be? Blake then produced a baby carrier, which was really just a glorified backpack with an open top. With Isabel strapped between my shoulder blades, Blake and I marched toward the chaos.

Ethan's house was lit up like an overdecorated Christmas tree, in stark contrast with the black night sky above and all the other houses on the block, which appeared to be inhabited by a series of people with great talent for falling asleep to loud, overplayed pop music.

"I guess we'll do this like they did in the Middle Ages, since you don't have a phone," Blake said as we climbed the front steps.

"I'm pretty sure no one had to go on missions to wild teenage parties to rescue their drunk ex-girlfriends back then."

Blake snorted, then looked mad that he'd laughed.

The ceilings in Ethan's entry hall were two stories high and heavily chandeliered, but below, the room was packed with sweaty, bikini-clad, board-short-wearing bodies that were all jumping in rhythm to the Justin Bieber song being blasted through Ethan's surround-sound stereo system. Over the music, someone belched loudly from somewhere to my left, adding to the thick, heavy stench of alcohol that plagued the building. And it wasn't just loud, smelly, and cramped in here. It felt like I had just stepped into a furnace.

This was hell.

"Nope!" I shouted over the music. "Nope, we're leaving."

I turned back to the door. Isabel let out a little cry of protest.

"Pa-tree!" she exclaimed. *Party.*

I'd never been to a house party before. Most of the students at Huntington Prep weren't partying people—unless we were counting weekend outings and overnight trips for sports tournaments, debate competitions, and performance art festivals. Alcohol and loud music wasn't exactly something we could slap on a college application. But even the toddler strapped to my back seemed to realize that this was a special opportunity.

Maybe this was my chance to be the kind of girl who went to parties.

With a deep breath, I nodded. Blake took my hand, which I hadn't expected, and tugged me into the crowd. We pushed through the mob of dancing teenagers, some of whom were bouncing up and down on the cushions of a sleek leather couch that looked more expensive than anything I had ever owned. Several people stopped to watch us. My social anxiety had only a moment to take flight before I realized why I was suddenly the center of attention.

"A baby!" someone gasped in delight.

"Oh my gosh, *so* cute."

"Look. At. Those. Cheeks."

By the time we made it to the kitchen, Blake still tugging me along with him, Isabel was positively basking in the attention, shooting gap-toothed grins at anyone who noticed her. The kitchen was blessedly emptier, but I barely had time to appreciate the fresh air before a pair of arms wrapped around my neck and pulled me into a tight hug.

"Lena!" I cried in relief.

"What are you doing here?" she asked, releasing me from her arms and grabbing both of my shoulders so she could look at me. "And why do you have Isabel?"

"She's my drinking partner, obviously."

"Par-tee," Isabel intoned again.

Lena let out a surprised laugh. "Did Blake drag you both along?"

As if summoned, Blake appeared at my side with Jesse at his heels.

"Hey, Waverly!" Jesse greeted. "And guest."

Isabel reached over my shoulder, grasping for him.

"Have either of you seen Alissa?" Blake asked the twins.

The Fletchers exchanged a glance. For a moment, I thought they were communicating telepathically, and I was jealous that I didn't have a twin to do the same with. But then they both opened their mouths to speak.

"Nope," Lena said at the same time that Jesse replied, "She was with Ethan."

So much for twin telepathy.

"She's with *Ethan*?" Blake repeated, eyes suddenly wide and wild.

"But maybe she—" Lena started to attempt damage control, but it was too late. Blake had already grabbed the front of Jesse's short-sleeved button-down shirt and dragged him into the mob of people dancing in the living room.

"That went well," I said. "What's wrong with Alissa?"

Lena sighed and played with Isabel's little, round, sock-clad foot. "Aside from the usual theatrics? She came here to let Ethan know that she's done with their relationship."

"But then why—"

"Is she with Ethan right now? Because she's drunk. I swear to God, I turned my back on her for one second, and next thing I knew, she's giggling like a maniac and bouncing on that Louis Vuitton couch in the living room."

"Louis Vuitton couch?" I repeated.

"Ethan's dad owns a chain of seafood restaurants," Lena explained. "Anyway, how'd Blake rope you into coming to this?"

She leaned back against the kitchen's marble countertop, which had become the foundation for a mountainous heap of crushed soda cans, half-empty potato chip bags, and uneaten chunks of pizza crust. There was an architecturally impressive stack of plastic red cups constructed like a modernistic sculpture next to the sink.

"He needed a car," I admitted, "so we had to take Rachel's."

Lena's jaw dropped. "You *stole* your aunt's car?"

"I know." I grimaced, reaching over my shoulder to untangle Isabel's fist from my hair. "I'm so dead. I don't know what I was thinking—"

"You *rebel*. Holy shit. You're going to *drive* Alissa *home* in Rachel's car? What if she, you know, pukes or something?" Lena asked, grimacing as she visualized the interior of Rachel's car splattered like the world's worst mural.

"Then I'll send Blake the bill for the upholstery detailing."

Lena laughed. "Come on," she told me, still chuckling as she grabbed my arm. "I bet we can find Alissa before the boys do."

Together, Lena and I wove through the kitchen and darted down a hallway filled with several couples engaged in heated make out sessions (I angled Isabel away so she couldn't see). When we reached the end of the hall, we found ourselves standing in a giant game room. The emerald-green walls were lined with vintage-looking pinball machines, and in the center of the room were three large, mahogany pool tables.

The whole room screamed *This family has too much money*.

"How big is this house?" I asked, mostly to myself since I knew Lena wouldn't be able to hear me over the music, which Isabel was kicking her legs along to the beat of.

Lena stood on her tiptoes and craned her neck, trying to see if Alissa was anywhere across the room. When she sat back on her heels again, she was frowning.

"Let's try upstairs," she said.

I grabbed hold of her arm and steered us to another hallway, this one much shorter than the last, that led back into the living room. The crowd parted for Isabel like the Red Sea for Moses.

Except Isabel didn't have a beard, and she was parting a mob of drunken teenagers instead of a large body of water.

"The baby's back! See, I told you there was a baby!" someone shouted.

We climbed the grand staircase and made our way to the second floor, which seemed just as crowded as the rest of the house. Lena and I stopped at the top of the stairs and found ourselves facing a dilemma: the hallway in front of us branched out, one part winding to the left and one curling to the right.

"You two go that way," Lena told me, pointing down the left hallway, "and I'll take the other hall. Let's meet back here in three minutes. If you find Alissa, just stay put and I'll know to come that way and find you. If I'm not back here, then you'll know she's this way and you should come find me."

With that, Lena went right and I went left.

"Alissa?" I called.

The hallway was long and the walls were painted pale cream. Hung along the walls, at four-foot intervals, were professional-looking family photos. Some of them were small portraits but most were large group shots of ten or eleven people. If I hadn't been on a mission to find Alissa, I would have stopped and tried to pick out which of the boys in the photos was Ethan.

But I had more important things to worry about.

The hallway, aside from being ridiculously long, was also lined with an enormous number of doors, most of which were bedrooms occupied by couples making out. I did pass one bathroom, though, and had to stop and make sure none of the brunets waiting for their turn to grab the porcelain toilet seat and heave were Alissa.

Nope, not there.

I groaned and kept walking.

"Come on, Alissa!" I called. "Come out, come out, wherever you are!"

"Come out, come out!" Isabel added helpfully.

One of the doors farther down the hallway popped open and a short girl with long, copper-red hair stuck her head out. She stared at me for a moment, taking in my oversized shorts and the toddler on my back.

"Did you bring a *baby* to a party?" she demanded.

It seemed like a rhetorical question, given that Isabel certainly hadn't arrived on her own and just bumped into me.

"Have you seen Alissa Hastings?" I asked.

"Lissa?" The copper-haired girl raised an eyebrow at me, again looking down at Rachel's shorts, which I had tied around my waist with a piece of ribbon saved from one of last year's Christmas presents. "Are you her friend?"

"Yes. Well, sort of. Acquaintance, really."

"She just went downstairs, like, two minutes ago," the ginger told me. "Seriously, is the baby like a political statement or something?"

I had my lead. That was all I needed.

I spun around and hurried back to the top of the grand staircase. From behind the railing, I scanned the crowd in the living room for any sign of Alissa before I heard thunderous footsteps coming from the hallway I had just been down. I turned just in time to see several large, shirtless guys bounding through the hallway, laughing and throwing toilet paper rolls at everyone who threatened to step in their way. I threw myself flat against the wall just in time to dodge them, shielding Isabel's tiny body with my own, but didn't manage to escape the snowstorm of toilet paper.

"Assholes!" I shouted, plucking a sheet of toilet paper off of my head as I watched them continue down the hallway.

"Ass-oles," Isabel repeated, because of course she'd caught that through the earmuffs.

"No, no, no. Don't say—oh, this is just getting worse."

And then I saw Lena. Like me, she was covered in toilet paper.

"I hate these frat boy–wannabe assholes—" she began.

"Don't swear in front of the kid. She picks up *everything*. Look, I just ran into this girl who told me she saw Alissa head downstairs a couple of minutes ago."

"Awesome!" Lena cried.

"Come out, come out!" Isabel supplied.

The living room seemed to have become even more crowded in the short time Lena and I had been upstairs; now the crowd was so dense that I decided to hover on the edge to keep Isabel safe and out of the crush.

"Lena!" I called over the music. "I don't like this!"

Judging from the look on her face, I could tell she wanted to get out of here too. As we started a loop around the crowd and toward the kitchen, the song changed. For a moment, we were serenaded by the cute, sugary sweet, country-pop voice of *Fearless*-era Taylor Swift. Then, suddenly, the bass started thumping like a jackhammer.

Leave it to Ethan to play a techno remix of a Taylor Swift song.

I rose up onto my tiptoes and tried to look over the crowd. I was taller than just about every girl in the room, but the crowd was so thick, and the room so poorly lit and packed full of beach bums.

Speaking of beach bums, where was Blake?

"Where are Blake and Jesse?" I asked.

Lena turned to frown at me over her shoulder and pointed to her ear. She couldn't hear me. I took a deep breath, preparing to shout.

But then the music stopped.

I sighed in relief. And then a bulky blond boy in SpongeBob-print swim trunks climbed onto the Louis Vuitton couch. He was well over six and a half feet tall and probably weighed twice as much as I did, at bare minimum. Everyone turned to watch him as he held up a meaty hand and pointed to a small circle that was forming on the other side of the living room.

"Fight!" he bellowed.

All hell broke loose.

The kids who were standing around me, no longer upset over the sudden disappearance of the music, quickly rushed forward to the scene of the fight.

"Kick his ass, Ethan!" one guy cheered.

"That's unfair! Home court advantage!" another protested.

"Anyone got some popcorn?"

I swung Isabel off my back and hooked her around my front so I could better shield her and locked eyes with Lena in the hysteria. We reached a silent, mutual agreement almost instantly, and together we turned and sought out high ground on the stairs.

I already knew who was fighting, even before Lena and I were high enough to see the two grunting, grappling boys in the middle of the circle over the crowd. Because, really, who did I know who had a history of starting fights with Ethan? And who, therefore, would be the most likely person to start a brawl at Ethan's party?

Ethan's nemesis, of course.

And, as fate would have it, my ride home.

Talk about déjà vu.

As I pushed through the crowd toward the circle around Blake and Ethan, things were starting to seem like they couldn't possibly get any worse than they already were.

But, of course, the universe doesn't seem to like me very much.

I'm not sure who threw the first punch. In fact, I don't even care who started it all. But someone in the crowd thought that right now would be a good time to take out their anger on some poor drunk kid standing next to him. And once the first punch was thrown, the shouting started. And right behind the shouting came more punching.

Soon enough, everyone in Ethan's living room was fighting.

"We need to get out of here," Lena said.

"Can you carry Isabel?" I asked. "My arms are going numb." I shifted Isabel out of my arms, offering her to Lena.

Lena's eyes briefly went wide with panic. "I'm not great with kids, Waverly, I—"

"Here's Aunt Lena!" I announced, shoving Isabel into her arms.

"Ass-oles!" the kid cried, demonstrating her new favorite word.

"All right, she's kinda cool, I guess," Lena said, holding Isabel as stiffly as one might hold a bag of rotting lemons. "Let's get you out of here, babe."

I was just about to step out of the living room when something came flying at my face.

In retrospect, I totally deserved an elbow to the cheek. I really did. Not only had I let Blake Hamilton convince me that coming to his arch nemesis's party was a good idea, but I had also stolen my aunt's car and essentially kidnapped a two-year-old. I'd been an idiot all day, and since karma has a habit of coming back and biting me in the ass, I should've seen it coming.

And I did, for a moment.

But then it hit me.

I don't remember what the impact felt like, because the next thing I knew, I was sprawled not so elegantly across the floor of Ethan's living room and staring up at Lena, who looked almost as surprised as I felt, and Isabel, who had the nerve to laugh.

"Oh my God! Waverly! Are you all right?" Lena cried.

I wasn't sure if I was. I could still wiggle my toes, which was always a good sign, but there was a dull throbbing in the back of my head that didn't feel right. Lena reached down, grabbed one of my hands, and pulled me to my feet.

The throbbing in my head became worse.

"Waverly?" she asked, snapping her fingers in front of my face.

"I'm okay!" I argued.

Lena pursed her lips and held up her hand.

"How many fingers am I holding up?" she demanded.

"Tree!" Isabel supplied.

"Three," I repeated.

"You cheated," Lena huffed.

"We don't have time for this," I insisted. "We need to find Blake and Jesse. We need to—we gotta go. It's probably decades past her bedtime."

Lena narrowed her eyes for a moment, and I could only assume that she was mentally debating whether she should perform a proper medical exam on me or give up and help me find her brother and his friend.

"Par-tee over," Isabel said.

"Fine," Lena finally sighed. "Party over. Let's go."

We turned and had taken no more than a couple of steps before I spotted dark curls hovering above the crowd. I grabbed Lena's shoulder to get her attention and pointed him out. Lena hiked Isabel up on her hip and we started toward the other end of the room.

As we got closer, the guy with the curls turned around.

I was glad to see that it was, indeed, Jesse Fletcher.

But why did he look like he was clueless?

I mean, he was clueless. But usually, he just had a big idiotic grin on his face. His eyes scanned the crowd nervously, searching for someone. When Lena and I finally broke through the crowd, we realized why he looked so distressed.

He had a girl in his arms.

It was Alissa Hastings, passed out and wearing a little neon-orange bikini.

"Where'd you get the baby?" Jesse asked.

"Where'd you get the girl?" Lena shot back.

"She was in the home theater," Jesse said, his voice a couple of octaves higher than usual and his cheeks turning bright red as Alissa's head rolled to the side and landed against the crook of his neck. "Blake and I found her trying to put on a movie. I think she threw up in the popcorn machine. And of course, Blake's convinced it's all Ethan's fault, so I decided I'd try to get Lissa out of here as quick as possible to cool him off, but then . . ." Jesse trailed off and, at a loss for words, settled for motioning his head at the chaos in Ethan's living room.

"Right." Lena nodded. "Let's get her out to the front porch."

The three of us (four if you count Isabel; five if you count Alissa, unconscious and snoring) made our way through the crowd. By the time we finally spilled onto Ethan's front porch, we all looked like we had just walked through the eye of a tornado. Jesse's shirt was askew and his curls had deflated a bit on one side of his head. Lena's bun had little corkscrew curls poking out in every direction. Alissa was still completely out, but even her slick, black hair had been mussed up on the side that wasn't resting against Jesse's shoulder.

Isabel was pink cheeked and grinning like she'd just had the best night of her young life.

"Did you bring the car?" Lena asked her twin.

"Yeah," he replied. "I parked just around the corner."

Lena pressed her fingers to her lips for a moment in thought.

"Okay, go ahead and drive Waverly back to Blake's, and then drive Alissa home," she told Jesse, already turning to me to hand over Isabel.

"Wave-ree," she said in greeting.

"Hey, kiddo." I sighed.

"What about you?" Jesse frowned at his sister.

"You can come pick me up in a half hour or so," she explained.

"Lena." Jesse sighed. "I really don't want you joining the fight."

"I'm not going to!" she argued. "I'm first-aid certified, Jesse! It's my duty to go back in there and help those drunk, injured morons. Besides, we're still missing someone."

Jesse's eyebrows drew together.

"Who?" he asked, glancing around the porch.

"Blake!" Lena cried. "Who else do you think, you—"

"Baby listening," I interjected.

"—cucumber!" she finished, flustered.

Jesse cocked an eyebrow. Lena looked ready to fight him.

"Why don't you go back in there and play Mother Teresa?" I suggested, tapping her shoulder.

Lena sighed and spun around. After shooting one final glare at Jesse over her shoulder, she slipped back into the chaos that had encompassed Ethan's living room.

I turned back around to face Jesse, ready to ask him where exactly he had parked his car. But what I saw before me made the words catch in the back of my throat.

Jesse had shifted his weight so he could hold Alissa, who really looked quite small compared to Jesse's tall frame, in one arm. He had brought his free hand up to push the tangled mess of long, black hair from Alissa's eyes, and was gazing down at her like she was the prettiest girl he had ever seen in his life. When he realized I was watching him, Jesse froze, his fingers still hovering over Alissa's cheek.

We stared at each other for a moment, me with my mouth hanging open and him with eyes as wide as golf balls and a faint, pink blush spreading across his entire face. His ears turned bright red.

"Waverly, it's not—" Jesse began, his voice cracking.

And at that moment, I realized something. Back when I had first met Jesse, in the ice cream parlor, he'd seemed so ticked off by how upset Alissa was about being dumped by Blake. He'd wanted her to just get over him already. I thought he just couldn't stand her wailing about the breakup because it was annoying.

But now, it was clear.

"Oh my God!" I exclaimed. "You're in love with her!"

Jesse lunged forward and clapped his hand over my mouth. Isabel cackled.

"Keep it down!" he told me. "I don't want anyone to know!"

"But it's true?" I gasped into Jesse's palm.

Jesse narrowed his eyes at me in the least intimidating glare I'd ever seen. I raised my eyebrow at him, and he sighed and gave up. Even Jesse had to know that in comparison to his sister, he was about as threatening as a puppy.

"Can we talk about this in the car or something?" he asked sheepishly.

"Fine," I said, slapping his hand away from my mouth.

Jesse turned and started down the porch steps.

I followed him, and together we walked in silence down the street. Jesse went a couple of steps ahead of me, but occasionally he stopped to shift Alissa in his arms so she wouldn't tumble onto the sidewalk. We turned at the corner of the street and kept walking, the distant thump of the music blasting back at Ethan's house growing softer.

Eventually, we arrived at Jesse's beat-up Jeep, with its dented rear bumper and faded forest-green paint that was starting to chip around the door handles. I guessed that what with Jesse's general obliviousness to everything around him, the poor car had been through a lot. The image of the Fletcher twins bickering in the front seat, with dark curls and lanky limbs flying everywhere, popped into my head. I couldn't help but snort with laughter.

Jesse lay Alissa across the bench in the backseat, then hopped into the driver's seat.

"Are you getting in?" he asked when he noticed I was still on the sidewalk.

"I don't have her car seat," I said, nodding at Isabel. "It's in my aunt's car. Which Blake has the keys to."

"I can drive really slow," Jesse offered. "It's like a mile back to Blake's place, and there's no traffic this time of night. I know it's not, like, legal. Or safe. But I've gotta get you home."

And I had to get there before Blake's parents did. I couldn't imagine how worried they'd be if they came home to find Isabel missing.

I slid into the passenger's seat apprehensively and placed Isabel on my lap. She bounced her feet against my knees as I buckled in.

"Superslow, okay," I insisted. "Seriously. Grandma slow."

Jesse nodded and pulled away from the curb delicately, settling on a pace slow enough that I could've gotten out of the car and walked next to it. The clicking of the Jeep's hazard lights and the low rumble of the road beneath our tires lulled Isabel to sleep within thirty seconds.

When we were a couple of streets away from Ethan's house, I turned to him.

"So," I prompted.

"What?" Jesse asked warily.

"How long have you been in love with her?" I asked, smirking slightly.

"Could you *not* use that word, please," Jesse mumbled, sinking into his seat a little.

"What word?" I frowned.

Jesse turned a shade redder.

"Love," he said, wincing as if it was painful to say.

"Fine. How long have you been in *like* with her?"

Jesse sighed heavily.

"Three years, seven months, and eight days," he told me, sounding dejected.

Jesse didn't just have a little crush on Alissa Hastings. No, he was seriously and uncontrollably in love with her. When a guy counts the days he's been head over heels for a girl, you know it's serious. But I had been expecting Jesse to say something in the time frame of a couple of weeks. Not three and a half years.

"Wait a second," I said. "When did she and Blake start dating?"

Jesse shrugged. "The start of last year."

He was hunched over the steering wheel now but, he kept shooting glances at the rearview mirror so he could check on Alissa. I wasn't sure if he was worried that she'd wake up and hear our conversation or that she'd puke all over the interior of his car.

Or maybe he just liked to look at her.

"But didn't you ever tell Blake that you liked her?" I asked him. "Why would he go after her if he knew that you were in love with—"

"He didn't know," Jesse said miserably.

"You've never told him?"

"He always said he thought Alissa was stuck up. You know, he'd call her names and make fun of her for being so high maintenance. I couldn't tell him I liked her. He would've made fun of me too."

I pursed my lips. "Why did he change his mind?"

"I don't know," Jesse said with a sigh. "He never told me."

Well, that didn't help. Now I had a million more questions, and it looked like Jesse couldn't answer any of them. My stomach twisted as I imagined several different scenarios, all in which Blake and Alissa first fell in love. Maybe they had bonded over their love of the ocean; I pictured them swimming together, smiling and laughing and splashing each other.

"How far is Blake's house?" My voice sounded odd and strangled.

"A couple of blocks," Jesse said.

His eyes lingered on me, and for a moment I was worried that Jesse knew what I was thinking. Could he tell that I was about to cry? Could he tell that I had a massive, embarrassing crush on his best friend?

"Eyes on the road," I snapped.

"Okay, okay!" Jesse said, facing forward again before mumbling to himself. "God, it's like having a second Lena."

I would've laughed if I hadn't been so miserable.

When Rachel's sunset-orange house rolled into view, I felt only slight relief at the sight of the empty driveway. The Hamiltons' driveway, too, was empty, and the only lights on inside the pale-green house were in the living room. It was only once Jesse pulled his Jeep up against the curb in front of the house that I realized I didn't have a set of keys to the Hamiltons' house.

I turned to Jesse.

"Hey, do you by chance have a—"

I stopped halfway through my question when I noticed the silver key Jesse was holding out to me, a slight smile on his face. I held my hand out and he dropped the key into my palm.

"Thanks, Jesse," I told him. "You're a lifesaver."

"No problem," Jesse replied, then reached up a lanky hand to scratch the curls at the back of his neck. "Could you do me a favor?"

"Sure. Anything," I said as I unbuckled my seat belt and started to open the door.

"Could you not tell Lena about . . . you know." Jesse tilted his head toward the backseat, where Alissa had begun to snore audibly. She was a picture of elegance, passed out in the backseat of Jesse's Jeep wearing that little neon-orange bikini with her tan limbs bent at odd angles. It seemed unfair that anyone could look like a *Vogue* cover model under such conditions.

"I pinkie swear I won't say a word," I said.

"Thanks. I meant it, Waverly. I owe you one."

I slid out of the car as gently as I could, trying not to jostle Isabel. Thankfully, all the activity of the evening had exhausted her. The kid was sleeping like a rock.

"Good luck with your sleeping beauty," I said, jabbing my thumb at the backseat.

Jesse snorted. "Yours too."

I shook my hand in a half wave, then turned and marched across the Hamiltons' recently watered front lawn.

Just as I put my foot on the first step, a car honked very gingerly behind me.

I clapped my hand over Isabel's ear (although she didn't so much as twitch) and spun around, scared shitless that I was going to see George and Chloe Hamilton pull into the driveway in their silver sedan. But it was just Jesse, who had leaned across the passenger's seat to poke his head out through the window, face twisted in a wince.

"Sorry," he called, "I just thought you should know that he likes you too."

"What?" I whisper-hissed.

"Blake likes you too."

And with that, Jesse leaned back into the driver's seat and pulled away from the curb. I watched his beat-up Jeep jolt and bounce down the street until it disappeared around the corner.

Then I was alone, standing at the base of the Hamiltons' front steps, unsure what to make of what had just happened. It was a quiet night in Holden, Florida; the pavement was still radiating heat from a long day under the scorching sunshine, but there was a cool breeze that carried over from the Atlantic Ocean. After a few moments, I shifted Isabel in my arms and climbed the porch steps.

Float

As much as I wanted to write off what he had said as Jesse being his goofy self, I couldn't bite back my smile or shove down the feeling bubbling up in me.

It felt an awful lot like hope.

Chapter 11

Isabel snored. And not those soft, almost kittenlike murmurs that you'd find adorable. No, Isabel sounded more like one of those heavy-duty lawn mowers they sell at Home Depot. A broken lawn mower, at that. It's hard to believe a child so small could generate that type of noise.

Aside from the horrific electric gardening tool impersonation she was doing, Isabel looked angelic when I set her down in her crib. Her wispy curls were like a halo.

With the toddler safely delivered, I went back downstairs to the living room, where I collapsed on the couch. Now that I was finally alone, I noticed that the throbbing pain in the back of my head hadn't disappeared. Not to mention, my cheek was pretty tender where I'd been jabbed by that unidentified elbow.

I closed my eyes and exhaled wearily.

"Well," I said aloud, "that went about as well as predicted."

I was never going to follow along with one of Blake Hamilton's ludicrous plans ever again.

Speaking of which: where was he?

I kicked my legs over the side of the couch and hopped up, then crossed the room to stand by the curtain-framed window that had a decent view of the Hamiltons' front yard and the houses across the street. I cupped my hands against the glass, trying to block the reflection of the living-room lights to see if Rachel's neon-green Volkswagen was back in front of her house.

It wasn't.

Fucking Blake Hamilton. He was more trouble than he was worth.

I marched back across the room and into the kitchen, anxiety twisting my stomach into knots. I knew I didn't really need a snack, because I wasn't actually hungry, but I raided the Hamiltons' cupboards anyway, eventually locating a large box of Ritz Crackers. With the family-sized box tucked under my arm, I headed back to the living room to claim my lookout spot under the window. But before I could plop back down on the couch, I heard the unmistakable clatter of house keys against the front door.

Someone was home.

For a moment, I thought Chloe and George might be back. Which wasn't good, considering their son hadn't gotten home yet and was, for all I knew, still hunting down Ethan. I braced my arms around my box of crackers and held it up in front of me like a shield as the front door swung open—and there stood Blake Hamilton, looking like he'd just been hit by a bus.

"Holy shit," I cried. "What happened to your face?"

A dark, shadowy spot had appeared on the right side of his jaw, along with an angry red scrape over his right eyebrow. And maybe it was just me, but I thought I saw a bit of dried blood on his cheek.

"What happened to *your* face?" he shot back.

Of all the immature things to say.

"I'm serious," I said, chucking my emotional support box of Ritz onto the couch.

"So am I." Blake kicked the front door closed behind him and crossed the living room to where I stood, ducking his head and narrowing his eyes as he scanned my face. "What happened? Did you run into a wall or something?"

Now I was really confused. "What are you even talking about?"

Blake glanced around the living room. Then, suddenly, he stepped forward, grabbed me by the sleeve of my shirt, and dragged me over to an ornate gold wall-mounted mirror.

Hamilton was right. I looked like I'd walked into a wall cheek first.

"Oh no," I breathed, lifting my fingers and pressing them softly to the large, purplish spot directly under my eye. It was exactly where I'd been elbowed at Ethan's party. "Oh, it's bad."

"What did you do?" Blake asked. "Shit. Is Isabel all right?"

"She's fine." I spun around to face Blake again. I hadn't realized he was standing so close behind me, though, so I nearly whacked him in the chest with my hand. "And I didn't do anything. It's not my fault some douche bag has hard elbows."

Blake's eyebrows furrowed. "What do you mean?"

"Some jerk elbowed me in the—"

"Who?" Blake demanded, voice deathly low. "Who did this to you?"

"I didn't see his face. And even if I did, I only know, like, seven people in this town by name."

Blake opened his mouth again, eyes ablaze with righteous fury, but seemed to struggle to get any words out. He ran a hand through his dark, already-disheveled hair. How had I never noticed how big and sun kissed his fingers were before? I wondered, vaguely, what they'd look like intertwined with mine.

I hoped that was the elbow to the head talking.

"You look like shit," Blake said at last, which was certainly a reality check.

"Thanks."

"I didn't mean it like—" He stopped halfway through his sentence to let out another frustrated grunt. He closed his eyes and pinched the bridge of his nose for a moment before taking a deep breath and looking back up at me. "How did you even get back here?"

"Jesse drove us."

The corner of Blake's eye twitched.

"Jesse?" he repeated.

"Yeah."

"Why didn't you come find me? I would've driven you home. And Isabel. Shit, I had the car seat—"

"We went slow," I snapped. "And you were a little busy."

Blake was supposed to give me a ride back. That had been the plan. But then Blake had to go all mixed martial arts on Ethan's ass, and all hell had broken loose. And for what? The two of them were still disputing over Alissa Hastings, who, might I point out, had been unconscious in the backseat of Jesse's car for a good part of their toxic masculinity–fueled fight.

"I would've driven you home," Blake said again, his deep voice a bit softer now.

He sounded chastened. Maybe even a little remorseful. It was at that moment that I became aware of the fact that we were alone in the house, except for Isabel. But I could just barely make out the thunderous rumble of her snoring, so I knew she wasn't about to intrude or anything. Which meant that Blake and I were standing there, two feet apart, unaccompanied.

"Waverly?" Blake asked, his voice low and loud in the silent living room.

"Yeah?" I replied, my throat suddenly very dry.

Then his hand was coming toward me, and for a moment, I was reminded of the time at the pool when Blake had touched a strand of my wet hair. I kept my eyes locked on Blake's face, unable to look anywhere but his eyes, as I felt his fingers brush ever so slightly against the top of my shoulder.

"Why do you have toilet paper on you?"

Blake pulled his hand back, pinching a single sheet of white toilet paper in his fingers.

My cheeks flushed.

"Damn shirtless toilet paper throwers," I mumbled, snatching the sheet from Blake's hand and quickly shoving it into the pocket of my oversized shorts. Then, ignoring the befuddled expression on Blake's face, I stepped over to the couch and picked up the box of Ritz. I plopped down, reached for the remote, and clicked on the television.

As I flipped through the channels, Blake disappeared into the kitchen. He treaded back and forth across the tile floor, opened the refrigerator door once, and then headed back into the living room. I didn't turn around to look at him because my cheeks still felt a little warm, and the last thing I wanted to have to do was explain why I was blushing.

Blake took a seat at the far end of the couch.

"Here," he mumbled.

I looked over to see that Blake was holding something out to me. I frowned at the strange, round, deep-blue object for a moment before realizing that it was an ice pack and reached out to grab it. Then I tilted my head back and placed the cold compress over the side of my face, wincing a little at the frigid temperature.

"Thanks," I mumbled back.

"No problem," Blake replied.

I glanced over at him out of the corner of my uncovered eye.

Blake was slouched back just like I was, cradling an identical blue ice pack against the right side of his face. He was staring straight back at me, blue eyes unblinking. We were close enough for me to see the small, barely visible scar above his left eyebrow again.

I frowned slightly.

"How'd you get that?" I asked him, motioning my hand at the faint white mark.

"Boating accident," Blake croaked.

He suddenly leaned forward and cleared his throat. Then, shaking his head slightly as if angry with himself, Blake snatched up the remote from where I had set it down on the couch cushion between us. I let myself stare at his profile for a moment as he clicked through the channels, his shoulders tense and the ice pack still against his face.

Neither of us spoke for a long time.

"I'm sorry," Blake finally broke the silence.

"For what?" I practically whispered.

"Dragging you along to that party," he explained. "It's my fault you got elbowed."

I couldn't disagree, so I said nothing in response.

"And toilet papered," Blake added. "I can't believe those ass-holes did that."

"Is it completely embarrassing for me to admit that I actually found that part fun?"

The corner of Blake's mouth that wasn't covered by the ice pack curled into a smile. I couldn't help but smile too. We turned our attention to the television screen, although I doubt either of us was really interested in watching the evening news. I already knew what the weather forecast for the week was. Hot, with a chance of *holy shit it's hot*.

"Did you kick Ethan's ass?" I asked casually.

"Of course," Blake said, puffing his chest out a little. Cue my eye roll.

"If you don't mind me asking," I said, pausing to flip over my ice pack and press the colder side against my cheek, "why'd you two decide to beat the snot out of each other, anyway? Do you really think physical violence is the key to solving your problems?"

"Ethan and I have never been friends," Blake muttered.

"How come?"

I couldn't help but be curious. It felt like I kept getting crumbs of history and drama, but no one was sitting me down and giving me answers.

"It's a long story," Blake said, somewhat ominously.

"You know, I'm here all summer."

Blake didn't respond.

I sank down into the absurdly plush cushions of the sleek sectional couch. There was still a sharp pain in the back of my head, and now my hand and half of my face were going numb from the cold of the ice pack. I kicked my feet onto the coffee table and closed my eyes, letting out a little moan as I realized that the throbbing in my head wouldn't stop.

"Waverly?" Blake asked.

I grunted halfheartedly.

"Are you sure you're okay?"

"I'm just tired," I slurred out, too exhausted to say anything more.

Blake was weirdly quiet for a moment. "How hard did you get elbowed?"

"Not that hard." I shook my head, then immediately regretted it. I grimaced and added in a pained mumble, "It was the floor that really hurt, to tell you the truth."

Blake shifted on the couch. "How many fingers am I holding up?"

I cracked open one eye to see Blake's sun kissed fingers wiggling in front of my face. The movement of them made me feel nauseated almost instantly, so I squeezed my eyes closed again and leaned my head back, trying not to feel sick.

"Not again," I groaned. "Lena already tried this. It's three."

"Two, actually."

"That's what I said, right?"

"Waverly, I think you might have a concussion."

"Your face is a concussion."

Admittedly, I'd had better comebacks, but the throbbing pain in the back of my head was making it really hard to think straight. I briefly considered what Chloe and George would think when they came home and found Blake and me sitting on the couch, both holding ice packs and one of us nursing a possible concussion. We were in so much trouble. Of course, the one night I decided to pretend I was cool would end in head injuries.

"Stand up," Blake told me.

I watched, with my good eye, as he pushed himself up from the couch. He tossed his ice pack onto the coffee table, then turned around and looked down at me expectantly.

"C'mon," he coaxed. "Up."

I scoffed. "I'm not a toddler."

"Waverly, just stand up for, like, one second. Please."

With one hand still clutching the ice pack to the side of my face, I rose from the couch, counted out *One Mississippi* in my head, and then collapsed back onto the soft cushions. I kicked my legs up on the coffee table and smiled sardonically up at Blake.

"There," I said. "I got up for a second."

"No one likes a smart ass," Blake said.

"Fine." I pushed myself up from the couch again. The sudden change in altitude, albeit only a few feet, made my head spin like the wheel on *Wheel of Fortune*. I groaned, trying not to feel sick, and reached out to grab the back of the couch to steady myself.

"Stay right there," Blake told me, taking a couple of hesitant steps back. "I'll be back in, like, one minute. Don't sit down, and whatever you do, don't fall asleep."

"Why not?" I demanded.

"Because you might be concussed, and the worst thing you could do right now is nod off and let that little head of yours swell up. I'd really prefer it if you aren't in a coma when Chloe and my dad get home. I'm already grounded for eternity as it is."

"My brain isn't little."

"Just stay right there, okay?" Blake pleaded, already starting up the stairs.

"What are you—"

He was already gone. The cloudlike couch was calling my

name, but I decided to follow Blake's advice. He was a lifeguard, after all—they were trained to deal with minor medical emergencies. Besides, how embarrassing would it be if I fell into a coma? I might drool all over the Hamiltons' couch. Talk about classless.

Blake came padding back down the stairs again a minute later, carrying a large rectangular box in his hands. I watched him walk over and set the box down on the little white coffee table beside me and frowned when I realized that it was a board game.

I arched an eyebrow. "What's that?"

"Scrabble."

"And you brought it down here because . . ."

"We're going to play."

With that, Blake plopped down in the matching armchair at the end of the couch. He wiggled back and forth, nestling into the cushions, and leaned forward to pull the top off of the cardboard box. Blake pulled out the dark velvet sack of tiles, embroidered with the word *Scrabble* in gold, and tossed it to me. I squealed in surprise and dropped my ice pack, then flailed my arms out. Somehow, I ended up grabbing a hold of the corner of the sack before it tumbled to the floor.

"Pick out seven tiles," Blake instructed, ignoring my marvelously graceful catching abilities and unfolding the board on the table.

"I don't want to play Scrabble."

"Look," Blake snapped, "I'm trying to keep you from falling asleep. If you sit down and watch television or something, you'll be out in five minutes, tops."

He wouldn't let me watch television, but he wanted me to sit down and play what was possibly the slowest, most boring board game ever invented?

"And Scrabble won't put me to sleep?" I drawled.

"It's mentally stimulating," Blake said, reaching out his long, tan arm to snatch the sack of tiles right out of my hands. He shoved his hand in the bag and pulled out a couple of tiles for himself, then set about arranging them in his little wooden tile holder.

I let out an admittedly overdramatic groan and plopped down on the couch.

"Give me the bag," I grumbled, jabbing my hand out at Blake.

He tossed me the sack of tiles, a stupid, smug smile on his face. I narrowed my eyes at him and shoved my hand wrist-deep into the bag. Blake and I were silent for a moment as we arranged our tiles and planned out our first moves. I decided to go first.

Slug.

It was only six points, but it was really all I had. Blake quirked an eyebrow but didn't say anything. I watched as he picked up a few of his own tiles and laid them out on the board perpendicular to mine.

Gravy.

"This is embarrassing," I grumbled.

"It's *invigorating*," Blake corrected, picking up a pen to scribble down our moves on the score sheet, "and you're just mad because I got twenty-three points. Your move, Lyons."

"What?" I gasped, leaning over to look at the score sheet. "How did you do that?"

"Double letter score."

"No big deal." I shrugged. "I'm going to win, anyway."

There was no way I would lose a game of Scrabble to Blake Hamilton. Granted, I wasn't a genius. Not by any stretch of the imagination. But I liked to think that I was smarter than some bipolar lifeguard who couldn't go two days without getting into a fight of some sort.

"If you're so sure you're going to win," Blake said, the corner of his mouth pulling up in a devious smile, "then why don't we make this game a little more interesting?"

I narrowed my eyes at him.

"How so?" I asked, trying to sound more indifferent than suspicious.

"Winner gets to ask the loser three questions," Blake proposed, leaning his elbows against his knees and placing his fingertips together, "and the loser—that'll be you, Waverly—has to answer two of them entirely and truthfully. Loser can take one pass."

Answers.

It was the one thing I wanted from Blake. Already I had thought up a million questions I wanted to ask him. How did he first fall in love with Alissa? What happened to his mother? Did he think I was as attractive as I thought he was? Okay, maybe not that last one. But still. The possibilities were endless, and he'd have to answer two of my questions honestly.

"Deal," I said, extending my hand.

Blake reached his right hand out to meet mine and we shook on it.

It was only once our fingers untangled that I started to wonder what on earth Blake might ask *me* if *he* won. Would he ask why Jesse was acting so weird, especially around Alissa? Would he dare to bring up my parents? My lack of a social life back in Fairbanks? Maybe I'd been impulsive to agree to this. What if I ended up having to answer a really terrible question?

I couldn't let him have the chance.

I had to win.

Blake and I both leaned down to peer at our tiles, planning our next moves and occasionally shooting each other intimidating *I'm going to beat you* glares. It was my turn, though, so eventually I had to stop glaring long enough to place my tiles.

Vet.

It was ten points, which was pretty good for only three letters. Blake mumbled something under his breath, which sounded suspiciously like he was criticizing the length of my word. I ignored him and drew two new tiles from the bag.

Tropic.

Blake got eighteen points, double letter score. Again.

Penis.

Twenty-two points, triple letter score. It was my first decent move. Blake's eyebrows shot up and a sort of strangled sound came from his throat, but he quickly composed himself and sent me a reproachful glare.

"Seriously?" he asked. "This is a children's game, Waverly."

"It's in the dictionary," I argued. "And you're only mad because I'm catching up."

Blake glanced at the score sheet and his eyes went wide with disbelief. Before I could gloat, he hunched over his tiles and rearranged them, preparing to make his move. This wasn't fun and games anymore. This was high-stakes Scrabble.

North.

Thirteen points.

Hamster.

It was thirty-two points, thanks to a double word score. Blake cringed and reluctantly wrote down the number underneath my name on the score sheet. I was in the lead. But that didn't last long, because Blake's next move was good.

Arctic.

The game went on like that for a while.

Run.

Ukulele.

Lump.

It wasn't long before I reached into the bag of tiles and felt myself grasping at nothing but velvet. We had almost covered the board at that point, leaving little space for any decent moves. Blake had five tiles left while I had two, one of which was a *Z*, the hardest letter to use. I watched Blake lift up all five of his tiles to place them on the board.

Tickle.

And, just like that, he was ahead by twenty points.

My palms were sweating as Blake leaned back in the floral armchair. The corners of his mouth tugged up like he was proud of himself. I would have been much angrier at his smug little smirk if he hadn't winced a little and brought his finger up to delicately prod the bruise on the right side of his jaw, which was apparently making it painful for him to smile. I had the sudden urge to swipe the Scrabble board and tiles off of the coffee table, launch myself over it, and plant my lips on Blake's. I shook my head and forced myself to look down before I could impulsively hurl myself at the boy across the table.

The next time I played Scrabble, I needed to choose a less attractive opponent.

I glanced back and forth between my tiles and the board.

"Hurry up," Blake grumbled impatiently.

"I'm thinking!" I snapped.

"Just let me win already," he groaned.

And then, I saw it.

The perfect move. It was almost too wonderful to be real, like when school gets snowed out on the day your biggest test of the year was scheduled or someone gives you two free samples instead of one at See's Candies. Shaking with excitement, I lifted up my two tiles, a *Z* and an *O*, and set them down on the board.

Zoo.

Triple word score.

"Eat it, Hamilton!" I cried, leaping up from the couch and pounding my fists in the air.

I almost didn't feel the throbbing in my head. Almost.

Blake's smirk dropped instantaneously.

His blue eyes went wide as he lunged forward, leaning over the board and lifting both my tiles to check that I had, indeed, just kicked his ass at Scrabble. I grinned triumphantly as I waited for him to look up at me and say the magic words. Finally, after making sure I had actually scored more points than he had, Blake pushed himself up from his armchair reluctantly, folding his arms across his chest and refusing to look me in the face for a moment.

The corner of his eye twitched when he finally saw the idiotic smile on my face.

"Fine." He sighed. "You win, Alaska."

"What's that?" I asked, cupping my hand to my ear. I knew I was being an asshole. I knew it. But I couldn't stop from leaning over the coffee table a bit and saying, "I don't think I heard you right. Could you repeat that?"

Blake muttered something under his breath.

"I said you won. You beat me."

"Damn straight!"

And then, with absolutely no shame or conscience, I did a little victory dance. It wasn't much of a dance, really, so much as me jerking my limbs around as I spun in a little circle and made myself a beat of little *whoop-whoops*. When I finally stopped spinning, I noticed that Blake, still with his arms across his chest, was fighting back a grin.

"What?" I asked innocently.

"You're so weird." He shook his head at me.

"But you love it," I teased.

I hadn't meant anything by that. It had been an almost knee-jerk response, the type you use when a best friend points out how awkward or embarrassing you are. But Blake's blue eyes flashed with something I didn't recognize and darkened a shade. For a moment I was worried I had offended him by suggesting that we were friends, or at least knew each other well enough to exchange a bit of friendly banter.

And then, all at once, I felt like he was getting closer.

Or maybe I was getting closer. Or maybe we were both getting closer at the same time. It was hard to tell, because all I could focus on was Blake's face. Those eyes, the scattering of light freckles across his cheeks and the bridge of his nose, the little white scar above his eyebrow, and, finally, his mouth. All of it coming steadily closer.

It didn't feel real. What I thought was happening couldn't possibly be happening.

Are we about to kiss?

The thought brought on a burst of panic. Which way was I supposed to tilt my head? I hadn't brushed my teeth since breakfast that morning—would Blake be able to tell? Was I actually reading him right, or was this another one of those situations where he was just leaning in to take the tag off my bathing suit or comment on my dripping wet hair?

The riot of worries in my head manifested physically: I *flinched*.

Blake noticed—because of course he did—and went still, his eyes flaring with concern.

But before I could course-correct and lean in again, to make it clear that I definitely wanted to kiss him before the moment slipped through my fingers, I heard two pairs of footsteps coming up the front porch, one distinctly high-heeled. Blake heard them at the same moment I did, because his eyes went wide and he immediately stepped back from me, dropping his arm. I hadn't even noticed he'd brought his hand up. My God—had he been planning to grab my chin? Cup my cheek? Run his fingers over my hair?

I didn't have time to process it all.

The Hamiltons' front door swung open, and Chloe and George stepped into the living room, smiling a little and laughing at some joke Blake and I hadn't heard. They were still smiling when they saw the Scrabble board on the coffee table. Their smiles dropped just a bit when they saw I was awkwardly leaning halfway over the table. And then their smiles vanished altogether when they took in my bruised eye and Blake's battered face.

"What the hell happened to you two?" Chloe cried in horror.

"Uh . . ." Blake trailed off, glancing around the room for any sort of inspiration.

I glanced down at the coffee table. "Scrabble!"

Chloe and George looked at me in disbelief. Out of the corner of my eye, I saw Blake bring a hand up to his face and clap it over his eyes.

"Scrabble?" George repeated, raising one eyebrow and folding his arms over his chest.

Float

I glanced at the dark bruises and scrape on the side of Blake's face, then turned back to George and gave him one short nod, fully committing to my terrible bluff.

"It got *really* competitive."

Chapter 12

The next afternoon, there was a knock on the door.

Rachel and I were seated on opposite ends of the living room, both of us still dressed in our pajamas and neither of us showered. We had done a good job of ignoring each other all morning, except for the occasional heavy sighs and worried glances Rachel sent my way, but the silence in the house was starting to eat away at me. To be completely honest, I was considering breaking out into song—just to fill the void—before we heard the knock.

"I'll get it," I said, making a move to get up from the armchair I was seated in.

"No," Rachel snapped. "*I'll* get it. *You* stay there."

She leaped up from the couch and shuffled across the living room, soles of her fuzzy blue slippers slapping against the hardwood floor. Sinking back into the armchair, I buried my miserable face in my hands. Whatever trust Rachel had given me, I had managed to lose it in one evening of bad decisions. I'd followed Blake Hamilton to a party. I'd kidnapped a toddler. I'd technically stolen my aunt's car. I'd gotten one tiny whiff of freedom—one solid chance to be one of those kids who didn't spend every single night in their bedroom surrounded by a swath of homework— and I'd turned into a monster.

Rachel pulled the front door open. I listened, a little curious to know who would be dropping by Rachel's house.

"Lena," Rachel said.

"Hi, Ms. Lyons." Lena's voice sounded cheerful, but there was a hint of calculation in it. I dropped my hands back into my lap only to see Lena standing in the front doorway, her curls pulled up into a bun and her dark eyes bright and well rested. At least *one* of us had gotten some sleep last night.

"What brings you here so early?" Rachel asked her on a yawn.

"It's almost three o'clock?"

"Oh." Rachel blinked at Lena as if she'd just told her that the earth was square.

But I couldn't exactly blame Rachel. She'd had a long night, and it had been mostly my fault.

Rachel had taken Margie Kim's brother's van to the art supply store and then to Marlin Bay, where she'd painted for over eleven consecutive hours. When she'd finally trudged into the house, covered in paint splatters and looking like it was all she could do not to fall to the floor and pass out, I'm sure the last thing she wanted to see was her niece with a black eye.

The next three hours had been dedicated to figuring out what the hell had happened and what we needed to do before I could fall asleep. Rachel went on her computer and searched the word *concussion* on one of those medical websites, but after five minutes of reading, she was convinced that I had some form of tetanus infection—which, might I point out, could only be acquired in the waters off the port of Acapulco— and was going to die a slow, painful death. I made her shut down the computer and call the hospital down in Marlin Bay so a very kind nurse could explain that I was definitely going to survive the night.

I'd made it halfway upstairs before I realized I hadn't apologized for making Rachel's night so long. But by the time I had spun around at the top of the stairs, a weak *I'm sorry* hovering on the tip of my tongue, Rachel was already fast asleep on the couch, decorative pillows strewed across the floor.

I had sighed and then trudged off to bed.

But even in the cocoon of soft blankets and lush down pillows, I'd had trouble nodding off. Whenever I closed my eyes, all I could see was Blake Hamilton's face coming closer and closer, ever so slowly, but never touching mine. Jesse's words from earlier that night echoed in my head.

Blake likes you too.

The thought had left an odd feeling in my chest. It was wonderful and uplifting, almost like the kind of feeling I got when I saw any kind of sign advertising free food.

Blake Hamilton had wanted to kiss me.

Needless to say, I hadn't slept very much last night.

"What brings you here, then?" Rachel asked, rubbing her eyes.

"I wanted to stop by and make sure Waverly's alive," Lena explained. I shot her my best I need to talk to you right now look, and she nodded.

"She's all right," Rachel said, jabbing a thumb in my direction. "Just concussed."

"I suspected as much." Lena sighed. "Would you mind if I came in? It's a little muggy out today, and my hair—"

Rachel had a brief internal debate that played out entirely on her face. Obviously, she had never had to ground a child before, so she had no idea what the proper protocol was for visits from friends. And I had never actually been grounded before, so I wasn't much help aside from pointing out that I had a shift at the bookstore I probably shouldn't miss.

It seemed like everyone else my age had stories to tell about wild shenanigans and the resulting period of house arrest, but I'd disappointed my parents in much subtler ways. It was always a steady drip of mediocrity rather than a flash flood of poor decision making. I'd been benched every game of my volleyball season. I'd been passed over for a speaking role in middle school musical theater. I'd brought home report cards that weren't so bad as to warrant a parent-teacher conference, but certainly never got pinned on the fridge.

When Rachel had told me—with her best I'm stern and parental and refuse to put up with your shit look—that I was grounded, I did something I don't think either of us was expecting: I'd thanked her.

"Here are the rules," Rachel finally announced. "Waverly doesn't leave the house. You two can talk in the living room or the kitchen, but no going upstairs. I don't want anyone trying to sneak out through the second-story windows. Given her"—she jabbed a finger at me—"track record, she'll break both her arms. And today's my day off, so I *really* don't want to have to drive down to Marlin Bay to take her to the hospital. Got it?"

"Got it." Lena and I nodded in unison.

Rachel eyed us warily before stepping aside and letting Lena into the house.

"Thanks, Ms. Lyons," Lena said, the epitome of polite until she shot me a wicked wink behind my aunt's back.

I had to bite down on my tongue to keep from giggling.

"Can I get you anything to drink, Lena?" Rachel asked as she padded back into the living room, the rubber soles of her fuzzy slippers scuffing against the hardwood floor.

"Water would be great," Lena said.

Rachel nodded and started across the room. Lena and I both held our breath as we watched her walk past the sofa. The second she disappeared into the kitchen, Lena lunged at me and grabbed me by my shoulders.

"Look at your *eye*, Waverly," she cried, turning me back and forth to examine the purplish bruise. "Holy shit, you look like you were in an action movie."

"I'm glad one of us is getting some enjoyment out of this."

"Sorry," Lena mumbled, releasing my shoulders and falling back onto the couch. "It just looks so badass. Anyway, did Jesse get you home okay last night? He didn't run over any stop signs again, did he?"

Again? How bad of a driver was he?

"No, he didn't run over anything. We had to drive slow, because of Isabel."

"How long are you grounded for?"

"Two days," Rachel answered before I could.

Lena and I both looked over to see her trudging back out of the kitchen, a glass of water in her hand. She passed the glass to Lena, who muttered a timid thank you. "And before you tell me that two days is nothing, consider the fact that Waverly is only here for twenty-eight days. If that two months was eighteen years,

I'd be grounding her for more than a year. Now, I don't know about you, but that's what I call stern parenting."

Lena laughed.

"I'm loving the logic, Ms. Lyons," she said.

Rachel nodded and, although I could tell she was trying to keep a straight face, the corners of her lips twitched upward. It was probably the first time she'd ever had anyone compliment her on her parenting skills. Rachel must've realized that Lena and I had noticed her smile, because she cleared her throat and hurried back into the kitchen.

When I was sure Rachel was out of earshot, I turned to Lena.

"Nice," I whispered appreciatively.

Lena grinned.

"I try." She shrugged. "But this is good news, you know. You'll miss Jesse's volleyball tournament tomorrow, but at least you can come to the beach with us later this week."

"The beach? Is Blake coming too?"

The question tumbled out of my mouth before I could stop it.

"I knew it." She grinned.

"Knew what?"

My cheeks were on fire. How could she know? How could she tell from one little question that I was falling in love with Blake Hamilton? Was I really that obvious? Ugh. Cross professional actress off my list of potential future jobs.

"I should've guessed before," Lena said casually.

"Oh God," I moaned, leaning forward in my chair to rest my elbows on my knees and hide my face in my hands. "Please don't tell Alissa."

"Why shouldn't I tell Alissa?" Lena's eyebrows furrowed.

I gaped at her.

For someone who seemed so smart, Lena sure was acting like an idiot.

"Because she'd probably claw my eyes out!" I cried. "Can you imagine? 'Hey, Alissa, I know I'm new to town and it's only been, like, two weeks since we met, but I think I'm in love with your ex-boyfriend!' She'd eat me alive if—"

I didn't get a chance to finish that thought.

"You're *in love* with Blake?" Lena demanded, her hazel eyes as wide as golf balls.

It took me two full seconds to realize what a giant mistake I'd just made.

"No," I choked out. "I mean, obviously, that's an exaggeration, but I—I do like him. Which you knew already. Right? I thought you said you knew."

"I meant I knew you weren't going to be upset about missing Jesse's volleyball tournament after what happened on the beach, the whole riptide thing! Because you didn't even *try* to sound disappointed . . . that's not important. Don't try to change the subject. Are you *serious*?" Her voice dropped to a whisper and she leaned toward me. "You're really *in love* with Blake?"

There was no way I was *in love* with Blake Hamilton. I'd met him less than two weeks ago. I didn't even know the boy's favorite color. How could I be *in love* with someone I knew so little about? I'd only used the word *love* because it was shorter than *abnormally large and incredibly embarrassing crush*.

"It's just a little crush," I croaked.

Lies. It was the size of fucking Texas.

"Wow," Lena said, sprawling back in the chair. "I mean, I thought you hated him. I was *way* off."

"Please don't tell Alissa," I said. "I swear I'll leave you guys alone for the rest of the summer. I won't go within two hundred feet of Blake. Except, you know, when we're in our houses. But aside from that, I won't—"

Lena's eyebrows knit together. "What are you talking about?"

"Please don't be mad at me," I begged, digging my fingernails into the upholstery of the armchair I was sitting in. "I don't want to step on anyone's toes."

Oh God. I could see it. My entire summer, slipping right out from underneath me.

"Mad at you?" Lena repeated, sounding confused. She frowned for a moment before her face lit up with understanding. "I'm not mad at *you*, Waverly. I'm mad at myself."

I stared at her for a moment, completely confused.

"I'm mad I didn't see this earlier," Lena explained.

And then, all at once, it hit me.

Lena wasn't mad at me. She didn't hate me, and she didn't think I was some sort of parasite in her perfect summer, and she wasn't going to storm out of my aunt's house and demand that I never try to contact her again. A wave of relief crashed over me, and I had the sudden urge to launch myself onto the couch and give Lena a bone-crushing hug.

But I realized that, with my luck, I'd probably just end up injuring the both of us. So instead, I let out a little high-pitched laugh.

I sounded borderline hysterical but Lena was nice enough not to act creeped out.

"So you won't tell Alissa?" I asked again.

"Of course I won't tell." She snorted. "I'm not stupid, and I don't have a death wish."

"Thank you!" I sighed.

"Don't thank me just yet," Lena said, the corner of her chapped lips pulling up into a devious smirk. She leaned forward and propped her elbows on her knees, then rested her chin in her hands and batted her eyelashes, looking extremely suspicious.

She's up to something.

"What's that look for?" I demanded.

"What look?"

"The one you're doing right now. The one that looks like you're plotting a murder."

"I'm not plotting a *murder*!" she argued.

"But you *are* plotting," I insisted.

"Well, yeah," Lena admitted, rolling her eyes. "But can you blame me? This is like that awesome moment when you realize that your two favorite characters on a television show are in love with each other! Now all you two need is a little bit of guidance and—"

"Lena."

"—you'll be dating and then—"

"Lena."

"—I'll be the maid of honor and—"

"Lena!"

She stopped mid-rant.

"What?"

"Look," I said, leaning over the side of the armchair. I glanced at the doorway to the kitchen out of the corner of my eye, checking to make sure that Aunt Rachel was completely out of earshot. "No one else can know, okay? Not my aunt, not Mr. and Mrs. Hamilton, and definitely *not* Alissa."

Lena nodded. "I won't tell Jesse either."

"Oh," I said, thinking back to last night. "That won't be an issue."

"Why not?"

"He already found out. That, you know, I like Blake."

Lena's mouth popped open, and for a moment, she just looked shocked. Then her face twisted into a grimace.

"*Jesse* knew?" she cried indignantly. "You told *him* before you told *me*?"

"I never told him anything! He found it out—"

"*Found it out?*" Lena repeated, then threw herself backward across the couch—her legs swinging up and nearly kicking me in the face before she draped them over the armrest—and grabbed a decorative orange pillow. She buried her face into it, moaning, "I am an *idiot*!"

Rachel chose that moment to pad back into the living room, a steaming mug of something—coffee, most likely—clasped in her hand.

"Lena, dear, not with my nice pillows," she scolded, sipping her drink.

"Sorry, Ms. Lyons," Lena grumbled, sitting up and setting the pillow back in place.

Rachel plopped down in the other armchair.

"Now," she said, snatching the remote up from the coffee table, "what should we watch?"

I opened my mouth to voice a suggestion but was interrupted by the doorbell.

"Who's that?" Lena asked.

"Let me consult my crystal ball," I deadpanned.

Lena shot me a look that could only mean *I'm getting real tired of your shit.*

"I'll get it," Rachel announced but didn't move right away. Instead, she glanced first at her left hand (the one holding her mug of coffee) and then her right hand (the one clenched around the remote). I could tell that she was having an internal battle about which object to put down on the table so she could answer the door. But Rachel couldn't decide between her caffeine and her reality TV, so she tucked the remote under her left arm and rose from her chair slowly, her eyes locked on her cup of coffee. She managed to stand up without spilling even a drop. I considered giving her a standing ovation, but she'd probably think I was just being a sarcastic smartass.

"Five bucks says it's Blake," Lena whispered as Rachel started toward the door.

My heart did the funniest thing. It lurched, like I was on a roller coaster. Just the idea that Blake Hamilton might be at the front door sent a shot of adrenaline running through me.

"Five bucks says it's not," I whispered back, my voice sounding oddly high pitched.

Rachel pulled open the door slowly so she wouldn't spill her coffee.

Standing in the doorway was Chloe Hamilton, wearing a little yellow sundress and carrying a white designer handbag on her arm.

"Damn it," Lena swore.

I laughed, half relieved and half disappointed.

"You owe me five bucks."

Lena groaned and sank farther down on the couch.

"Hi there, Chloe!" Rachel greeted her, the friendly grin on her face wavering a little as she compared her attire—fluffy robe, slippers, and haphazardly constructed bun—with Chloe's impeccably cute outfit. "Would you like to come inside?"

"Yes, thank you," Chloe said, stepping into the house. Even

in her wedge heels, she was shorter than Rachel by a good four inches.

"What's up?" Rachel asked, kicking the front door closed.

"I came to see how your niece is doing," Chloe answered, glancing around the living room for a second before her dark eyes landed on me. Her face twisted into a grimace for a split second before she could compose herself. "Waverly!" she cried. "You look . . . better."

Lena snorted.

"I feel better," I replied.

Aside from the throbbing pain in my eye.

"I, ah, have something for you," Chloe said, reaching a perfectly manicured hand into her white handbag. After a moment of digging around, she pulled out a little blue envelope with my name scribbled on the back of it. "This is from Blake."

I could practically feel Lena smirking at the back of my head as I shot up from the armchair and hurried across the living room. My cheeks suddenly felt like they were on fire, and I nearly lost my footing and tripped on the edge of the rug under the coffee table.

"Thanks," I murmured, snatching the letter from Chloe's tiny hand.

"I made him write it," Chloe admitted, smiling sheepishly as she tucked a curl of platinum-blond hair behind her ear. "It's an apology note."

"Oh," I said, my cheeks burning even hotter. "He really didn't need to—"

"He did." Chloe interrupted me.

I didn't have the balls to argue with her, so I just smiled awkwardly. Rachel was suddenly staring at me like she expected me to rip open the envelope and read Blake's note aloud, so I decided I wanted a bit of privacy.

"I'll go read this," I said, waving the letter around for emphasis, "in the kitchen."

I spun on my heels and started walking.

"I'll come with you!" Lena cried, tumbling over the back of the couch.

The kitchen was bright, partly because it was sunny outside and partly because the walls were painted an incredibly reflective white. I sprinted toward the little kitchen table—which was covered in a menagerie of art magazines, paint swatches, and unopened packets of brand-new paintbrushes—and launched myself into one of the cute little chairs that were made of driftwood and painted vibrant orange, green, and blue. Lena grabbed the chair next to mine and yanked it over so our legs and shoulders were pressed together.

"Open it, open it!" she cried.

"Shush!" I hissed. "Stop acting like a four-year-old! It's just a letter."

But I was excited too. So excited I felt like giggling.

"Oh, come *on*!" Lena said, slapping me on the shoulder. "This is *so* romantic!"

"It's a sorry I inadvertently gave you a black eye note, Lena."

"But—"

"That his *stepmom* forced him to write."

"Could you stop being such a downer and open the goddamned letter already?"

I sighed and looked down at the envelope.

My name, Waverly, was scrawled on the envelope in thick blue crayon. I had to laugh at that. Blake must've borrowed one of Isabel's or something. The sudden image of him, plucking his favorite color crayon out of a box, flashed through my mind. It was oddly endearing.

I flipped the envelope over and tore it open.

Inside, I found a piece of standard paper, folded into fourths like the little birthday cards I used to make all my friends in second grade, with a large "I'm sorry" printed across the front—in blue crayon, again—and a sticker of Dora the Explorer with her purple backpack.

"This is the most adorable thing I have ever seen in my life," Lena cooed. "When you two get married, I expect a *Dora the Explorer* sticker on my invitation."

I shot Lena a death glare.

Then I tucked my hair behind my ear and prayed I wasn't blushing too noticeably.

I opened up the letter.

> *Dear Waverly,*
> *I am really sorry that I made you come to that party*
> *with me, and I am really sorry that I started that fight.*
> *I am also sorry that the guy at that party had a hard*
> *elbow, and I am sorry that you were standing next to*
> *him. I am sorry I made you play Scrabble too. And I*
> *am sorry I got you grounded (Chloe told me that) and I*
> *am sorry that your aunt is probably making you watch*
> *Andy Warhol documentaries with her. Again.*

"I'm going to have a fucking heart attack," Lena said, snatching the letter out of my hands and reaching for the pocket of her shorts, "but first, I'm instagramming this."

She poised her cell phone about the note.

"No!" I cried, snatching the letter back. Lena made a sound of protest as her cell phone's camera went off a second too late, leaving her with a blurry picture of the kitchen table. "No one can see this, okay?"

"Waverly!" she moaned. "This is comedic gold! You can't just—hey, what's that?"

Her thin eyebrows scrunched together and she leaned forward, narrowing her hazel eyes at the letter.

"What's what?" I frowned.

"Hold on," she mumbled, tilting her head to the side, "unfold it."

"Unfold it?" I repeated.

The note was, as I said, folded into fourths. I grabbed the bottom of the note and pulled it up, completely unfolding the piece of paper. There, in the center of the page, were a few more words. These ones were messier, obviously jotted down in a hurry.

> *I am also sorry for that thing I tried to do after you*
> *won Scrabble. I will not try to do it again, I promise.*
> *Just please forgive me. I will see you at the beach on*
> *Monday.*

"What's he talking about?" Lena asked me, her voice low and urgent. "What did he try to do after you won Scrabble?"

I tried to open my mouth to answer, but my lips were suddenly dry. There was an odd sort of burning feeling in my throat, like I couldn't breathe. My eyes scanned the note again, this time lingering on one sentence. The sentence that made me feel nauseated. The sentence that made me remember how frizzy my hair was and how pale my skin was and how awkward and rambling I could be. The sentence that reminded me that I wasn't from Holden.

The sentence that told me Blake Hamilton couldn't possibly like me the way I liked him.

I will not try to do it again, I promise.

"It doesn't matter," I croaked.

Chapter 13

There are two ways I hate being woken up. The first is with the false promise of food, because there's nothing worse than getting up for some scrambled eggs and hash browns only to find out that your mom lied and you're going out to drill ice samples instead. The second is on a Monday morning, because ever since I've started working at the bookstore in town, Mondays—my day off—have been totally sacrosanct when it comes to sleeping in until noon.

But apparently Lena Fletcher doesn't respect my beliefs.

"Rise and shine!" she hollered.

I had just barely opened my eyes when she yanked back the curtains, letting the harsh Florida sunshine beam me right in the face.

"Lena! It burns!" I cried in agony, floundering around in my bed as I tried to grab hold of anything—a pillow, a blanket—to shield myself with.

"Quit being so overdramatic," Lena scolded.

I couldn't see her because I had my eyes squeezed shut, but I knew she was smirking.

"You are evil incarnate," I grumbled, finally grasping the edge of my down pillow.

"Waverly, don't be such a—"

The last word got muffled as I smashed my pillow down over my head, sealing out the rest of the world. Unfortunately, *the world* happened to include oxygen, which I sort of needed. When I pushed the pillow up so I could take a gulp of air, I found myself six inches from a pair of dark, unblinking eyes.

I let out an almost inhuman shriek and tumbled off the side of the bed, landing flat on my back, my legs bouncing as they hit the carpeted floor with a resounding *thud*. From the other side of the bed, I heard Lena gasp, then erupt in laughter.

"You—I—I'm sorry, Waver—ly!"

"Yeah, yeah," I grumbled, grabbing a fistful of the fitted sheet on my bed and using it as leverage to pull myself to my feet. When I was upright again, I adjusted my pajama shorts and looked back up at Lena.

Her lips quivered as she fought to hold back her laughter.

"Good morning?" she offered innocently.

"Watch your back, Fletcher."

Then I turned and stalked off to the bathroom, snatching my towel from its designated spot on the floor next to the dirty clothes hamper along the way. The second I kicked the door closed behind me, I heard Lena erupt into laughter again.

"Not funny!" I shouted through the door.

"Wear your bathing suit, Lyons!" Lena shouted back.

I heard her footsteps thump out of the room and down the stairs, so I assumed she was probably headed to the kitchen to raid Rachel's fridge.

It was a whole forty-five minutes before I finally padded into the living room, dressed in a big white T-shirt and a pair of Rachel's jean shorts over my blue and white striped bikini, at Lena's request. I had already guessed that we'd be wading into the ocean—why else would Lena put me in a bikini? It wasn't like I needed to even out my tan lines—but I figured that if I stayed in the shallow water, I'd be fine. I couldn't drown in six inches of water. Right?

I found Lena standing in the kitchen, munching on a granola bar as she poured herself a large bowl of frosted flakes. Rachel had left for Marlin Bay earlier that morning, and by the looks of it, she'd overslept and left in a hurry; her coffee mug was sitting on the edge of the kitchen counter and she'd left her favorite strawberry-flavored SPF seventy lipstick on the table with her paint swatches and collection of brushes.

"Feeling better?" Lena asked me through a mouthful of whole grains.

"Slightly." I nodded. "But you should still watch your back."

Lena rolled her eyes at my threat, and I couldn't help but smile. We both knew she could take me in a fight.

It took Lena less than three minutes to wolf down her bowl of cereal. As she was finishing off her second granola bar, she shot Jesse a text message asking him to drop by the house and pick us up. I was too focused on the butterflies in my stomach to think about anything other than the note that'd been delivered the other night. Blake had said—or rather, written, in crayon—that he wanted to see me at the beach today, which meant that he was sneaking out of his house to tag along with the Fletcher twins, Alissa, and me.

I wasn't sure whether to be excited or pee my pants.

The past two days on lockdown had given me plenty of time to read, reread, and overanalyze the absolute shit out of Blake's adorable little note. I had almost committed the whole thing to memory. There was one line, however, that kept popping into my head even though I wished I would forget it.

I will not try to do it again, I promise.

"You all right there?" Lena asked me, peering across the kitchen at me, her eyebrows knit together in concern. "I think you're about to grind your own teeth off."

It was only then that I realized I'd been clenching my jaw.

"So, when's Jesse getting here?" I asked, trying to change the subject. I reached up and ran my fingers through my hair. I hadn't bothered to blow it dry, much less take a brush to it, so my fingers promptly got stuck in an abnormally large knot.

"He said—" Lena began, but was cut off as a car horn sounded outside.

"I'm guessing that's him?" I prompted, wincing as I yanked my fingers free from the bird's nest that was my hair.

Lena nodded and set her empty bowl in the kitchen sink, then wiped her hands off on her light-blue tank top. She snatched her cell phone from the counter and then we both tore through the living room like professional sprinters. Well, Lena was like a sprinter. I was like a three-legged dog galloping along behind her.

The second I stepped through the front door and onto the porch, I realized that there was something off.

It wasn't boiling.

I mean, it was still pretty warm outside compared to my hometown, which averaged a high of fifty-two degrees during the month of August. But I wasn't instantly drenched in a sheen of sticky sweat, and I didn't feel like the humidity had smacked me in the lungs. The only thing that was smacking me was the wind, which was so strong it had blown my soaking wet hair back from my face, tangling it behind me.

Lena didn't seem to notice; I watched her as she tore across the front lawn, her flip-flops clapping against her feet, and lunged for Jesse's busted-up Jeep.

"Shotgun!" she hollered.

Jesse leaned over from the driver's seat and waved at me. I decided to stop standing on the porch like an idiot and just embrace the fact that, for once, I could walk outside in Holden, Florida, without feeling like a giant, pale, melting popsicle.

"Hey, Waverly!" Jesse greeted me when I pulled open the car door. He and Lena were, as usual, matching, today in baby blue that made their beautiful skin gleam. His corkscrew curls bobbed gently in the wind. "Sorry about the mess in the back."

The Jeep had one long, leather bench in the back—which had been good for when Alissa got drunk at Ethan's party and was too unconscious to stay upright—with three semidistinct seats. The far seat was completely occupied by a large box of black fabric and two foam boards that looked like larger versions of the kickboard Blake had made me use during our last swim lesson.

"What's all this?" I asked, taking the seat behind Lena and closing my door behind me. I reached out and ran my fingers over a dark strip of fabric hanging over the edge of the box in the other seat. It was thick and smooth to the touch.

"Those are wet suits," Jesse explained, watching me prod the material in the rearview mirror, "and those big things are boogie boards."

"Boogie boards?"

"Yeah. We had to put 'em in the backseat because Lena was worried the wind would blow them out of the trunk. I doubt we'll use them anyway, though. It's so windy the waves are probably hitting five foot."

His words bounced around in my head for a moment, my brain not really sure how to process them.

"Oh, there's Blake!" Lena said, pointing through the passenger-side window.

My heart did a little hiccup in my chest.

Sure enough, when I turned my head to follow Lena's finger, Blake Hamilton was sprinting around the side of his house, wearing a pair of black swim trunks and a white T-shirt with some logo I didn't recognized printed across the front. His hair was messy and his cheeks were flushed. It took me a second to realize that he'd probably slipped through a second-story window and scaled down the side of the house to avoid running into Chloe or George. Part of me, the part that had always loved James Bond movies and squealed over the mere mention of Jason Bourne, couldn't help but think that Blake's little escape—and the mischievous sparkle in his blue eyes—was the hottest thing I'd ever seen.

"Waverly, you should probably scoot over a bit," Lena suggested.

"Huh?" I mumbled back.

I was too busy staring at Blake to notice that Lena had a point: Blake was running full speed at the car. More specifically, the back door of the car. I realized this too late and had only shifted over about an inch when Blake yanked open the door, letting in a large gust of wind, and threw himself into the seat I was trying to occupy.

Which, of course, left me crushed.

"Rude," I choked out as he pulled the car door shut behind him, sealing us in like sardines. Blake was sitting halfway on my lap—like an extremely heavy baby—and our legs were tangled together at odd angles. He leaned backward a little and I had to turn my head so he wouldn't crush my nose in with his shoulder blade.

"Drive!" Blake commanded, ignoring the fact he was turning me into a human pancake.

Jesse nodded furiously and brought his foot down on the gas pedal.

The Jeep lurched forward, and we were off.

"Hey, mind moving?" I rasped.

"Oh," Blake said, sounding surprised and slightly flustered to hear my voice coming from below him. "My bad, Waverly."

He leaned his body against the car door as far as he could go. I wriggled out from underneath him and pushed myself into the middle seat of the bench. But even though Blake and I were sitting as far apart as we could manage, we still didn't fit; Blake's right shoulder was pressed up against the car window, and the left was dangerously close to my jawbone.

"Good job, genius," I snapped at him.

I would've elbowed him in the ribs, but I couldn't move either of my arms. One was trapped behind Blake, squished between his muscular back and the leather seat, and the other was pressed against the box of wet suits.

"It's not my fault," Blake told me gruffly.

"Not your fault?" I repeated.

I looked up to tell him off and was promptly struck silent by how close we were in the cramped backseat of Jesse's car. The words I had planned to say dissolved in my throat, leaving me gaping up at his bright blue eyes. He still had a bruise on the right side of his jaw. It was purple and yellow and blotchy, like a grotesque flower. The scrape underneath his right eyebrow had started to bruise, too, but it didn't look nearly as bad. It almost balanced out the thin white scar above his left eyebrow.

"Yeah," Blake continued, oblivious to the fact that I was gaping at him, "it's whoever put all that crap in the other seat's fault." He motioned to the box of wet suits. "I mean, why is there a box of—"

He stopped talking abruptly.

"Hey, Jesse?" he asked, his voice pinched. "What are all these wet suits doing back here?"

Jesse laughed, like Blake's question seemed dumb to him. Lena snorted, too, and turned around in her seat to give us both a smirk.

"Do you want to surf *naked*?" she asked, cocking an eyebrow.

Two things happened very suddenly.

First, the image of Blake Hamilton standing on the white sand of the beach wearing nothing but his birthday suit flashed through my mind. I made a strangled noise at the back of my throat, like a startled cat, and a rush of blood went straight to my cheeks . . . and some other places I don't *ever* want to talk about ever again.

Second, the word *surf* set off blaring panic alarms in my head. This was a *horrible* idea. I couldn't even tread water yet. I couldn't even hang out in the shallow end at the Holden Public Pool without managing to swallow a gallon of chlorinated water. How did these people expect me to get on a surfboard and *not* get myself killed in a tragic accident?

Oh right. Two out of the three other people in this car had no idea I couldn't swim.

Today's forecast, 30 percent chance of rain and 99 percent chance of my death.

"I thought we were going to the beach," Blake protested. My hand—the one trapped between Blake and his seat—was starting to go numb. I fidgeted and he leaned forward so I could pull my arm out from behind him. "I mean, the usual beach. You know, to hang out, play some volleyball. What happened to that?"

Blake leaned back again, and his shoulder blade nailed me right in the boob.

"Ouch!" I hissed, resisting the urge to grab my chest.

"Huh?" Jesse asked from the front seat.

"Not you," I snapped.

"Sorry!" Blake grimaced, leaning forward again.

He looked back over his shoulder and our gazes met.

"Um," he said, eyebrows furrowing, "do you want to be on top?"

Yes, please, the hormonal voice inside my head chirped.

Blake seemed to realize how what he'd said could be taken a beat later, and the faintest trace of pink appeared across his cheekbones. He hurried to correct himself.

"I mean, do you want to be in front?"

If anyone else had made this many unintentional sexual innuendos, I would've been howling with laughter. Instead, I was light headed.

"I mean, your shoulder," Blake added. Finally deciding that

he'd made the situation sufficiently awkward, he reached out a hand and pushed me forward far enough so that he could lean back against the leather seat. When he pulled his hand away, my shoulder fell back against his. In front of his shoulder. On top of his shoulder.

This made so much more sense.

"Oh," I said, sounding like a total idiot.

Blake shifted his arm—the one that was now pinned behind my back—and tried to find a more comfortable spot to put it. He ended up draping his arm over the back of my seat, just far away enough that we weren't touching but close enough that I could feel the heat of his skin radiating against the back of my neck.

I glanced up and caught Lena's gaze in the rearview mirror. She winked.

"Jesse and I decided we should go surfing instead," she explained, not even trying to conceal her full-blown maniacal grin. In the seat beside her, Jesse had his eyes narrowed at an upcoming stop sign like he was preparing to do battle with it. Which, given Jesse's infamous driving skills, he probably was.

"Why?" I asked, trying not to sound too distraught.

Why did we have to do the *one* activity that could get me killed?

"There's supposed to be a storm rolling in these next few days, and I heard the waves out by Marlin Cove are getting up to seven foot." Lena shrugged. "How could we pass this up?"

The Jeep rolled to a halt at the stop sign.

Jesse reached forward and clicked a button on the dashboard.

After a second of silence, the radio crackled to life, and the car was filled with the sound of a thumping drum and the voice of a singer I didn't recognize.

"Any suggestions?" Jesse asked, fiddling with the dial.

"Here, let me," Lena said, knocking Jesse's hand aside so she could choose a channel.

Jesse mumbled something about an *overbearing sister* under his breath as he looked both ways and pulled forward into the intersection.

"So, how far away is Marlin Cove?" I asked.

And by that, I meant *How long am I supposed to sit here pressed up against Blake Hamilton and be expected to keep my emotions intact?*

"Eh, twenty minutes or so," Lena said, looking at Jesse for confirmation.

"Yeah." He nodded. "Twenty minutes. Unless we hit traffic."

Oh. My. God.

Twenty minutes was going to feel like a lifetime.

Was I just supposed to ignore the fact that the last time Blake Hamilton and I were this close he had been about to kiss me? Were he and I just going to ignore the elephant in the room? Or, rather, car. Because there certainly wasn't enough room in the backseat for an elephant.

"Have you ever gone surfing before, Waverly?" Lena asked.

I resisted the urge to laugh in her face.

"Um, no," I replied, swallowing hard as I tucked a piece of wet hair behind my right ear. "I never really got around to trying it out."

I felt Blake shift beside me.

"Well, you seem like a fast learner," Lena told me, pulling her corkscrew curls up into a bun on top of her head. "And Jesse gave surf lessons all last summer. He can teach you."

Jesse nodded and beamed at me in the rearview mirror.

"Thanks," I told him, grinning back at him.

Blake cleared his throat.

"Is Alissa meeting us at the cove?" he asked. His voice, deep and slightly rumbly, reverberated through my whole body, starting at the point where my right arm was pressed against his ribs. It gave me the chills. *Say something else,* I begged silently. *But this time don't mention your ex-girlfriend.*

"Yeah, she said she'll meet us there with the surfboards," Lena replied.

We pulled up at another stop sign. Jesse bent over the dashboard and fiddled with the dial for the radio. Lena let out a grunt of protest as her choice of music was suddenly cut off by static, then mariachi music, then more static, then the riff of a guitar, then static again.

"Cut it out!" Lena told him, trying to slap his hand away. "I was listening to that!"

"No you weren't," Jesse argued.

One of their hands collided with the volume knob, and suddenly some country singer was screaming at us about how much he loved his truck. Blake and I both jumped, startled, and I shrank back into the leather seat, clapping my hands over my ears and trying to ignore the fact that Blake's arm had slipped off the back of my seat and was now resting across my shoulders.

"That was your fault!" Jesse and Lena cried in unison, two accusatory fingers pointed.

"Turn it down!" Blake shouted over the music.

Lena reached forward and turned the knob. My ears rang.

"You're such a douche bag, you know that?" Lena scowled at her brother.

"Your face is a douche bag!" Jesse shot back.

While the Fletcher twins continued to bicker in the front seat, Blake bent his head down so his lips were only an inch or so from my ear.

"Did you get the note?" he asked me, his voice low and his breath warm against the span of cheek directly adjacent to where my ear met my jawbone. I pulled my head back, worried that if he did something like that again I'd pass out, and looked him in the eyes.

"Yeah." I nodded, the corners of my mouth curling up as I thought about Blake's crayon-scribbled handwriting. "The *Dora the Explorer* sticker was a nice touch, by the way."

"I thought you'd enjoy it."

And there, just like that, it was easy enough to believe that I'd been wrong. That maybe I'd misread or even misinterpreted his note. That maybe "I will not try to do it again, I promise," actually meant *I'm so going to try it again, so please chew a stick of gum and wear some lip balm the next time I see you.*

It was easy enough to believe that Blake Hamilton didn't regret almost kissing me.

"Hey, Blake?" I asked, trying to ignore the sudden swarm of butterflies in my stomach. "I sort of wanted to talk to you about—"

Blake shook his head, cutting me off in the middle of my sentence.

My heart lurched.

Was this rejection, then?

"We don't have to talk about it," Blake told me, his face suddenly becoming hard. His jaw locked and his lips tensed into a line. He glanced out the window, then looked back at me. Or, more accurately, at a point directly above my head. "It won't happen again."

There was a hint of apology in his tone, and it took me a second to realize what it meant.

He was trying to let me down easy.

"Okay," I mumbled, nodding once before I turned and pretended to suddenly be very interested in the fabric of the wet suits. Tears prickled behind my eyes, and I had to start picturing a bunch of dancing bananas to keep myself from crying. It's really a handy trick, actually. When my parents had finally sat me down to tell me that they were getting a divorce, I had bitten my tongue and stared at the fruit bowl on the dining room table. I had pictured the fruits coming to life—sprouting little arms and legs and growing faces—and performing a choreographed dance number, just for me.

I didn't cry. Not even a tear.

But at least after my parents had announced their divorce I'd been able to run up to my bedroom and bury myself in a Harry Potter book. This time, I was trapped in a car with the entire side of my body pressed against the person who'd broken my heart.

I could get over this. I *would* get over this.

I straightened up in my seat, trying to feel empowered—*I am fierce, I am independent, I am Beyoncé* was my new mantra—and sent a glare at Blake Hamilton out of the corner of my eye. His elbow was propped up on the sill underneath the car window, and his forehead leaned against the glass. His eyes, usually so blue and warm, looked grey now.

Fuck it. I'd never be over him.

The next thirty-five minutes in traffic seemed to go by in slow motion. I didn't risk another glance at Blake. In fact, I tried to ignore his existence completely. Which was difficult because his knee kept knocking against mine, and I could feel the steady thump of his heartbeat against my arm.

The truth was, I had never been *more* aware of Blake Hamilton.

Lena managed to win monopoly over the radio and played pop song after pop song. She knew almost all the words to every song that came on and howled along to the tune—much to Jesse's annoyance. I was glad she was enjoying herself, but I was even gladder that she hadn't noticed the tense silence in the backseat. Blake hadn't said a word, and neither had I, since our attempt at a conversation.

"Oh look," Jesse said.

"What?" Lena asked, turning down the radio so that we could actually hear him. "Where? What is it?"

"The clouds are rolling in."

I leaned over the box of wet suits and peered through the window. We were driving on a winding road right by the cliffs overlooking the Atlantic Ocean. Far off in the distance, where the sky met the water, was a giant, menacing mass of grey. It seemed so out of place against the sunny blue sky.

"Do you think it'll rain today?" I asked no one in particular.

Maybe if it poured, I wouldn't have to get in the water.

"No," Lena said, shaking her head. "Not today. The storm isn't supposed to get to Holden until Wednesday. I'm sure it'll be another day or two before those clouds hit the cove."

"Which means it'll be perfect surfing weather today!" Jesse chirped.

My entire body felt tense and cold, which was strange consider-ing the inside of Jesse's Jeep was pretty warm and shielded from the wind. I sat back in my seat, but my eyes remained locked on the ocean. It was huge. Huge and powerful and destructive. And I was about to jump into it with nothing but a giant board and a wet suit to protect me.

I debated telling Jesse and Lena my secret.

What was the worst that could happen if I suddenly blurted out *I can't swim*?

An image of the Fletcher twins, their faces twisted in disgust and betrayal, popped into my head. I sank down farther in my seat, suddenly feeling very carsick. I squeezed my eyes closed, the sight of the ocean too much to bear. I wished Blake would say something. Anything. He didn't even have to ask me if I was all right, he just had to crack a joke or ask a question or *something*! The silence was stifling.

Speak, I screamed in my mind, testing out my telepathy.

Blake didn't say anything. My superpowers were still a work in progress.

I opened my eyes again and glanced over at Blake's lap. Not in a perverted way, but just in an I'd rather look anywhere else but outside way. His leg was pressed up against mine, his shorts dark beside my pale white thigh. Resting on the middle of his leg, palm down, was his left hand. God, his fingers were *long*. Long and tan and really, really boyish. I had never seen someone with more attractive hands.

"How much longer?" I asked, sighing shakily.

"About five minutes," Lena replied, too busy tapping away at her cell phone to notice that her estimation caused all the blood to drain from my face. Five minutes. I had five minutes to prepare myself for my impending death. I glanced back out the window. Sure enough, the road had started to swoop down at a slight decline, and I could make out the details of Marlin Cove—rocky beach, rough water, and huge waves. The perfect recipe for disaster.

I gulped and looked down at my hands again.

They were shaking harder, almost violently so. I curled my fingers in, trying to form the tightest fists I could, but it didn't help. My stomach wasn't just doing somersaults anymore; it was doing an Olympic gold medal worthy routine. I remembered what it felt like to sink into the ocean, churning water pushing and pulling at my limbs. Salt scratching at my nose and throat. Sunlight fading above me. Blake had saved me that first time I walked into the water—but what if he couldn't save me this time?

I shook my head.

This was ridiculous. I could save myself—that was what the swimming lessons had been for. I just needed to calm down, get a grip, and stop shaking like a Chihuahua. I was a big girl, and I could handle a couple of waves. Besides, didn't surfboards float? Wasn't that the whole point?

I glanced at Blake out of the corner of my eye. He was staring forward stoically, right at the back of Lena's headrest. Why wasn't he freaking out like I was? I mean, didn't he care *at all* that I was about to break every bone in my body? Didn't he care about me?

Please hold my hand.

The words threatened to tumble out of my mouth, but, to my relief, I managed to stop them. It sounded pathetic, even in my head. What was I, some damsel in distress begging my knight in shining swim trunks to come save me? I scowled at the dashboard of the Jeep and started chanting my mantra again.

I am fierce, I am independent, I am Beyoncé.

I am fierce, I am independent, I am Beyoncé.

I am fierce, I am independent, I am—fuck it, I need my Jay-Z.

I took a deep, shaky breath.

But before I could turn to Blake and make my pathetic request—*Please hold my hand? I'm so very fragile and weak and willing to throw away decades of women's rights movements*—a tan, long-fingered hand appeared seemingly out of nowhere to cover my shivering right fist.

It is very possible that, in that moment, I flatlined.

"Hey," Blake breathed softly, coaxing my fingers out of their death grip with his own. I glanced up at him; his bruises looked much worse when his eyebrows were furrowed like that, like he was concerned. His voice was quiet, almost a whisper, and I was positive Jesse and Lena couldn't hear it over whatever ungodly pop song Lena was humming to on the radio. "Your fingers are gonna fall off if you keep this up."

He forced a chuckle, his breath white-hot against my bare arm.

"Sorry," I replied, my voice weaker than I had hoped.

Blake didn't say anything, but kept his hand on top of mine. By definition it wasn't exactly holding hands, but I'd take it. My mind raced a million miles a minute, but strangely enough, none of my thoughts were about surfing anymore. Instead, I found myself thinking about the three questions I could ask Blake. Our Scrabble agreement had been pretty simple: I got to ask three questions, and he could skip one but was required to answer two truthfully.

What should I ask about?

His mom? Alissa?

Me?

Suddenly the Jeep jolted to a stop, interrupting my scheming. I was thrown forward into the space between the two front seats but managed to catch myself before I face-planted into the dashboard.

That, kids, is why you always wear a seat belt.

"We're here!" Lena hollered.

Chapter 74

From the edge of the parking lot at Marlin Cove, I looked down onto the beach. Lena and Jesse had dragged the box of wet suits halfway down the sandy slope and were both shrugging off their T-shirts. Blake was standing a little farther off, his hands tucked in the pockets of his black swim trunks as he stared out at the ocean. What a hipster. Didn't he have anything else to do besides stare at the horizon and contemplate life? Like, for example, start stretching, so he could help me with my rain dance.

"Hey, Waverly!" Lena called.

I squinted down at her, shielding my eyes from the sun.

"Pick out your wet suit!"

Damn it.

I'd been hoping no one would notice that I hadn't set foot on the sand yet.

"Coming," I called back.

I tried to sound enthusiastic. I really did.

"Blake!" Jesse called as I trudged down to where the twins had set down the box of wet suits. "Let's go, man!"

The roar of the waves almost drowned him out; the ocean, stretched out before us like a bluish-grey oversized carpet, looked menacing today. The water was choppy and filled with foam, and the waves were higher than I'd ever seen them before.

"Waverly, are you a small or a medium?"

Lena's chipper voice snapped me out of my so this is where I'll die train of thought.

"Uh." I looked down at myself, almost like I was expecting a large *S* or *M* to be printed across the front of me. If I said small and ended up not being able to fit into it, I'd look like an optimistic fatso. Then again, if I said medium and it was too big, I'd be flapping around in an oversized wet suit. But that was better than looking fat. "Medium, probably."

Lena tossed me a suit.

I twisted the fabric around for a moment. It was heavier than I'd been expecting—the lining was thick and the seams were double-stitched. After a couple of minutes of examining the thing, though, I realized I had no idea how to put it on.

"Hey, Lena, how do I—"

When I looked up, she had already stripped off her shorts and shirt and had her legs in the wet suit.

I decided to follow her lead.

The wind whipped my hair into my face as I shrugged off my shorts, kicked off my flip-flops, and stepped into the snug legs of the wet suit. Lena noticed my struggle and handed me a hair tie. I formed a tiny bun on top of my head, then hiked the suit up to my waist. That was where my understanding of how to put the thing on ended.

There were ties and zippers all up and down the front, like a complicated menagerie meant to showcase my incompetence. I glanced over at Lena, silently pleading for assistance.

Blake stepped around me, oblivious to my struggle, and grabbed a wet suit out of the cardboard box. I pretended to be adjusting one of the elastic ties on the side of my suit and watched him strip off his shirt out of the corner of my eye. If I was going to drown today, I wanted to go out with a picture of Blake Hamilton shirtless burned into my memory.

The blare of a car horn shook me out of my ogling.

Jesse, Lena, Blake, and I all looked up at the parking lot at the same time. A large white Range Rover with several surfboards strapped to the top had just pulled in. Through the tint of the windshield I could make out Alissa Hastings, her hair impeccably curled and a pair of sunglasses perched on her nose.

"I'll go help with the boards!" Jesse blurted.

I think I was the only one who noticed the sheepish look he shot over his shoulder before he started up the sandy slope, Lena lagging behind and mumbling something about making sure Jesse didn't drop a surfboard on his toe again. Unable to help myself, I grinned and chuckled at his love-struck eagerness.

My happiness was short lived, however, when I found Blake scowling at me.

"What?" I demanded, the grin on my face disappearing.

Blake's eyes dropped to my wet suit. It was still resting around my hips, the top part flapping around in the wind. The frown on his face deepened.

"Aren't you going to put that thing on?" he asked.

"Yeah," I huffed.

I reached for the sleeves of the thing and pulled them up, but they were twisted around. Blake watched me, his expression blank, as I spun in a circle, trying to figure out how to untangle the suit. Finally, he got impatient enough to step forward, grab me by the arms, and hold me still.

"Here, let me do it," he said.

"Fine." I sighed.

At Blake's insistence, I held my arms out at my sides as he walked around me and untangled the sleeves of my suit, which I'd practically tied into a knot. He pulled the back of the suit up to my shoulders, then grabbed my right hand and guided it into the right sleeve. Once that was secure, he grabbed my other hand and poked it through the left sleeve. The material of the wet suit was heavy and rubbery, but it slid over my skin like cotton.

"There," Blake said, stepping back around me so we were face to face. His blue eyes sparkled with triumph. "Now you just have to zip it up and—what'd you do to the elastic?"

I followed his gaze.

The elastic tie I'd been tugging on in an attempt to look like I knew how to put on the suit was poking out at my side, forming giant loops.

"Dunno," I mumbled.

"Do me a favor," Blake said. "Don't touch anything."

He dropped to one knee and reached for the elastic to untangle the loops. While his fingers worked against my hip, I looked up at the parking lot. Lena had two surfboards stacked on top of her head and was starting back down the beach. Alissa was standing against her car, her hands clutched over her mouth as she fought to hold back a laugh. Jesse was beaming at her, his arm slung around a surfboard he'd propped on its tail end.

Attaboy, Jesse.

I felt a sharp tug on my side and squealed.

"Sorry," Blake said, not sounding in the least bit apologetic.

When he finished fixing the elastic, I thought he'd stand up and be done with it, but then his hands went to my other hip and started pulling at a different elastic tie.

"What are you—"

"It's too loose here," Blake explained, cutting me off and pinching at the bulging excess of rubbery fabric around my waist. "It's supposed to be skintight. What size is this suit, anyway?"

"Medium."

Blake's lips twisted.

"Yeah, I guess you're too tall for a small," he said. "I think Lena might have an extralong one somewhere, though. You can try that next time."

"Next time?" I snorted comically. "What, are you planning on burying me in a wet suit?"

Blake stopped fiddling with the elastic and stood up, so I was staring directly at his chin.

"You're not going to drown," he told me.

I glanced up at his eyes. They were soft, comforting.

"How do you know?" I asked.

I'd meant to sound snide and teasing, but my voice came out a little bit hoarse and very, very small. I sounded pathetic even to my own ears. Blake must've heard the fear in my voice, too, because he reached out and grabbed my chin between his thumb and forefinger.

I stopped breathing for a second.

"Trust me," he said, his voice rumbling straight through his fingers and into my bones. "I won't let anything happen to you."

I took a deep breath.

"Promise?"

"I promise," he replied.

I felt heat rush to my face and wondered if he could feel it beneath his fingers.

"Because, you know, if I die, I'll come back from my watery grave to haunt the shit out of you, right?" I teased, trying to break the invisible tension that'd appeared between us.

"I figured you would," he said, releasing his hold on my chin and tapping me once on the tip of my nose with his finger. It was painfully endearing.

"Blake!"

The high-pitched wail of Alissa Hastings shattered the moment. Blake and I both turned to see the offending girl skipping down the beach, her tank top billowing in the wind and her tanned skin glittering in the sunlight.

She was so pretty. It wasn't fair.

"Hi," Blake responded.

I turned to look for Lena, not wanting to witness Blake and Alissa's interaction. I'd have rather put my own hand in a blender and made a cannibal smoothie.

"Long time no see, huh?" Alissa quipped. "I heard I really stole the show at Ethan's house."

The self-deprecation was unexpected. Even more unexpected was the little twitch of her eyebrows and mouth that betrayed the truth: Alissa was embarrassed that we'd had to rescue her from the party.

"I wouldn't know," Blake said. "I took a few punches to the head. Don't remember much."

He sounded . . . civil. Not flirtatious, not love struck. Just like he was talking to an old friend.

"I'm good, I'm good." Alissa nodded, then set her hand against his arm, briefly, before letting it drop. "How are you?"

"Good," Blake replied instantly, glancing over at me. I took the opportunity to pull my lips back into a grimace and stick out my tongue. I even crossed my eyes, just for added effect. The corners of Blake's lips curled upward a little, like he was holding back a laugh, and he turned back to Alissa.

"Really?" she asked, eyebrows quirking up.

"Great, actually," he revised. "I'm great."

Alissa smiled. "Good. I'm glad."

And she sounded like she genuinely was. Which made me feel like I was intruding on some very important *getting over each other* moment. I turned and looked for Lena, trying to resist the urge to grin like an idiot. Now Jesse and Alissa would be in the clear to have whatever sort of romantic relationship an idiot like Jesse could manage, and Blake and I could—could what?

I thought back to the note he'd left me.

I am also sorry for that thing I tried to do after you won Scrabble. I will not try to do it again, I promise.

He regretted almost kissing me. The thought blew a hole through my heart and sent it sinking into my feet. Just because Blake was single now didn't mean I had any more of a shot with him than I had at the start of the summer.

I was still the weird, pale chick from Alaska.

He probably just wanted to be friends. But hey, that was better than nothing, right?

"Oh, hi there, Waverly!" Alissa said, as if only just noticing my presence. "I didn't know you could surf!"

"I can't," I replied.

"I'm teaching her," Blake interjected.

"That's sweet of you!" she chirped.

It was right then that I realized Alissa Hastings naturally sounded flirtatious; she wasn't trying to win Blake back, and she wasn't trying to compete with me for his attention. She just had those eyelashes that naturally fluttered and a voice that naturally took on a squeaky quality. Which, now that I thought about it, was probably why she had so many guys falling for her.

Including a certain lanky goofball.

Jesse suddenly appeared at my side, kicking up sand and grinning from ear to ear. He threw a bony arm over my shoulder and flicked the bun on top of my head.

"You excited, Waves?" he asked.

Waves? Was that my new nickname? Oh, the irony: death by nickname.

"Superpumped," I lied, throwing a fist up halfheartedly.

Blake's eyes narrowed.

"Why don't you guys all go ahead and hit the water," he said, nodding at Alissa and Jesse. "I've gotta teach Waverly some of the basics so she doesn't eat foam all day."

Jesse gave me a squeeze and wished me good luck, then tagged along behind Alissa like a lost puppy. I watched the two of them meet up with Lena, who was already at the edge of the water, and pick out their boards.

I took a deep breath and turned to face Blake.

"Do you think they'd notice if we ditched and went to get some burgers or something?" I asked hopefully.

"You know I'd never let you drown, right?" he asked. I pursed my lips, pretending to think.

"Oh, c'mon," Blake grumbled, reaching out to punch my arm so lightly I barely felt it. "Give me a little credit."

"But what if—"

"No."

"But you never know—"

"Stop."

"But—"

"Waverly," Blake said. "Shut up."

I snapped my mouth shut and clenched my teeth, willing the nervous chatter to subside. Why did I always talk so much around Blake? I was the type of person who never put up their hand in class. So how come I could suddenly tell another human being—an attractive one, at that—everything?

"Sorry," I mumbled.

"It's all right. You're allowed to be nervous. Go grab a board."

"What? Why?" I croaked in terror.

"Calm down," he huffed, grabbing me by the elastic tie on my hip and dragging me farther down the beach. "I'm not letting you anywhere near the water yet. We'll do the basics on land."

I stumbled after him, my heart still pounding erratically.

Blake grabbed two surfboards and dragged them a bit farther onto the dry sand. I alternated between watching the muscles in his arms flex and staring out at the tumultuous ocean, where Lena, Jesse, and Alissa had already started paddling out to the taller and more violent waves.

"Hey, space cadet," Blake called. "Get over here."

I jumped and turned around to see Blake several yards up the beach, rubbing his hands together to rid them of sand. I hurried up the slope to join him.

"Which one's mine?" I asked, nodding at the boards.

"The smaller one," Blake said, tapping the board in question with the side of his foot. "Just go ahead and sit down on it."

I plopped down on one end, the rubbery fabric of my wet suit screeching against the board. Great. That was *so* attractive. Before I even had time to adjust my seat so I didn't look like I was straddling a plank of wood—which, essentially, I was—Blake was crouching in front of me, fiddling with a thin line of black rope attached to the end of the board.

"What's that?" I asked.

"It's your tether," Blake explained, holding up a circular band of Velcro. "This part goes around your ankle, so you and your board stay attached."

"That's good," I said.

Yes, attached was good.

Please tie me to a flotation device before you throw me head-first into the Atlantic Ocean to fend for myself.

"Here, give me your left foot," Blake said.

But his fingers were already wrapped around the back of my calf and he had my foot a good several inches in the air. He wrapped the Velcro band around my ankle and pulled it tight, making sure it stuck. Then he let my foot drop.

"Are you sure it won't come off?" I asked, tugging the band.

"I'm positive." Blake swatted my hand away from my ankle. "Now roll over and lie down on your stomach."

I climbed onto my hands and knees, and then, with all the grace of a beached whale, plopped down onto the board. Which, of course, was painful. Especially considering whoever invented the surfboard clearly hadn't possessed boobs.

"This is so stupid," I muttered. "Why do people do this?"

"It's *fun*," Blake argued.

"That's nice," I said, propping myself up on my elbows so I could look up at him. "You guys must also enjoy ripping your own fingernails off, too, huh? Since you're clearly a bunch of sadists."

"Just paddle."

I reached my arms out and dragged both of them through the sand on either side of me.

"Not like that," Blake snapped. "Like you're swimming, not making a snow angel. Come on. Don't tell me you've never seen anyone do a front crawl or a doggy paddle."

"What does that even *mean*?"

"Please end my suffering."

"I'm sorry!" I howled. "I'm stupid, okay. Explain it to me like I'm stupid."

Blake winced and opened his mouth, like he was about to argue that I wasn't stupid. Instead he took a breath and said, calmly: "You have to alternate strokes. Pull your arms back one after the other, not at the same time. You want one forward when the other's back."

I did as he said, pulling my arms back one after the other. I felt like a windmill; a windmill that was getting sand shoved underneath her fingernails. But Blake was nodding at me and kept mumbling things like "There you go," so I could only hope I didn't look nearly as silly as I felt.

"Like this?" I asked.

"Exactly. Now for the fun part."

"Oh no." I highly doubted we had the same definition of *fun*.

Blake smiled to himself as he straightened out the surfboard beside mine, kicking a bit of sand onto my board as he scooted his closer. Then he dropped into push-up position over the longer board before lowering himself onto it, and I had to twist my features into a scowl to keep from letting my jaw drop open. Stupid boys with their stupid athleticism and stupid arm muscles and stupid floppy hair.

"Once you're out on the water," Blake said, still wiggling on his board as he tried to find a comfortable position, "you'll have to wait for the right wave."

His elbow bumped against mine.

"How am I supposed to know what—"

"I'll be right next to you the whole time, so I'll let you know the second I see a good one."

I glanced back out at the ocean. Lena was standing on her board, legs apart and knees bent, careening across the top of a wave that was taller than she was.

"I have to do *that*?" I croaked.

"No." Blake propped himself up on his elbows just in time to watch Lena slip off her board and tumble into the water. "Of course not. I'm not letting you take on anything bigger than a four footer."

I nodded. That didn't sound too horrifying.

"But you *are* going to have to stand up on your board," he added, turning to give me a resolute look.

Oh fuck me.

"Can't I just paddle?" I asked, batting my eyelashes at him.

I'd only meant to be teasingly persuasive. But suddenly Blake's blue eyes got a bit wider, and the muscles in his arms tensed up as his fingers tightened on the edge of his surfboard. He swallowed— hard—before turning back to the ocean in front of us, blinking.

"Don't be a coward," he mumbled, his voice hoarse.

I couldn't tell whether he was talking to me or himself.

"All right," I huffed after a minute of silence—him staring out at the ocean and me picking the sand out from underneath my fingernails. "Let's get this over with, then."

Blake snapped out of his daze. He cleared his throat. "You'll have to be able to pop up when you catch a good wave."

"Pop up?" I frowned.

"You know, get up on your feet."

"Okay."

"Grab each side of the board," he said, tapping the back of my hand that was closest to him.

I wrapped my fingers around the board, level with my chest, and then did the same with my other hand.

"And then what?" I asked.

"Then—all in one move, okay—you're gonna push yourself up with your arms"—he straightened out his arms so he was hovering above the board with his knees bent—"and then you pull your feet under you."

In one movement he brought his legs underneath him so he was crouching with his hands still clamped on either side of the surfboard. He smiled nonchalantly, acting as if he hadn't just pulled out a regular James Bond move.

"I can't do that," I told him.

"Yes, you can," he insisted, still smiling.

"I'm going to break my leg."

"You're so overdramatic."

"Both of them."

"Well, it's a good thing the Marlin Bay General Hospital is only three minutes away then, isn't it?"

I narrowed my eyes at him, and he narrowed his back mockingly. His lips curled upward, though, and within a few seconds he was snickering like an idiot.

"You're incorrigible," I huffed, looking down at my board and tracing patterns across the waxed surface with the tip of my finger. I wished I hadn't pulled my hair up; it was harder to hide my unwilling smile when I didn't have a curtain of tangles to hide behind.

"C'mon," Blake said merrily, knocking his elbow against mine, "your turn now."

Positioning my hands on the sides of the board again, with as much strength as I could muster, I pushed myself up and brought my legs underneath me. My left knee dragged a little on the wax, but at least I made it up without falling over and eating sand.

Blake laughed.

"What?" I hissed, challenging him to make any sort of remark about my poor coordination.

"Nothing." Blake shook his head, still laughing, and a lock of his dark hair fell across his forehead. "Why don't you try it again, though. Maybe a few more times, actually. Just for practice."

The next several minutes were painful, especially for my knees, which kept scraping against the wax on my board. I did manage to fall over a couple of times, and so when Blake finally declared me an expert at popping up, I had sand in my hair and all over the side of my wet suit.

"This is torture," I grumbled. "I hate surfing."

"Why do you always get so pissed off when you're not good at something right away?" Blake asked, getting to his feet and dusting sand off his legs. "How do you think anybody gets good at anything? You're not supposed to be good at it right away. You're allowed to suck. How can you possibly decide you hate surfing when you haven't even been in the water yet?"

His words were like a physical slap to the face. Maybe I needed it, but it still stung.

"Right," I quipped as I stood up along with him. "I'm sure this'll be much more fun when I'm inhaling salt water."

Blake's expression was one of annoyance, but the slightly pained clench of his jaw told me he didn't find talking about my impending death funny. I thought of our lessons, and how quick he always was to drag me to the surface, even when I was only under a few seconds longer than was comfortable, and even in the controlled environment of an unoccupied public pool. He was constantly on edge. Constantly anxious. Even when he hadn't liked me very much, he'd dived into the Atlantic Ocean to save me.

There was something there. And I wasn't so self-centered as to think it was entirely about me, because I also remembered what he'd said about his mom.

She'd drowned. I didn't know how, or when, but she'd drowned.

Maybe that was the question I needed to ask him.

"Last chance," I whispered. "We could still go get burgers."

Blake laughed, but it was strained. For a moment, it looked like he was considering it.

"Waverly!"

Lena's shout carried across the beach like she was screaming into a bullhorn. I looked out at the water to see her sitting on her surfboard, bobbing on the waves a little ways out. Alissa and Jesse were farther off, trying to tackle a set of large waves that'd appeared.

"Get in the water already!" Lena bellowed.

I laughed nervously.

"I'm coming!" I shouted back.

Blake clapped his hands down on my shoulders and turned me to face him. I stared at the faint freckles on his nose for a second before allowing myself to meet his gaze, seeing a hint of concern in his eyes.

"You'll be fine," he told me.

"You're psychic now?" I grumbled.

"I'll be next to you the whole time."

I closed my eyes and took a deep breath, trying to center myself. If I was going to die out there, I at least wanted to remember this moment—the wind on my face, the sand between my toes, and the weight of Blake's hands on my shoulders.

"Okay," I breathed.

When I opened my eyes again, Blake was staring down at me with a funny sort of look on his face. My cheeks went red hot, but I willed myself not to chicken out and start blabbing about the weather or something.

"Waverly?" Blake asked, his eyebrows knitting together and his lips flattening into one straight, serious line. His gaze, locked on mine, drifted down—briefly—to my lips.

"Uh-huh?" I asked, my heart starting up its imitation of a chimpanzee beating a pair of bongo drums.

Kiss me.

Please.

I'll pay you.

"Hurry up!" Jesse's shout broke through whatever tension our little staring contest had created. "Jeez. And you guys say *I'm* the slow one!"

Blake's hands shot off of me like he'd been burned, and he spun on his heels and grabbed the front end of his surfboard. I watched his back muscles go tense and knew I'd lost him. Whatever he'd been about to say—or *do*—was forgotten.

And I was going to die having never kissed a boy.

Chapter 15

The Atlantic Ocean rolled out like a wide grey carpet in front of me, stretching as far as the eye could see. I walked forward until the sand underneath me stuck to the bottom of my feet and made sloshing sounds with each step I took. I stopped walking at the edge of the water and lined my toes up with the line of residual foam along the shore.

I heard the shrill sound of Jesse's scream, followed by a splash and then Lena's boisterous and slightly maniacal laughter. Maybe if I turned, dropped the surfboard I had tucked under my arm, and sprinted for the parking lot, they wouldn't see me.

A large, warm hand settled on the small of my back.

Blake was standing beside me, and the look in his eyes said *Don't even think about it.* Not to mention, the hand he had on my back kept me from making a break for it.

"Go on," he said, pushing me forward.

I stumbled one step into the water and shrieked as a little wave of foam rushed over my bare feet.

"Nope!" I cried, spinning on my heels and taking a leaping step back to dry land. "Nope, nope, nope!"

But Blake was faster than I was.

His arm shot out and looped around my stomach, and the next thing I knew, he was pulling me along with him. And I was heading—backward—into the Atlantic Ocean, both my heels and the little rudder at the end of my surfboard dragging in the sand.

"Quit being such a baby," he said, sounding amused.

I opened my mouth to make an admittedly lame comeback about his face being a baby, but a wave of salt water smacked against the back of my thigh; I could feel the cold through the heavy fabric of my wet suit, although it was a bit muted.

"Mother of all that is holy!" I wailed.

"I thought you were supposed to like the cold," Blake pointed out, releasing his hold on my middle so he could grab my shoulder and spin me around. We were knee deep in the ocean.

"It's not the cold I'm bad with," I snapped, "it's the water."

"Which is *why*," Blake said, "I'm going to be right next to you the entire time. Now put your board down and let's go; Lena's gonna wring our necks if we don't hurry up."

I knew he had a point.

Blake took a few more steps into the water until it came up to the middle of his thighs and set his board down; it floated, bobbing up and down with each wave that rolled by. I watched him sling a leg over the board so he was straddling it, and then lean forward until he was on his stomach. He looked over his shoulder and frowned at me.

"Are you coming or what?"

I dropped my surfboard into the water, following his lead. Paddling turned out to be a lot more strenuous when there was actually some form of resistance. Blake, with his massive swimmer's shoulder muscles, had to stop several times and wait for me to catch up as I panted, dragging my arms through the water and wincing every time my fingers brushed against slimy seaweed.

"You need to work out more," Blake told me.

"I know," I conceded.

"Seriously, no wonder you can't tread water."

"Okay, I get it."

Blake kept his mouth shut for the next minute and a half while we paddled farther out into the ocean. I was relieved when he stopped paddling and sat up again; my arm muscles throbbed in protest. I rested my chin on my board and let my sore limbs dangle in the water, trying not to think about how many hundreds of feet below me the ocean floor had to be.

"Lena's heading over," Blake said suddenly.

I lifted my head and turned to look over my shoulder. Sure enough, the Fletcher twin in question was paddling our way, her face framed by a few dripping-wet curls that'd slipped out of her ponytail. I sat up—with a great deal of struggling and so much teetering that Blake reached out a hand to steady me so I wouldn't capsize my surfboard—and turned back to grin at Lena.

"Hi!" I called as she got closer.

"So." She beamed back at me. "How do you like the water?"

I really hope I didn't grimace.

"It's great!" I croaked.

"See! Told you it'd be fun!" Lena said.

Her arm shot out and, before I could brace myself, clapped me on the back in what I think was supposed to be a friendly gesture. But Lena could probably bench press a live grizzly bear, and so I was sent pitching forward from the sheer force of her patting me on the back.

My surfboard tilted.

I let out a noise of distress from somewhere at the back of my throat and my hand shot out, as if I could somehow turn into Jesus and catch myself from hitting the water.

And I did.

Well, at least I thought I did, for a second. Then I noticed I hadn't spontaneously become the Son of God; Blake Hamilton had reached out and grabbed my board with one hand and the wrist of my outstretched arm with the other.

"Careful there," he chuckled, steadying the surfboard.

I let out a breathless laugh of relief.

"Whoops," Lena said, grabbing the back end of my board and holding it steady so I could sit back up. "Sorry about that. I'm used to surfing with Jesse. He's steadier than he looks."

Lena's eyes narrowed suddenly.

Blake's grip on my wrist had slipped somewhere in the midst of me trying to get back on the middle of my board and find my balance, leaving our hands braced together. The warm tingle of a blush spread from my neck to my hairline and I immediately pulled my hand out of Blake's grip. But it was too late. Lena had seen us practically holding hands, and the smug expression playing on her lips told me I'd never hear the end of it.

"Really?" I cleared my throat, flustered and suddenly hot all over. "I always thought Jesse seemed sort of, I don't know . . . uncoordinated."

Lena's smirk grew wider, but she decided to humor me.

"He used to be a gymnast, actually. I think my mom might still have some photos of him from sixth grade. He had to wear these stupid spandex tights—"

"Lena! Shut up!" Jesse screeched from across the water.

"Okay, okay!" she bellowed back, then turned to me and added in a hushed tone, "I'll show you them later. You should come over for dinner or something. My mom wants to meet you, and my dad's always happy for an excuse to break out the barbecue. He makes a mean steak."

Well, how could I argue with that?

"I'm so in," I told her.

"You're invited, too, Hamilton," Lena added. "We could make a whole event out of it, have a big family dinner in the backyard."

I took this as an excuse to look over at Blake.

The bruise on the right side of his jaw, the one he'd gotten at Ethan's house party, was already beginning to turn a putrid shade of yellow. I wondered if the spot underneath my eye, where I'd been elbowed, looked just as nasty. But Blake's smile distracted from any ugliness the spot on his jaw might've caused.

"Sounds fun," he said. "I'd love to."

A big gust of wind carried over the water, ruffling through Blake's hair and slapping me directly in the face. I winced and turned, blinking briny mist out of my eyes.

Several yards off, Jesse and Alissa were sitting atop their surfboards, just talking. Jesse had a hand on Alissa's board to anchor her to him; it was just about the cutest and most romantic thing I'd ever seen, even if they were a bit of a mismatched pair.

Blake still had a hand on the edge of my board so I wouldn't drift away from him.

"So," I said, realizing I was starting to get a funny feeling at the pit of my stomach, "I'm hungry. Any chance we can leave soon and get some burgers or something?"

"Not so fast," Blake chided, tilting his chin up in a teasingly authoritative manner. "You haven't surfed yet."

Why would he bring that up?

The asshole.

"But I—"

"C'mon, Waverly!" Lena jumped in, punching me on the arm as lightly as she could—which would probably still leave a bruise. "It's easy once you get the hang of it. You have to at least *try*."

"I don't really—"

"You'll do fine," Blake said, moving his hand from my surfboard to my knee. I could feel the heat of his skin through the thick fabric of my wet suit. "Just one wave, and then I'll take you to the best diner in Marlin Bay. Deal?"

I *was* hungry.

"Deal," I said halfheartedly.

Lena giggled gleefully and started paddling farther out in the ocean, toward the bigger waves, where Jesse and Alissa sat. At first I was glad she'd left so I could fail in private, but when I looked over again, she was grinning and pointing in my direction, obviously trying to get Alissa and Jesse to watch.

I had an audience now.

"Oh God," I groaned under my breath.

"What's wrong?" Blake asked.

"They're watching," I whispered, nodding in their direction. Blake looked over my shoulder and huffed.

"You'll do fine," he said.

"I'll fall off this damned surfboard, and then I'll sink to my watery grave. I'll wind up in Dennis Jones's locker."

"Davy Jones?"

"Yeah, him." The corner of Blake's mouth quirked upward. "What?" I snapped.

"Nothing," he said, shaking his head. "Let's find you a wave."

Blake turned and started paddling but looked back over his shoulder to make sure I was following him and not making a break for the shore. As if I was *actually* considering sprinting up the beach, breaking into Jesse's Jeep, hot-wiring it and hightailing it out of here just to avoid surfing . . .

Preposterous. I didn't know how to hot wire a car.

"Keep up!" Blake called back to me.

I made a point of sighing loudly before shoving my arms back into the ocean and paddling as hard as I could. Blake stopped moving for a moment and waited until my board was beside his before he resumed paddling, matching my pace.

"Why are you making me do this?" I grumbled.

"Because," Blake said, "it'd look weird if you drove all the way out here just to sit on your board for five minutes and then ditch. No one's expecting you to be a good surfer, Waverly—"

"Well, *thanks.*"

"But they *are* expecting you to try."

Damn him for having valid points all the time.

I squinted at the expanse of ocean before me. The waves looked significantly higher than I'd ever seen them in Florida; the incoming storm wasn't due for a couple of days, but the wind had already swelled enough to trigger a stronger tide. I watched a wave reach its crescendo fifty yards out, then come crashing down in a heap of foam. A couple of seconds later, the residual ripple made my surfboard bob and a piece of seaweed glued itself to my ankle.

"Oh ew." I grimaced, kicking my leg wildly under the water.

"C'mon," Blake said, ignoring my struggle and releasing his grip on my board. "Let's get this over with."

He began paddling out farther into the water. I dropped forward onto my surfboard a little too quickly, sending a splash of salt water directly into my face, and hurried after him.

The thing nobody ever tells you about surfing is that even someone who's had years of practice can end up face-planting right into the ocean. One second I was staring ahead, trying to convince myself that I was looking at the ocean, *not* Blake Hamilton's wetsuit–clad rear end. The next, I heard Alissa and Lena cheering Jesse's name. By the time I turned to see what all the fuss was about, I only just caught a glimpse of Jesse standing upright on his board before he pitched to the side and tumbled into the water.

I tried to scream, but the sound came out wrong.

Blake turned to look over his shoulder—probably convinced that I'd suddenly decided to check the acoustics out on the water by practicing my yodeling techniques.

"What is it?" he asked, eyebrows drawn together.

"Jesse—Jesse fell! He—oh my God, he fell!" I cried.

Blake's eyes drifted over my shoulder, then back to me.

"Surfers fall all the time, Waverly."

I swallowed the lump in my throat.

If Jesse could fall, I was *definitely* going to fall.

"Did anybody call to warn the paramedics yet?" I asked, digging my arms back into the water as I tried to keep up with Blake. "Because they really should know someone's about to drown out here. Or did you just skip ahead to calling the cemetery and telling them what I want carved into my gravestone?"

"Waverly."

Blake's tone was dark, warning.

"I'm thinking we could skip the classic RIP and go for something hip. You know, like YOLO."

Blake stopped paddling and sat up on his board.

"I told you I wasn't going to let you drown," he said, turning over his shoulder to shoot me a glare. "Now stop being a smartass and hurry up. We just need one good wave, and then I'll tell Lena the two of us are bailing to get you some food."

The two of us?

As in, Blake was going to take me to lunch? Just me? No Jesse to interrupt with some dumbass question about whether or not we thought hot dogs would be advocates for democracy if they had functioning brains, no Lena to butt in with her bony elbows and shout at Jesse for being such an idiot, and no Alissa Hastings to sit there and shine like gold while I, in comparison, rusted away like an old penny?

I was going to have a heart attack.

"Let's go!" Blake called.

I snapped out of my moment of possible cardiac arrest to find Blake Hamilton several yards ahead of me again. I cursed and plunged my arms back into the water, furiously trying to catch up with him but only really succeeding in splashing sea water all over myself.

We stopped a moment later.

I gulped when I saw how far out from the beach we were.

"What now?" I asked, cracking my knuckles just so I had something to do with my hands; I was worried they'd start shaking if I didn't *move*. My nerves were going haywire.

"We wait for a good wave," Blake said, narrowing his eyes

as he scanned the ocean ahead of us. "I'll tell you when we get one. You're just going to keep on your stomach for a second, and when I tell you to pop up, you do it. Just try not to stand up all the way."

"Why not?" I frowned.

"You're too tall," Blake said.

Ouch. That was like a punch to the stomach. As if I hadn't already known I was practically monstrous next to someone petite and dainty like Alissa, Blake had to go and make that clear.

You take up too much space, I reminded myself.

"Yeah, I know," I replied, my voice dry.

Blake shot me a funny look.

"I mean you'll want your center of gravity lower to the board so you don't fall over so easily," he said. "I didn't mean—"

He coughed, seemingly unable to finish his sentence.

Well, this was sufficiently awkward. I turned to the beach, hoping that if I angled myself away from the sun, Blake wouldn't be able to see me blushing like a freaking tomato.

"Hey, hold on," Blake said, grabbing the back of my surfboard and towing me backward until I was staring right up into those blue, blue eyes of his. For a heartbeat, I imagined him opening up his mouth and saying something sappy. Something that you only ever heard in bad romance movies. Something like, *You're just the right height.* Instead, I got, "This wave looks good."

My stomach damn near flipped over.

"Wait, I don't think I'm—" I started to protest, but Blake was already on his stomach. He reached across and slapped a hand between my shoulder blades, forcing me to join him in the ready position on my own board.

"Keep low, okay?"

Float

If you've ever ridden a roller coaster, you know what it feels like when you're going up the incline before a steep drop. As the wave beneath us swelled, lifting our surfboards forward and up, I knew what kind of drop was coming. It was the type of drop that made your heart plummet into your feet and ripped a scream out of your throat. I just hoped it didn't involve any splashes.

"Pop up!"

I barely heard Blake's command over the roaring in my ears.

Somehow, as if on their own accord, my hands slapped down on the board beneath me and pushed my shoulders up. I swung my legs forward until my feet were planted beneath me and then I rose, my arms poised outward to steady the rest of me.

For a moment, I was flying.

And then came the drop.

I don't really know what happened, and I probably couldn't articulate it even if I tried. All I really know is that I must've looked really fucking hilarious to anyone watching as I tumbled forward, four parts flailing limbs and zero parts grace, and smacked my forehead against my own surfboard.

My arms and legs, splayed in every different direction, curled up and locked around the board beneath me in a desperate attempt to keep me from slipping into the water.

A wave crashed onto my back.

For a moment, I was submerged. I was trapped in a dark, cold, soundless void, and all I could do was cling to my surfboard. What felt like minutes but was probably only seconds later, Lena's hearty laughter rang in my ears as I broke the surface again and bobbed, slowly and steadily, up to the edge of the beach.

I pried my arms out of their death grip on my board and rolled back so I was sitting upright. My legs only managed to stretch out a few inches before I felt sand squish beneath my toes.

"Good try, Waverly!" Lena bellowed.

I turned over my shoulder.

She and Alissa were doubled over in laughter, but Jesse was whooping and hollering and clapping for me. I offered them a weak wave, still not sure how exactly I'd managed to survive. I heard water sloshing at my side and turned to see Blake walking up to the beach, knee deep in the water, dragging his surfboard behind him. The ghost of a laugh hovered on his lips, and his eyes were bright and teasing.

"I must admit," he said, "your surfing techniques are a little unconventional, but I'm glad to see you're alive."

I winced.

"On a scale of one to ten, how graceful was that?" I asked, suddenly very aware of the fact that Blake stood well over six feet tall and I was still sitting on my board, which hovered a good two inches off the ground. I had to squint to look up at him.

"A solid negative seven," Blake replied without hesitation.

"*Nice*. So when can I go pro?"

"I'll call the World Surf League immediately."

We stared at each other for a minute, me enjoying the moment more than I should've, before Blake cracked a smile and offered me his hand.

"See?" he asked as I hooked my fingers around his. "I told you I wouldn't let you drown."

Being as oversized as I am, I'm used to people not being able to lift me up. I didn't consider the fact that Blake, with his thick arms and swimmer's shoulders, could toss me over his shoulder in a way a lot of people couldn't.

So I overcompensated.

As Blake yanked on my hand, I planted my feet in the sand and pushed myself up. I was unsteady, partly due to the uneven ground and partly due to the fact that I still had that I'm about to die adrenaline rushing through my veins, and so I hurtled forward. My chest smacked against Blake's, our wet suits squishing together with all the dignity of two soggy Pop-Tarts.

"Sorry," I blurted.

I planted my hands on his shoulders and pushed myself back, trying desperately to escape the awkward situation I'd managed to create. My heel clipped the edge of my surfboard, which was still resting behind me in the shallow water, and I tumbled backward. Blake's arms shot out to catch me, but he wasn't quite quick enough.

I landed on my ass, hard, and the rear end of my surfboard sent a geyser of sea water into the air.

Lena's laugh was explosive, even from out across the water.

"Are you okay?" Blake asked.

His lips quivered as he tried to hold back a laugh.

Lena was still cackling in the distance.

"You know what?" I huffed, clapping wet sand off of my hands. "I think I'm ready for that burger."

Chapter 16

Blake and I dragged so much sand into the front seat of Jesse's beat-up Jeep that the car could've been considered a mobile island nation. I felt guilty about the mess until Blake reminded me that Jesse had a collection of empty gum wrappers and used tooth-picks in the glove box, so he had no right to complain about a little sand on the floor. Still, I couldn't help but feel like a certified asshole as I dusted little grains from the crease behind my knees.

"Where are we going again?" I asked as Blake pulled the car out of the lot by the beach.

"Only the best diner in Marlin Bay," he replied, tapping the steering wheel in time to the faint beat of the pop song playing on the radio. He paused at the edge of the lot and shot a grin at me, then hit the gas and took a sharp turn onto a cliff-side road.

"Do they have burgers?" I asked.

Blake nodded, still smiling. "Milkshakes too."

"Drive faster, please."

I sank back into the worn leather upholstery of my seat and closed my eyes, savoring the deep, rumbling sound of Blake's laughter. For a moment, while I'd been peeling off my wet suit and Blake had been paddling back out to tell the others we were heading off for lunch, I'd been so worried about being alone with Blake in a car with nothing but a few feet of air between us.

The last few times we'd been sitting side by side like this, I hadn't had sand in all my nooks and crannies and my hair wasn't matted with salt water. And I probably hadn't smelled like seaweed either. But even if I did reek of the ocean, Blake didn't seem to notice.

Or maybe he did, and he was too nice to point it out.

We drove for two minutes before we passed a large sign made of driftwood painted with pastel blues and greens. MARLIN BAY, it read in elegant white script.

The nice thing about Blake Hamilton was that he didn't feel the need to fill the silence with mindless small talk. He was perfectly content to keep his hands on the wheel and his mouth shut while I watched the small seaside town roll by. We passed a little white stucco chapel and a gas station that looked like it'd fallen straight out of a '50s movie.

Blake took a turn at a fork in the road, and we started down a street lined with little shops. Marlin Bay was so different from Holden; the town felt older and more sophisticated with its red-brick façades and black wrought-iron railings on second-floor balconies. Holden was a place for tourists and rich vacationers. Marlin Bay looked like the kind of place only locals and history enthusiasts would care to see.

"Where is this diner?" I asked, my eyes scanning the shops we drove past. I didn't recognize a single one of them; they were all family owned and local. Not a McDonald's in sight.

"Last building on the right," Blake replied.

On the corner of the block, across the street from a small parking strip perched at the edge of the cliffs overlooking the ocean, sat a window-lined restaurant that looked like it'd dropped out of a small midwestern town from the '50s. The exterior walls were brick and the awning over the front door was striped white and pale blue. Written on one of the awnings, in cursive script on a doily-shaped patch of orange, were the words *Bayside Burgers*. It was quaint, the type of place Aunt Rachel would've added to her Pinterest board in two seconds flat.

Blake pulled the Jeep into an empty space across the street, and my heart nearly did a backflip when I realized that we were separated from a fifty-foot drop into the Atlantic Ocean by only a less than trustworthy-looking wooden guardrail.

"Is it safe to park here?" I asked warily.

"I've parked in this spot at least a thousand times," Blake replied, pulling the keys from the ignition. "Not once have I come back to find my car missing."

"There's a first time for everything," I grumbled.

I released the buckle of my seat belt, tugged down the hem of my white T-shirt, pushed open the passenger-side door, and was promptly smacked in the face by a gust of wind. I spat hair out of my mouth as Blake exited on his side.

"Hold on one second," he called as he started toward the trunk of the Jeep. "I think Jesse has some sweatshirts back here."

I was still trying to figure out where the pieces of hair plastered to my lips were connected to my scalp when Blake jogged around the car, a sizeable bundle of wadded-up sweatshirts tucked under one arm. He held up the first—a navy-blue crew neck—and sent me an inquisitive look.

"Will this work?" he asked.

I grabbed the top and tugged it on over my head. The sleeves were several inches short of hitting my wrists, and the hem was so high it look like a crop top on me.

"It's a little small." Blake snorted.

I shot a glare at him, but it was really hard to be mad when he was grinning at me like that. I sighed and pulled the crew neck back over my head, cringing as I realized my hair was probably starting to resemble some form of wildlife. Blake was smart enough not to comment on my appearance as I handed him back the child's size medium crew neck.

"Jesse really needs to clean out his car," he said. "I'm pretty sure that was Lena's when she was, like, eight. Here. Try this one."

Blake handed me a faded dark grey sweatshirt with a hood—one that was big enough to slip on over my massive tangle of windblown hair—and frayed drawstrings. The sleeves were just a little long and the hem hit so close to the bottom of Rachel's shorts that I was sure, from one angle or another, it probably looked like I wasn't wearing any pants. But the sweatshirt was thick and warm and, compared to the crew neck, fit pretty well.

"That works," Blake said, his tone odd.

"Who do you think this one belonged to?" I said, patting down the front pocket. It was only then that I noticed the little white logo on the left breast of the sweatshirt, the unmistakable lifeguard cross.

Damn. I looked *so* legit.

"It was mine," Blake said.

My head shot up, but all I got was an eyeful of Blake's wide,

T-shirt covered back as he walked around to the trunk and tossed the rest of the sweatshirts into their designated spot. He tugged a dark-green crew neck on over his head, mussing up his already windblown hair in the process, and slammed the trunk shut. Then he turned to me and smiled.

"You ready to have the best burger of your life?" he asked.

I was a little caught off guard by how utterly happy Blake Hamilton looked. I'd sort of been worried that he didn't want me wearing his old sweatshirt, which in turn led me to worry about whether or not he wanted to be seen in public with me. During my first couple of days in Holden, Blake had made it perfectly clear that he didn't want to be seen with me. But maybe, just maybe, he considered us friends now.

"Bring it on," I said, rubbing my palms together.

Blake spun on his heels, crossing the tiny parking strip and heading toward the crosswalk. I trailed one step behind him, so when he stopped abruptly to look both ways for oncoming cars, I stepped on the back of his shoe and smacked him in the back with my right shoulder.

"Sorry," I mumbled, wincing.

Could I go, like, *five minutes* without fucking up? Although by that point, Blake had already learned from experience that I had all the grace and coordination of a giraffe attempting en pointe ballet, so there really was no recovering.

Blake chuckled, the sound coming from somewhere deep in the barrel of his chest. I was standing so close that I could feel the heat radiating off his back. But then he stepped into the street, and cold air flooded the place where he'd previously been. Blake's hand drifted back toward me, as if he was going to make a move to hold my hand, but then, suddenly, he straightened his back and shoved both of his hands in the pockets of his black shorts.

I shivered and hurried after him.

Bayside Burgers looked like the kind of ice cream parlor you'd see in an old black and white film. There was an *L*-shaped bar that took up most of the restaurant, and behind the white marble counters and large menu placards hanging from the high ceilings, I could just make out the hustle and bustle of the kitchen. The interior of the shop was warm and smelled like some enchanted combination of chocolate sauce and hamburger patties. There were two families and a group of senior women in some of the booths along the windows and a handful of individuals scattered around the bar.

Blake strode right up to the hostess's podium, his hands still tucked in his pockets. The woman standing there looked to be in her late sixties, although her bright eyes gave the illusion of youth, and was incredibly short. When she saw Blake, she smiled the kind of smile a grandmother would use to greet her favorite grandson.

"Well, look at you!"

"Hi, Carol." Blake grinned back at her.

He pulled his hands out of his pockets as the woman—Carol, according to the golden nametag pinned to her apron and Blake's greeting—stepped around the podium and gave him an appraising once-over. She tucked a piece of pale grey hair behind her ear, and I caught a flash of her pearl earring.

"You're too thin," she chided, reaching out to prod Blake's sweatshirt-covered abdomen. "This is what happens when you don't visit me often enough."

"I was here last weekend."

"And you didn't order any dessert," Carol said, resting her

hands on her hips and tilting her head back so she could look Blake in the eye. He was well over six feet tall. She, on the other hand, looked like she couldn't be over four foot ten.

"I wasn't that hungry," he said.

"You'll be skin and bones before long," Carol scolded. "Don't you dare turn into one of those skinny little hipsters, you hear me?"

Blake laughed. "I promise we'll order the monster sundae today."

At his use of pronoun, Carol's gaze shifted and settled on me. I straightened my spine and tried my best to smile, but I felt more nervous than I'd been to sit down and take my AP biology test just a couple of months earlier. And I was *horrible* at biology.

I wondered, briefly, if this was what meeting your boyfriend's parents felt like.

Shut up, I scolded myself. *This isn't a date.*

"Hi," I offered up, my voice a little higher pitched than usual.

"Oh, this is my friend Waverly," Blake told Carol, shifting a couple of steps to stand so close our shoulders bumped. "She's visiting for the summer. Her aunt is Rachel Lyons."

"The artist working on that mural over by the hospital?"

"That's her." I nodded.

Carol took a moment to stare at me, her gaze assessing, before she looked over at Blake. Her eyes scanned his face for a moment before making their way back to me, but not before focusing in on the lack of air between our touching shoulders.

The corners of her lips quirked upward.

"It's very nice to meet you, Waverly."

I took her outstretched hand and shook it, praying to God that my palm wasn't too clammy or anything.

"It's nice to meet you, too, Carol," I returned.

Carol beamed at me. Blake shifted beside me, tugging at the sleeves of his crew neck, as Carol hurried back around the podium. She returned with two laminated menus tucked under her arm.

"Table, booth, or bar?" she asked.

"Booth, please," Blake responded immediately.

Carol started across the restaurant, the short heels of her shoes clicking lightly against the black and white marble tiles of the floor. Blake tilted his head, motioning for me to follow her, and fell in line behind me. We passed several perfectly decent looking tables, but Carol didn't stop until we reached the booth tucked into the very farthest corner of Bayside Burgers. She slapped the menus down on the table and turned to face us, smiling like a toddler proud of her crayon masterpiece on her mommy and daddy's bedroom wall.

"Thanks, Carol," Blake mumbled.

Carol hurried around him to attend to a man at the bar who had his empty coffee mug raised, her lips flattened into a thin line as if she was trying to hold back a laugh.

I slipped into the booth, choosing the bench with a better view out the windows so I could keep an eye on Jesse's precariously parked Jeep. But the second Blake Hamilton dropped onto the opposite bench, his bare knees brushing mine underneath the table, I was pretty sure that the car outside could've burst into a giant ball of flames and billowy, black smoke and I wouldn't have noticed.

God, he was big. His shoulders were broad and his long legs didn't fit all that well under the table—especially not when my too-long legs were occupying the same space—and his hands looked huge as he picked up one of the laminated menus Carol had left for us.

Blake was a physically imposing presence.

I grabbed my own menu and willed my heartbeat to stop fluttering around like a stupid bird. There was no reason to be nervous. Blake was my friend now. He'd said so himself, to Carol. I'd be better off in the end if I tried to remember that this was *not* a date, Blake was *not* interested, and I was *not* going to get any action anytime soon.

I must have sighed self-deprecatingly.

Blake glanced up from his menu and quirked an eyebrow. I couldn't help but think back to the first time Blake and I had been forced into association, at the bonfire party, and how he'd quirked his eyebrow at me the same way. Then, it had been the kind of subtle expression you make when another driver cuts you off only to ease up off the gas until he's doing twenty under the speed limit. It was the kind of move that said *You're kidding me*, with just a dash of *F you*.

Now, it was gentle. Familiar. Teasing.

What had changed so drastically in just a handful of weeks?

I tugged at the sleeve of my sweatshirt, pursing my lips as I tried to select my next couple of words as carefully as possible.

"Hey, Blake?" I asked, almost in a whisper.

He leaned over the table just the slightest bit.

"Yeah?" he whispered back.

"Can I ask my first question?"

Blake's back stiffened and he slid his elbows off the table. He leaned back in the opposite bench—trying to get as far away from me as physically possible, I guess—and eyed me warily. For several seconds, his eyebrows remained furrowed as he tried to figure out what sort of intrusive, malevolent questions I might've come up with.

"You're well within your rights," he said.

Carol chose that exact moment to appear with a glass of ice water in each hand. The moment she set them down, Blake snatched his glass and started to chug it. Carol turned to me.

"Can I get the two of you anything else to drink?" she asked.

"Water's fine," I said.

"Are y'all about ready to order?"

"I think I need another minute to choose," I admitted, smiling a little sheepishly. I hadn't even started to read the menu.

"Sure thing, dear." Carol nodded.

She was halfway across the restaurant before Blake finally slammed down his glass, rattling the ice inside of it.

"You good?" I asked.

Okay, I probably could've sounded less amused. The poor guy probably thought I was about to ask something superintrusive or devastatingly embarrassing.

"Fantastic." He nodded. "So, what's the question?"

I took a moment to review the wording in my head, then nodded and set my hands on the table—fingers clasped—like I was about to interview Blake for the executive position as my new friend.

"Why did you hate me when we first met?"

Blake stared at me for a second, and then his face scrunched up.

"I didn't hate you."

"Yes, you did."

He was reaching for the ice water again. I slid my hand across the table and snatched it away before he could use it as an excuse to further evade my question.

"I honestly didn't," Blake insisted, sighing as he propped his elbows up on the table again. "I mean, I know I probably acted a little like an asshole—"

"A lot," I corrected under my breath.

Blake winced.

"Okay, *a lot*. I was a really big asshole. But I didn't hate you."

It was my turn to eye him warily.

"But you—"

Carol materialized at the side of the table, almost out of nowhere, and I was cut off halfway through my rebuttal. The older waitress beamed at us, seemingly delighted at the way the two of us were both bent over the table and speaking in hushed voices.

"Y'all ready to order?" she asked.

We were. Carol smiled to herself as she jotted down our order and collected our laminated menus—and let out an audible laugh when Blake requested something called the Beluga Whale Sundae for us to split for dessert.

"It'll be ten minutes, tops," she told us.

Blake waited until she was gone to turn to me again.

"You were saying?" he prompted, reaching across the table to snatch his glass of water before I could stop him.

"I was *saying*"—I scooted forward on the bench, back to business—"that you acted like you hated me at the bonfire party. And on the drive home, too, but you were pretty hammered, so I don't think you remember it that well."

"I don't," Blake admitted.

"Which is sort of a bummer, because I was hoping someone would be able to vouch for my awesome driving skills."

"I'm sure you're NASCAR material."

"Thank you," I said, trying my absolute hardest not to smile. "But don't distract me. You hated me, and I know it. You couldn't even look at me without glaring. And I just want to know what I did wrong."

Blake looked down at the table again, tracing his fingertips over the grain in the faux wood.

"You didn't do anything," he mumbled.

"See, that's *exactly* what you said in the car."

I remembered that part vividly. He'd said something about how I'd ruined his night—there'd been an expletive in there somewhere—and I'd told him I hadn't done anything to warrant his hostility. His reply had been one word, peremptory.

Exactly.

As if, somehow, the whole situation made perfect sense in the world of teenage-boy logic.

Blake fidgeted on the other side of the booth, his knees knocking against mine underneath the table. Leave it to Carol to put us in what had to be the smallest booth in the entire restaurant. Blake's presence was nerve racking enough when I didn't have to feel the heat of his skin against mine.

"I just thought, you know, that you'd tell everybody at the bonfire about what you saw. You know, when Chloe yelled at me."

His words startled me.

I had to sit still for a moment to process them.

"When she grounded you and took your phone?" I asked, frowning.

Blake winced.

"Yeah, that," he mumbled. "I just had this idea that you'd want some sort of icebreaker, you know, so you could talk to people. I thought you'd be all like, *Do you know that kid Blake? I just watched him get his ass handed to him by a four-foot-eleven blond chick.*"

"She's really four foot eleven?"

Blake shot me an incredulous look.

"Sorry, sorry," I said, straightening in my seat and reaching for my glass of water. I didn't bring it up to my mouth to sip it, though. I just wanted something to occupy my hands. "Jeez, you really thought I'd do that to you? Talk shit about you and your family?"

Blake shrugged.

There was such defeat in the hang of his head, the slump of his shoulders. It made me furious.

"Who the fuck even *does* that?" I growled.

Blake must've thought my anger was directed at him, because he straightened suddenly and looked me dead in the eyes.

"I'm sorry, really, I am," he told me. "I realized once I saw you talking with Lena . . . I mean, I guess I figured out that you weren't going to do that to me. That you wouldn't. And by then I'd already had a couple of drinks, and I was still pretty pissed about the whole thing with Chloe, and then on top of that I was mad at myself for being such an asshole to you, and then Ethan came over and, well, you know Ethan."

I nodded. "I want to punch him when I'm sober," I offered.

"The urge is only intensified when you're drunk," Blake replied. "I shouldn't have bothered with him, though. I was more mad at myself than anything else. He was just *there*."

"Wasn't he hooking up with Alissa, though?" I asked.

Way to rub salt in the wound, I chided myself the moment the words left my mouth.

Blake shrugged and reached for his water.

"But I knew about that already," he admitted, then tipped his glass back and took a long drink.

Carol arrived with two large, white, porcelain plates balanced in the crook of her arm. I tried to focus on smiling appreciatively and saying thank you the appropriate number of times, but my head was still reeling from Blake's admission. He'd known Alissa and Ethan were having some sort of relationship on the side, and he didn't seem all that upset about it. Where was the cringing in heartbroken agony, the stares into the distance as he reminisced, the clench of his fists as he imagined making contact with Ethan's nose?

Blake seemed pretty unperturbed for a guy who was talking about his ex-girlfriend's infidelity. In fact, he looked nothing less than thrilled as he thanked Carol and turned his attention to the massive burger sitting on the plate in front of him.

I watched him pop a couple of French fries in his mouth.

Apparently, I was gawking at him like he'd just told me he had a part-time job working for the Russian mafia, because Blake met my gaze and frowned.

"What?" he asked.

"You never hated me?" I asked again, just to be sure.

"No, never."

He said it with such conviction, I had to believe him. And so, with the matter of Blake's initial attitude toward me finally settled, I was able to focus my attention on more important matters. Namely, how fantastic the burger in front of me smelled.

The next few minutes were filled by the same sort of pleasant, comfortable silence we'd experienced on the car ride up to Marlin Bay. Blake and I were actually pretty good at the art of silent communication. When he lifted the top bun off his burger, I'd already grabbed the bottle of ketchup and passed it his way. When I felt a dollop of mustard perched on my bottom lip threaten to slide down my chin, Blake already had a napkin held out. I tried not to focus on how pretty his eyes were or how his smile made something in my stomach feel light and fluttery, but instead on how nice it felt to have a friend by my side.

A friend I wanted to have push me up against the nearest wall and kiss me so hard it'd make a romance novelist blush. And here I'd been doing so well at keeping my mind out of the gutter.

Twenty-five minutes later, Blake had polished off everything on his plate, garnishes included, and I'd given in to his longing gazes and offered him a handful of my fries. Carol gave us a satisfied nod when she came to collect our plates—both of them empty—and said she'd bring out the Beluga Whale Sundae in just a moment.

"I don't think I can eat any more," I admitted.

"Fine." Blake shrugged. "More for me, then."

But when the sundae did arrive, I found myself reaching for a spoon and leaning forward to calculate the perfect first bite. It was the biggest ice cream monstrosity I'd ever seen in my life. There were at least three chocolate-chip cookies wedged into the side of a mountain of chocolate and vanilla scoops, and, if I wasn't mistaken, it looked like there was a giant, gooey brownie at the bottom of the large, glass dish the sundae was served in.

Three minutes later, the dish was empty, and I'd be lying if I said I hadn't had half of what'd been in it.

"I can't believe we did it," I moaned, pressing my forehead against the table. Blake was too busy licking hot fudge sauce off his spoon to comment on my state of distress. "I'm so proud of us. But I think I need a nap."

"You can sleep in the car."

I tilted my head so I could peer out the window. Jesse's beat-up Jeep hadn't rolled off the cliff during our meal, but it did look pretty far away in my current state.

"I'm not carrying you," Blake said, as if he could read my mind.

I sat up and reached across the table to smack him on the shoulder, but he just chuckled at my efforts. His laughter proved contagious, because by the time Carol strode up to our table with the check, Blake and I were snickering like five-year-olds.

"Here you go," Carol announced.

It wasn't until Blake reached for his wallet that I realized I didn't have any money with me.

"I'll pay you back," I declared as Blake pulled out a few crumpled bills and tucked them into the black booklet with the check.

Blake shook his head. "No, you won't."

"Yes, I will. I swear, I'll write this down so I don't forget—"

"I mean I'm not letting you."

Blake slid the check onto the edge of the table. A moment later, Carol plucked it up.

"Thank you," he told her, "it was delicious, as usual."

"You'll be back and visit me next week, then?" she grinned, casting a look in my direction that seemed to ask, *And you'll come too?*

"I've got the day off on Thursday," Blake replied.

"It's a date!"

I felt my cheeks flush at her choice of words. *Not helping, Carol.*

"Goodness, boy, I wish you'd quit that lifeguard job," she continued as she gathered up our empty sundae dish. "You're too busy, and it's too dangerous. I don't like those Holden beaches."

"I'm always careful, Carol," he insisted.

Carol paused for a moment, her lips pursed into a tight, lipstick-stained line as she gazed down at him with a sort of maternal worry I hadn't seen in person in a long time. She reached out a wrinkled hand and brushed her thumb across the pale white scar above Blake's left eyebrow, her eyes flashing with untouchable melancholy. She blinked, as if to collect herself, and the pain was replaced with a teasing glint.

"Do me a favor and get yourself a haircut before Thursday," Carol scolded, flicking the locks of dark hair that'd fallen over his forehead, and then she was gone.

Blake was still smiling, the gesture a little sad and his eyes a little unfocused, when we stepped out of Bayside Burgers and back into the gusting wind, which had picked up strength considerably during lunch. I trailed along at Blake's side as we crossed the street and made our way to Jesse's Jeep, my brain working in overtime as a second question started to take form inside my head.

Blue eyes, not like George's.

That little white scar above his eyebrow.

The way he'd completely panicked at the pool a few weeks ago when he'd seemed so convinced that I'd drown in four feet of water and had sputtered about some big secret.

It was all so obvious. But I wanted to hear it from him.

So when Blake turned to me from the driver's seat of Jesse's car, smiling contentedly and patting his stomach, and asked, "Didn't I tell you that was gonna be the best burger of your life?" I replied with, "How did your mom drown?"

Waverly Lyons, Queen of Tact. Bow down.

Chapter 17

I truly believe that every person on this earth has one special talent.

Some people are naturally gifted when it comes to athletics. Others are better at performance arts or painting or composing classical music. I once read a news article about a guy who recited, like, fifty thousand digits of pi. It took him three days. The Guinness World Records officials wouldn't even let him go to the bathroom by himself in case he had the digits written inside his underpants or something. Sometimes I can't even remember my parents' cell phone numbers, so I sort of wish that I'd been born with a useful gift like that.

But no, my special talent is something far less helpful. My brain has the unique ability to calculate the exact combination of words that are least appropriate for a situation.

Basically, I'm really good at sticking my foot in my mouth.

The smile Blake had when he'd turned to face me from the driver's seat, still completely and utterly unaware of the verbal punch I was about to unleash on him, was still on his face. Only it kind of looked more like a grimace now. I'd never wanted to disappear so badly before in my life. I wanted to push open the Jeep door, army roll out of the vehicle, and hurl myself over the nearest cliff.

Which, conveniently, was only a couple of steps away.

It felt like a small eternity passed before Blake made a strangled noise at the back of his throat. He suddenly straightened his spine, faced forward in his seat, and flattened his lips into a thin, expressionless line. Then he reached out to turn the keys in the ignition and grabbed hold of the steering wheel.

He didn't look at me again as he pulled out of the parking space.

He didn't look me as we started down the street either.

He still wasn't looking at me when we rolled up to a stop sign.

"Is that your second question?"

He'd spoken in monotone, his words slow and deliberate, cautious even. His face didn't give away anything. I thought I could see a pinch between his eyebrows, but it was hard to tell when I was staring at his profile.

Please, don't do this, I pleaded in my head. *Don't shut me out.*

He'd been so open in the restaurant, so willing to welcome me in. Maybe, if I hadn't been so tactless with my last question, he'd still be smiling. I clasped my hands in my lap, squeezing my fingers until the bones ached and my skin stung.

I shook my head, feeling breathless.

"That's not, um—I mean, I know she drowned, I just . . ."

I squeezed my eyes shut, desperately trying to grasp onto any idea as to how I could close the distance I felt growing between Blake and me.

"I'm not here by choice," I blurted.

For a second, silence hung in the air.

"I didn't force you to come." Blake's tone was dark, bordering somewhere on angry, but his voice cracked a little.

"No, no, that's not what I meant," I cried, clamping my hands over my face and sinking into my seat. "I meant I didn't ask to be in Holden this summer, to see Rachel. It wasn't my choice. I'm only here because my parents didn't want me on either of their expeditions."

Out of the corner of my eye, I saw Blake's hands tighten on the steering wheel. But now that I'd started to speak, the words just kept bubbling up in my throat and spilling over.

"I'm dead weight. I'm not good at math or science or navigation or basic survival skills. And I'm not good at any of the arts, like Aunt Rachel, so it's not like I provided any entertainment value. I'm just . . . there. No talents. No skills. Nothing to bring to the table. My parents finally cracked and sent me out here because it was getting embarrassing to have to cart me around in front of all their colleagues. Neither of them have called me yet to ask how my summer's going, and I know I should give them the benefit of the doubt, because cell reception can be so spotty up there, but I don't think they care. I really don't. I could probably drown in the Atlantic Ocean and they'd—"

The car jerked to a stop.

I looked out through the window for a moment before I realized the front wheel of the Jeep was two inches from the curb.

Blake had pulled over.

Shit.

I'd thought that maybe, if I opened up a little, he'd feel more comfortable telling me about his mother. Friendships are about trust, after all. I couldn't just sit here and interrogate him. But I'd dug a little bit too deep into my own story, and somehow I'd ended up telling him exactly how miserable I was.

Miserable and untalented and useless.

I kept my hands clasped in my lap, refusing to look anywhere else but out the window. My breathing was rapid and a little uneven—the same way it was after I tried to do anything that involved running farther than the distance between the living-room couch and the refrigerator—and I sounded like I was panting in the silence of the car. For what felt like the longest time, it was just the sound of my erratic breath in that beat-up Jeep.

Finally, Blake shifted in the driver's seat.

I squeezed my eyes shut, half expecting him to unlock the doors and tell me to take a hike.

"Hey," he said.

The word was spoken softly, but not in that gentle tone people use to comfort you at someone's funeral. It was calm, asking for a moment of my attention. I peeled my eyes open and took a deep, steadying breath before I met Blake's gaze. There were no signs of pity in his expression, like I'd been both expecting and dreading.

Instead, he looked determined—sure of himself.

His hand came out over my lap, and I felt his fingertips brush against my clenched fists. Almost immediately, the tension in my muscles unraveled. The fingers on my right hand untangled themselves from my left, only to be replaced by Blake's.

His palms were hot and a little bit sweaty, but I didn't mind.

"I wanna show you something," he told me.

His fingers tightened around my hand just a fraction, silently asking me if that was okay.

I nodded.

Blake nodded back, and then he slipped his hand from mine and grabbed the steering wheel. The warmth of his skin lingered, though. He pulled Jesse's Jeep away from the curb and started back down the street but took a left turn at the next intersection. We drove for another two minutes before I spotted a large, clinical blue and white sign emerging up on the left.

MARLIN BAY MEDICAL CENTER.

I bit my tongue as we turned into the hospital parking lot because even though I was really curious about where he was taking me, I didn't want to end up saying anything stupid. *Again.*

Instead of blurting out all the questions I had, I turned to peer through the car window. The hospital at Marlin Bay looked like it'd been painted white when it first opened but had since faded to a slightly muddy shade of cream. The building wasn't anything fancy, really, just a pair of rectangular blocks stacked atop one another—the bottom horizontally, the top vertically. There was blue trim around the windows and a blue awning over the front sliding-glass doors, but other than that, the whole structure looked pretty bland.

Blake didn't stop to park in the front lot.

Instead, he kept driving. It was only once we'd started down a little street that ran along the side of the building that I noticed the rest of the hospital, which had been completely concealed by the main building from my view back in the parking lot out front. There was another large building, just as cream-colored and plain as the first, which appeared to be connected to the front building by a fully enclosed bridge lined with glass walls.

Blake turned the Jeep down the street between the two halves of the Marlin Bay hospital. The road was wide enough so that perpendicular parking spaces ran along both sides of the road, but two cars could still drive past one another without clipping mirrors. The two structures flanking us weren't all that tall—maybe five stories, at most—but if the small trees planted at the back of the front building were any indication, the buildings blocked out most of the wind.

I gripped the seat belt across my chest with one hand as Blake slowed the Jeep. Most of the parking spaces along the street were empty, so he didn't have any trouble pulling into one. He cut the motor, pulled the keys from the ignition, and opened his door without so much as turning to face me.

I figured I should follow him, so I popped open my own door and scrambled out of the Jeep.

And then I saw it.

I don't know why I hadn't spotted all the bright blue tarps on the sidewalk across the street, or the three ladders propped up against the wall at varying heights. But there, on the flat façade of the back building, was a gigantic, half-completed mural.

Rachel's mural. It had to be.

My feet moved as if they had a mind of their own, and I walked around to the rear of the Jeep so I could get a better look at the artwork. It was an ocean scene, full to the brim with marine wildlife. Dolphins and swordfish. Starfish and barnacles. A school of shimmering silver fish weaving through vibrantly colored coral and disappearing into the unpainted expanse of wall where I could make out the faint outline of seaweed tendrils and giant sea turtles.

"Wow," I breathed.

I glanced to my side to find that Blake had walked around the back of the car to stand next to me. But he had his back to the mural, and his eyes were trained on the other building behind me.

"*Psst*, Blake," I whispered theatrically, "mural's this way."

Blake didn't respond for a moment.

"Third floor, second window from the left," he told me, nodding up at the building behind me. "That was my room."

It took me a second to figure out what he was talking about, but when my brain finally processed his words, I took a couple of steps until he and I were both standing away from the Jeep. My eyes flew up to the building, counting out three floors up and two windows over. I waited to feel some sort of all-encompassing feeling of knowledge wash over me. When it didn't, I looked at Blake.

My eyes locked on the little white scar above his left eyebrow.

"What happened?" I asked, my voice quiet but not soft. I knew Blake Hamilton well enough to know he'd hate it if I suddenly started treating him like some kind of wounded baby animal.

"My mom was a competitive swimmer," Blake said, his eyes still locked on that window. "She almost made it to the Olympics back in her twenties, actually. But then she met my dad, and she sort of gave it all up to settle down and raise a family. She kept swimming, though. She was still really good at it. She just didn't compete."

There was a knot forming in my stomach.

"When I was about twelve or thirteen, Hurricane Dean went through the Caribbean. We all thought it'd completely missed Florida, so there wasn't any reason to worry about it. My mom went out swimming one morning, like she usually did, and . . ."

I was going to throw up my Beluga Whale Sundae. Blake

seemed to have trouble starting another sentence. He looked down at the ground for a minute and shook his head.

"We—my dad and I—heard about all the residual rip currents that afternoon on television. Hurricane Dean didn't even brush us, and we'd thought maybe the Gulf would get some weird tides, but we had no idea . . . God, there was this horrible moment when we just both looked at each other and went, *Mom's usually back by now*."

I'd started shaking, but I didn't dare move.

"Dad called the Coast Guard right away. But I couldn't just sit there and wait to hear if Mom was alive or not, so I sprinted to the harbor, and I just jumped in Mr. Fletcher's boat—you know, Lena and Jesse's dad, he had this dinky little sailboat—and I took it out to sea."

He shrugged then.

"That's where this came from?" I asked hesitantly, reaching up to brush my fingertip along the little white scar on his forehead. Blake shivered under my touch, and I realized my hands must've been cold.

"It was so fucking stupid," Blake said, squeezing his eyes closed and letting out a single huff of bitter laughter. "I thought I could just sail out there and I'd find Mom and everything would be okay. I didn't even make it out of the harbor; currents pulled me right into a wall of rocks along the shore. Mr. Fletcher's boat flipped and I ended up pancaked."

Blake shook his head again.

"Just fucking stupid," he breathed.

"It wasn't stupid," I insisted. "It was brave."

He turned so his back was to the hospital building where he'd no doubt received a couple of stitches, and eyed the mural. It was obvious from the slump of his shoulders and the weary look on his face he didn't want to talk about his mom anymore. I turned to the mural, my shoulder brushing against his, and changed the subject.

"It's amazing, isn't it?" I prompted.

Blake nodded wordlessly.

"I mean, I knew Rachel was a good artist, but this is—this is amazing."

My captive audience nodded again. For what felt like the millionth time since I'd arrived in Holden, I felt that ridiculous urge to keep talking.

"You know, I really wish I'd inherited some of the talent genes. I'm no good at science and math, but I can't draw for shit either. Sometimes I think Rachel must've made a deal with Satan to get her talent, because my dad is, like, the least creative person I've ever met. I mean, I guess climatologists don't exactly have the freedom to get *creative*—"

Blake's soft, barely there chuckle rang in my ears.

"—but the man can't even draw stick figures—"

"Waverly."

"Really, sometimes it's like the entire right side of his brain never fully developed—"

"Waverly."

I jumped as Blake's elbow shot out and nudged me in the ribs, knocking me a little off balance. When I turned to ask him what his problem was, I practically lost all the air in my lungs.

Blake's smile was devastating.

He was smiling. Actually smiling. Almost laughing, in fact.

"What?" I asked, breathless and completely caught off guard by the fact Blake Hamilton was grinning at me like I was the most entertaining thing he'd ever seen in his life.

Blake let out a laugh at the baffled look on my face.

"Do you always talk this much?" he teased, prodding me in the ribs with his elbow again.

And I'll never be sure why I said what I said next.

I guess I must've felt like Blake had just entrusted me with something sacred. Because, really, that's what he'd done. He'd willingly given me a part of him I had a feeling very few people knew about—a part of him that was young and helpless and had been so brave but hadn't been able to save his mother. And I guess I felt like, since Blake had been so honest with me, it was only right that I was honest too.

"Only around you," I admitted.

Blake's smile froze.

I ducked my head and stared down at an imaginary pebble at the toe of my sneaker, hoping my windblown hair was polite enough to cover the way I was flushing red as a tomato. Had I really just said that? It was like my brain knew the exact combination of words that would make Blake feel completely uncomfortable and ruin the—

A couple of large, tan fingers slipped underneath my chin and tilted my head up. And then, heaven help me, Blake Hamilton stepped so close to me that our chests were pressed together and bent his head down to meet mine.

Our lips collided.

And it was *completely* intentional.

Which meant that, mother of all that is holy, Blake Hamilton was kissing me. On purpose. His right hand was warm against my cheek and his other hand was a gentle, supportive pressure against my lower back and—good *God*—it was all I could do to keep my knees locked so I didn't turn into a pile of Jell-O in his arms.

Float

Nobody ever tells you that when you're kissing someone you really want to kiss, you find out that you'd rather die of asphyxiation than tear your lips away from theirs for even one minute. And nobody ever tells you what to do with your hands, either, so you'll stand there for a moment doing a perfect impression of a block of wood before you end up throwing your arms around his neck and dragging him into you with so much enthusiasm that you worry, for a second, that you might've broken both your noses. But he'll keep kissing you anyway, and you'll be so caught up in how soft and warm his lips are that you'll completely forget about the world around you and how inappropriate it is to be full-on making out with someone in a hospital parking lot.

This I know from first-hand experience.

Blake Hamilton's lips tasted like hot fudge sauce and, if we're being honest, his abdominals were rock solid. I didn't realize the two of us were backing up until I felt something cool press against the back of my legs. Blake pulled back at my gasp of surprise. Somehow, we managed to keep our arms tangled together as I glanced behind me to find that Jesse's Jeep was the culprit.

Damn. Even when they weren't there, the Fletcher twins managed to ruin the moment.

"You good?" Blake laughed. "Sorry, I didn't see that there."

"What, the Jeep?" I asked, cocking an eyebrow.

"I was a little busy," he admitted, tightening his arms around my waist. "You'll have to forgive me."

I rolled up onto my toes and planted a kiss on the tip of his nose, realizing, belatedly, that we probably looked like one of those annoying couples who were always in the midst of a public display of affection. To my surprise, I also realized that I didn't care who saw us or who rolled their eyes and fantasized about running us down with their car—the way I always did whenever I saw two lovers who seemed a little too interested in swallowing each other's tongues for my liking.

Blake Hamilton had kissed me.

You could've punched me in the face, and I'd still be smiling like a love-struck idiot while my nose bled. I was pretty damn sure that, in that moment, nothing could've brought me down from cloud nine.

That was, until Blake suddenly went rigid in my arms.

I looked up, ready to tease him about not needing to flex for me and to reassure him that his biceps were indeed bigger than his ego, but his eyes were locked on something over my shoulder and his face had gone very pale. When I finally managed to twist around in his grip, I saw the reason for his alarm. A car was driving down the little street between the two halves of the Marlin Bay hospital, heading toward us at a reasonable five miles per hour.

I recognized the big, white Range Rover instantly.

It was Alissa Hastings's car.

Somewhere, in the back of my mind, my severely messed-up sense of humor rang out in its best wrestling announcer voice.

Ding, ding, ding.

Smackdown!

Chapter 18

Alissa's obscenely large white Range Rover pulled to a stop in front of Blake and me. One of his hands was still resting on my hip, his index finger pressed against the tiny sliver of skin bared between the waistband of my shorts and the hem of my sweatshirt. *His* sweatshirt, I reminded myself with a great deal of chagrin. As if our little parking lot escapade could look any worse.

"On a scale of paraplegic turtle to Usain Bolt, how fast are you?" I demanded out of the corner of my mouth.

"What?" Blake hissed back.

"Here's the game plan. On the count of three, we turn and go for the car. You do one of those cool over-the-hood slides and get in on the driver's side, and I'll—"

"We're not running away," Blake said firmly.

I shifted my weight between my feet, trying to shake off Blake's hand so I could give in to my instinct and run in the complete opposite direction of the ex-girlfriend of the boy I'd just kissed. But his fingers just tightened resolutely around me, as if to say, *We're definitely about to die, but damn it, we're gonna die together.*

The tinted passenger-side window of Alissa's car rolled down at an excruciatingly slow pace. I squeezed my eyes shut and held my breath, not ready to face Blake's ex-girlfriend like this.

"Dude, you pick the weirdest places to hang out."

Funny. Alissa sounded a lot like a teenage boy.

I peeled open one of my eyes. Jesse Fletcher grinned back at me from the passenger's seat of the Range Rover, his dark curls pinned back by a hot-pink elastic headband. Behind him, Alissa sat upright in the driver's seat, her face hidden by a pair of oversized sunglasses.

"How did you find us?" Blake asked.

Jesse held up his phone. "Your location's on."

"Where's Lena?" I asked, frowning.

At this inquiry, the rear passenger's side window started to roll down. Lena was slouched, a bun of corkscrew curls perched on the top of her head like one of those fancy wedding hats, with her arms folded across her chest and her eyes narrowed at the back of the seat in front of her.

I turned to Jesse, confused.

"Don't mind Lena," he said. "She's just bitter I got shotgun."

"Only because you cheated," Lena snapped, kicking the back of her brother's seat.

Jesse let out a cry of outrage and twisted around, jabbing himself in the face with his own seat belt before managing to get a clear view of his twin.

"I did *not* cheat."

"You broke shotgun rules. You called it before the car was in sight. Everyone knows that's a violation."

"Your mom's a violation."

"Once again, moron, we have *the same mom*."

I shot a wary glance at Alissa, wondering if she'd seen more than the incredibly oblivious Fletcher twins had. But her face was impossible to read behind those stupid hotel heiress slash part-time model sunglasses, and since she wasn't getting out of the Range Rover and demanding that someone hold her earrings while she punched me out, I was starting to think maybe none of them had seen Blake and me kissing just a minute ago.

Blake seemed to realize this at the same moment I did. His hand dropped from my side and he cleared his throat.

"What's the plan?" he asked.

Jesse abandoned his attempts at defending himself to turn to us.

"We have work, dude," he said. "Lissa was going to drive Lena and Waverly home and you can take us to—"

Lena's hand shot out. Her fingers hooked underneath the hot-pink elastic headband Jesse was wearing and pulled it half a foot from his face. I winced, already knowing what was coming.

The sound of elastic smacking skin was audible.

"*Lena!*" Jesse roared, cradling his forehead as he spun back around in his seat. "I'm gonna rip all the posters off your bedroom walls, and I'm gonna eat all your favorite flavors of those stupid protein bars Mom keeps buying, and I'm gonna cancel all your recordings on our TV, and I'm—"

But Lena was laughing too hard to hear his threats.

I glanced over at Blake.

For a solid three seconds, the two of us just stared at each other. Then the relief set in. Blake was the first to crack a smile and release a breathy chuckle.

"You have work?" I asked.

Blake nodded.

"Lifeguarding," he said.

"Oh," I managed, dumbly. "Uh, have fun."

"I'll try."

"Don't drown or anything."

"Thanks," Blake said.

"I mean it," I insisted, and I might have sounded a bit too serious, because suddenly Blake's smile was sympathetic. His arm jerked up, as if he was going to reach for my hand. But the Fletcher twins were still tossing insults at each other not even ten feet from us, and Alissa Hastings could have been watching us from behind those enormous sunglasses of hers—although we'd never know, since her shades were about as tinted as the windows on the presidential limousine. In any event, it definitely wasn't the time for Blake and me to act like anything other than platonic friends.

"So," Blake began, then cleared his throat. "I'll see you at the Fletchers' house. For the barbecue?"

Jesse's head poked out of the front window.

"Saturday." He coughed. "Eleven o'clock. Parents and stepparents and guardians of the aunt persuasion are welcome. But you're gonna have to bring your own ketchup."

"Our own ketchup?" I echoed.

I'd never been to a barbecue before, so I didn't know what was customary.

Lena's head appeared out of the back window.

"Dad's allergic to tomatoes," she explained, "so we don't keep any tomato products in the house."

Jesse took advantage of Lena's momentary lapse in focus to slip out of Alissa's Range Rover and tumble into the hospital parking lot, a mess of spindly limbs and dark curls.

"And he sticks the landing," Blake muttered in a huff.

Jesse, who'd managed to pick himself up and was dusting grains of asphalt off his shorts, shot Blake a scowl as he slammed the passenger-side door.

"Just for that," he said, stabbing a bony finger in the air as he started toward his Jeep, "I'm not letting you sit shotgun."

"Fine." Blake shrugged. "You can be my chauffeur."

I watched dumb and dumber bicker all the way to Jesse's Jeep, where—after a moment of debate—Blake yanked open the passenger-side door and stepped onto the ledge over the wheel. He paused for a moment, sending another glance in my direction, and only ducked into the car once I'd given him a reassuring nod.

"Hey," Alissa called from behind me.

I turned over my shoulder and, stupidly enough, was surprised to find she'd spoken to me. Her sunglasses were pushed onto the top of her head and her eyes were trained on me.

Naturally, her winged eyeliner was on point.

"I'm driving you home," she said.

But what I heard was: *I'm gonna pretend to drive you home but actually throw your dead body into the ocean, you ex-boyfriend stealer.*

"Okay," I swallowed. "Sure. Great. Thanks."

I stood there for a second, debating whether to run around the Range Rover and hop into the backseat next to Lena or risk my life and sit shotgun. But then Alissa leaned over and popped open the passenger-side door, and the choice was made for me.

The leather seats of the car were smooth and cool against my bare thighs, but I couldn't help but feel like I'd just slid into the fiery depths of purgatory. Dante hadn't accounted for the tenth circle of hell—sitting in an intimidating girl's car five minutes after messing around with her ex-boyfriend in a parking lot.

"God, I'm exhausted," Lena groaned from the backseat.

I heard the shuffle of limbs as she squirmed into a more comfortable position and was struck by the sudden realization that, if Lena was to fall asleep, she wouldn't be witness whatever wrath Alissa unleashed on me.

Do not fall asleep, I willed Lena in my mind. *Don't you dare—*

Not ten seconds later, Lena let out a massive snort that most accurately resembled the anguished cry of a dying whale. There was an awkward pause, and then the sound came again. And again. My impromptu bodyguard was *snoring.*

I sank into my seat, my chest tightening with dread.

For one long, drawn-out minute, the inside of the car was totally silent except for Lena's rhythmic, lawn mower–esque snores. Alissa sat ramrod straight in her seat, but her hands were resting lazily on the steering wheel, her wrists slack. She glanced at the dashboard, and for a moment I thought she was going to turn on the radio. Instead, she opened her mouth.

"I know you're a thing," Alissa said. "You and Blake."

Well. There it was. The elephant in the Range Rover.

It felt like every blood cell in my body was migrating to my face. I sank a fraction lower in my seat, my mouth opening and closing several times as I dug through my scattered brain for something to say.

"I'm not mad, Waverly."

And just like that, the excuse I'd started to word in my head collapsed.

"You—huh?" I asked, fumbling my words. "You? Aren't—are not—mad? At me? Mad at me? You're not . . . *what*?"

Alissa let out a little sigh and executed an impeccable left-hand turn.

"We broke up," she said simply. "We're over. He should move on."

She must've seen the way my eyebrows furrowed in suspicion because she pushed on, her cheeks flushing the slightest bit pink.

"Blake is important to me, obviously. I mean, we dated for a year and a half. But . . ." We pulled up to a stop sign. She turned in her seat to face me. "We, like, grew up, I guess."

"I thought you wanted him back," I said. "You seemed so upset when you guys broke up, I just assumed you were still . . ."

"In love with him?" Alissa finished for me, falling back in her seat.

"Well, yeah."

Alissa took a deep breath and adjusted her grip on the steering wheel.

"I don't know if I ever loved him," she admitted. "I mean, I guess I loved him in a way. But I wasn't *in* love with him, you know? He was, like, my first *real* boyfriend. And it was a good relationship while it lasted, but—"

Alissa's face screwed up, her mouth twisting to one side.

"But what?" I prompted.

Alissa glanced over at me again, then up into the rearview mirror. When she saw Lena was still asleep, sprawled across the backseat, she let out a gushing breath.

"His mom was dead and mine was in Milan boozing it up on a yacht with some guy twice my dad's age," she said, shrugging. "Our relationship was built on being pissed off."

I didn't reply for a long time.

The girl sitting next to me in the plush leather driver's seat of a car that must've cost a year's college tuition was a picture of perfection. Her hair was pin straight, though dented where her sunglasses hit it when she wore them on top of her head, and dark against flawless olive skin. She was gorgeous and wealthy and terribly, horribly unhappy.

Something heavy settled in my stomach. *Guilt.*

I hadn't known a thing about her, and I'd gone and painted her a villain in my head, all because she'd been pretty and wealthy and carried herself like someone with half a brain and was dating the boy I had a crush on.

"How did you and Blake start dating, anyway?" I asked suddenly.

Alissa's hands twitched on the wheel, then went for the air-conditioning dial.

"We had class together second semester sophomore year, and someone said his stepmom was hot. He got up and walked out of class, and we didn't see him at school again for a week. I offered him my notes when he got back." She shrugged. "It was good, for a while. We needed each other. But I—I think I got bored. Which I know sounds just, like, *terrible.* But . . . I don't think we're good for each other. As friends, maybe. But not like we were."

I peered out the car window to watch the roll and crash of the waves down in Marlin Bay, one guardrail and rocky cliff's drop away from us.

"Why Ethan?" I blurted.

I mean, why had she chosen to mess around with *Ethan*, of all people? Alissa clearly had enough horrible people in her life. Why would she go looking to add another to the mix? I mean, who had ever looked at the cast of people they knew and gone, *You know, I could really use an egotistical jerk with the fashion sense of someone in an early-2000's music video in my life. And I should date him.*

To her credit, Alissa didn't even wince.

"Because the first time we hung out, my mom shouted at me. *Screamed* at me, actually. She didn't trust him at all. She didn't want me hanging around him."

"A teen rebellion thing?" I asked, smiling a little.

"It was the first time my mom had talked to me in four months."

Alissa slipped her sunglasses back down over her eyes, and I couldn't help but worry that she was tearing up behind her shades. I was relieved when she reached forward and turned on the radio, settling on a country music station. I hadn't pegged her as the type, but soon enough I caught her tapping the steering wheel and mouthing the words to a couple of songs.

Who would've guessed Alissa had a thing for Tim McGraw?

While acoustic strumming and banjo plucking drifted through the car, I kept glancing into the backseat to check on Lena, whose face was plastered against the car window. At some point during the ride, Alissa pushed her sunglasses back on top of her head, and I pretended I didn't notice the way her winged eyeliner had smudged at the corners.

"Is she drooling yet?" Alissa asked as we drove past a sign alerting us that Holden was less than ten miles away.

I craned my neck.

"Uh-huh."

Alissa handed me her phone, the corner of her lips curling up mischievously. "I need a new screensaver."

When Alissa finally pulled her car to a stop against the curb outside Aunt Rachel's sunset-orange house, I was exhausted from the forty collective minutes in the car, the one attempt at risking my life to sit on a board out in the ocean, the impromptu lunch date, and the kiss (the *kiss*). I still had sand and salt tangled in my hair, but at least Blake's too-large sweatshirt was clean and soft. Alissa tucked her phone into her pocket, promising me she'd forward all the photos I'd snapped.

"Thanks for the ride, by the way," I told her as I hopped out of her Range Rover.

It was just as windy as it'd been that morning, but I figured I already looked homeless, so what was a little hair in my face?

"It's no problem," Alissa told me, smiling sheepishly. "I'm sorry if I scared you earlier. I—look, I'm really happy for you and Blake. And I know I can't say that without sounding like I'm totally lying, but I mean it. I'm not mad at you guys for getting together. Like, at all. I promise."

"Thank you," I told her. It was all I could think to say. I had no idea how to articulate my relief without coming across as an imbecile.

Alissa glanced into her lap, hesitant, and then sent me a nervous smile.

"To be honest, I'm sort of relieved you're with *him*," she told me, her cheeks flushing pink again. "For a while there, I sort of thought you and Jesse were, like, *a thing*."

The little burst of annoyance I felt was immediately trampled by the realization that Alissa was *relieved* to find out that Jesse and I weren't together. I thought of them again at Marlin Cove, sitting out on the water together, their surfboards tethered by Jesse's grip on hers.

Jesse, you suave son of a bitch.

"We're definitely not a thing," I told Alissa with a shake of my head.

"Oh?" She bit down on her lower lip.

I turned toward Rachel's house so she wouldn't see the amused grin spreading across my face. "Trust me," I called over my shoulder as I started up the front walk, "he likes girls who can actually surf!"

Chapter 19

The Friday afternoon crowd at the bookstore was a surprisingly slow trickle, so at three o'clock, Margie came to the front of the empty shop, set her hands on her hips, and announced that Lena, Alissa, and I should all clock out for the day.

"Go," she urged. "Be free. Embrace your youth."

We didn't have to be told twice.

I finished restocking the display stand, Alissa collected her tote bag and a beach towel from her stash behind the register, and Lena whooped out a cheer as she grabbed her sunglasses.

"I want to sit under the sun until I turn into a little raisin," Lena announced as the three of us slipped out onto the sidewalk, the bell tied to the door trilling in good-bye. "I want to put my headphones in, listen to my new playlist, and *nap*. I haven't napped in weeks."

"Maybe we can stop and get some ice cream," Alissa proposed, not meeting our eyes as she rummaged around in her tote. "I'm in the mood for some double chocolate fudge."

I snorted before I could stop myself. Alissa shot me a wide-eyed look.

"Well, *I'm* not going in the parlor," Lena said. "Jesse used the last of my coconut curl cream this morning. I'm not speaking to him again until he buys me a new jar."

Alissa pressed her lips together tight.

I nabbed her beach towel, tucked it under my arm, and looped my other arm around Lena's elbow. "Why don't you go get your ice cream, Alissa, and we'll go find a spot to sit on the beach. You can meet us there."

Alissa smiled at me, her eyes communicating a nonverbal thank you. She turned on her heel and took off at an acceptably normal speed to see the boy she liked.

"I'm so excited for this weekend," Lena said, giving my arm a squeeze.

"What are you supposed to wear to a cookout?" I asked.

"I have a dress you can borrow," Lena offered. "I'll bring it to work tomorrow. You can do another bathroom fashion show."

We stopped to kick off our shoes before we marched into the hot sand. The beach was packed with locals, the volleyball nets in use, the handful of picnic tables all occupied, and all the prime real estate claimed by big umbrellas and scattered towels. Lena and I wove through the chaos, dodging kids the height of my hip who ran past with plastic buckets and seashells in their little hands, until we found a relatively open spot not too far from what looked like a treehouse in the middle of the sand, painted teal blue and with a little wraparound porch and a ramp.

A lifeguard tower.

My heart leaped, then sank when I realized the guy in red board shorts leaning against the railing and peering out at the water was blond, not brunet. I hadn't seen Blake since yesterday (since we'd *kissed*), which meant that the mere idea of him was enough to make me giddy to a point of dysfunction.

"Waverly," Lena said, clearing her throat. "Can you put the towel down before the bottoms of my feet burn off?"

"Right! Yes, sorry."

We rolled out Alissa's towel and collapsed onto it with matching grunts.

"Oh, this is nice," I said as we settled, the warmth of the sand seeping through the towel under us. "This is very, very nice."

Lena sighed in agreement and popped one headphone in, offering me the other.

I took it, slipped it in, and exhaled a long breath.

A minute passed. Maybe two. I wasn't sure because the sun was on my skin, the sound of crashing waves was in one ear while some indie pop song I'd never heard played in the other, Lena was next to me, and Alissa and Jesse were together in the ice cream parlor (probably flirting in that nervous, hesitant way of theirs). I was perfectly at peace.

And then a shadow fell over me.

I peeled open one eye and found Blake standing over me, bare chested and glistening in his red swim trunks. He was *glorious*. My heart actually hiccupped at the sight of him.

"You're blocking my sun," I blurted, smooth as ever.

"I know," Blake said without flinching. "You're welcome. Please tell me you've applied sunscreen in the last half hour."

"We've literally been here for five minutes," Lena piped up.

"Also, if you're going to flirt, please let me turn up my music first."

I blushed and spluttered.

Lena took her headphone back, shoved it into her ear, and proceeded to lean back and turn up her music until I could hear it.

"I can't talk long," Blake said, offering me an apologetic smile. "Technically, I'm on duty. My shift started ten minutes ago. I just wanted to ensure everyone over here's practicing good defense against skin cancer."

"Oh," I said, unable to hide my disappointment.

Was I supposed to spend the next hour just staring at him longingly from across the beach?

"But I'll see you tomorrow," Blake offered.

"Do you want to carpool to the barbecue?"

"I'm actually lifeguarding at the pool tomorrow morning. I start at seven."

"Yikes. Well, have fun."

For a brief moment, Blake hovered, like he had something else he wanted to say—or do. But he was standing, and I was sitting on Alissa's beach towel with Lena beside me, mumbling the lyrics of the song rupturing her eardrums, so it wasn't the ideal time or place for romance.

"I'll call you before my shift," Blake said, then took off toward the lifeguard tower. "Six o'clock. Your aunt's landline. You'd better answer, Lyons."

O

On the morning of the Fletchers' barbecue—which should have been a day of celebration because, c'mon, *free food*—I woke up at the ungodly hour of 5:55. It was dark. It was cold. For a solid eight and half seconds, I thought I might actually rather die than get out of bed.

"Fucking *morning people*," I grumbled at my ceiling.

I tossed my duvet aside and got to my feet, very much alive and very much unhappy to be *up and at 'em*. With all the stealth and finesse of a newborn elephant, I nudged the bedroom door open (it creaked) and tiptoed into the hallway (where the floorboards also creaked, because *of course*). In a rare stroke of luck, Aunt Rachel's door was closed. I slipped past it and down the stairs, my arms braced in front of me as I felt my way through the pitch-black living room.

The kitchen was dark, too, but luckily the windows that looked out at the ocean let in a bit of dim blue light. I snatched the home phone off the charging dock on the counter and plopped down on the tile floor, folding my legs and looking up at the display of the microwave. Five fifty-nine. Perfect.

I braced my thumb over the Talk button.

In the same instant that the clock on the microwave clicked to six o'clock, the handset in my lap lit up and the opening bar of the ringtone played (Rachel had customized her home phones to play an instrumental rendition of Snoop Dogg's 2004 hit single "Drop It Like It's Hot"). I hit Talk before the xylophone could start up and pressed the phone to my ear.

"Hi," I grunted.

Blake Hamilton's laugh carried through the speaker.

"*Goooooood* morning, Holden!" He greeted me with the smarmy affectation of an anchor from one of northern Florida's lower-budget news stations. "Today is Saturday, August 5. The weather looks like—well, actually, it looks like total shit. It'll probably rain. Now, for a special report on the Fletcher family barbecue, we're going to turn to Waverly Lyons, who has just woken up. Waverly?"

"My mouth tastes like expired yogurt."

"That might be one of the top five most revolting things I've ever heard."

"I can't believe I woke up for *this*," I said.

"You know," he huffed, "we wouldn't even have this problem if you had a cell phone. Like any other person living in this decade. Then I wouldn't have to wait to tell you about all the shit that happened the day before. I could just text you, like a civilized person. And send you memes. Do you know how hard it is to *describe* a meme, Waverly?"

I scoffed. "You're such a *youth*."

"Even my dad doesn't call people anymore."

"Hey," I said, feigning offence and trying not to laugh. "George is ahead of his time. A trendsetter. An *icon*."

"He wears long-sleeved shirts under Hawaiian T-shirts."

"Because he doesn't want to get sunburned! Do not start with me on this. You don't know what it's like to fear the sun."

"Speaking of," he drawled, "how are your shoulders?"

"Um . . ."

It'd taken two whole bottles of aloe vera, but my shoulders had finally faded from purple to red, and then from red to a brown that peeled in itchy flakes. I prodded at one shoulder with my finger and winced. *Still tender*.

"You know," I finally said, "I've had worse."

"That's really upsetting."

"Yeah, well. It won't happen again. Rachel's not letting me out of the house without sunscreen on."

"Good," Blake said.

"What's the Fletchers' house like, anyway?" I asked, picking at the lint on my socks. "I'm picturing that house from *Home Alone*. People running around everywhere. Lots of booby traps. Children flooding basements and letting tarantulas loose."

"You know"—Blake laughed—"you're not that off."

We talked for what felt like hours—and, simultaneously, only a few minutes—before Blake suddenly went quiet, and I could hear the muffled wailing of a toddler somewhere on the other end of the line. Isabel was awake. Which meant Chloe and George would be up any minute too. It was only then that I glanced up at the microwave and realized how long we'd been talking.

It was 6:52.

"Oh yikes," I whispered. "You're gonna be late."

"Shit. I've gotta get to the pool." There was a great deal of rustling on the other end of the phone and a few unintelligible grunts of exasperation. "Where're my *fucking* shoes—okay and my whistle. Shit. I don't even have time to brush my teeth."

I scrunched up my nose. "You're gonna do that before the barbecue, though, right?"

"Of course. Soon as I'm done, I'll shower and brush my teeth."

I opened my mouth to protest the shower—I kind of liked the way Blake had a tendency to smell like chlorine and sunshine—but decided there was really no way to say all that without sounding creepy.

"I'll see you at the barbecue," I whispered.

"See you there," Blake whispered back, and then hung up.

I sat on the kitchen floor for a moment, phone cradled in my hands as I let myself readjust to the silence of the house.

I pictured Blake next door, running around the house with

his hair all disheveled and his cheeks flushed pink while Isabel hollered in her crib. Blake had been an only child for most of his life. I wondered what it was like to have a sibling drop into your lap—all chubby cheeks and flailing limbs. Part of me envied him. I'd always kind of fantasized about having a brother or sister. A partner in crime. Someone on my team. A living being who understood how frustrating and disappointing my mom and dad could be.

I hadn't quite realized how used to being left alone and to my own devices I'd gotten until about ten o'clock that morning— after I'd tucked myself back in bed and then woken up again, at a more reasonable hour, to hop in the shower—when Aunt Rachel bumped my bedroom door open with her hip and bounced in with a basket of laundry tucked under her arm.

"My darling little polar bear, I just folded your—oh."

She blinked at me. I blinked back. A single dollop of sunscreen rolled off my foot, which was lifted in the air with all the grace of a drunk man attempting pointe ballet. I'd just used about half a bottle of SPF 100 to slather my arms and legs the way a small child might paint a pristine white canvas—messily and with great enthusiasm. I wasn't wearing pants, obviously. Or a shirt. My bra did not match my underpants.

"What's up?" I asked, as casually as one can when half naked and dripping with sunscreen.

"I folded your dress," Rachel announced, lifting the folded square of cobalt blue.

"Oh. Thanks. My hands are a little—sticky."

"I'll put it on your bed," Rachel said, doing an admirable job of pretending she wasn't debating whether to laugh at me or apologize for barging in without so much as knocking.

"Great. Perfect. Yes."

"See you downstairs in fifteen?" she asked.

"Affirmative. Yep. You got it."

She slipped out of my room, and I let my foot hit the carpet with a little wet thump.

I finished rubbing in my sunscreen—a feat that took fourteen of the fifteen minutes Aunt Rachel had allotted me—and tugged on Lena's dress, which had been church with grandma length on her but was just barely family friendly on me. I tugged at the hem of it and darted into the bathroom to spin in front of the mirror, checking that a gust of wind wouldn't turn the barbecue into an unasked-for, low-budget Victoria's Secret fashion show.

When I was sure I was good, I dug a tube of mascara from the drawer beside the sink. I tried to ignore that my usual foundation—SPF 40, shade 001—didn't match my face the way it had at the beginning of the summer. I tried not to pinch my split ends and wonder when all the sun I'd been getting had managed to bleach them brilliant gold. I didn't like to think about how much Holden had changed me (outside *and* inside) because my summer had an expiration date that couldn't be compromised.

I had eleven days left. I'd have to make the most of it.

When I made my way downstairs, still tugging self-consciously at the hem of Lena's dress, Rachel was sitting at the kitchen sink, perched on a stool, with a bucket of solvent and a cup of stained paintbrushes. Her hair was pulled back into what might've been a French braid—it was hard to tell with all the stray curls—and she'd put on her *fancy shoes*, which meant a pair of espadrilles that didn't have duct tape or paint splatters on them.

"Oh, look at you!" She beamed as I started for the fridge. "Figures you'd wait until we've got a storm coming in to put on a dress."

"Funny," I huffed.

"You look very pretty, Waverly. Very grown up."

I tugged open the refrigerator door and ducked behind it so Rachel couldn't see the sudden flood of warmth in my cheeks. Her words were a comfort I packaged away in my head for later, if I started to doubt myself again.

I'd been up way too late the night before practicing my eyeliner and soaking my hair with homemade leave-in conditioner, wondering if Blake would use the Fletchers' barbecue as an opportunity to reintroduce me to Chloe and George as his *girlfriend*, or if he'd already told them about us, or if he'd decided he didn't want his parents knowing that he'd started canoodling with the girl next door.

He was already grounded until New Year's, after all.

In any case, I was suddenly terrified of rolling up to the Fletchers' in my usual oversized T-shirt and sloppy ponytail. The fact that Rachel had noticed my sudden burst of caring about what I looked like was somewhat reassuring.

"We're taking the pie, right?" I asked.

"Yes, ma'am. Second shelf, next to the eggs. Oh, and remember to grab the ketchup from the back. Gummer's allergic."

I frowned.

"Gummer?"

"Yeah. Lena and Jesse's dad. Gummer."

"His parents named him that?"

Rachel gave me a look that said *Don't be silly*.

"It's short for Montgomery," she explained.

His parents named him that? I wanted to ask again.

I decided to hold my tongue, tucked the ketchup under my arm, and grabbed the key lime pie Aunt Rachel had baked the night before while we watched three consecutive hours of Meg Ryan movies and I marinated in aloe vera.

"All right, I'm just going to soak these brushes in some turpentine all day while we're gone," Rachel announced. She stood and patted down the front of her long-sleeved denim dress—another of the *fancy* staples she kept at the very back of her closet. "Gosh, I'm hungry. I think I'd kill a man for a turkey burger right about now."

I slipped my flip-flops on and hustled out the door before Rachel could get homicidal.

I was halfway onto the porch, my eyes straying to the Hamiltons' empty driveway, when a gust of wind barreled down the street and nearly lifted the tinfoil covering off the pie. I let out an unattractive squawk and slapped my hand down on top of it just in time.

"I guess the storm's really rolling in," Rachel commented as she joined me, keys in hand and head tipped up as she squinted at the gloomy sky. "I hope it doesn't ruin our barbecue."

Rachel and I climbed into the neon-green Volkswagen together, key lime pie nestled safely in the backseat and ketchup bottle stowed by my feet. Rachel claimed it was too chilly to leave the windows of the car rolled down, what with the malevolent wind and all, so we bumped up the volume on the radio and sang along with songs I knew would be stuck in my head later, the way overplayed hit singles have a tendency to get.

The Fletchers lived about ten miles inland from Holden Point, where the palm trees and tall grass gave way to wetlands. Rachel didn't know the route by memory, so I had to read her directions from her phone. When the GPS indicated our destination was on the left, I looked up and saw a wide driveway that trailed up to a big one-story house with an enormous front porch and a raspberry-red front door.

There was a lone, live oak tree in the front yard. Moss hung in threads from the upper branches, along with a tire swing and a pair of sneakers—Jesse's, it looked like—that'd had their laces tied together before someone chucked them into the thick of the tree.

There were four cars in the driveway, including Jesse's mud-splattered Jeep and the Hamiltons' silver sedan. Rachel pulled her neon Volkswagen in behind them. Outside, the air smelled damp and green, somehow—like the produce aisle of a supermarket or the botanical garden I vaguely remembered visiting on a third-grade field trip.

It was significantly warmer inland than it was out by the ocean, warm enough that I could've run around in a bathing suit if I was really determined to cling to summer, but the sky was still decidedly overcast.

I gathered the key lime pie from the backseat of the car. Rachel discreetly pointed out a spot on my neck where I hadn't rubbed the sunscreen in all the way.

We marched up the rest of the driveway side by side, the hem of Lena's cobalt dress swinging around my thighs. The wind was gentler this far inland, but it still whispered across the front yard and made Aunt Rachel tug at the sleeves of her denim dress.

There were eight different sets of wind chimes suspended from the beams over the front porch. Rachel rang the doorbell, and I wondered if anybody would be able to hear us over the cacophony.

Lena was the one to open the door.

Her hair was loose around her shoulders, curls blown out in every direction with the humidity, and she had on an apron—one of those novelty ones, with a cartoonish depiction of a muscular man's body in a red Speedo. She took one look at me before beaming and clasping her hands like a mother seeing her daughter off to prom.

"Do not say anything," I warned.

"Not even *hot damn*?"

"No."

"You're no fun," Lena whined, stepping back from the doorway so Aunt Rachel and I could step inside. From the foyer, I could see through to the living room and what appeared to be a library. Everything in the house was a cluttered mix of new and old—grand chaise lounges arranged around a fireplace with an enormous flat-screen television mounted over the mantle; framed prints of Miami and Orlando in the early twentieth century hung between photos of a young Jesse posing with a soccer ball tucked under one arm and a little Lena smiling, gap toothed, in an all-white uniform with a yellow belt around her waist. It was a full house, lived in and warm. I'd never been somewhere like it. I felt like an astronaut exploring an alien world, my spacesuit too bulky and restrictive to let me pretend this was my own home planet.

"Hi, Ms. Lyons," Lena was saying behind me.

"Hi, dear." Rachel greeted her. "I love the apron."

Lena chuckled. "Thanks. Dad put Blake and me on grill duty."

My stupid heart hiccupped at the sound of his name and I spun around a little too quickly. It was unbearably pathetic.

"Where should I put this?" I asked, trying to keep my voice even as I held up Aunt Rachel's pie.

Lena, of course, saw right through me.

"Why don't I take that," she said, reaching her arms around

her waist to untie the strings of the apron, "and you can go be on grill duty."

We traded. Lena hustled off with the pie, Aunt Rachel at her heels, and me trailing a few steps behind as I looped the apron over my neck and tied the strings in a sloppy bow at my back.

The Fletchers' kitchen was enormous.

They had two industrial-grade refrigerators and a marble-topped island surrounded by eight or nine mismatched bar stools. There was food everywhere—potato salad and fruit salad and actual salad and a two-gallon pitcher of what had to be sweet tea were scattered on the island. In the middle of it all was a tall woman who had long box braids and almost the exact same profile as Lena.

"Boss!" Lena singsonged, announcing us with a flourish.

Her mom looked up, spotted me, and clapped her hands.

"You. Must. Be. Waverly."

"Hi, Mrs. Fletcher."

Lena's mom tossed two handfuls of lemon wedges into the pitcher of sweet tea, then rounded the island and came to a stop right in front of me so she could put a hand on each of my shoulders and give them a soft, tight squeeze. My face grew hot with what I could only describe as stage fright. How on earth had I earned such an affectionate greeting from a woman I'd never met? Had Lena and Jesse really said nice things about me to their parents?

I felt, all at once, like I might cry.

"It is *so nice* to meet you," Mrs. Fletcher said, then stepped back and offered me her hand to shake. "I'm Amanda."

"But we all call her Boss," Lena chipped in from behind me.

Mrs. Fletcher—Amanda—Boss? had the kind of smile that

made you feel like you were in on a joke together. It was the same kind of generous warmth Lena had shown me when I first met her at the bonfire party back at the beginning of the summer. I felt a terrible pang of jealousy. What must it be like to have a mother who welcomes you home with a hug and a laugh? Would I be a happier person, a better friend, if my parents weren't so cold?

"You have a beautiful home, Boss," I croaked.

Amanda Fletcher laughed and flicked her wrist.

"Oh, that's too sweet of you," she said. "This place is a pigsty. I can't get any of my kids to pick up after themselves. Even the big one."

I was about to ask what she meant when the tallest man I'd ever seen in my life ducked into the kitchen from a hallway off to the right, an enormous bag of ice tossed over one shoulder.

Amanda Fletcher groaned.

"Gummer, you're trailing water on my hardwood floors."

Montgomery Fletcher looked a lot like his son, except that his hair was shaved flat against his head. That, and he wore glasses and ankle-length socks with New Balance sneakers, which meant he definitely had more of a dad vibe going on than Jesse did. He had Jesse's devil-may-are smile, though.

"Good thing we own a mop," he teased.

"Your shirt's getting soaked," Boss said.

Gummer shrugged. "Nature's air conditioning. George is hosing down the cooler in the garage. Someone spilled some Coke in there the last time we used it."

"You're the only one in this house who drinks Coke."

"*Someone* spilled some Coke in there. Didn't say it wasn't me."

Lena cleared her throat.

"Dad, this is Waverly. Rachel Lyons's niece. And I'm going to go put her on grill duty, so if you'll excuse us—" Lena grabbed my apron and tugged me toward the back door.

"Hi, Mr. Fletcher," I said, waving.

"It's nice to finally meet you, Waverly."

Lena already had me halfway out the door.

"It'snicetomeetyoutoo—"

And we were gone.

"C'mon, you've got burgers to flip," Lena told me, sounding far too proud of herself as she steered me across the back porch.

The Fletchers' backyard was enormous. From up on the porch, I could see over the tall wood fence that encircled the slightly scraggly lawn; in the distance were cypress trees and murky green water. I remembered that, once, Jesse had joked about having recurring nightmares about finding alligators in his bathtub. I hadn't realized he lived a hundred yards from a swamp.

The lawn was wet with dew that covered my flip-flops and soaked my toes as we marched toward an enormous stone patio centered around a bean-shaped swimming pool with a dinky little plastic slide and a diving board.

There were white plastic lounge chairs everywhere; Chloe Hamilton was sprawled out on one, looking entirely too pristine for a mother of a young child while wearing a stainfree white one-piece swimsuit. At the far end of the patio sat a few outdoor couches and a big built-in grill station with a mini fridge. But the mysterious allure of a mini fridge stocked with who knows what had almost no effect on me, because two feet to the right of it stood Blake Hamilton.

Shirtless.

Grilling.

I'd always kind of rolled my eyes at obnoxiously *masculine* things like screaming at the TV during a football game or pretending *The Real Housewives of New York City* wasn't quality entertainment, or having construction site–scented body wash because apparently smelling like dirt was better than smelling like—*gasp*—an apricot.

But, you know.

Blake. No shirt. All that red meat. I was kind of into it.

And then, when Lena and I were rounding the pool, he turned— spatula in hand—and I caught sight of the apron he was wearing.

I glanced down at the Speedo-clad male torso on my own apron.

"I guess these are a matching set, huh?" I called out.

Blake squinted in the sun, one side of his mouth curling up in a lazy smile as he watched us approach, and ran his free hand over the front of his apron, right over one of the enormous, balloon-shaped boobs on the cartoon female body that was wearing a red bikini two sizes too small for her physically impossible proportions.

"I called dibs on this one," he said. "I'm not trading."

Lena huffed.

"Stop feeling yourself up," she told him, releasing her hold on my apron and positioning me beside him at the grill, where eight perfectly round, still-pink patties were sizzling.

Blake glanced down at his chest.

"I feel like these would be really heavy," he mused.

Lena's hand shot out to smack his wrist.

"Cut it out, pervert."

"Maybe they're filled with air," I suggested. "Like pool floaties. Or beach balls."

Float

Blake hummed thoughtfully. "Versatile."

"I'm gonna help your dad with the cooler," Lena said.

He flipped his spatula up in the air and caught it by the handle, pointing it at her with a flourish. "You got it, superstar."

She turned to me. "Make sure he doesn't burn the burgers."

"Will do."

Lena took off toward the house, and I was finally—*finally*—alone with Blake. Well, except for his stepmom, who was lounging on the other side of the pool. But she was on her stomach, her head tipped in the other direction, and she had headphones in.

I'd take what I could get.

"So," I said, turning to survey the grill and setting my hands on my hips in a down to business fashion. "What are we—"

Blake caught my wrist in his free hand, gave me a little tug toward him, and ducked his head to press his lips to mine.

I was so surprised, I forgot to kiss him back for a half second.

Just as my brain came to terms with what was happening, he was pulling back. So I, being a complete dork, grunted and rolled up onto my tiptoes to follow him. I was pretty enthusiastic about it. I think my tongue touched one of his front teeth. Blake growled low in his throat.

I swayed back.

"Sorry," I blurted.

Blake blinked down at me, looking stunned.

"Sorry," he repeated. "You're sorry."

It was half a question, half a statement.

I didn't know what to do with it.

"Yes?"

Blake tipped his eyes at the sky.

"Lord, give me strength," he murmured. Then he hooked one

arm over my shoulders and tugged me into his chest, his lips pressing into my hair at my temple.

"I didn't mean to *maul* you," I said, cringing.

"You can maul me anytime," he said.

I flushed bright red and sent a nervous glance at Chloe. Hopefully, she was the type to blast her music.

"Don't worry about her," Blake told me, bumping my hip with his and prodding a few of the patties with the tip of the spatula. "She's *out*. Crashed the second she put her head down. Isabel had a nasty cold this week, so the two of them have slept, like, *maybe* four hours over the last three days."

I shot the tired mom a sympathetic look.

"Don't look at her like that," Blake grumbled. "She's been a complete bitch for the past seventy-two hours."

I winced a little.

Blake and Chloe still weren't on great terms. I couldn't say I was surprised, but my heart sagged a little.

"How's Isabel?" I asked.

"She bounced back fast," Blake said. "Jesse's on baby duty. He's somewhere around here. Think he took her inside to see if he could find one of Lena's old taekwondo outfits."

It didn't slip past me that there was a tiny note of resentment in Blake's voice, and, if the way he scraped a patty up and bashed it back down on the grill was any indication, it was safe to say he was upset.

"How come you got grill duty?" I ventured.

"Because Jesse's good with kids," he said with a shrug. "And the last time I was on baby duty, I kind of fucked it up monumentally. You might remember it. You were there."

He tapped his forehead, as if I needed reminding of the night

I'd taken an elbow to the face and played the most sexually tense Scrabble game of my life.

"Jesse *is* a kid," I said, deciding to ignore the second half of his explanation.

Blake snorted a little.

Still, he didn't go any easier on the burgers.

I leaned my hip against the mini fridge and cast another glance over the backyard, trying to think of something to say—anything to say—that might make him feel better.

If I was being totally honest, then no, Blake wasn't great with Isabel. I'd seen him interact with her a few times. He was awkward. Too stiff, too unsure. Kids usually picked up on that kind of stuff. But Isabel seemed to adore him, no matter how rigid and pissy he was with her; I'd seen her watch *Sesame Street* with him. She'd been giddy to have him there—her *brother*. She was too young to understand the difference between a brother and half brother.

But Blake was old enough. And maybe that was the problem.

I yawned loudly before I could catch myself.

"Am I boring you?" Blake asked.

"No. Just woke up superearly this morning. Some idiot thought it'd be nice to have a chat at six a.m."

"Well, I'm sure he wouldn't have to call you so early in the morning if you just had a cell phone, like the rest of the modern world."

I leveled a glare at him. He smiled back at me, unfazed.

"We're not having this argument again," I grumbled.

Luckily, Lena and Blake's dad chose that moment to march onto the back porch carrying a jumbo-sized cooler. Well, Lena was carrying it. George was walking behind her, eyeing her with something like wonder and acting as a (kind of unnecessary) spotter.

Lena set the cooler down beside the outdoor couches and smacked her hands together, looking quite proud of herself. George put his hands on his hips—God bless the dad uniform of khaki shorts, white tube socks, and polo shirts—and eyed her warily.

"What do you bench press?" he asked.

Lena just laughed.

"Oh, Mr. Hamilton," she said, shaking her head and giving his arm a little pat. "I'll go help Mom bring out the sweet tea."

"I'll get some napkins or something," George offered.

I watched Lena jog back to the house and bound up the steps just as Rachel and Gummer came outside—Gummer with a bowl of salad tucked in each elbow and Rachel with several tinfoil-sealed pans stacked in her arms. It seemed it was almost time for the party to start. Jesse and Isabel were still in the house, I guess, and Alissa was running a little late, but soon, we'd all be digging in to some much-awaited and much-hyped lunch.

George rounded the pool and stopped briefly beside his wife, bending down for a moment to brush her hair off her face and over her shoulder, and then shook her gently.

It was such an intimate moment, I had to look away.

I turned to Blake, who was watching his dad and his stepmom with a slightly sour expression. I could read his face too well—the bitterness, the guilt, the hurt. It was eating at him, that he didn't know how to get along with the new half of his family. He played it off with smooth teen angst, but I knew him too well now to not see it.

Blake Hamilton was a big, bruised softie.

Right.

Say something. Cheer him up.

"You know," I said, nudging his side with my elbow, "today is perfect. It's not too sunny, not too cold. There's *food*. I've never been to a real family barbecue. You know"—oh hell, here came the nervous oversharing—"I've never really had real friends. And my parents would never come to something like this. This is, like, really, really cool. And there's sweet tea and key lime pie and a bunch of other stuff I've never tried before—"

Blake made a choked sound.

"Waverly," he said, very softly.

I refused to meet his eyes. Or stop talking.

"—and it's gonna be *great*. Literally, the best day. Perfect."

It was at that moment that Jesse burst through the back door and pounded down the porch steps. Isabel was seated on his shoulders, wearing the smallest white taekwondo *dobok* I'd ever seen and an enormous, gap-toothed grin. She had two fistfuls of Jesse's dark curls in her tiny hands and was tugging at his hair like she was handling the reins of a horse.

But her steed didn't look all that great.

Jesse raced across the lawn, each thump of his bare feet on the grass urging a gleeful squeal from Isabel's tummy. He slowed to a cautious walk as he made his way around the pool (it was then that I noticed he was breathing heavily and clacking his tongue rhythmically in time with his steps, making a noise that resembled the trotting of a horse) and then came to an exaggerated halt in front of Blake and me, which he punctuated with his impression of a horse's whinny.

Then Jesse slumped, as if exhausted, and tried to catch his breath.

"Hey, there, Secretariat," Blake said.

Jesse held up one hand.

"Gimme—a minute," he panted. Then, "Hey—Waverly—so glad—you made—it."

"What's up, Jesse?" I asked.

Isabel giggled.

"Horsie! Go!"

"Horsie no," Jesse huffed.

"Jesse," Blake urged, "what's up?"

He stood up straighter again, his hands still clamped around Isabel's little ankles, and shook his head at Blake.

"Alissa's here," he said. "With her mom—"

Blake wrinkled his nose.

"Ugh," he groaned. "The *supermodel*. Well, I guess we can try to wrestle up some diet soda or something. Or maybe she can have a wet piece of lettuce to eat—"

But Jesse was still shaking his head.

"—and her dad," he added, ominously.

Blake's spatula clattered to the ground.

Chapter 20

The Hastings arrived at the barbecue in three separate cars, each worth more than a year's tuition at a private liberal arts college, which was the first warning sign that things had taken a turn for the shitty.

Blake, upon hearing that his ex-girlfriend's parents were in the vicinity, promptly attempted to strangle himself with the ties on his novelty bikini-girl apron. At least, that's what it looked like he was doing, given how violently he was struggling to get the thing off.

"Calm down," I snapped as I tried to undo the knots with my fingernails. "Would you stop *moving*? You're going to choke yourself."

He let out a single panicked laugh.

"That's a great idea, actually. Quick. No one's looking."

I huffed and smacked him on the back of the head.

Ugh. His hair's softer than mine. How's that fair?

"Don't joke like that," I told him. "It's not funny. And what am I missing? What's so bad about Alissa's dad?"

"It's not her dad," Blake said, shaking his head. "It's her mom and dad *together*. They're—"

They're here. On the back porch.

I'd missed the first warning sign. The second was that Alissa's mother looked like an Instagram model. She was a walking embodiment of the sponsored post on your feed that you don't really want to see because it reminds you that your last vacation was spent on your couch and also you are, in the grand scheme of things, not very pretty. Her hair was dark and blown out in perfect curls, and her eyeliner was so sharp it could've slit a man's throat.

She didn't smile, and she'd brought her own bottle of rosé and didn't look like she was going to share it.

Then there was the last red flag of the day. Alissa's father, the founder and owner of Hastings Yachts, had shown up to a casual family barbecue wearing white linen pants, a white button-down shirt, crocodile leather shoes, and a Rolex watch nearly the size of my fist. He barely came up to my shoulder when we stood on level ground, but he had the ego and the bank account of LeBron James, so he carried himself like he was closer to seven feet tall than to four.

Standing between them on the back porch was Alissa, whose face was blank in a way that screamed *I am dissociating*.

Jesse and Lena's mother, Boss—who was both the host of the party and the bravest matriarch at the family barbecue—welcomed the Hastings without batting an eyelash.

"Penelope!" She greeted Alissa's mother just loudly enough for me to hear from across the yard. "It's been months. You look phenomenal, as always. What've you been up to?"

"I've been doing business abroad," Penelope replied shortly.

"We're glad you could make it," Boss said, smile unwavering as she turned her attention to Alissa's father. "And you must be Santiago! It's wonderful to finally meet you. I feel like I know you already—your daughter's told me so much about you."

Santiago Hastings cocked one eyebrow.

"Has she?" he drawled.

Blake was still very tense beside me, despite the fact that he was no longer wearing an apron with cartoon boobs on it, and had resorted to giving his undivided attention to the grill.

"You're going to burn the burgers," I whispered.

He hummed noncommittally.

"Blake," I whispered again and set my hand on his bicep.

The tension in his shoulder eased almost immediately (which was kind of flattering and made my heart feel all melty). He leaned into my touch and sighed.

"Her parents suck," he grumbled.

I scoffed, and because I was both painfully oblivious to all the ominous warning signs and blissfully optimistic, I squeezed Blake's arm and said, "They can't possibly be *that* bad."

I totally jinxed it.

Boss called us all to come take a seat at the two folding tables that'd been set up end to end across the length of the back porch. There was enough food to feed half of Holden—turkey wraps and chicken wings and zucchini fries and pie and chocolate chip cookies and grilled vegetables and burgers and hot dogs and literally every variation of salad that I could think of—and the whole setup was large enough that we probably could've seated twenty people comfortably. This all proved deeply ironic, given that there were just thirteen of us and we somehow managed to achieve the exact opposite of a comfortable dining experience.

Blake and I had to make two trips to the table to transport all the platters of meat and grilled vegetables. On our return lap, halfway back to the grill, he started dragging his feet a little. I shot him a look—an eyebrows-raised You good? kind of look—and he responded by grimacing like he might actually throw up.

"Sit next to me," he whispered in a tone that suggested this was life or death and not hot dog or hamburger. "Please."

I chuckled in a way that retrospectively makes me want to kick myself in the face just a tiny bit and bumped my hip against his.

But by the time we got back to the porch, everyone else had taken a seat and started filling their paper plates. Two chairs remained. They were at a diagonal across the table from each other—not far, given the size of the table, but still not, like, *together*. Blake and I exchanged a quick glance before taking these seats. I was a bit disappointed. Blake, on the other hand, looked like the world had come to an end.

I watched him slump in his chair and wished, more than ever, that I had a cell phone so we could communicate privately. He looked like he could use a meme.

"Dig in, everybody!" Boss informed the table.

And so the barbecue began—memeless and with a great deal of obvious discomfort for the majority of parties involved.

I sat at the center on one side of the table. To my right, George and Aunt Rachel debated the pros and cons of using different brands of waterproof exterior paint on window trim—a topic so obscure and mundane that I was sure they'd started talking about the first thing they could come up with just to break the awkward silence. Across from them sat Gummer, who was listening far too intently to their paint debate. Then there was Blake, who'd consumed four glasses of sweet tea in quick succession out of sheer discomfort.

To my left, Isabel—still dressed in Lena's old taekwondo outfit—jumped between the laps of Jesse and Chloe, who were comparing notes on schools in the district. Across from the future PTA stars sat Lena and Boss, who were both loading potato salad on their cheeseburgers in what was clearly an old and beloved mother-daughter ritual. Directly across from me sat Alissa, who kept one hand shielded over her manicured eyebrows and squinted like the sun was blinding, even though it was so overcast I was half expecting it to rain.

I could see it in her posture; she was *mortified*.

Her parents clearly hadn't come to the barbecue together because they wanted some quality family time. Penelope and Santiago had chosen to sit at the opposite ends of the table, facing each other, and did little else but glare and set down their plastic cutlery with unnecessary force for the sheer dramatic effect.

Everyone at the table felt the heat of their mutual hatred and was withering under it, unsure what to do. Twice, Boss tried to start a tablewide conversation to cut through the awkwardness. Twice, she failed. Then Chloe tried her hand.

"I absolutely love your dress, Penelope."

"I do too," Alissa's mother replied, eyes fixed resolutely on her ex-husband. She took a long sip of rosé and said nothing else.

Emboldened by this tiny measure of progress, Gummer turned to Santiago and attempted some similar small talk.

"You're in the boating business, I hear," he said.

"Yachting," Santiago corrected brusquely, then turned to fix the glare he'd been giving his wife on Gummer. "I hear that your son is dating my daughter."

Beside me, Jesse gasped, then coughed, then made a gagging noise. When I turned, his eyes were watery and he had a wet grape in his palm.

"I think I inhaled this," he wheezed, then set the grape back on his plate gingerly.

"Daddy—" Alissa groaned.

"It's true, isn't it?" Santiago insisted.

Gummer looked at Jesse, who was a bit red but had managed to dislodge the grape from his windpipe, and then back at the short, leathery man at the end of the table.

"Well, yes," he admitted, "I think they're hanging out."

"And your son," Santiago began, looking Jesse up and down. "He's a senior this year, too, I presume. What's his sport? Has he had any scholarship offers yet?"

There was a brief silence in which no one at the table seemed to know how to handle this inquiry. And for one brilliant and horrible moment, I realized that Alissa Hastings and I had the very same brand of parents, even if hers looked like they'd stepped out of a perfume advertisement set on the Amalfi Coast and mine were probably wearing parkas zipped up to their noses while their glasses frosted over.

"He surfs," I spoke up. "And he's really good."

Penelope laughed, and it was exactly the kind of laugh you'd imagine belonging to a woman getting hammered by herself at a family barbecue while her ex-husband picked fights with his daughter's new boyfriend.

"Mom, please," Alissa moaned.

"I'm on your side, darling," Penelope said. "You don't need to land a professional athlete just yet. You're young. Enjoy yourself."

Santiago barked out a cruel laugh.

"Oh, I think she's enjoying herself *plenty*."

Several things happened at once.

Rachel, who had the same wide-eyed look she got when shit hit the fan on one of her reality shows, gasped audibly. Blake, who'd just polished off his fifth glass of sweet tea, pushed back his chair and stumbled over an excuse with the word *bathroom* somewhere in it before darting inside the house and slamming the screen door behind him. And Jesse, who'd only just recovered from inhaling a grape, looked even more distressed than he had during his episode of accidental asphyxiation.

"Leave her alone," he said, his voice stronger than I'd ever heard it.

Santiago arched an eyebrow. "This one has a spine, eh? That's a minor improvement over the last." He tipped his head toward Blake's vacated chair.

"Mr. Hastings," George cut in, sounding so stern that the entire table went silent, "I think it's time for you to go."

It was all such a familiar routine—the backhanded compliments, the accusations of moral debauchery and personal failures—but something about George's interruption made me feel like I was watching it all from a new angle. Alissa's parents were children. *My* parents were children too. Big, overgrown children who'd never learned how to keep their conflicts and ego trips from hurting others. And it wasn't Alissa's fault, and it wasn't my fault, and everyone else at the table could recognize how utterly selfish and destructive they were being.

Santiago's eyes narrowed. "Excuse me?"

I saw what happened next out of the corner of my eye, for the most part. At the other end of the table, Penelope downed the last bit of rosé in her plastic cup, poured herself a refill, then stood abruptly, knocking her chair back, before tossing the full cup across the length of the table with a precision and grace that could've made Tom Brady fall to his knees and shed a tear.

The cup collided with her ex-husband's chest, its contents splattering across his crisp white shirt and pants, staining them like a Jackson Pollock.

Isabel, who was propped up on Chloe's knee, cackled.

"*Mom!*" Alissa cried. "Oh my God, would you *chill*?"

Santiago wiped a drop of rosé from his cheek.

"See, *mija*? This is where you get your dramatics," he said evenly. Then, with a surprising amount of pride for a man covered in the drink of choice of nine out of ten Real Housewives, he stood from the table and stormed inside the house. Thirty seconds later, we heard a car engine roar to life.

"Good riddance," Penelope murmured.

I glanced across the table at Alissa. Her hands covered either side of her face as she hunched over her plate full of untouched food, so I was the only person at the table who could see the anguish on her face. It was more than just humiliation. It was the kind of pain a child feels when her parents have let her down, irredeemably and unapologetically. I knew what that looked like, because I'd felt it. When Alissa stood abruptly and tore down the porch steps and across the lawn, I slapped my napkin onto the table and stood too.

Lena pushed her chair back to follow me.

"Let me talk to her," I said.

Lena scrutinized me for a moment, looking torn. "Don't be

funny. She's got no sense of humor when she's upset. You've gotta compliment her hair, and then remind her she got a five on the AP bio exam and—"

"Lena," I interrupted. "I've got this."

She pressed her lips together tightly and nodded.

I turned and padded down the porch steps. Alissa was already across the yard, sitting on the ledge of the bean-shaped pool with her feet in the water and her back to the house. I marched across the grass and tried to think of an opening line that *wasn't* a joke. Which was tough, because humor was kind of my go-to coping method.

Alissa sighed and sniffed when she heard my footsteps approaching. I plopped down on the cobblestone pavement with all the grace of a wet sponge, scooted forward until I was sitting next to her, and threw off my flip-flops to stick my feet in the water.

The pool was cold—way too cold to be enjoyable, much less comfortable, given the overcast skies and cool breezes.

"This weather sucks," I blurted.

Nailed it, I thought. *Just absolute slam dunk. Home run. Everyone else go home.*

I fought the urge to dunk my head in the pool and inhale.

But beside me, Alissa barked out a laugh.

"It's the *worst*," she spat, kicking her foot out and splashing water across the width of the pool. Her toenails were painted robin's egg blue, the color the sky should've been. "Fuck this whole tropical storm thing. It's August. Where's the fucking sun?"

"Yeah," I agreed, because she seemed pretty fired up.

"The whole reason I spent the summer here instead of taking bogus art history classes in Madrid was so I could *enjoy* it." She punctuated this with a kick of her heel against the surface of the pool, sprinkling us with a few drops of chlorinated water that dotted her floral romper and also landed directly in my left eye, because that's just the way things go for me.

"You could've gone to *Madrid*?" I cried, sounding a bit more alarmed than I actually was because, hello, chlorine in my eye.

"Yeah," she grumbled in response. "My mom knows a professor at some university there. She had an affair with him, I guess, and she was gonna blackmail him into letting me enroll late. I think his wife is, like, important in politics or something. Whatever. So, yeah, I was going to spend the summer in Madrid, but then—then I started hooking up with Ethan, and my mom got mad."

Alissa shrugged, as if this was a perfectly common chain of events that could happen to any high schooler.

"Your mom's kind of cool," I said without thinking.

Then, with the kind of sudden burst of panic that you might feel after stepping on an upturned thumbtack or closing your front door and realizing your keys are on the kitchen table, I remembered that Alissa had told me she'd liked hooking up with Ethan for the sole reason that her mom had been mad enough about it to talk to her for the first time in four months.

"I mean," I hurried on, "awful. She's just the worst."

Alissa sighed and offered me a half smile, like she'd gotten used to my foot-in-mouth routine and didn't fault me for it.

"She's my mom," she replied with a shrug. "I mean, I guess I love her. You're supposed to love your mom, right? But . . . I wish, sometimes, that she was better at it."

She admitted this last bit in a very quiet voice and followed up by clearing her throat and gathering chunks of her long, pin-straight hair over one shoulder. She flared the tips in front of her face, examining them for nonexistent split ends.

A hard breeze whisked across the yard, ruffling the grass.

It was cold. Not Arctic cold, but still.

"My parents are divorced," I said suddenly, staring ahead at the water in the pool and twisting a bit of fabric at the hem of my dress. "They're professors at the same university. Same field, but they have totally different views. And they're both brilliant—I mean, truly, some of the nerdiest people on earth—but they're *idiots* for ever getting married. I think they just wanted the challenge. Trying to change the other's mind, you know?"

Alissa was quiet for a long moment.

"My mom's on her seventh marriage," she finally said.

"I think mine's sleeping with one of her students," I offered.

"My mom has told me—on multiple occasions—that she regrets having me because I messed up her modeling career."

"Nobody's ever helped me with my homework," I admitted. "I failed physics my freshman year. I had to retake it over the summer to catch up. And you don't even want to *know* how bad AP bio kicked my ass last year."

Alissa sighed, then mumbled, "I got a five."

"I got a two. I don't even get college credit for my suffering."

She laughed. And I laughed, too, because all these things seemed smaller now that we'd laid them out side by side.

I knew talking about things didn't change them. My parents still weren't what I wanted them to be, and they probably never would be. I still dreaded going home to Alaska, even though I had an impending return flight and one last year of high school to finish before I got to flee the state and never look back. I'd still gotten a two in AP bio and couldn't go five minutes without saying something I regretted.

These things were true.

But I'd be all right. I had Aunt Rachel, who had *tried*, unlike either of my parents, to appreciate me in all my mess-ups and mediocrity. I had Jesse and Lena, who'd shown me, for better and for worse, what I was missing as an only child. I had Alissa—the kind of girl I thought I hated, with her perfect hair and overflowing confidence—who'd proved to be a lot more like me than I'd ever thought possible. And I had Blake. I had a *boyfriend*. And he was patient when I rambled, and he was actually quite funny when you got past the social awkwardness he'd buried beneath mountains of broodingly handsome glaring, and he always kept my secrets, even at the beginning, when I hadn't trusted him as far as I could throw an empty red Solo cup.

I'd found my people.

And in one week, I'll have to say good-bye.

"You wanna have a belly flop contest?" Alissa asked, nudging my shoulder with hers and beaming in a way that told me she was feeling a lot lighter too. I'd once thought there was some kind of unspoken competition between us, some contest where the prize was the cute lifeguard next door. I'd been so utterly wrong.

"Fuck, yeah I do," I said.

We both scrambled to our feet, giggling like two twelve-year-olds who'd gotten their hands on their mom's copy of *Fifty Shades of Grey* and had no idea what they were in for. And maybe it was the sudden kinship I felt with Alissa that made me say what I said next.

"You know," I told her as we scampered across the patio and into the grass to get our running starts, "before I got to Florida, I didn't even know how to swim. Isn't that crazy?"

"*You couldn't swim?*"

The voice wasn't Alissa's.

It was Lena's.

I turned over my shoulder and saw that we'd gotten closer to the back porch than I'd realized. Lena and Jesse were sitting on the steps, both staring up at me with wide, unblinking eyes. Everyone else had heard, too, it seemed, and was staring at me—Rachel, Gummer, Boss, George, Chloe, Penelope (the rosé was gone, but she was not), and even Isabel (who, to be fair, probably didn't give a shit if I could swim and was just watching because she thought Alissa and I were going to take a running leap into the pool and make *big splashy*).

I glanced back at Alissa. She was frowning at me like I'd just told her I ran a Twitter account dedicated to posting overzealously graphic Fifty Shades fan art.

It was happening.

The thing I'd had nightmares about was actually happening.

They knew. Everyone knew that I couldn't swim, and they were looking at me the way I'd always known they would. *Outsider,* their eyes said. *You don't belong here.* What kind of pale, long-armed, flat-haired, lopsided-breasted creature crawled off the plane from Alaska and thought she could go unnoticed in Holden? What made her think she could walk in here and pretend we're her friends, her family?

You don't belong here. You don't belong anywhere.

The wave of anxiety I felt was so intense it nearly knocked my feet out from under me. And maybe, if it'd happened at the beginning of the summer, I would've let it. Maybe I would've allowed the roaring in my head to drag me under and drown me.

But not now.

Not when I knew how to float.

I shrugged with an easiness I didn't quite feel and smiled like someone who has nothing to lose, even though it sort of felt like I could lose everything.

"Nope," I admitted. "But I learned."

Lena was the first to react.

"Oh my God," she said, pinching the bridge of her nose and squeezing her eyes shut. "Oh my God, we took you *surfing*. In the *ocean*. Please, Waverly. Please tell me you knew how to swim when we went out there to surf." Her eyes opened, briefly, and then shut again almost immediately when she saw how red my face had turned. "Oh my God, you didn't. Oh no."

"It was great practice," I insisted, rubbing the nail of my right index finger into the side of my thumb so hard I took off some skin.

I glanced around the yard again.

The realization I came to was long overdue, really. Nobody was staring at me because of the admission that I'd arrived in Holden seventeen years old and unable to swim. They were staring at me because I'd been deeply, fundamentally, atrociously self-conscious, to the point of voluntarily putting myself in an extreme position of peril.

"You idiot!" Lena growled.

Yeah. Yeah, that was fair.

I shrugged again, feeling very small and very young suddenly.

The incredulous look on Lena's face slipped. She frowned at me for a moment, like she was trying to fit together puzzle pieces, and then shook her head. She pushed herself up from the porch and took three long strides across the grass.

"You *idiot*." She sighed, throwing her arms around my neck and hugging me so tightly I wheezed. "I would've been your friend, you know. Even if you'd told me."

I buried my face against her shoulder, humiliated.

"It was embarrassing," I said very quietly.

She laughed hard, and I felt it rattle in her chest. I threw my arms around her, too, and squeezed. She squeezed back, a little harder, and I quickly ditched any thoughts of engaging in a hugging contest. It sort of felt like I was a first grader trying to arm wrestle John Cena. It just wasn't gonna work out in my favor.

Lena finally released me and stepped back.

"You could've told us, Waverly," Jesse piped up from beside his sister, offering me a lopsided smile. "I mean, it's not that big a deal, but Blake and I are both trained lifeguards. We could've—"

He stopped, abruptly, his mouth still hanging open as he blinked.

Oh no.

"Wait," he drawled, narrowing his eyes at me.

Oh *no*.

"He knew. Blake knew," Jesse concluded. Then he gasped and beamed at me. "He was teaching you, wasn't he? That's why he kept sneaking out of the house and going to the pool! He was teaching you!"

I tried not to make eye contact with Blake's parents.

Oh my God, if they knew how many hours I'd spent staring at their son's bare chest—

"He *what*?" Chloe snapped.

For one short and terrifying second, I thought her sudden burst of anger was directed at me.

Then Blake stepped onto the porch, as if summoned to return from his anxiety-driven bathroom break by the sheer willpower of his stepmother's wrath, and I remembered that he'd been grounded for most of the summer.

Well. Oops.

Blake went from cautious, as he glanced at Santiago's chair, to relieved, seeing as it was now empty. But then he looked up at Chloe and saw that the parental hellfire wasn't over yet, because his tiny, blond stepmom was staring at him like a warrior Viking goddess preparing to vanquish some dumbass man.

My dumbass man.

"Mrs. Hamilton, it was my fault!" I blurted. "I asked him to!"

But Chloe didn't listen.

"Jesse," she said, eerily calm. "Hold the baby."

He scrambled up the porch stairs and collected Isabel from her outstretched arms. Isabel, delighted by the new development in the chain of events that'd caused the Fletchers' casual backyard barbecue to more accurately resemble the season finale of a tele-novela, twisted wildly in Jesse's arms to watch her half brother receive what was sure to be the ass whooping of the century.

"He was only helping me!" I insisted. "It's *my* fault!"

Blake glanced at me, eyes wide in confusion, and then back at his stepmother, who was—luckily for him—stuck on the opposite side of a very long table (which was, unluckily for him, also covered in things she could easily throw at him, should the urge strike her).

"You were *grounded*," Chloe seethed.

Blake's face sank.

Yeah, he'd realized what she was all fired up about. For a split second, I saw everything on his face—the sheepishness, the terror, the embarrassment—before he squashed it down and leveled her with a very cold, very bored expression.

"I'm almost eighteen," he said, rolling his eyes and folding his arms across his chest. "I'm not a kid anymore. You can't just ground me. That doesn't mean anything."

"Well, you're still seventeen," Chloe pointed out. "And until your next birthday, you abide by *our* rules. I made the decision to ground you after you took your sister to that stupid party. If you can't respect my call, then—"

"Then *what*?" Blake asked, his voice tight.

It was only then that I noticed his hands, which he'd balled into tight fists and shoved under his armpits, were shaking.

This was his greatest fear.

I mean, he'd been a complete asshole to me the first night I'd spent in Holden all because he was worried I'd tell all his friends that I'd seen him get chewed out by his stepmom. We'd wasted so much time being hostile and snapping at each other because of it. And now, here, in front of all his friends, it was happening.

For me, it was déjà vu to the first time we'd met.

"Then you've lost the privilege of having your phone," Chloe said, grinding her teeth together. I winced when she reached across the table and said in a low voice, "Hand it over."

Blake stared down at her hand, manicured fingers arched like claws, and shook his head.

"I'm not giving you my—"

"Blake," she snapped. "Phone. *Now*."

His eyes drifted. He looked around the porch, where the other parents were watching in tense and solemn silence (save for Penelope, who was chuckling ever so slightly, because I guess that's what one does when one has had an entire fucking bottle of wine to oneself). Then he looked across the lawn at his friends. At me.

His face flushed red.

He looked very young all of a sudden—young and unsure.

Chloe didn't look much better. There was something wild in

her eyes that reminded me what Blake had said, about the fact that she hadn't slept much the last seventy-two hours because Isabel had been fighting a cold. She was probably exhausted. And it wasn't her fault that she didn't have the first clue how to raise a teenage son who'd never asked for a replacement mother.

She was *trying*.

Trying counted for a lot.

Chloe quirked her eyebrows and glanced down at her empty hand, huffing in impatience. I knew she was just acting so tough on Blake because she had an audience; she didn't want to look like the woman whose stepson walked all over her.

Blake stared at her for a long moment before he shoved his hand into the front pocket of his shorts and dug out his phone.

Chloe exhaled, her shoulders hunching under the intensity of her stepson's glare. She didn't look the least bit triumphant as he dropped his phone into her open palm.

"Thank you," she said.

Blake leveled her with a look so cold it sent a shiver up my back.

"There," he said. "Now you can stop pretending to be my mom."

"Blake!" George exclaimed, standing up in a rush from his seat at the table and fumbling out something about having respect and, in more eloquent terms, not being a total dick to your stepmother.

But the damage had been done.

Chloe flinched, as if Blake had slapped her clear across the face. I watched, completely helpless, as her hand went slack and Blake's phone slipped through her fingers. She tried to catch it—I saw her. I caught the flare of panic in her wide, dark eyes and the little twitch of her arm as she moved to correct the mistake. She didn't do it on purpose.

But it was too late.

Blake's phone plunged into a pitcher of sweet tea.

It went without saying that the party was over.

Chapter 21

The rain started about five minutes after Rachel and I got home. We were in the kitchen playing fridge *Tetris* with all the leftovers the Fletcher family had forced upon us when I heard it—little pitter-patters against the roof, like the world's tiniest drum circle.

I gasped in delight and said, "It's raining!"

It was like all my brain cells had jumped ship, and only Captain Obvious remained on deck. Rachel shoved the last of our reusable glass containers into the few remaining square inches of fridge space, then stepped back to admire her handiwork.

"Well," she said, "it's a shame the barbecue ended like that—"

With the complete decimation of Blake and Chloe's relationship, she meant.

"—but look at all this food! I think we've got enough leftovers to last us until the end of week, if we freeze some."

Float

The end of the week. The end of my time in Holden.

I shook off the thought and crossed the kitchen to stand at the sliding glass doors and watch the rain come down. Behind me, Rachel puttered around cleaning up, then—

One new message.

"Rachel," my dad's voice said from the machine. "Hi. I just landed in Fairbanks. Our trip got cut short because of a pretty bad snowstorm, and I just saw the news that you've got a tropical storm moving in down there in Florida."

My heart stuttered with a spark of hope. *Say I can stay longer,* I thought. *Please give me more time. Even if it's just a few more days.*

Instead, my father's crackling voice said: "I just booked a new flight to Holden tomorrow, and I got our flights home bumped up to Monday morning. It was the soonest I could get. Hopefully, we'll beat the storm. I'll email you the confirmation. Give me a call back when you can, okay? All right. Take care."

The answering machine clicked.

I felt it like a physical blow to the chest.

My dad was coming early. He wanted me to *leave* early. How was I supposed to tell my friends? How was I supposed to tell *Blake*? I turned to Rachel, who was wide-eyed and watching me with something like concern, and had the brief and strange urge to ask her to hide me. To let me stay here, like a stowaway, in her house. Forever.

"Do you have any books I could read?" I blurted.

I needed to be away from myself for a while. If I was left to stew in my own thoughts, I'd undoubtedly come up with a laundry list of things I'd miss about Holden, and then I'd end up sitting on the bench under the window in my bedroom with my forehead against the rain-streaked glass, like some kind of early-2000s music video, and I didn't want to be that girl.

It was thus of the utmost importance that I dive headfirst into a book, immediately.

"Check the bookshelf in the living room," Rachel said gently. "I've got some good ones."

I was a little distracted, so I didn't really stop to think about what Rachel's standards might be for *good* fiction. Instead, I loped into the living room and squatted in front of the bookshelf, completely unprepared for the sight that greeted me.

Two words: Romance. Novels.

We're talking a gross abundance of male torsos. Every book I pulled out had some kind of half-naked man on the cover. Doctors with stethoscopes around their necks. Professional athletes with their biceps flexed around footballs. Firemen carrying hoses in what was clearly an attempt to appeal subliminally to heterosexual women.

And not a single one of them was wearing a shirt.

Isn't that, like, very unprofessional? was my first thought.

The second was, *Oh my God, my aunt reads porn.*

I tugged more books out by their spines and slammed them back into place, searching frantically for something that looked even remotely family friendly.

And then, on the bottom shelf, I found it. It was a romance novel, like all the others, with a similarly obscene stock photo of a male model on the cover. But this particular book caught my eye. And I wish I could say that I pulled it off the shelf and tucked it under my arm because I found the plot summary on the back to be well written and intriguing. I wish I could say that I recognized the author, or knew, somehow, that I was in for a good story with a fine-tuned plot, complex characters, and feminist undertones.

Nope. The shirtless pirate on the cover just looked a lot like Blake.

I darted across the living room and bounded up the stairs like a gunslinging bandit on the American frontier who'd just heisted bars of solid gold from a moving locomotive.

The pale blue of my bedroom walls looked washed out and grey in the dim light that poured through the white plantation shutters. I pulled the door closed behind me and hurried to my dresser so I could tug off Lena's dress and slip into a pair of flannel pajama pants and an oversized T-shirt. Then, after a moment's hesitation, I jogged back to the door and turned the lock until it clicked softly into place.

Aunt Rachel was great—and this was *her* book, after all, which she'd seen in the store and made the conscious decision to buy with her hard-earned money—but I really didn't need the embarrassment of her knowing what I was reading.

I crawled into bed, tugged my duvet up over my legs, and settled in.

The cover really was a work of art.

I think the man on the cover was supposed to be a pirate. He had a rope from the ship's rigging in one hand and a sword in the other, and behind him was a hint of crystal-blue water. I wasn't all that concerned with the context. What really mattered was that his cream-colored shirt was unbuttoned and billowing in the wind, he had abs for days, and his dark hair and (photoshopped) blue eyes sort of resembled Blake's, if you squinted.

The Prince of Turning Tides.

Yeah, who cares.

I flipped it open and scanned the first few pages for any grammatical errors or strikingly misogynistic sentiments. Thankfully, it passed inspection.

And ten pages later, I was no longer in my aunt's guest room waiting for the best summer of my life to end. I was on a ship docked in a quasi-European coastal town, where nobody had to worry about graduating high school or mediating between their divorced parents. They were just getting in a lot of fistfights at the local pub and thinking about stealing shit.

And then there was the hero, Jem Blackheart, whose name was eye-roll inducing but, in my mind, looked exactly like my boyfriend, so I wasn't complaining. Jem Blackheart needed a ship and a crew, fast. It was all very contrived. But then, in the middle of what had to be the tenth bar fight in three chapters, something plunked against my window. I assumed it was a very fat raindrop or water falling from a crack in the gutters that lined the roof.

But then, about a minute later, there was a heavy thump outside—like someone had climbed onto the roof of the wraparound porch—followed by the gentle but insistent tap of knuckles against my window. I looked up from my book. There were really only a handful of people who could've been knocking on my bedroom window. One lived next door.

I chucked off my duvet and stomped over to the window to flip open the shutters. Sure enough, there stood Blake Hamilton, his hair plastered to his head with rain and his hands pressed to the glass of the window.

He smiled sheepishly.

"Son of a—" I muttered, tossing my book over my shoulder and tearing open the shutters so I could grab the bottom pane of the window and lift.

I had the muscle mass of a small tropical fish. It took me a moment of grunting and grappling to get the window open.

When it was, I stuck my head out, glaring as a few drops of rain smacked me in the face.

"What are you doing?" I demanded.

Blake blinked at me like it was the dumbest question I could've asked. "Trying not to fall off your roof."

"You know what I meant. Why are you on my roof?"

"Well, Waverly, I was just wondering if you had a minute to talk about our lord and savior—"

I grabbed a fistful of his sweatshirt (the dark-green crew neck he'd worn on our date at Bayside Burgers after my surfing career began and ended in the same afternoon) and yanked him in through the window, stepping aside so he didn't crush me as he fell into my bedroom and landed on the hardwood floor in a heap.

"Jesus Christ," he groaned.

I tugged the window shut behind him.

It closed with a heavy wooden *thunk* that made me flinch.

"You have to be quiet," I whisper-hissed at the boy sprawled at my feet.

Blake grunted as he sat up. "It's not like Rachel would actually kick me out of here. Right?"

He had a fair point. She was pretty laissez-faire about the whole *guardian* thing. It was more that I didn't want her knowing that I had a boy in my room. I turned and stared down at Blake, who was soaked from the rain—his hair, his sweatshirt, his jeans, his canvas sneakers, everything. He was leaving a puddle on my floor.

I had a *boy* in my room. What an odd turn of events. I'd never had a boy over before. Not like this. Was I supposed to provide snacks and beverages? I had a half-eaten box of parmesan-flavor

Goldfish on the desk and tap water from the bathroom sink, but that didn't seem very hospitable.

"Could you please take your shoes off?" I asked.

He grinned.

"And then what?" he teased, using the toe of one shoe to scrape off the heel of the other as he blinked up at me through his unfairly thick eyelashes.

I huffed and folded my arms over my chest, quietly relieved that I'd been so pumped to read my book that I hadn't stopped to take off my bra.

"And then put them in the corner so you don't get mud all over the floor."

"Not the dirty talk I was hoping for," he mumbled.

I pressed my lips together, willing myself not to crack a smile.

Blake got to his feet and set his sneakers against the wall under the window. Then he ran his fingers through his hair, pushing his bangs back from his forehead so they stuck straight up, and took a seat on the edge of my mattress.

"Not on the bed!" I scolded. "You're all wet."

Blake's smile was scandalized.

"If your aunt hears you talking like that—"

I grabbed the sleeve of his sweatshirt and tugged.

"Get *off*."

"Again, you're saying things that could really be taken out of context."

He let me pull him to his feet and position him in the middle of the room so he wasn't dripping onto any furniture.

"Better," I said, more to myself than to him.

"So this is fun. I'll just stand here," Blake deadpanned.

I frowned and hurried across the room to my dresser.

"Let me see if I have anything . . . here we go!"

I tugged out the largest sweatpants I could find—a pair of grey Fruit of the Loom ones with holes in the pockets and a frayed elastic band. They were Rachel's, from a distant period in time she referred to as her *stress-baking phase.*

Blake plucked them from my hands and held them up against his waist.

"They'll fit you," I insisted. "Just don't knot the elastic."

Blake shrugged. Then he reached down to unbutton his jeans.

"What are you doing?" I squawked, clapping my hands over my eyes.

"Well, I'm not gonna put them on *over* my pants."

I jabbed a finger at the bathroom door. "Go change in there."

"It's gonna take me, like, four seconds. Just close your eyes."

I huffed loudly and overdramatically so he'd know I wasn't happy about it and buried my face in the crook of my elbow. What I should've done was covered my ears, too, so that I wouldn't hear the slide of his zipper or the wet thump of his jeans hitting the floor.

There's a boy in my room, and he's taking off his pants.

Aunt Rachel would have a heart attack if she knew.

"Coast is clear," Blake announced.

I sighed and dropped my arms. Now, here's the thing about grey sweatpants: for whatever reason, when we as humankind decided to make these a thing, we accidentally stumbled upon an article of clothing that's simultaneously the most unassuming and the most revealing thing a boy can wear. I cast my eyes toward the ceiling, my face on fire.

"They're a little snug," Blake commented, fidgeting with the waistband.

"Mm-hm."

"Can I sit on your bed now?"

I was going to pass out. Blake would be too slow to catch me, and I'd hit my head on the floor and get my second concussion of the summer, and my aunt and all the nurses and doctors at the hospital would ask, *How did this happen?* and I'd have to point at my boyfriend's crotch.

"Well, your sweatshirt is soaked, too, so maybe you should just sit on the—"

Blake grabbed the back of his crew neck between his shoulder blades and tugged it off over his head. His plain white T-shirt rode halfway up his chest.

"Would you quit undressing?" I snapped.

Blake offered me a grin as he dropped his pile of wet clothes on top of his shoes, then sprawled on my bed.

His foot nudged *The Prince of Turning Tides* off the mattress.

It tumbled to the floor.

"Whoops. Sorry, I got it—"

Blake rolled onto his stomach and stretched one arm off the side of the bed to grab the book.

In moments like this one (in which a boy who happens to resemble the shirtless pirate on the cover of the romance novel you've just been reading—with all the guilt-ridden secrecy of someone on a diet who's stashing packets of Oreos under their bed—is reaching for said romance novel) you have a choice to make. And whenever I face tough decisions, I think of my nana, who used to spend hours in the rocking chair in the living room of my mom's apartment listening to the Bible on tape.

"Waverly," she'd say, voice all shaky and, I don't know, *old*.

Float

"There's no reason to feel lost. You'll find your way. You just gotta ask yourself, what would JC do?"

She meant, of course, Jesus.

But as Blake reached for my book, another JC popped into my mind: John Cena.

What better way to distract someone than to body slam them?

Chapter 22

I launched myself onto the bed with all the might (and none of the grace) of a professional wrestling champion. When I came down on Blake's back, I landed hard—which was great, because my pirate romance novel tumbled out of his hand, but also decidedly *not* great, because when I bounced my momentum carried me right off the side of the mattress.

I hit the floor with a thud so tremendous it shook the walls.

Blake coughed (I'd knocked the air out of both of us, it seemed) and stuck his head over the edge of the bed to peer down at me where I lay sprawled on the carpet.

"Is it just me," he asked, "or are you *super*aggressive today?"

Then, in unison, we turned to regard my fallen book. And as my luck would have it, the damn thing had landed cover up.

"Wait a second—"

I lunged for it, but Blake somersaulted off the bed and beat me to it.

"—what is *this*?"

He leaped to his feet, examining the cover with wide eyes and a shocked smile. I popped up, hair in my face and chest heaving, and made a move to grab it from him. He just held it up out of my reach and stared at me, mouth open with amusement.

"Nothing," I blurted. "It's nothing."

The corners of Blake's lips twitched.

"Well, I had no idea I was interrupting your—uh, *reading time*."

I folded my arms over my chest, trying to look stern rather than humiliated.

"The plot's really captivating," I said.

"Right," he replied, nodding solemnly. "The *plot*."

I narrowed my eyes at him.

"Did you just come over to mock my taste in literature?"

"No," Blake said. "I came over here because my stepmom dunked my phone into a pitcher of sweet tea, and to be honest, it's been kind of a shitty afternoon. I just wanted to see your smiling face. But apparently, you just want to beat me up and then read—I don't know, some stupid pirate romance novel."

My shoulders fell. "Blake."

He shouldered past me and crawled back onto my bed. "Don't give me that look."

I watched him settle so his back was propped upright against a blockade of pillows, his eyebrows pinched and his lips curled into a slight frown despite how utterly comfortable he looked. He turned *The Prince of Turning Tides* over in his hands and scrutinized the back cover, then set the book down on his lap.

"You want to talk about it?" I asked.

Blake shook his head.

"You sure?"

His chest rose and fell with a breath. "I shouldn't have said it. That thing about her pretending to be my mom. I know it was a dick move. It just came out, like—like it wasn't even me."

I plopped down on the edge of the bed, the mattress dipping under my weight.

Blake reached out one hand and traced the plaid of my pajama pants with his fingertip.

"She just treats me like a *child*," he added.

"Well, her only experience being a mom *is* with a toddler."

Blake was quiet for a moment.

"I guess," he mumbled, stubborn as ever.

"Look," I told him. "I think Chloe's trying her best. Neither of you has any idea how to do this—this whole *stepmom, stepson* thing. You're *both* crap at it. You need to sit down and have a conversation about what you want from each other."

Blake tugged his hand back from my leg to rub the heels of his palms against his eyes.

"We've *tried*," he groaned. "Every time we talk, we just end up *fighting*."

He let his head fall back against the wall, then dropped his arms to his sides.

The hurt in his eyes was more than I could bear.

So I blurted out the first thing I could think of.

"Knock, knock."

The corner of Blake's mouth twitched.

"Who's there?" he asked.

It occurred to me, suddenly, that I didn't know any knock-knock jokes.

"Give me a second."

"Give me a second who?"

"No," I huffed. "I mean—ugh. Sorry. I really thought something would come to me."

Blake blinked at me for a moment. And then he absolutely lost it.

His laughter was the heaving, silent type—the kind that made your shoulders shake and your eyes well with tears. I sat there and watched him, my arms folded over my chest and my face what surely had to be the brightest shade of red ever witnessed.

"I was *trying* to cheer you up," I snapped.

"I know," Blake said, wiping his fingers under his eyes. "It worked. How the hell do you not know a single knock-knock joke? What about 'Orange you glad I didn't say bananas'? You had, like, hundreds of years of comedic discourse to pull from."

I huffed and threw myself back on the mattress so my head was beside his hips and one of my legs dangled off the edge of the bed.

"All I wanted to do," I grumbled, "was read my book in peace, so I don't have to think about the fact that my dad is coming to Holden tomorrow."

I'd meant to deliver the news more delicately, but there it was.

"What?" he asked, eyebrows furrowing. "I thought he wasn't coming for another week."

"Change of plans. His research trip ended early, so he's trying to fly in before the storm hits." I swallowed hard. And then, more softly, I added: "He rescheduled my flight out. I'm leaving on Tuesday."

"Tuesday," Blake repeated. "You're—that's—*Tuesday*."

I didn't know what to say. And he didn't, either, clearly,

because the silence dragged on for several seconds, the pattering rain drowning out my shattering heart. At last, Blake picked up *The Prince of Turning Tides* and began flipping through pages.

"Where'd you leave off?" he asked, voice hoarse.

"Chapter three," I whispered. "Bar fight with the duke. Why?"

Blake muttered something under his breath about historical accuracy, then, having identified the page on which the aforementioned bar fight began exercising some real artistic license, cleared his throat and started to read aloud.

"'Jem Blackheart'—really?—'sliced his sword through the air and struck down Duke Morningbright'—these names are just getting worse—'where he stood.'"

"I could go without the commentary, Blake."

"Yeah, and I could go without the shirtless dude on the cover," he grumbled.

"He looks like you, you know."

Blake sputtered out a surprised laugh.

"That's the meanest thing you've ever said to me."

"It's not an insult! He's hot. That's why I picked it up in the first place."

"Because this shirtless man turns you on?"

"No, dipshit. You do."

I had all of two seconds to be mortified by what I'd just admitted before Blake chucked my book clear across the room—something I was determined to admonish him for later—and rolled on top of me so his hands were braced on the mattress on either side of my head and his knee was wedged between my thighs.

"Waverly?" he asked.

I nodded and tugged him down by the sleeves of his shirt.

Thank God I locked the door, I thought vaguely.

And then we were kissing.

Here's the thing about making out—I don't think anybody really knows what they're doing the first couple of times. You kind of just move your lips around and put your hands on their shoulders and hope you're not doing anything flagrantly weird. So even though Blake and I had kissed before, several times, the moment his lips touched mine, my worried little brain started working overtime to assess how badly I was doing.

Okay, what am I even doing with my tongue? And what's with the hands on his shoulders?

What is this, a middle school dance?

Blake must've noticed I'd gone stiff, because he pulled back.

"You good?" he asked.

I am the opposite of good. I am the worst.

"Yeah," I lied, tugging at his shoulders a bit desperately. "I'm supergood."

But he didn't kiss me again, and immediately, I was panicked.

I knew I should've brushed my teeth after the barbecue. Way to go, hot dog breath.

"I can just, like, get off of you. If this is weird," Blake said.

It took me a second to realize he was nervous.

"No," I blurted, "no, this is nice."

Blake looked skeptical.

"We don't have to *do* anything," he insisted. "I just wanted to kiss you."

"I know!" I hurried out, then sighed. "I know. It's not—it's not that."

He frowned in question.

I took a deep breath and swallowed my pride.

"I just have no clue what I'm doing. Or where to put my hands."

Blake's shoulders went slack beneath my fingers.

"Oh," he said, sounding a little relieved. "Wherever you want."

I looked down, between our bodies, at the waistband of his grey sweatpants. And then I immediately snapped my eyes up to his face, mouth pressed into a thin line as my face flushed what had to be the deepest possible shade of red.

Blake blinked at me for a moment, equally pink cheeked.

"You've really got your mind in the gutter, huh?" he asked.

I burst out laughing. And just like that, when he bent down to kiss me again, it felt easier. I tossed my arms around Blake's waist, my body slack beneath his, and let my eyes fall closed. I ghosted my fingertips up and down the length of his back, raking my nails against his shirt. Then—because he'd said I could—I let one of my hands wander down to where my grey sweatpants were stretched over his butt.

I giggled, because I had the emotional maturity of a twelve-year-old boy.

"Are you *really* grabbing my butt right now?" Blake asked against my mouth.

"You said wherever I want," I argued.

He laughed. The mattress dipped and bounced. I felt, rather than saw, Blake reach around his back to drag my bedsheet up over us, so we clung to each other amid a sea of white fabric.

I could've kissed him forever.

This is something people say all the time, but I'd never really understood. I'd always sort of thought that kissing was something people had to get bored of, like, fifteen minutes in. You move your mouths around for a few minutes and then one of you says *Hey, I'm kinda hungry, do you wanna grab some burritos?* and you call it a day.

I didn't think it could be fun.

Every brush of fingers against skin, every bump of my legs against his, every little exhale.

When we finally broke apart, what felt like an hour later, we were both breathing hard.

"Okay, I think I need a sec," I admitted. "I'm really winded."

"You should try swimming," Blake panted. "Great cardio."

I pinched his arm. He squirmed, jostling the sheets over us and brushing our thighs together.

God. Bless. Grey. Sweatpants.

I grinned up at Blake. His face hovered inches above mine, so familiar to me now—the freckles across his nose, the little white scar above his left eyebrow, the bright-blue eyes. We stared at each other as our breathing evened out.

"We should just stay under here," I whispered.

"I think we'd get hungry, eventually."

"I have some Goldfish on my desk."

"Sweet. We're set then."

I laughed. Then I lifted my head a few inches to kiss the tip of his nose.

"You'd get sick of me," I mumbled. "Even I get sick of me."

Blake frowned in question.

"I worry," I explained. "A lot."

He hummed thoughtfully. "That makes sense. I mean, you *did* choose to risk drowning in the ocean just to avoid having people think you were lame."

My face flushed.

"That was dumb," I conceded.

"I don't think I've ever met someone who second guesses herself so much."

He said it kindly. Like it was absurd that I could be so anxious about who I was and what people thought of me, but that he didn't hold it against me. He understood. He cared about me, in spite of myself.

"You're gonna be so glad to get rid of me," I teased, my throat oddly tight.

Blake's head fell down against my shoulder so his hair tickled the side of my face and his lips ghosted over my skin just above the collar of my T-shirt.

"I can't believe I only have you for three more days," he murmured.

It was the worst thing he could've said.

Every little worry and anxious thought I'd carefully packed and vacuum sealed into my metaphorical emotional suitcase came tumbling out. I was going to leave. It seemed so cruel that everything I'd never let myself daydream about—friends, a family member who genuinely cared about what I wanted, a boyfriend— had been thrown into my lap just long enough so that I could know what I'd be missing when it was all ripped away again.

I had to go back to Alaska.

Back to my mother, self-assured and intelligent and judgmental.

Back to my father, brilliant and awkward and mean.

Back to my crappy cell phone, filled with the numbers of classmates who'd texted me about group projects or homework and then never again, and back to a high school with people who were not Blake and Alissa and the Fletcher twins.

Blake felt me tense beneath him and lifted his head.

I stared up at his face, willing myself to hold it together. The tears came anyway. They welled up and spilled over, dribbling down the sides of my face and soaking my hair at my temples. I managed to stay quiet for one long, agonizing moment before I finally had to take a breath. It caught in my chest.

I sobbed.

"Hey, hey, hey," Blake said, his face falling.

I screwed my eyes shut. It didn't help stop the tears. I buried my face under my hands, wishing my mattress would just swallow me whole.

"I don't want to go," I croaked, then sobbed again. "I'm sorry."

Blake's fingers ghosted through my hair.

"Hey," he whispered. "Why are you apologizing?"

I huffed in frustration and wiped my hands underneath my eyes, then held them up for inspection and saw wet mascara smudged everywhere.

"I'm so gross," I blubbered.

"Do you want me to grab you a tissue or something?"

I nodded. "That would be"—a sniffle—"really great."

Blake shot off the bed and disappeared into my bathroom.

I heard him riffling around, opening the cabinets under the sink and knocking over shampoo bottles and what sounded like my tweezers, before he marched back into the room with a pack of makeup removing wipes.

"Chloe uses these," he muttered in explanation as he peeled back the plastic tab and tugged out two wipes by accident. "Here. Let me—I don't really know what I'm doing, but—"

He motioned for me to close my eyes. And so I folded my hands one over the other against my stomach and tried to steady my breathing while Blake rubbed mascara stains off my eyelids with a cleansing towelette.

"Okay, open," he murmured.

I did. He wrapped a wipe around one finger and, very delicately, ran his fingertip along the tender skin under my eyes.

"I think I got it all," Blake announced, sounding quite pleased with himself.

I sniffled again.

"Hey, Waverly?" he whispered.

"What?"

"Knock, knock."

I didn't stand a chance. I burst out laughing. It didn't matter what the punch line would've been. What mattered was that I knew, without a single shred of doubt, that Blake Hamilton cared as much about me as I cared about him. I grabbed him by the shoulders of his shirt and pulled him down, kissing his forehead—*Thank you*—and nose—*I'm so glad I met you*—and, finally, his lips—*I love you.*

Distantly, I heard footsteps out in the hall.

But this is so nice . . .

Someone was coming.

Two more minutes, please. Just give me more time—

A stern knock sounded against the door, so jarringly loud that Blake lurched off me and tumbled off the edge of the bed onto my floor.

"Open up!" Rachel demanded.

My inner monologue was an endless train of swear words.

"Um, I fear rejection!" I blurted, scrambling off the bed and searching wildly for a place to hide a whole-ass person in a room that I was only now realizing had very little storage space.

"All right, I'm letting that one slide because it was funny," Rachel said. "But I'm serious, Waverly, open the door. I know Blake's in there. I'm middle aged, not blind, deaf, or a raging idiot."

Blake and I looked at each other over the bed. Yeah. *Mortified* was an understatement.

I swallowed my shame and hurried over to unlock the door. Rachel stepped into the room with one arm slung over her face and the other stretched out, feeling around so she wouldn't bump into furniture.

"Is everybody clothed?" she asked.

My face could not possibly be redder.

"Yes! Oh my *God*. We weren't—that's not what—"

"We were just working on her knock-knock joke delivery," Blake blurted.

"I don't even want to know what that's code for," Rachel said, dropping her arm to her side and shooting him a withering look. "Sorry to crash your party, but, Blake, your dad just called me. He figured you'd be over here. He wanted to know if you said anything to Chloe before you left—or if *she* said something."

She looked uneasy. When she ran a hand through her hair, which had gone wild in the humidity, I could see her fingers were shaky.

Something was up.

"No," Blake said, drawing the word out long and slow as his eyebrows pinched in confusion. "We haven't talked since the barbecue."

Rachel huffed.

"What's wrong?" I asked, folding my arms over my chest.

"Well, Chloe left," Rachel said. "And George doesn't know where she went. She took the car without saying anything. He was hoping she mentioned something about an errand she needed to run or something. I'm not sure. In this weather, you'd think it could wait."

She shrugged helplessly.

Chloe was probably still upset about what'd happened at the barbecue. Maybe she'd decided a little drive would calm her down, or maybe she'd thought to do a quick run to the grocery store so she could channel her nervous energy. I, for one, understood the innate urge to buy eggs and flour and cocoa powder when in distress. But I wasn't too worried about her. I had a feeling that Chloe just needed some space.

I turned to look at Blake, to say as much.

She'll be back soon. I bet she's fine.

But the sight of him made the words turn to ash in my mouth. Blake had gone very still, and very pale.

"She's gone?" he whispered.

Chapter 23

Here are the symptoms of a panic attack.

Accelerated or pounding heart rate, palpitations, sweating. Chest pain or discomfort, shortness of breath, trembling. Nausea. Dizziness. Faintness. Unsteadiness. Derealization—the sense that you are no longer connected to reality. Depersonalization—the sense that you are no longer yourself. Fear of losing control. Fear of death.

I didn't know any of this at the time.

But I knew, instinctively, that Blake wasn't okay.

He stood on the far side of the room, my bed, seemingly as wide as an ocean, between us. There were still happier traces from a few minutes ago—the rumpled hair, the twisted shirt, the flush in his cheeks—but now they were buried beneath a blanket of icy panic.

"She's gone," he said, again. "She *left*."

"I mean," I mumbled, "*technically* yeah, but—"

Blake interrupted me with a stilted, mangled laugh.

"She didn't even take Isabel!" he cried in disbelief. "She—what a *bitch*. She left the kid."

Rachel, who was still standing beside the door, took a step toward him with her palms out. Blake seemed to look right through her.

"She didn't take Isabel because *she'll be back*," Rachel explained very calmly. "I didn't mean to startle you, Blake. I'm sorry. George was just worried that the two of you had talked at home and things had escalated. That's all. Chloe didn't—"

"She ditched us."

Blake shoved his hands into his already-messy hair, fingers tugging it up into unruly peaks, and shook his head in disbelief. His movements were jerky. Strained. His whole body was a rubber band that'd been pulled too tight and then plucked.

"She wouldn't do that," I pointed out.

"No."

"Seriously, Blake, she—"

"No, no. *No.*"

He buried his face in his hands and rubbed at his eyes. Then he dropped his arms to his sides and started toward my bedroom door with frightening determination.

"I need to—shit." He spun on his heels and rushed back to where he'd left his muddy sneakers under my window. He stood on one foot, then the other, to tug them on. He didn't even bother untying the laces. "I need to borrow your car, Ms. Lyons."

Rachel blinked at him.

"Blake," she said, "I don't think that's a good idea"

It was actually the *worst* idea, but it seemed like a dick move to make that clarification when Blake was clearly on the verge of a nervous breakdown.

One of the heels of his sneakers was giving him trouble.

He roared with frustration and dropped to the floor to fumble with the laces, eyebrows knit together and mouth twisted in a scowl.

"I have to find her," he insisted, shaking his head. "She can't do this to my dad."

"Let's wait until it stops raining," I said.

Blake lurched to his feet, sneakers on, and yanked on his dark-green crew neck sweatshirt.

"I'm not waiting."

He turned, yanked open my bedroom window, and slipped out onto the roof. I took two steps after him, then thought better of it, because scaling a roof in the pouring rain seemed like the kind of thing I'd break both my legs attempting.

"What just happened?" Rachel blurted, looking as horrified as I'm sure she would've been if she'd barged into my room without knocking.

"I don't know," I admitted. "But I'm going with him."

It was possibly the most dramatic thing I'd ever said before exiting a room. I sprinted across the hall and tore down the stairs, where I paused at the front door and searched frantically for a matching pair of shoes that weren't flip-flops.

Rachel's footsteps thundered down the stairs after me.

I steeled myself for an argument.

"Waverly, it's pouring out there—" she began.

"I have to go!" I blurted, one sneaker clutched in my hand as I turned and squared my shoulders. "We can't let him run around alone. He needs someone. He needs a *friend*. I can't—"

Rachel interrupted my heroic monologue by tugging a giant clump of bright-red plastic out of the front hall closet and chucking it at my chest.

"I know, I know! Take this."

The clump of plastic was, on closer inspection, a cherry-red poncho with Mickey Mouse on the front (giving a somewhat mocking thumbs-up) and the Disney World logo on the back.

"You—you're okay with this?" I asked, a little dumbstruck.

Rachel nodded.

"I don't know the first thing about parenting," she admitted. "But I *know* you kids don't need parents right now. You need each other. Go catch up with Blake. I'll call Lena and Jesse and let them know what's happening."

I made a little choked sound in the back of my throat.

Then I lurched forward and threw my arms around my aunt's shoulders, tugging her into a tight hug.

"Thank you," I whispered.

She rubbed her palm between my shoulder blades and then stood over me, her eyes suspiciously watery, as I laced up my sneakers and tugged on her poncho. She pulled open the front door. I took off into the storm—and made it about halfway down the front lawn before I lost my footing in the mud and absolutely ate shit. Distantly, over the thunderous pounding of rain, I heard Rachel inhale sharply through her teeth.

"You good?" she hollered from the front porch.

I climbed to my feet.

My flannel pajama pants were caked with mud. I turned back to the house, so me and Mickey could both shoot my aunt a thumbs-up.

"Maybe don't run?" she suggested, eyebrows pinched in a way that said she already regretted letting me out of the house.

"Got it!"

I took off into the storm, again, but slower.

Float

There was nothing romantic about trudging through the rain in pursuit of Blake. The grey skies and relentless deluge didn't feel like some poetic reflection of his inner turmoil, and there was no Adele song layered over a montage of me marching down the sidewalk with a mud smear on the ass of my Mickey Mouse poncho.

It was cold and wet and miserable.

The air in Holden was so thick with condensation that I couldn't see more than four or five houses ahead of myself.

It didn't help that the wind was brutal. The palm trees shivered and the rain cut down at sharp angles, so even the hood of my poncho couldn't protect my face from the stinging spray. Somewhere in the back of my head, I was glad Blake had already helped me remove my eye makeup, because it wouldn't have stood a chance against a tropical storm.

I made it three and a half blocks before I spotted Blake through the haze of rain.

He was soaked from his hair to his sneakers, his shoulders hunched against the wind. He seemed to be losing the frantic momentum he'd had back at Rachel's house, because I was able to catch up to him without breaking my promise about not running.

I didn't know what to say to Blake, so I didn't say anything.

I just fell into step beside him.

He must've been deep in thought, because it took him a solid five and a half seconds to notice that I'd appeared. When he did, he stopped walking abruptly.

"What are you doing?" he demanded.

I turned to face him and shrugged, a bit sarcastically.

"Felt like a walk."

Blake sighed and shook his head.

"Go home, Waverly," he said.

And then he had the nerve to shoulder past me and keep walking down the street, footsteps a little harder and faster than they'd been before.

"Where we headed?" I asked, jogging after him.

Blake ignored me.

"Can we make a pit stop at the corner store?"

His hands balled into fists.

"I'm feeling snacky."

This proved to be the last straw. Blake stopped walking.

Gotcha, I thought. My triumph was short lived, because when he spun around to face me, his expression was something awful.

"*Stop* talking," he snapped.

It hurt like he'd prodded a bruise.

"I will when you start using your brain!" I shouted back. "This is stupid, Blake. This is the stupidest thing you've ever done. But I'm not letting you do it alone. So, once more, *where are we going*?"

He clenched his teeth and shook his head, his eyes roaming to the other side of the street—anywhere but me.

"This isn't your problem," he said.

When someone is under extreme stress, they can say things they don't mean. I know this, logically. I knew that Blake was lashing out because he was angry and afraid that his relationship with Chloe had reached a point of no return. Maybe I should've been gentle. Maybe I should've been a doormat, with a big *Welcome* scrawled in cursive across me. But instead I lurched forward and shoved his chest.

Blake stumbled back a step, wide-eyed with surprise.

"What the fuck?" he demanded.

My heart was hammering. I was angry. Furious.

"It *is* my problem," I said, my voice shaking with rage. "I have your back and you have mine. That's how it works."

"How what works?"

"Love!"

All at once, the tension in Blake's shoulders deflated, like he was a balloon that'd been inflated to the point of popping.

"You take care of the people you love," I barreled on, my words coming like a giant boulder I'd accidentally shoved over the crest of a hill. "You don't ditch them. *That's* how I know Chloe didn't leave for real. Because you're a *family*, and you don't ditch your family."

Blake shook his head.

His breathing was as shaky as my voice.

"I'm not her son," he argued.

"It doesn't *matter!*" I screeched. "Who gives a single, flying shit about technicalities like that? I'm not Rachel's daughter, but who's been feeding me? Who's been asking me about my day when I get home? Who let me read one of her romance novels? *Her*. Families are messy, Blake. But Chloe isn't a replacement part. You don't have to swap her out for your mom, you just have to give her a fucking chance."

It was not lost on me that the gravitas of my words did not at all match with the cherry-red Mickey Mouse poncho and flannel pajama pants I was wearing. But sometimes life's biggest moments happen when we're severely underdressed for them.

The rain, at least, suited the occasion.

Blake sniffled.

Then he started to cry in earnest. I worried he might crumple to the sidewalk and curl in on himself, so I stepped forward and wrapped my arms around his waist, squeezing him tight enough that I could feel the erratic thumping of his pounding heart against my chin.

A moment passed before Blake returned the embrace, the plastic of my poncho crinkling under the weight of his arms.

He croaked out a weak laugh.

"What are you *wearing*?" he asked, voice hoarse.

"Talk later," I grunted against his chest, "hug it out now."

I don't know how long we stood there, clinging to each other as the rain pelted down and the wind tossed palm fronds onto the sidewalk around us. Blake's breath caught in his chest every now and again, hitching with a muffled sob, but he just pressed his lips to my shoulder and held me closer.

We finally broke apart when a pair of high beams cut through the rain, casting us in light.

From the haze of the storm emerged a white Range Rover. It rolled to a stop at the curb beside us so that I could see Lena's face in the passenger-side window. Her eyebrows were furrowed with worry.

I waved.

Then I tipped my head up to look at Blake. His eyes were red and puffy, and his nose was a little bit runny, but he'd calmed. He looked like himself again, to me.

"Can we get out of this rain now?" I asked him.

He nodded.

Then he sniffled.

Then he leaned forward and brushed his lips against my cheek.

"Thank you," he whispered.

"Anytime," I whispered back.

He kissed my cheek one more time, for good measure, before pulling back.

"Also, you look really hot in that poncho."

"Don't push it."

The back door of the Range Rover flew open and Jesse's head popped out into the rain, curls bouncing and eyes squinted.

"This isn't *The Notebook*. Get in the car already," he said.

Distantly, I heard Lena say something that might've been "Knock it off, Jesse."

Blake crawled into the backseat first. I followed, cringing when I realized how much mud I was about to smear all over Alissa's leather interior, and tugged the door shut, sealing out the wind and rain.

"I'm so sorry about your seats," I blurted.

"Don't worry about it," Alissa said, the corner of her mouth twitching as she twisted in the driver's seat so she and Lena could both face the back in the gap between the driver's and passenger's seats. "I'll just get it cleaned and send my dad the bill."

I beamed at her and settled back in my seat.

For a moment, the car was quiet, save for the patter of rain against metal.

"You all right?" Jesse finally asked, resting a hand on Blake's knee.

Blake took a shaky breath and nodded.

"Yeah," he said. "Yeah, I'm okay."

I put a hand on his other knee and gave it a squeeze.

"You scared us," Alissa murmured.

Then she stretched out her hand.

Blake took it.

Lena slapped hers on top of theirs, and then Jesse added his to the pile before nodding at me, which was my cue to set my hand on top of everyone else's. It was a little awkward, and slightly clammy, but it said what we didn't have to.

We're here for you.

We have your back.

We're a family—messy and disjointed and glorious.

Chapter 24

We sat in Alissa's car for a long time.

At first, we just talked—quietly, candidly. But after a while, someone handed Jesse the auxiliary cord so he could plug in his phone and introduce us to a Spotify playlist made up exclusively of pop songs by Norwegian girl bands. Most of us gave him some shit for it, but Alissa just sat forward in the driver's seat and smiled to herself while she swayed to the drumbeat.

Blake's hand wandered into my lap to wrap around mine.

Eventually, when the wind was battering the side of the car with rain so hard that I began to wonder if it was possible for the storm to tip over a massive Range Rover weighed down with five people, we decided it was time to head home.

When we reached our street, Blake tensed. It didn't take a genius to figure out his sudden shift—we could all see the

Hamiltons' silver sedan parked in their driveway, sitting there as ominously as a 2014 Honda Accord could.

Chloe was home.

"Look, Blake! She's—" Jesse began, just as Lena said, "I'll fight her for you—" and Alissa chimed in with, "Who fucking cares if—" and I cried, "This is good!"

Blake sighed as we talked over each other, supplying words of encouragement and advice that he hadn't asked for.

"Guys," he finally said, shutting us all up. "I'm fine."

This statement was almost as unassuming as his family's car but equally ominous given the context. Alissa, Lena, Jesse, and I all exchanged looks, eyebrows raised and eyes wide, each of us trying to work out if anyone knew Blake well enough to predict what he was going to do.

He seemed calm. I couldn't figure out if that was a good or bad thing.

Alissa pulled into the driveway behind the Hamiltons' sedan and Jesse's Jeep. Jesse unplugged his phone, cutting off the music mid–bongo drum solo, and we all slipped into the rain and made a mad dash for the porch.

We found Chloe and George in the dining room. They sat next to each other on one side of the circular table, their chairs pushed together and their heads bent as they talked in hushed voices. George had his arm slung over the back of Chloe's chair, his hand tracing shapes on her back, as she fiddled nervously with the handle of a hard-to-mistake white bag resting on the table. I hated to intrude on what looked like such a private moment, but as soon as Jesse slammed the front door shut behind him, there was no hiding.

Chloe jumped to her feet.

"Kids," George said in greeting.

His eyebrows furrowed as he took in his son and me. We had to be quite the sight—Blake in his sweatshirt and sweatpants combo, me in mud-smeared pajama pants and a cherry-red Disney World poncho, both of us still decently soaked from our little stroll. Alissa, Lena, and Jesse stopped in the doorway between the living room and the dining room. I hung back with them, watching as Blake stepped forward to face his stepmother.

I couldn't read him. Not his blank expression, not his body language. Chloe seemed to be having an equally difficult time gauging his emotional status, because she seemed jittery with nerves as she wiped her palms against her jeans and met his eyes.

"I'm sorry," she blurted, tucking her hair behind her ears. "I didn't—I didn't realize I'd be gone so long. I thought—I just ran to the Apple store in Marlin Bay—I wanted it to be a surprise."

She scooped up the bag on the dining table.

Then she turned back to Blake and held it out by the handle. A peace offering.

"I'm so sorry about your phone," she said.

Blake looked at the bag for a long, terrible moment. He reached out and took it from her. Then, without looking inside, he set it carefully on the floor next to his feet.

And he hugged her.

It was poorly coordinated, like two people who'd never had a hug in their lives and had only read about them in academic texts. Blake had to hunch significantly to wrap his arms around her middle, and one of Chloe's arms was trapped between them. Her eyes, which I could see over Blake's shoulder, were wide with stunned surprise. But after a beat, she realized what was happening. She tugged her arm free. And then, very tentatively, Chloe looped her arms around the wide stretch of Blake's shoulders.

Her eyes welled up. She squeezed them shut.

George stood from the table and nodded at the doorway, motioning for the rest of us to clear the room so the two of them could have a moment alone.

"That went really well," Lena whispered as we shuffled into the living room.

"Anybody else feel like this has been the longest day of their life?" Jesse asked, dropping into an armchair and slouching so low that his chin essentially rested against his chest.

George and I raised our hands simultaneously and exchanged glances.

"Your aunt called," he said. "She told me you were the one who chased down my son."

I nodded.

"Thank you."

"Of course," I said, like chasing down your boyfriend while he had a panic attack during a tropical storm was typical weekend fare.

"Can I get you a towel?"

"Please."

George saluted me and disappeared upstairs.

"I really wanna hear what they're saying," Lena murmured, craning her neck to peek over the back of the couch and through to the dining room.

Alissa plucked up a decorative pillow and whomped her with it. "Don't be rude. Give them some—oh, look at them. They're actually *talking*. Like, inside-voice talking. This is wild."

"Right?" Lena exclaimed. "Waverly, what did you do to the boy?"

The three of them looked up at me from their seats.

My face flushed. I shrugged.

Alissa grinned wickedly. "You told him."

"Told him what?" Jesse demanded.

"That she loves him," Lena said.

"Oh. That." Jesse waved us off.

I folded my arms over my chest and grunted in outrage.

"Does everyone just *assume* that—"

"Okey dokes!" George Hamilton announced as he came plod-ding back down the stairs. "Got you a towel!"

I closed my mouth so fast I nearly bit my tongue. My friends watched me towel dry the tips of my hair with shit-eating grins on their faces.

Chloe and Blake chose that moment to appear in the doorway, both of them a bit puffy eyed but visibly happier.

"We're done," Chloe announced with a sheepish laugh. "Sorry about that, everyone."

Blake smiled.

He met my eyes and nodded once, in a way that said, *We fig-ured it out.* There was a moment of contented silence as we all stood there, basking in each other's company.

And then Jesse said, "So. Who's down for a sleepover?"

Parents and guardians were called and boundary rules were quickly established and negotiated—no girls upstairs, no sharing sleeping bags, and no touching the cabinet where George kept the good whiskey. Chloe said this all while wringing her hands, glancing at Blake every now and again to be sure she wasn't being too pushy or out of line.

When she was done, he nodded and said, "Yes, ma'am."

Her shoulders sagged with relief. "You guys want some cookies?

I'll make some cookies. Chocolate chip? S'mores? I can do both. I'll just do both."

Chloe trotted off into the kitchen, bouncing with excitement at the prospect of getting to play hostess. While Blake and Jesse ran upstairs to round up some sleeping bags, blankets, and pillows, Alissa, Lena, and I pushed the coffee table to one side of the living room so the carpet was clear. The two of them started talking logistics, like a pair of architects. I stood back as they mapped out how five people could sleep comfortably in the room, my thoughts still on our conversation.

You told him.

I hadn't. Not really.

Should I? Oh God. My stomach was in knots.

I managed to recover from my stress-induced nausea (miraculously) when Chloe brought out an enormous platter of cookies.

"Waverly, hon, do you want to borrow some pajamas or something?" Chloe asked, eyeing my outfit.

"That would be fantastic!" I said through a mouthful of chocolate chip cookie.

Fifteen minutes later, when I stepped out of the downstairs bathroom wearing a pair of hot-pink pajamas with little snowflakes all over them, I regretted this. The sleeves didn't reach my wrists. The pants hit me midcalf. It didn't help that I'd taken a very hot shower, so my face essentially matched.

"I am a strawberry popsicle," I announced.

Alissa tried not to laugh and failed miserably.

"Stand still for a second," Lena murmured, holding up her phone. "Just—checking"—the flash went off—"my email."

I huffed.

"At least you're dry," Alissa offered.

It *was* a nice consolation. Besides, I'd worn worse that summer. At least Chloe was too bougie for polyester—I was rocking 100 percent cotton.

With my wet clothes tucked away in a plastic shopping bag under my arm, I left Alissa and Lena to fight over the sink and padded back into the living room. Blake was rolling out a sleeping bag next to the couch I'd claimed. He'd changed into a clean pair of pajamas—sweats and a long-sleeved shirt—and by the look of his wet hair, he'd showered too.

"Where'd Jesse go?" I asked.

Blake shook out his pillow.

"He's upstairs, grabbing a few more blankets. Should I flip my sleeping bag around? Jesse's gonna be on the floor over there, and he kicks in his sleep, so I'm kind of scared he's going to break my nose in the middle of the night. But his morning breath is honestly worse than a kick to the face, so—"

"I love you."

Oh dear God, I thought in horror. *That was me. I said that.* Why in the ever-loving fuck was I so bad at timing these things?

Blake's mouth twisted into a frown, and he set his hands on his hips.

"Damn it," he grumbled.

And now it's worse. My shoulders slumped and I clapped a hand over my eyes, wishing there was some kind of eject button that would catapult me out of the Hamiltons' living room.

"I did *not* mean to just blurt that—"

"I wanted to say it first."

My breath whooshed out of my body. I let out a half laugh, half croak of relief. Then I lurched forward and punched Blake in the arm. I tried to scowl and look reprimanding, but I was pretty sure I was laughing.

"You—big—*idiot*. I got all nervous!"

Blake darted forward and kissed the tip of my nose, wrapping his arms around mine before I could sock him again.

"I'm sorry, Waverly," he said, laughing against my forehead. "Obviously, I love you too. But I had this big plan and—ugh. This living room is, like, the least romantic place on earth."

"Porta potty," I mumbled into his shirt.

"This living room is the *second* least romantic place on earth," he corrected.

I pulled back my head so I could meet his eyes. Electric blue. All lit up with joy.

"You love me," I teased.

He nodded vehemently.

"I do. Waverly, you—"

"Bro! Feel this blanket!" Jesse shouted as he stomped down the stairs, the upper half of his body completely hidden behind the massive stack of blankets piled in his arms. "It's the softest fucking blanket I've ever felt in my life."

Blake sighed and squeezed his eyes shut.

"It was going to be so romantic," he murmured.

I shrugged. "I think it was pretty romantic. You. Me. Mood lighting from the storm. These awful pajamas. Jesse. What more could I ask for?"

Jesse dropped the pile of blankets beside us. "Are we gonna watch a movie or what? Because I haven't seen *Mamma Mia!* in *ages*. That's my vote."

Jesse was quickly overruled by Lena, who wanted to

watch *The Godfather* and was perhaps the most gifted rock paper scissors player I'd ever witnessed.

Chloe and George hovered for a while, seemingly concerned that we would soon trade our cookies and classic cinema for some edgier teenage behavior. But eventually they determined that we were, in fact, just a bunch of dorks having a nice, wholesome night in and that George's good whiskey was not in any danger.

"Good night!" Chloe called as the two of them headed upstairs. "See you all in the morning. Do you guys like French toast? Scrambled eggs? I'll just do both—"

George put a hand on her back and gave her a firm push up the stairs.

"Night, kids!" he shouted.

I'd never had a sleepover before. It was nice. Even if the movie wasn't exactly my cup of tea—I liked that Lena knew every line and did a pretty solid Sicilian accent. I liked Chloe's cookies. I liked sitting on the couch next to my boyfriend, who loved me, and whom I loved.

I tried not to think about tomorrow and my dad's impending arrival.

The present was too good to waste.

And later, in the dark, with the rain thrumming on the roof and Lena's steady snoring like surround-sound ambient noise, I rolled onto my side so I could look over the edge of the couch cushions. Blake was on his back, the top of his sleeping bag pulled up to his chest so his arms were free. And, without a word, I stretched my hand down just as he lifted his up to meet mine.

We locked fingers and held on tight.

Chapter 25

I dreamed that the storm came early. I dreamed that the public pool overflowed, and the Fletcher twins drifted past me on the flooded street on their surfboards, and that Dad called to tell me that every flight in and out of Holden was cancelled indefinitely.

It was a really, really good dream.

But I woke up to the muted blue glow of morning light streaming into the Hamiltons' living room, the gentle (and-not-so-gentle) snores of my friends the only sound. It was peaceful, until I realized that the rain wasn't coming down anymore.

Mother Nature wasn't going to save me.

O

I felt a sense of impending doom as Rachel and I pulled into the airport terminal in her neon-green Volkswagen. It was strange to be back here, where my summer had begun, and even stranger to be watching it all from Rachel's perspective.

Dad was one of the only people standing on the platform outside of the arrivals gate. He was in his usual attire—glasses, button-down shirt, khakis, hiking boots—and had the straps of his enormous camping backpack braced over his shoulders. There were half-moon stains under his armpits and two spots of pink high on his cheeks that told me he was flustered and out of his element. It was the most I'd related to my father in a long time. I wondered if I'd looked this awkward and terrified the afternoon that Rachel had picked me up.

Rachel rolled up to the curb carefully, determined not to hit it, and rolled my window down.

"Jeffery," she called out, "you need a haircut."

Dad looked mildly offended. "Well, it's good to see you too."

His disheveled brown curls—so identical to Rachel's—*were* a little unruly, but I was used to that. Dad was the kind of person who got so absorbed in his research that he forgot to do simple, human things like eating breakfast, lunch, and dinner and getting his hair trimmed.

"Hi, Dad," I said, popping open my door to step out. I realized, a beat too late, that I'd forgotten to plaster on the smile I'd rehearsed. But Dad pulled me into a quick hug without missing a beat, then held me at arm's length so he could examine me for damage.

"Waverly," he said on a sigh. "You're sunburned. I knew you'd be sunburned."

"It's not even bad," I murmured.

"She's fine," Rachel called as she slipped out of the driver's side and came around to swoop in and distract her brother with a hug so tight he grunted. "A little sun never hurt anybody."

"Well, that's just not true," Dad said. "Oh—and I have your phone, Waverly. It's in my bag."

I popped the trunk and helped Dad heave his backpack into it, determined to get away from the airport as quickly as possible. The longer we were here, the longer I had to envision myself hurtling through the air at three hundred miles an hour away from all the people I gave shits about. And I wasn't prepared to cry this early in the morning.

Dad sat shotgun for the drive back to Rachel's house. I fidgeted in my seat. He'd been in Holden all of ten minutes, and already, I felt unsettled. Restless. Hyperaware of how I was holding myself and what came out of my mouth.

"Waverly picked up a job at the bookstore in town," Rachel said, meeting my eyes in the rearview mirror briefly. I caught the flicker of worry. She'd noticed I'd gone quiet. "She'll have to point it out to you when we drive by."

I did. Dad said, "Ah." I knew his tone well. He was unimpressed.

Back at Rachel's house, Dad examined the cluttered book-shelves and bountiful decorative pillows and scattered art supplies with the same level of enthusiasm. I knew, of course, that he'd always been baffled by Rachel's life choices. Her career, her personal style, the unashamed and outgoing energy with which she moved through the world. But Rachel was successful. Rachel was talented and bright and loved by the people she knew in this town. The only reason my dad didn't see it was because her name wasn't in the bylines of any major research journals.

Dad would never be satisfied with my success unless it looked like his.

"Well, what should we do for lunch?" Rachel asked.

This tropical storm wouldn't save me. But maybe I could save me.

"I think," I began, then caught myself. "Actually, no. I *know* I want to stay."

"Sure, we can eat here."

"No. I mean in Holden."

She and my father both stilled, and I saw the moment that they caught on. Rachel pressed one palm to her chest, right at the base of her throat. I thought I saw her eyes well up. Dad, for his part, just let out a long and weary sigh.

"The tickets really aren't flexible, Waverly. I already changed the date—"

"I want to stay longer than another week," I interrupted. "Like, the whole school year."

Dad did the worst thing he could've done.

He laughed.

"Jeff," Rachel said, her voice surprisingly stern. "Hear her out."

I shot her a thankful look. With one little nod, she told me everything. That she was proud of me. That I was welcome to stay. That she would let me try out a million different hobbies and part-time jobs and never once make a comment about how it would look on a college app or resume.

"I like who I am here, Dad," I said, my voice cracking. "I didn't realize how miserable I was in Fairbanks until I got here. And I love you and I love Mom, I do—I'm not trying to ditch you guys. But I feel like I just get in your way."

"That's absurd, Waverly," Dad said with a huff. "When have I ever said you get in my way? Is that what you think this summer was about? Because your mother and I have always made a point of including you in what we do—"

"Well, maybe you shouldn't," I blurted. "Maybe you should let me do my own thing."

"We've tried that. Your mother and I have always supported your extracurriculars, Waverly. We took turns shuttling you around when you had debate meets and volleyball games, but you quit both of those. I told you I'd help you get into that marine biology program in Marlin Bay. We've paid *years* of Huntington tuition . . ." He trailed off, shaking his head again. "And you want to get a degree from a public high school in Holden? What a waste of all that time, all that money. And what will you say on your college applications? How will you explain this?"

"I don't know," I admitted, hugging my arms tight across my chest. "But it's not like I'm getting into an Ivy League, anyway. I'm not like you and Mom. I'm not smart." The words sounded wrong, so I frowned and tried again. "I *am* smart, just—just in a different way. I'm just not good at the things you're good at, and I haven't tried enough things or gotten enough practice to figure out what I *am* good at."

Dad shook his head. It seemed I'd stunned him into silence.

"Let me stay," I whispered. "*Please.*"

Rachel's eyes were wide and imploring. Dad's mouth was a terse, flat line.

"It just isn't practical, Waverly," he said.

The words were like a door slamming shut in my face.

O

We ate at the restaurant at Holden Point—the one where I'd had my first meal with Rachel, Chloe, and George—in miserable silence. I ordered a milkshake but lost my appetite a few sips in when Dad slid my cell phone across the table.

"You'll have to charge it," he said.

I stared into the void of the dark screen for the remainder of the meal.

"At least come and see the mural, Jeff," Rachel said when the check came. "You flew all the way out here. It's not quite done, and the unveiling ceremony is not for another week, technically, but it's going to be so crowded and pretentious, anyway. And since the two of you won't be here . . ."

The knife in my chest twisted again.

"We'll see the mural," Dad said. "We have time."

"Can we invite everyone else too?" I asked.

Dad frowned. "Who else is there?"

"Her friends," Rachel said sharply. "The neighbors' son, his best friend, and her co-workers from the bookstore in town. They're great kids. And they're all pretty broken up to see her go."

I felt Dad's eyes on me, but I couldn't look at him.

I'll never forgive you for this, I thought.

I hoped his big, brilliant brain was capable of telepathy.

O

Blake, Jesse, Alissa, and Lena were still at the Hamiltons' house, their sleeping bags rolled up and tucked out of the way while they sat on the living room floor together, the loose wrappings and leftovers of a burrito lunch scattered on the coffee table.

"Do you guys want to come to Marlin Bay to see my aunt's mural?" I asked.

There was a great deal of muttering and looking for shoes and jackets and wallets and Jesse's car keys, which had somehow migrated out of the back pocket of his jeans and onto the top of the Hamiltons' microwave. He couldn't offer an explanation for this phenomenon, but Lena assured us that it happened all the time and was no cause for concern.

Outside, the pavement was still wet and glistening. I tipped my head up and prayed the clouded sky would crack open again and drench us all.

Dad introduced himself to my friends as Dr. Jeffery Lyons, Ph.D., which only added to my humiliation and hostile feelings.

"Waverly, why don't you ride with the kids," Rachel said, directing me to follow my friends into Jesse's Jeep while she shepherded Dad to her Volkswagen.

Blake called shotgun, so I was relegated to the backseat—which was fine with me, because that meant Blake had the responsibility of selecting the music, and I got to stare out the window while I secretly catalogued the songs he chose. He was surprisingly big on Coldplay. It could've been a pretentious thing, if it wasn't for the fact that I caught him mouthing along like the big nerd he was.

We reached the hospital just as the clouds cracked open to reveal a sliver of blue and streaks of glorious, buttery sunlight. This sight—when paired with the Coldplay—was an almost tear-jerking thing. Jesse pulled into a parking spot on the far side of the lot, where there were plenty of open spaces for Rachel and my dad to squeeze in beside us.

The air in Marlin Bay was a little warmer than in Holden. I

tipped my face up to the sky, letting the sunlight warm my skin as we all walked toward the alley between the two halves of the hospital. It dawned on me that Blake and I were returning to the scene of the crime—our first kiss. It seemed a little silly that the memory of it could make my entire face flush with heat, given that we'd progressed well beyond the nervousness and uncertainty of a first kiss. I'd told the boy I loved him. You'd think I could walk through a parking lot with him without turning into a puddle.

But this wasn't just any parking lot. It was the place where I'd had my first kiss. The place where my aunt had worked all summer. The place where a very young Blake had learned what it meant to lose a mother.

It was a very important parking lot.

I stopped for a moment. Felt the wind on my face. Took a deep breath. Smelled the ocean. Sometimes—when we're very lucky—we realize we're somewhere we'll always remember while we're still standing there.

The others walked on, laughing and chattering. Blake was the only one who noticed that I'd come to a complete halt in the middle of the parking lot. He circled around to face me, eyebrows pinched in question.

"You good?" he asked.

I nodded. "Just being sentimental. Give me a minute."

Blake rolled his eyes but stepped forward so he could hook one of his pinkie fingers around mine. I exhaled a shaky breath and gave his finger a squeeze.

"This is the most emotional I've ever seen anyone get about a painting of sea life," he said.

"It's the parking lot, actually."

Blake glanced around and shrugged. "I've seen nicer."

I opened my mouth to tell him to stop joking around and let me be dramatic about this. Instead, he beat me to it.

"Waverly," Blake said again, putting his hands on my shoulders.

Our eyes met. And I don't know how else to describe the feeling in my stomach, but it was like the sudden gut-deep panic you feel when you're in an airplane that suddenly drops in altitude. The floor and your seat seem to go out from underneath you. You think you might scream. You're definitely crying.

I cupped Blake's face in my hands. Then, because I needed to break the tension building in my chest, I smooshed his lips together so he looked like a fish.

"Why?" Blake asked, voice distorted and tone withered.

"Just trying to commit the moment to memory," I said. "All right. I'm done."

Blake nodded, like we'd just completed some kind of business transaction, and took my hand in his as we turned to follow the others. I looked up and locked eyes with Dad, who was staring at us like we were some kind of new and strange wildlife. It was, briefly, the most awkward thing I'd ever experienced. But then I decided that I couldn't afford to be embarrassed, because I only had so many hours left to hold Blake's hand.

The parking spots between the two halves of the hospital were roped off and cluttered with stacks of white plastic chairs and collapsible tables that'd been draped in tarps and weighed down with sandbags, to shelter them from the storm.

The façade of the back building, where I'd seen the half-finished mural just a week ago, was now a full wall of bright colors. Sea turtles and starfish and smiling fish wove through tendrils of seaweed and elaborate coral structures. It was like something out of a Pixar movie.

"We'll have a curtain covering this up for the big reveal," Rachel explained. "We kept it uncovered so the kids could watch us while we painted, but the board wants a big reveal for the donors. You know. Like, *ta-da*! Here's what your money paid for!"

Jesse, Lena, and Alissa showered her with compliments and questions, all of which Rachel took with a beaming grin. Dad alternated between staring at his sister and staring up at her mural.

"She's good, huh?" I asked, a bit sourly.

Dad winced, then nodded. The coward.

Admit you're wrong, I thought.

I'd started my summer wanting to become someone else. Someone cooler. Someone braver. But I hadn't become someone else—I'd become myself, but better. Myself, but a bit more at peace with it. And I hadn't realized just how much I'd grown until Dad had stomped on me. I felt myself wilting. Getting smaller, quieter, more anxious.

Blake squeezed my hand.

"I want to put my toes in the ocean," I said, turning to him. "Just one last time."

O

The nearest beach was Marlin Cove—the same beach where we'd gone surfing. The Fletcher twins raced onto the sand first, followed shortly by Alissa, who groaned loudly about just getting her pedicure done, and Blake, who walked with his hands in his pockets and his head down. I waited up for my dad and my aunt, but only Rachel got out of the car.

"He wants to wait," she said. "Says he's jet-lagged."

"Good," I muttered.

Together, we walked down the steps that connected the

parking lot and the beach. I kicked off my shoes and dug my toes into the sand. There would be swimming pools in Fairbanks, but there wouldn't be this—the glorious stretch of the Atlantic Ocean. There wouldn't be soft sand under my bare feet and salty wind whipping my hair in my face.

Rachel stood back while Blake, Alissa, Lena, Jesse, and I lined up at the waterline, sea foam tickling our toes.

We didn't speak. There was nothing to say that wouldn't hurt.

"Well," I said, a lump already forming in my throat. "We have an early morning flight, so I probably won't see you guys again."

I turned to Alissa, first, because she was closest. She threw her arms out, and with a startled burst of laughter, I stepped forward to hug her. She smelled expensive. Nice shampoo, nice laundry detergent, nice perfume.

"I'm sorry I thought you were a bitch," I mumbled into her television-commercial-grade hair.

Alissa sighed. "I'm sorry I was a bitch. Let me know if you're ever in the Mediterranean. My mom knows people. I can get you a free stay anywhere except Santorini. Don't tell people you know me in Santorini, actually."

I'd hated her, once. I'd thought that, somehow, one of us was in some way better than the other. One of us had to be prettier. Smarter. More reserved. More outgoing.

What a load of shit.

Alissa stepped back and smiled at me. "Travel safe, Waverly."

Jesse was next. He took a long pull of iced coffee, then set the cup on the ground by his feet. I had only a moment to anticipate his hug before his arms were around my torso, and I was a half a foot off the ground.

"Jesse!" I screeched. "Your hands are like ice cubes!"

He set me down and beamed at me.

"Just getting you ready for Alaska." He shrugged.

I rolled my eyes, but when I spoke again, my voice was hoarse.

"Thank you," I whispered. "Take care of everyone, okay? Even your sister."

"Watch out for bears and shit," he said, then shrugged. "*Alaska,* you know?"

"Bears really aren't a pressing threat in the city. But I'll do my best."

Before I saw her coming, Lena wrapped her arms tight around me and crushed me in a hug. I let out a miserable little wail of distress. She laughed and went to let go, but I held tight.

"I love you," I mumbled into her corkscrew curls.

"I love you too," she said into my shoulder. Her voice was tight.

"Are you about to cry?"

"*Obviously* not." Her sniffle betrayed her.

"Can I say something?" I asked. Lena grumbled in protest, but I pushed on regardless. "You were the first friend I had here. You were the first person who didn't look at me like I was a total weirdo—"

"You *are* a weirdo," Lena murmured affectionately.

"—and I'll always appreciate that. More than you know."

Lena and I stepped back and took a moment to detangle the bits of our hair that'd gotten tangled. We both had tears in our eyes and kept sniffling, so eventually the sight of each other became so comical we had to laugh.

"If anyone up in Alaska gives you trouble," Lena said, "you call me. I'll come kick their ass."

"I know you will," I told her.

There was only one person left to say good-bye to. I could

see him hovering off to the side in my peripheral vision. My whole body felt like an honest to goodness ice cube. I was frozen solid.

"His turn," Lena said, tipping her head to the side.

I stared at her, wide-eyed with panic.

"Hold on," Alissa murmured, stepping up to us. She stood on her tiptoes, so we were eye to eye, and ran her thumbs under my eyes. "Mascara. Okay. You're good."

Jesse leaned over and gave me an encouraging pat on the shoulder.

And so I turned, finally, and met Blake's eyes. The dull ache in my chest was physically painful. I wanted to scream, again. I wanted to sit down and throw a tantrum like the child I suddenly realized I was.

"Um," I began, eloquent until the very end. "Hey."

Blake's throat worked as he swallowed hard. His smile was tight.

"I want you to have this," he murmured.

His sweatshirt. The green crew neck. I accepted it delicately, like he'd passed me a sleeping newborn baby.

"Thank you," I said, my voice so wobbly it hit four different octaves.

Something flickered across Blake's face, but before I could dwell on it, he stepped forward and pulled me tight against his chest. I tried to memorize it. The heat of his body, the smell of laundry detergent when I pressed my nose against his shoulder, the way his chest rose and fell with one deep breath while his heart hammered against his ribs.

Don't cry, I told myself. *Do* not *cry.*

We broke apart. I tucked his sweatshirt under my arm. Blake

looked like he was going to say something else, but he hesitated, and in that little window of time I decided that I needed to go before either of us made this any harder.

"Bye, Blake."

I turned and took one determined stride.

And then I promptly lost it. I stopped, my whole body slumping in defeat as the tears I'd worked so hard to hold back poured over, and turned back around to face Blake. I felt like a broken vase a guilty child had tried to piece together with Elmer's Glue and hadn't given the time to dry. I lifted my arms and let them drop to my sides again, as if to say, *I almost had it*. He hurried forward to meet me just as the first real sob came on.

"Talk to me, Waverly," he said.

I blubbered something unintelligible to all humankind. Blake put his hands on my shoulders and kneaded his fingers into muscles I hadn't realized were tensed. I used the sleeve of his green crew neck to wipe at my tears.

"I knew you were being weird," he teased.

"I just—didn't want—to cry," I sobbed.

"Yeah, well, I'd rather my last visual of you be covered in snot than, like, not making eye contact with me."

I sighed and leaned into his hands. "I'm sorry."

Blake tucked a piece of my hair behind my ear. "You realize we *will* see each other again, right? Because I love this sweatshirt. You're gonna dry clean it after this, right? I think you got snot on the—"

I hugged him again. He hugged me back, his chest heaving with a heavy exhale.

"I love you," I said.

"Right back at you," Blake murmured, then yelped when I

pinched the skin over his ribs right up under his armpit. "Okay, okay. I love you too. Gremlin."

We let each other go. I made it only a step before I remembered something.

"Wait," I said. "My number."

Blake handed me his phone, and I tapped it in. It might've been the gloomy light, but I was sure I saw tears glistening in his eyes.

"As much as I want you to miss your flight," he said, "you should probably go pack and get some sleep. Here to Alaska's, like, three hundred bucks one way."

I didn't need to ask how he knew that.

With one last wave and a round of shouted good-byes, I turned my back to the ocean and the people I loved. Rachel was standing at the bottom of the steps up to the parking lot.

I felt the tears soaring up like someone had knocked over a fire hydrant with their car.

"Oh kiddo," Rachel murmured as I approached.

She held open her arms and I stepped into them, feeling very much like a child.

"Thank you for feeding me," I said. "And clothing me. And—"

Rachel stroked my hair and shushed me.

"You know you're welcome down here anytime," she told me. Then, softer: "I mean it. As soon as you're done with high school and you turn eighteen, you are your own person. You don't owe your mom and dad *anything*, Waverly. You could go to college. You could take a gap year. You could go to trade school. You could join the circus. I don't care. You'll always have a place to stay in Holden."

She really wasn't helping my efforts to not ugly cry in public.

"Maybe don't join the circus, though," Rachel added, as an

afterthought. "I've seen you in action, kiddo. That's a broken neck waiting to happen."

I laughed against her shoulder. Then I buried my face there.

"You're a really, really good guardian," I said, willing my voice not to wobble.

"Happy to be of service," Rachel teased, squeezing me and rocking side to side.

Dad was waiting at the top of the steps, his expression as moody as the clouds overhead.

"We need to talk," he said.

Rachel and I exchanged a look.

"What's up?" I asked, blotting my eyes and resisting the urge to blow my nose in my shirt.

Dad looked me up and down. "You're different."

"I put an aloe mask on last night. It really helped with the redness—"

"No," Dad said, shaking his head. "I mean you seem happier."

I exhaled shakily. "I am, Dad."

"I know your mother and I aren't always the best at collaborating, but I do respect her input when it concerns you. Let me make the call."

"Wait," I croaked. "Seriously?"

He nodded once, sharply, and turned to the car, only to immediately double back, his expression suddenly determined. "You're not a disappointment, Waverly. I never meant to make you feel that way. I just wanted you to have the chance to be as passionate about something as I am. I wanted to give you the best chance for success."

"Thank you," I croaked.

"Don't thank me yet," he said. "Your mother's impossible."

Rachel looped her arm around mine. Together, we waited for the verdict.

O

I took the stairs down to the beach two at a time, my heart in my throat and misty rain on my skin. The clouds were starting to open up. It didn't matter anymore—I didn't need the excuse to cancel my flight. I sprinted across the sand, which was really more of a slow-motion jog, since I still hadn't figured out how to get my footing. It was infuriating. But the feel of the sand between my toes was glorious.

My friends were still standing out on the edge of the water, their backs to me.

"I bet you thought you got rid of me!" I shouted.

They turned in unison, their matching expressions of startled confusion so hilarious and so beautiful that my chest squeezed. I let out a peal of giddy, almost frantic laughter as I picked up speed on the damp sand.

"Well, jokes on you, suckers!"

I launched myself at Blake, tackling him backward into the shallow water. We landed with an enormous splash. Salt water went up my nose. I snorted and laughed harder.

"What the—" Blake spluttered as we sat up.

"I'm staying," I said.

He went still. "You're serious? Your dad—"

"Said I can stay. He called my mom and everything. They said yes. I can transfer, and they'll ship anything I need, and—"

Blake cut me off with a kiss so sweet and so happy it made my toes curl.

Float

Jesse, in only the way Jesse could, broke up our private moment by tackling us. Lena joined the dog pile next, and then, belatedly, there was Alissa, muttering something about getting her hair wet before Jesse dragged her down with us, a mess of limbs and sand and salt water.

For the first time in my life, I felt like I was exactly where I was supposed to be.

The End

Acknowledgments

I began writing this book on Wattpad when I was fifteen years old, with a whole lot of feelings but no grand plans of publication. Now, over a decade later, I'm proud to present the final draft. This book is inextricably tied to my experience sharing it with an audience, so I have to begin by showing my gratitude to everyone who read this book while it—and I—were both works in progress. Thank you for waiting so long between updates while I tackled high school, then college, then my first big-girl job. Thank you for laughing at my jokes and being gentle when you pointed out my typos. Thank you for teaching me that there are always new friends to be found and chances to become a braver version of yourself.

To my editor, Deanna McFadden, who championed my work and saw right through to the heart of this story: thank you. Your optimism, your ever-sharp insight, and your patience have single-handedly gotten me through the editing process. To the rest of the Wattpad team, with special thanks to Monica Pacheco and I-Yana Tucker, thank you for advocating for me and my work. I feel incredibly lucky to have the support of such a talented, creative, and driven team.

To the group chat (Ivey Choi, Marianna Leal, Daven McQueen, Simone Shirazi, Em Slough, Natalie Walton, and Anne Zou) and to the Wattpad writers I have been mutuals with longer than the average marriage lasts: I am deeply honored to know you, you wonderful, insanely talented, wickedly funny people. And to my college friends who downloaded Wattpad just to read my book: I don't think I can ever properly thank you for hyping me up and making me feel like my work is cool and worth celebrating.

To Christopher, for having the biggest heart and most infectious laugh (and for lying about your driver's test results to make me feel better) and to Elizabeth, for being my best friend all these years we've spent sharing a bathroom (and for being exactly who I wish I'd been at your age): you both make me so proud.

And finally—perhaps most importantly—to my parents, Anne and Bill, who have always believed in me (even when I didn't believe in myself) and who encouraged my writing even when it was objectively awful. I love you. Thank you for telling me not to go to law school. Thank you for the sacrifices you made so I could do what makes me happy. Thank you for the good advice, the unconditional support, and for telling everyone we have ever met, even tangentially, that your daughter is an author. I will never take for granted what a privilege and an honor it is to have you as parents.

About the Author

Kate Marchant started writing on Wattpad at fifteen and now holds a bachelor's degree in creative writing from the University of Southern California. She lives and works in the San Francisco Bay Area. *Float* is her debut novel.